DOROTHY

The darker side of Oz

Written by

Scott Stanford

FASTPRINT GOLD PUBLISHING
PETERBOROUGH, ENGLAND

Based on the novel,
'The Wonderful Wizard Of Oz'(1900)
by Lyman Frank Baum.

For more information on 'Dorothy - The darker side of Oz',
or the author, please contact:
s.stanford@darkersideofoz.com

www.darkersideofoz.com

ISBN 978-184426-798-9

Illustrations and cover art by Stephen Trumble.

First published 2010 by
Fastprint gold publishing
Peterborough, England.

Printed and bound in England by
www.printondemand-worldwide.com

Acknowledgments

My grateful thanks to Megan, Victor, Catherine, family and friends for their constant support and encouragement.

I'd also like to thank; Dave Moody, Andrew J Kirby, and Iain Mckinnon, without their advice this book may not have made it to print, along with Stephen Trumble, for his amazing work.

Finally, a special thank you to the late Lyman Frank Baum, his wonderful work is the reason this novel exists.

If you are not used to darker fiction I recommend you still push through the more 'peculiar' chapters, because just as Dorothy's adventure, the novel itself is *'sometimes pleasant, sometimes terrible'*. Amidst the strange land you'll encounter horror, humour, the fascinating, and the beautiful. This may not be the exact tale you know, but I've kept the essence Baum intended, deepening Dorothy's amazing journey.

I'll see you along the yellow bricks soon.

For Catherine, Jimmy, and Dexter,
without you it wouldn't be the same.

DOROTHY
The darker side of Oz

Written by

Scott Stanford

<u>1</u>

As Dorothy awakes, nothing is strange in Oz.

She gasps for air, her nightmares sever with consciousness and she sits on the bed, sweating with her head burrowed between her hands. It's quiet and Mr Lairman's not at the door anymore, not waiting like he was when she fell asleep. With his thin frame he stood lingering outside 'her' room for an hour, tapping at the wood with his pin-like fingers, waiting for an excuse to open the door. Dorothy's skin crawls at the thought of him, his sickly wife and all the others before them.

Their names combine like cogs, nothing but pinions, faceless people forming a mechanical system she'd been trapped in since she was twelve. She'd been moved from one house to another and all the 'parents' were just pin-levers, roskopfs that couldn't function, even the ones who tried their best to play mom and dad. Dorothy was never meant to have a home until now and she knew it, smiling at the thought of being eighteen tomorrow, an adult, free from the system. Then she'll live with her aunt and uncle, away from fake parents and the orphanage. It's been too long coming and Dorothy smiles as she thinks of them, that old farmhouse in Kansas…but the sadness creeps in. She'd known about their ill health for years, that's why she couldn't stay with them from the beginning; they're only in their fifties but their disabilities made them unfit to look after a child. Despite uncle Henry's strength, or how aunt Em's hair refused to grey and her skin daren't wrinkle, internally time had taken its toll.

Trying not to think too far ahead Dorothy looks around the dark dingy room meant for a teenage girl, as she smiles slightly thinking of tomorrow with a stray tear dribbling down her face. 'It will all be over soon' she tells herself, no more lonely nights in the orphanage, being rejected by families she starts to care for, and best of all no more cogs. Dorothy feels nervous at the thought of moving back into uncle Henry's old farmhouse, she didn't think she'd make it the six years, and it's hard to believe the wait's almost over. Wiping away the tears she puts a hand under the blanket and grabs at Toto, holding him tightly in her arms as she closes her eyes. It may just be a stuffed cuddly dog but he was the only one that stayed after her parents died, even when she lived in the orphanage. That little black dog's never left her.

Taking a deep breath she stands from the bed, walking to the window as she holds Toto tightly. Looking out to the dark sky and city lights, she catches a glimpse of herself in the mirror and places a hand to her nose, feeling blood caked around her nostril. Licking her finger she clears it away and rubs it into the blue flickers on her gingham dress. Staring down at the empty streets, she can imagine the taxi pulling up tomorrow, ready to take her home. With a, *'Not long Toto,'* she nurses him like a child and watches as the street lights flicker. They shimmer at first, then row by row Dorothy watches them burn out systematically, quickly eyeing the houses and apartments across the street as their lights suddenly die. She feels her heart racing, beating faster as she sees the city in darkness, feeling a cold chill as her bedroom loses light.

Almost unable to see past her hand she stands still, shocked as she looks out at the city again before putting Toto on the bed, walking toward the door. Clenching her teeth, worried that Mr Lairman will be waiting outside she listens carefully but can't hear a sound, nothing from in the house, or even outside, not a car on the streets or the creek of floorboards underneath her feet. At the door with her fingers lingering on the rusted bolt she takes a deep breath, fearless as she draws it open and grips at the handle. Shuffling her feet quietly, expecting at least a call from the fake parents she clenches a fist tightly and walks out of the room. Unsure whether she should speak, unable to see in front of her she places a hand against the wall for guidance, as the other remains tense, waiting.

Moving forward, remembering the layout of the house she makes her way to the staircase as her fingers press against the wall, passing over odd doorframes as she keeps her eyes open, too nervous to close them. Gently her feet step one in front of the other as she hears nothing but her own controlled breath, and turns a corner to see a flickering light shine from the staircase. Her mouth dry, lips pulling apart gently she calls, *'Mrs Lairman?'* and begrudgingly, *'Mr Lairman?'* to hear nothing.

A little relieved by the dim light Dorothy walks to the staircase and peers over the banister, as a shimmer of candlelight catches her eye. She takes her first step down to hear her most recent fake mother humming, slowly descending as she calls again, *'Mrs Lairman?'* with a fist still clenched as she reaches the bottom of the stairs. Peering around the corner into the kitchen, a candle still flickers in the distance and she squints her eyes to see Mrs Lairman in her wheelchair, with her back to Dorothy as she continues humming. Curious, scared where the husband is, the young girl steps into the kitchen, calling, *'Mrs Lairman?'* again, to receive no reply. Turning her head quickly to the only door that leads from the kitchen

Dorothy peers past the dim light, checking if it's open as she continues to approach the fake mother, still wondering where the husband is.

The humming sends a chill over Dorothy's skin but she walks toward it, quietly stepping through the kitchen then stretching out an arm to the back of the wheelchair. With the humming loud in her ears Dorothy's fingers linger gently over the metal as Mrs Lairman groans, *'You're not happy here are you? I don't need eyes to see that.'*
Stepping backwards, her fist unclenching and heart racing Dorothy watches Mrs Lairman's frail hand reach for the counter. Her head slowly turns as the young girl watches, too petrified to scream, and her body shaking as Mrs Lairman's face haunts past the flickering candle. With her eyes sewn shut and skin cracked open, her thin teeth rotten and sharp she stands frailly. Mouthing the word, *'No,'* the young girl watches as the feeble woman starts to shuffle forward, with her twisted face shaking. Gently stepping back to the staircase Dorothy can feel she's close and hears the elderly woman's, *'Come to mommy little girl!'*
Turning her body, ready to run Dorothy feels the shock stab at her nerves as Mr Lairman bursts through the door, his face as tortured as his wife's. Stretching out a rotten limb his long thin fingers leer like twisted knitting needles, inches from Dorothy's eyes as *'I just want to love you!'* groans through his rotten sharp teeth. Looking at him in fear she turns to the wife quickly, watching her reach for the candle before glimpsing back at Mr Lairman's face, moving toward her as suddenly, everything turns black.
Running, scared, Dorothy clambers up the stairs to hear, *'You belong to us now!'* as their voices creep through the darkness. Feeling them touch at the back of her leg she screams as she reaches the upstairs landing, running her hands along the walls to feel her way through the black corridor. Turning the corner she hears them coming closer as their voices hiss, ringing clearly in her ears, *'Come to daddy!'* as she runs into her room.

Grabbing at the door Dorothy feels him coming closer and pushes her body against it, slamming the solid wood into him as the door clicks shut and she feels him twisting the handle. Hearing it turn rapidly she draws the rusted bolt, standing still for a second as the door's weight pushes against her, and the fake father screams, *'The witch is waiting!'* Dorothy trembles, locked inside the room and stepping away from the door as she jumps onto the bed, curling her body as she holds Toto tightly. Closing her eyes she hears them outside, their nails scraping against the wood as she cries, unaware of what awaits her in Oz.

2

Waking in a panic, jumping from the bed and clutching Toto Dorothy stares at the door. Clenching a fist the silence grows on her, stagnant in the air as she thinks of calling to the Lairmans. 'It was a dream' she tells herself, but she'd never had any as vivid as that, normally just dreams of her parents, occasional nightmares. That's one thing she liked about living with the fake families, she'd have her own room, and when the nightmares came no-one could hear her cry at night.

She always lets herself be as scared as she needs to be in 'her' bedroom, because as soon as the door opens she knows she has to change who she is, pretend she's happy with the fake families, not scared. Their faces may have kept changing, but their styles and expectancies of Dorothy stopped being unique years ago. She used to act shy, needy for the parents who wanted to nurture, the ones who felt good about themselves when they protected her. Others wanted her to be stronger; confident enough to maintain an adult conversation and sturdy enough not to break, she preferred these. Then there were the others; the early morning drinkers, some who couldn't interact, feel the connection, ones who thought they could handle a child but wouldn't be able to get themselves out of bed. She'd seen them all and things never worked out, she always ended back at the orphanage, waiting for the next family to come along.

Prying her eyes from the door Dorothy looks to the window as she pulls herself from the bed. The dream felt so real and her body still aches from clambering up the stairs. Trying to flush the thoughts away she looks out of the window expecting to see the dark sky, a city lit by streetlights as odd cars drive through the late night, but no.
Her limbs suddenly feel loose, almost dropping Toto to the floor she looks out to a midnight blue sky as it drapes over the city, leaving an azure glow through the streets as random lights flicker. Her eyes grow bigger at the wonderful sight as she looks into the sky to see something in the vast distance. Leering over the city, past odd chunks of countryside and forests, even towering above distant hills a tall baroque emerald castle rules the land. Oozing its dominance and demanding attention the twisted architecture stands like an island above the sea of skyscrapers in front of Dorothy's eyes. Tearing herself away from the landscape and looking down at the streets, the young girl watches what seems like a blanket of ants as they flood the road. Pouring through the darkness like sand, dozens

and dozens of bodies lock together as their voices mesh into one, and Dorothy shudders.

Pulling herself away from the window, unsure whether she's awake or not the young girl knows she can't stay here and puts Toto in a small bag, slinging it over her shoulder. Moving to the door she listens carefully, hearing nothing as she gently slides the bolt aside. Slowly, with her hands along the edges she opens the door, peering through the cracks as nothing seems unordinary. Almost shocked she moves into the plain hallway as the landing light flickers, and she thinks maybe the Lairmans' slipped something into her food, perhaps she shouldn't have…then suddenly a shriek comes from downstairs.

She walks toward the staircase, the familiar sounds of a carnivorous feast amplified; the vicious chewing and gnawing at meat slathering in her ears before it suddenly stops. Again, slowly descending just like before she waits, lingering at the bottom of the staircase as she peers into the kitchen, though this time with no candle-light, no Mrs Lairman in her wheelchair. Instead the horror presents itself brutally as Dorothy places a hand over her mouth, trying not to scream as she looks at a bloody body on the floor, Mr Lairman's. He wriggles in agony, the skin removed from his twisted body as his nightmarish face groans. Suffering he screeches for help, flailing his long rotten knitting needled hands as Dorothy looks around him.

Scared it could be a trick, afraid of what will happen next she presses her back against a wall and looks to the only room leading from the kitchen. The door's open and as she slowly edges forward she notices something walk toward her through the darkened room. Small in shape and followed by another, then another, Dorothy edges back to the staircase and looks at them as they walk into the dim light.

Standing less than three feet they're bulky creatures with chubby bellies, their naked bodies covered in boils. Hunching their bulbous heads and keeping keen hunter eyes on Dorothy they point with long fingertips, and smile with sharp teeth through lipless mouths. Backed into a corner the young girl watches as the creatures walk toward her, one poking at her thigh with a spiked fingernail as another wheezes, its voice stretched like a child's, *'Why do you wear white? Witch?'* Whimpering, *'No…what, what are you?'* under her breath Dorothy feels one poking at her again, this time pulling at the blue in her dress as he squeaks, *'munchkins…blue, we like blue. Colour of suffocation…'* Then another finishes the sentence, pointing a thumb at her own deformed skin as she smiles, *'But we'll have to take you to Avatonika.'* Turning its head, the female munchkin screeches into the other room, *'Bring the restraints, one for the queen!'* but Dorothy battles, pushing away the creature closest to her with, *'I'm not going anywhere!'* as the munchkins laugh.

Raising a finger to Dorothy then pointing it to the dying Mr Lairman one of them speaks with excitement, licking at its cheek, *'We skin the grown folk first...you look tall enough to eat!'* then another munchkin finishes, *'Don't make us hurt you, Avatonika wouldn't be happy with us if 'we' cut off your pretty face.'* Grabbing at a small skewered blade from its boot the munchkin waves the tip at the young girl, as two more walk into the room holding a gag and chains. Waving the knife steadily the munchkin growls, *'On your knees grown one, down here now!'* and Dorothy looks out at them, five in the room and more outside the house. For a second she feels her knees bending, scared and succumbing to them as the little creature cuts at her leg, aiming above her knees and just below her dress.

Abruptly Dorothy's legs straighten; she pulls her body into the wall and grits her teeth, screaming, *'NO!'* The munchkins look at each other, chuckle amongst themselves as one speaks out to the girl, *'We just want to play,'* and another smiles, *'We have lots of toys to use on you!'* Pulling herself from the wall Dorothy tenses every part of her body and steps toward the munchkins, feeling her skin crawl as one licks at her leg and another raises the gag, offering it to her mouth. Shouting, *'NO!'* she kicks at one of the munchkins and feels another sink its teeth into her arm. Flailing her limbs and crashing a fist against the boils on his skin he screams, and the others try to bite at Dorothy, stab at her with their blades. Pushing through them quickly, feeling their attacks against her flesh she squeals as blood trickles down her skin, and she runs away as they pursue.

Dashing past the living room and speeding through the open front door she stands still for a second, looking onto the street as dozens of the creatures stand, waiting. Staring at her with fresh blood dripping from their mouths they surround a dead Mrs Lairman. Standing in shock the young girl feels teeth cut into her flesh again and swiftly pulls away, running deeper into the city as the munchkins chase her. Moving quickly through the azure streets she doesn't look where she's going and ignores the decaying buildings, the spreading vines and moss as she looks behind her. Getting distance from the munchkins she can see the herd of them charging, their short fat bodies running out of energy as she turns a corner, then another, and hides in a dark alleyway.

Crouching amongst debris and smelling the foul refuse Dorothy hides, curling her body as she listens to hear the creatures in the distance. Alert and waiting for them to crawl from any crevice, their screams slowly change direction, getting fainter, farther away as they lose the grown one. Her cheeks wet with tears, the white and blue gingham dress stained with blood, Dorothy's skin is raw and she runs a hand along her pigtails. Touching at the hazel strands of hair she feels small wet drips slide between her fingers, matting the layers as they clump together with blood. Raising her head, she looks up at a telephone pole to see skin draped across the wire like dirty washing. Clasping a hand against her mouth she tries not to scream, moving out of the alley and looking around as she pauses at the sight; almost a hundred skins hanging from the wires, blowing with the slight breeze as she sobs to herself, clenching tightly to her bag with Toto inside, murmuring, *'Where are we Toto, where are we?'*

After calming herself, she walks through the azure streets and takes a deep breath, smelling earth and brimstone as she watches vines and roots prying from the ground, and entwining the buildings. Some are dead or dormant, but others shrill, stretching to grow as they turn their leaves against the breeze.
Dorothy's fascination tangles with her fear as she traipses through the barren maze of a city, scared to call out for help and dreading what will be around each corner. Lost in a place where she'd been moved from one home to another for the last six years, everything's suddenly different. The buildings are decrepit and frail, wrapped in peculiar vines as the silence deafens her, and there's not a cloud or moon in the sky, nothing but a dank midnight blue.

Walking for ten minutes Dorothy can feel herself on the verge of tears, wanting to scream and beg for an answer, but she feels herself confined in this land, wrapped in its unseen bondage as she hears a faint whisper. Coming no farther than a foot from her ears she walks to a wall as the sound echoes from a plant, growing amongst the sprawling vines. The whisper's no louder so she puts her hands to the wall and her head closer as the sound of a dying insect hums in her ear. Curious, she puts her nose against the plant and looks into one of the flowers to see a beetle with a human face, crushed in half and dying as Dorothy barely makes out its words. Stepping backward, feeling her stomach sink she hears a gnarl coming from around the corner and searches for a hiding place. Again finding herself in an alleyway she doesn't notice the rows of eyes coming from inside the darkness, watching her hide. She hears a scream in the streets, followed by another gnarl, and she watches as a creature falls to the floor. Frail with its eyes sewn shut and cracked open skin the tall creature's just like the Lairmans, and Dorothy observes, unable to turn away. Attacking it, a munchkin screams incoherently as a centipede waits by the side, holding the little torturer's tools on its back in a leather case. Unable to blink Dorothy looks at the centipede, two foot high and stretching yards in length as it looks at the victim hungrily. Horrified Dorothy unwillingly gives a screech and the munchkin turns, looking into the alley as it groans and runs toward her. Moving quickly, running deeper into the darkness Dorothy can feel the small creature behind her, followed by the centipedes' trail as suddenly she screams, losing her balance and falling into a pit seven feet deep.

Standing at the edge, the munchkin looks down at Dorothy and laughs, turning as he walks back into the alley, whilst the young girl hunches on the floor. Raising her head she looks up at the alleyway and then into the distance to a fruitful, almost tropical garden as she places a hand in front of her. Pushing away large amounts of grass she looks out to the vast green, so confused how something like this could grow in the city. Then it crosses her mind, why didn't the munchkin follow her?

3

Dorothy's eyes peel away layers of tall grass as she leers out to the green, feeling at the brick wall behind her, knowing she can't go back.

Hesitant at first with her eyes dry and skin lightly trembling she ploughs a foot through the grass, wading at the strands with her hands as she hears the faint buzz of insects. Her skin itches; she feels them crawl along her legs and looks down as the spindly limbs of roaches trek up her body. Swiping them away, feeling the fluttering of dragonflies in her hair she freezes in fear, spotting a coiled snake a foot from where she stands.

With her throat dry and her mouth open, she does nothing but watch as it attacks. Lunging in the air with fangs poised it snaps, its jaws hungry and body coiling as it misses Dorothy's face by an inch as she comes too. Running through the peculiar garden, pushing with all her weight and unconscious of where she stands, Dorothy feels the insects crush under her feet and stops when she reaches a mound of stone. Looking at the tall grass around her, and the odd bright flowers piling in the air, their heads move, petals bulge as if for breath and Dorothy fears the utopia. Standing on the rock, an island to the intrepid grass her legs feel weak and she looks down to her black dolly shoes, covered in insect blood and plastered in their skin. Then staring across at the brick buildings and tropical garden trapped in the alleyway, she watches the vines clawing at the walls, trying to escape. Scared to step back into the grass Dorothy looks across the way at a message on the wall; carved ruggedly, inches thick into the concrete she reads, *'Welcome! Sometimes pleasant, sometimes terrible!'*

Jumping at the odd hiss of a snake her head turns quickly, looking into a corner of the alleyway to see a path where the grass turns to mud. With her heart racing, mind unable to fathom what lies beyond the garden she runs, feeling the grass press against her skin and the brittle armour of insects crush under her feet. Deafened by the odd hisses she clenches her teeth, powering through the green with no thoughts as her feet touch mud and her body crashes into a wall. Stumbling along, refusing to fall so close to the garden she bounces off the hard stone and feels the skin on her legs tare open as she finally crashes to her knees.

With her eyes closed momentarily, cold water and stone pressing against her legs she wants to sob but won't allow it. Raising her head she looks up at the dark narrow path before her, standing to press a hand against the wet wall as she walks forward, scared to go back. She touches at a cut on her shoulder, 'only a scratch' she tells herself as she presses forward, her path merely lit by the midnight blue sky. Walking deeper into the unknown, she turns a corner to see the same dark narrow trail in front of her. Her nerves splintering and the end so far away she moves quicker and breathes harder, as what looked like nothing in the distance is another wall. She panics, slaps a hand against the stone and looks down the new path, the same as before she keeps going, turning a bend, and another to see the same. She screams, almost sure she's walked a mile through the maze as she starts to run. Her feet crash into the wet ground, her hands glide along the walls and she looks up to the midnight sky, turning another corner.

Out of breath, stopping dead she grabs at her pig tails and pulls hard to feel pain, shouting, *'I don't want to be here!'* Her voice echoes off the walls, trailing to the new path in front of her as she listens to it repeat and fade, unexpectedly changing. The pitch heightens, feels closer, taunting as it comes threefold. The words:

'I don't want to be here, I don't want to be here, I don't want to be here!'
entwine, following with sadistic laughter as Dorothy feels its presence behind her. She turns, clenches a fist and screams, *'What do you want?'* to hear the munchkin voices screech, mimicking, *'What do you want?'*, *'What do you want?'*, *'What do you want?'*, *'What do you want?'*, *'What do you want?'*, *'What do you want?'* Then a deepened cackle scorns, *'Just your skin!'* as Dorothy turns, continuing to run down her new narrow trail. Ignoring the darkness, the mud growing slicker underneath her feet she turns a bend and stands still to see nothing but nettles and brambles in front of her.

A wall ten feet high of nothing but cruel vines blocks her path and she tries to look through them, placing a hand against the stinging leaves. She hears the voices behind her, their high-pitched goads coming closer as she ignores them and pushes her hand deeper into the fray. She knows there's no other way out and endures the scratches along her skin, letting her hand dip further into the darkness as suddenly she feels a tight grip around her wrist. Squealing in surprise she tries to resist but feels her whole weight fall forward, pulled through the wall as thorns cut along her arms and nettles brush their sting against her face.

In mere seconds Dorothy's through the wall and stands cold with her eyes closed, expecting the nettles to brush along her eyelids again. Twitching her fingers, feeling the cool air along her legs she slowly opens her eyes to look around a grotto, feeling lost and vulnerable. Dark and dingy the cave smells of hot tar, seared meat and bears a solemn hark as a line of munchkins stand close to Dorothy, their hands gripping at weapons as they await command. Looking down at them quickly, ignoring the stinging of her skin she searches the grotto with her eyes, letting them heavily swoop as they flutter past the racks of archaic tools to a caged pale female. Then Dorothy's stare rests in the distance, watching a shadowed woman sit atop a throne, every inch of her shrouded from sight except for the ocean blue of her eyes, and the odd shine of her silver boots.

4

From her darkened throne, Avatonika's harrowing shrill commands, *'Bind her!'* as Dorothy's succumbed by the munchkins attack, unable to stop them as they pile upon her like maggots.

Savagely fighting back and trying to bite at their fingers Dorothy's survival instinct struggles as the horde pin her to the ground, forcing a gag between her teeth while its leather strap presses strongly to the back of her neck. Trying to scream, flail a clenched fist in the hope of freedom her hands are quickly tied, and suddenly like on salted ground the slug-like munchkins reseed.

Finally one of them straps a collar to Dorothy's neck and another clenches tightly at its chain with a smile. Weak and scared she stares into the darkness, feeling the munchkin pull at her lead as her head snaps forward and she struggles to look behind her, seeing several of the creatures follow, holding long black sticks tipped with razorblades. Dorothy crawls forward with her hands bound as she follows her leader, striving along the dark grotto to be seized at the foot of the throne. Slowly raising her head, feeling defeated and lost, the silver glare of the witch's boots catch Dorothy's attention before she looks into the darkness at a pair of ocean blue eyes. Staring deep into the shroud she witnesses the face of Avatonika and screams, making no more than a whimper as saliva moistens the gag in her mouth. Trying to pull away Dorothy feels her chain tied to the base of the throne, as Avatonika laughs grimly and the munchkins anxiously watch. Dorothy sobs, struggling to breathe through her nose, whilst from a shadowed veil the witch's rotten voice spits acid:

'You're the one my people have talked about, the one of white and blue. How nice of you to come to me of your own will, there may still be hope for you...if I let there be.'

Dorothy tries to speak, bite with her words and inevitably beg but Avatonika demands her silent, and taunts just to see the young girl's eyes widen in fear:

'Be careful with what words you try to speak outlander, or I might just take your tongue like I have some of our caged guests.'

In the odd silence, unsure where to look Dorothy peers across the grotto, just past a pit of hot tar as several peculiar bodies lay captive. Her eyes linger on the caged creatures, several of them resembling the wicked munchkins; yet their skin's unscarred, cheeks rosy and their height only a little shorter than her-own. They look as old as her uncle and aunt, and one points to the stubbed tongue in its mouth as he shakes his head, advising Dorothy. Her eyes then rest upon one captive in particular, this one older than the others. She sits broken and caged as Dorothy stares at her skin, pale white as if bleached and her eyes the brightest purple. Looking through the bars of her bondage, pulling strands of clear white hair away from her tear stained cheeks she tries to smile, comfort the young girl. Dorothy's daze is splintered, thoughts of what to come shattered by Avatonika's voice as she trembles, clenching at fists of dirt while the witch's words burn:

'I am torn between what to do with you, but either way you will suffer!'

Avatonika looks down to watch a munchkin hesitantly approach the throne as he places a deformed hand on Dorothy's face. He smiles wickedly with the contact, caressing the flesh with a grunt as he looks up to hear the witch's voice:

'It appears you may have a use to me. We are in need of a new breed, and with your qualities the outcome would be promising. You could mother my next generation.'

As Dorothy tries to scream, wriggle away from her chains she can feel the munchkins coming from behind her. Avatonika watches but doesn't flinch, not even out of excitement as she whispers the words *'Brand her,'* into the air. One lucky munchkin separates from the horde quickly while the rest groan in high-pitched excitement, surrounding Dorothy. Glancing in the distance as the brand heats on scolding coals the witch watches the slow torture, letting it proceed as she looks into the young girl's eyes. They're begging innocently as the munckins' rough flesh and jagged nails graze like razors, and their greedy breath sinks into her pores. Soon enough the lucky munchkin runs from the hot coals as he holds the scorching branding iron in his hands. With a simple, *'Part!'* from Avatonika's festered mouth the munchkins pull from Dorothy's side and the lucky one walks to the new meat as she struggles. Feeling the heat of the iron close to her skin Dorothy tries to barter, beg again with gagged lips as the witch commands:

'Look at me child. I don't know why you are in my land, but you're mine now!'

Distracted by the witch she looks at the shroud, feeling the intensity of the iron throb through her body as the lucky one presses the brand into Dorothy's thigh. Biting hard into her gag the young girl's body tenses then she sprawls to the floor, the brand scorning her skin with the thick symbol of a cross, its east point tipped with an arrow. Pulling the iron away with an expression of excitement the munchkin walks back to the hot coals as Dorothy lays weak at the foot of the throne. Blinded by tears her body feels frail but she refuses to pass out, she won't let them take advantage of it and struggles to her knees.

Smiling in the darkness Avatonika hasn't finished modifying Dorothy yet. She's only just begun as she utters the word, *'Pitch cap!'* to have it followed by the munchkins' excitement, as several of them run to the tar pit. The pitch cap's used to gather information from prisoners, letting hot tar disfigure their faces, but Avatonika doesn't want answers. The witch wants to scar Dorothy's pretty head and remove her blue eyes, as the ruler once proclaimed during the war, *'No-one prettier than I will live in this land!'*

Grabbing at her chain and untying it from the throne a munchkin leads Dorothy to the tar pit as several follow behind, holding the razorblade tipped sticks to the young girl's skin. With her hands still bound she feels the sharp stones on the floor digging into her palms, as the witch watches from her throne, pointing a finger to the pit as the asphalt starts to boil. With the heat from the scolding tar spreading along her face Dorothy's forced to wait beside it, watch as one of the munchkins holds the tip of the metal cap and scoops at the onyx liquid. Trying to resist, stand to her knees or pull backward she feels the edges of razorblades cut at her skin and trembles as the pitch cap's held toward her. Desperately mumbling the word, *'No,'* it's silenced by the leers of wicked creatures as she looks to the munchkin between her and the pit, holding the cap and ready to burn her skin. Dorothy's eyes glisten, and in a split second of strength she pulls her confined wrists with all her weight, attacking the munchkin as he stumbles backwards into the pit, screaming as he sinks into darkness. Happening so quickly the others slice at the young girl's skin with their razorblades as she rises forcefully to her knees, her chain free from their grip she reaches for the metal cap. Clutching it in her bound hands Dorothy looks through the darkness, slinging the hot tar into the witch's dark corner. With no time to move, not even enough words to cast a spell the agony overwhelms Avatonika, and the munchkins stare in horror as their ruler screams relentlessly. On instinct, remembering the bigger girls who bullied her in the orphanage Dorothy dives into the shadows, attacking the bully when they least expect it. Her weight crashes onto the witch, both of them in darkness as the munchkins hear the screams and watch their ruler's ocean blue eyes disappear, leaving only the glisten of her silver boots. Quickly the screams change, shorten without breath at first, and then in an agonising minute fall mute without life. Then silence.

Stumbling out of the darkness the munchkins watch Dorothy appear, her bound hands shaking and her eyes staring at the floor. Unsure whether to attack they look at her as one of them shouts, *'Evil...white devil!'* speaking for them all as they flee the grotto wearily, scared of what the new white witch will do to them if they stay. Her eyes still fixated on the floor and her mind blank, Dorothy feels the cold breeze on her skin as the tar pit cools. In the distance she can hear a voice, a sweet gentle tone mouthing the word, *'Sorceress!'* then repeating, *'Sorceress!'* as Dorothy lifts her head to look at the caged ones. The old white woman smiles warmly and the young girl stumbles to the cage, her mind in shock and her body almost given up as she falls to her knees. Pressing a hand to the metal bars Dorothy sobs, *'I want to go home!'* and smiling softly the wrinkled woman asks, *'What is your name?'* With no answer the young girl stares to the floor with her thoughts drifting silently, but as the white one continues, *'Please open the cage,'* Dorothy pulls away. Gentling mouthing, *'I don't know if I should,'* she feels the cold breeze on her back and her lips tremble as she turns to look at the silver boots, gleaming besides the late ruler's shrouded throne as she whimpers, *'Who, who was she?'* The white one peeks a sad smile, her skin taut and her eyes agleam:

'She was Avatonika, witch of the east, a tyrant. You've done nothing wrong child. You've saved the munchkins whether they know it or not.'

Looking to the floor, scratching at her bloody skin Dorothy grits her teeth as she mumbles, *'Killing isn't saving...'* Then lifting her head, new to the world her curiosity snags as she asks, *'Who are the munchkins?'* The white one replies, *'These are,'* placing a hand on the shoulder of the man next to her, *'They are pureblood, unlike the ones that have been tainted by Avatonika. They've been suffering for many years, and you've freed them from their bondage.'* Dorothy looks at her blankly, frail and weak as the white one sighs, unveiling the horrific acts of the eastern witch to feel sickness well in her stomach:

'Since Avatonika's rule over the east it had become a barren region that none dare to trek. The streets had turned black, and roots from under the yellow road had infected the concrete. She only welcomed those willing to suffer for her, and could not bear rule over a peaceful race.

At first she threatened the munchkins, ensuring she would slaughter their young if they did not become her slaves. They were powerless against the witch and carried out her every bidding, as under her their peaceful existence was exchanged for a prisoner's life. Forced by her hand they would commit unforgivable acts, scouring the other regions for races near extinction so they could be brought to her lair, and their bodies devoured. Content in the dark paradise she'd created, though often bored the witch would randomly torture odd civilians in the square as the others watched. Avatonika revelled in their suffering, though despite their slavery she would catch the odd smiles on the munchkins innocent faces. Soon she banished the gesture, punishing the slightest sign of happiness with scars. After that some of the munchkins tried to revolt, flee the east and escape the witch's rule in hope of finding refuge. Though it didn't take long for Avatonika to become suspicious, and soon enough almost all of them were caught.

Over a dozen had tried to escape, but brought back to the witch she showed them no bane, instead she let them spend the day by her side; resting in her dank grotto before feasting on gourmet foods they'd only served before. For a while, they thought their act had struck compassion in the witch and they ate until their bellies were full and drank until they were merry. Then after supper, they were escorted to the newly grown twisted trees that stood twelve feet high as they sprouted through the ruler's land. Avatonika had come to love the suffering plants that dare grow in her domain, and watched in awe as some persisted to live, deformed by the lack of light and her own dark presence as the weaker simply chose to die. Struggling to stand and drunk on ale the munchkins who had been pampered by the witch stood in front of the trees, watching as their loved ones; brothers, friends and children stood on the branches. Waving at first, unsure of the scene and their vision slightly a blur, they turned to the witch confused. So she smiled and looked out to the twisted trees, as with a point of her finger dozens and dozens of munchkins stepped from the branches.

Their bodies hung like decorations as their necks snapped within tight nooses.

Subdued, the munchkins caused the witch no more troubles, and she even sent them to war with the other corners, killing many. Then those who could simply not bear her ruling would be found hanging themselves from the trees.

In her slaves submission Avatonika found no more challenges, and the faces of the munchkins still shone prettier than her own, despite what she had taken from them. That's when she could suffer their skin no more, and decided to change their race.

The women were caged and force bred with vicious creatures from the west that were known for their carnivorous nature. Their race were known to keep its prey alive for days, sometimes weeks as it would feed on it bit by bit, torturing the food constantly until it expired. The witch could not resist such a combination, and sent the male munchkins out to hunt for flesh in the east. Then when the first wave of babies was born the witch felt a comfort in their deformities and doubled the breeding, making the women suffer the process as the males would either hunt or take care of the new babes.

As years went by the witch's new breed grew strong in numbers and they wanted nothing more than to cause pain. Their bloodthirsty nature made them perfect hunters, and although being slaves the witch would let them freely roam the land, knowing that they only lived to serve their mother. Her new race surpassed anything she'd hoped for the pureblood munchkins, and soon she had no need for them. With her new breed in the hundreds and her originals slaves, she wanted their pretty faces erased.

The massacre went on for days, and whilst a number of munchkins escaped to find refuge beyond the east, hundreds were killed by the hybrid they'd nurtured, and then simply eaten.'

5

With her skin trembling and tears dried to her cheeks Dorothy's still crouched on shattered stones in the grotto, trying to absorb the white ones story as she stares into the cage. Opening her mouth to taste the cold brimstone air she pushes out the words, *'Who are you?'* as the caged woman replies, *'I am Bopeia, witch of the north.'*

Dorothy sobs at first, and then laughs almost deliriously, *'G...goblins, witches. What's wrong with me ...If...if you're a witch why didn't you stop her?'*

Regretfully Bopeia answers, *'I'm not as powerful as she was, otherwise I would have ended it long ago. You must be careful now child, as Outika shall surely try to find you.'*

'W...who?'

'She is the witch of the west. Once there were four of us child, we were to govern the land's four points. Though Avatonika and Outika abused their power, they've changed the east and west, corrupted our world.'

Bopeia stretches a hand out of the cage and gently places it on top of the young girl's. Dorothy doesn't flinch, just feels the warm skin press against her cold fingers, slick with blood as she looks into the witch's purple eyes, *'I used to be like you, pink, fleshy, but Outika made sure I never forget who I am, pure, a white witch. She scarred me many years ago, confined my limbs and scolded me with burning liquid. It tore the colour from my body.'*

'What...what will she do to me?'

'...Oz has never been civilized, we are a separate world, and Outika is the wickedest of all. I do not envy you, I am sorry.'

'What...what's Oz...How can I leave?' The young girl asks softly.

'This land, our world is Oz; you don't belong here at all do you?' The witch answers, and scared, pulling her hand back quickly, Dorothy presses her weight toward the cage, grabbing at the bars as she begs frantically:

'I want to go home, please, please help me!'

'Where is home?'

'K, Kansas.'

'...That's not in our world child. You must go to the wizard; he is the only one who can help you.'

'The wizard?' Dorothy asks with a jolted whimper, as a faint cynical laugh creeps up her throat. *'I can help you find him, but please free me,'* Bopeia says, almost bartering for her freedom with Dorothy as the girl's bound hands shake as she removes the lock.

The cage opens and the young girl steps backwards, still sceptical as the witch walks free, holding out a sincere hand. Breathing harder, wondering if it's all a trick Dorothy looks around quickly, searching for a weapon as she feels at her fingernails, sharp enough to wound the old woman if she has to. Unbinding the young girl's hands Bopeia comforts her scepticism with the words, *'I'll help you find your way home,'* as she guides her past the tar pit. Dorothy feels tired, too worn to keep on guard as she puts her weight against Bopeia, deciding to trust her as she has no-one else in this strange world.

Walking her out of the grotto the witch stands still for a moment, pointing over to Avatonika's throne as Dorothy sees the gleam of the silver boots. Bopeia looks down at the girl's shoes, covered in insect blood and torn by thorns, her feet cut open and infected. *'Take her boots,'* offers the witch, *'Think of them as your trophy,'* and Dorothy walks to the throne, her feet too sore to argue. Stepping into the dark she places her hands on the boots, undoing the laces and removing them from the dead witch's feet without hesitation. Grasping them in her hands she holds her breath, looking down into the darkness one last time as she stares at the witch's hideous face to feel unnerved. Pulling away quickly Dorothy's stomach turns, her vision starts to blur. Before she can reach out a hand to Bopeia she crashes to the floor, as the boots fall from her hands and her body scrapes against the jagged stones.

Feeling cold metal under her body Dorothy twitches her hands, waking to the smell seared meat. In shock, gasping for air she spots unusual dead animal carcasses hanging from butcher hooks, and as her eyes focus on Bopeia she grabs tightly onto the metal table. *'It's okay child, you're safe, you've been asleep for hours,'* the witch comforts, but Dorothy snaps, *'Where am I?'* as one of the munchkins hands her a glass of water and tells her she's in Avatonika's kitchen, where her fresh meat used to be prepared. Taking the water gratefully Dorothy calms and quenches her thirst, looking down to her bare feet, clean of blood and her wounds sewn shut. She stares to the witch with confused gratitude, giving a, *'How...thank you,'* before rushing her words, *'Home, please, the wizard, I need to find him, can you help me?'* as Bopeia replies:

'You'll have to go to Emerald city my dear, it is in the midlands, there you'll find him. His castle is the largest in Oz and you may have already seen it, but be careful, the geography of our world is deceptive and your journey will be long.'

'Can you come with me?' Dorothy pleads, and the witch holds her hand with a sympathetic smile:

'I'm sorry my dear I can't do that, but I can guide you. You will find a road of yellow bricks and you must follow them, they'll lead you to Emerald city, but be careful, and do not stray from the path. To the north of the city is my country, and to the south Quadling country, home of the good witch Notou. Though you must remember, just because Notou and I are good that doesn't mean our countries are safe. Oz can be pleasant, but also dark and terrible, you must be careful.'

'I...I'm scared...' The young girl murmurs, as the witch looks to her with caring eyes:

'I know, and you need to be, it will keep you on guard. Whatever you do, no-matter who you find along your way do not journey to the west, it is the country where Outika rules over the Winkies. They are a calculated race cloned by the witch and their teeth and fingers are as sharp as razors, and even though their eyes are sewn shut you should never go near one.'

'I...I've seen them, the Lairman's they...'

'If you have seen winkies in the east I can assure you they are nothing compared to those in the west. This is where the rejected clones are brought so that they can nourish Avatonika's munchkins, they are nothing compared to the monsters Outika surrounds herself with.'

'Anything else?' Dorothy asks, as her eyes lay fixated on the witch. Quickly she accepts the strangeness of this world and simply wants to go home, no-matter what she has to go through. Trying to absorb Bopeia's warnings, she listens carefully to her words:

'Oz is like an island, surrounded by the moving desert. It is alive and will swallow you whole if you let it, digesting you slowly like a snake, as it has hundreds before. To leave Oz you must go to the Emerald city and nowhere else.'

'Will, will the wizard help me?' Dorothy asks,

'He is a powerful wizard, but whether he will choose to help you I cannot say. Some believe he is a monster, though others call him a saviour.'

Dorothy's chest quivers as silence falls, and she watches Bopeia remove a small black key from around her neck. With the necklace tied with simple string she places it in Dorothy's hand and closes it tightly as the young girl feels the cold metal in her palm.

'You will need this to get back, it will send you home when you need it the most, but only the key knows when, no-one can take it from you...I am sorry but I cannot protect you from the witch when she tries to find you, and she will. This is not Kansas anymore Dorothy and you need to be strong, or Outika will make you her slave and you will never leave.'

Opening her hand and looking at the key Dorothy hears one of the munchkins say, *'Have a safe journey Dorothy,'* and another stands in front of her, wanting attention as she smiles with a tear dripping down her face, *'Thank you, you've saved us.'* Still sitting on the metal table, looking back at the small key with an odd smile she hears Bopeia offer, *'There is food in the cupboards, help yourself, the road of yellow bricks is nearby and cannot be missed.'* Dorothy raises her eyes to watch Bopeia and the munchkins walk through an open door. She stands, moving quickly as she follows them out of the kitchen to see no trace of the white witch or the munchkins, only the cold streets and an azure glow.

Walking back into the kitchen and trying to ignore the skinned animal carcases hanging from the racks Dorothy opens a cupboard, then another. Finding odd pieces of food she throws chunks of bread into her mouth eagerly and drinks more water before eating again. Picking as she goes along Dorothy feels her empty stomach fill, and grabs at a small wicker basket as she packs it with food and water for the journey. Feeling the cold floor against her bare feet, she places the basket down and looks over to the witch's silver boots. Wondering if they will fit she knows she'll need them for the long walk, and puts them on to feel the cold leather touch her skin. A little loose Dorothy pulls the laces tightly then ties the small black key around her neck before picking up the wicker basket. Finally, she feels at the small thin bag around her shoulder and checks Toto's safe, sighing in relief.

Leaving the kitchen and stepping back onto the cold bleak streets she fears for a second that Avatonika's munchkins may find her and moves quickly. Unsure where she is Dorothy ignores the skin hanging from the wires above her and walks briskly past the tall buildings as vines pulse like veins. Walking further, passing the dark alleyways, bright blue eyes lurk inside and she feels her nerves bite, moving quicker, turning a corner and then another to look in amazement between two tall buildings. In shock, she stops dead in her tracks and almost drops the wicker basket as she looks out to the open countryside, the sky a different shade and the surroundings out of place. Dishevelled buildings lay scattered along the tall grey grass, the sky is a murky pale blue, and farmhouses stand next to modern day structures. Dorothy's amazed, as her eyes flow past the odd broken blue fences, in the distance to fields of dead crops, and to small blue huts amongst peculiar trees. Odd deformed crows fly, dead plants still continue to grow and Dorothy glances at the grass, then the sky to imagine how much colour they used to have before Avatonika drained it. Looking far ahead she can see the pale victimised countryside span, as a deep dark forest waits in the distance, and the wizard's ominous castle rules above it all, so far away from where she stands.

Scared but trying her best not to be she looks at the path in front of her, to the dull road of yellow bricks as their cracks fill with a black liquid and sparse roots try to pry free. Preparing herself for the journey, she sets a foot onto the path to hear a cry from the vast countryside, followed by the soar of a murder of crows as she grips to Toto's bag tightly, ready.

DOROTHY

6

As her heavy boots crush at the peculiar tiny bodies of insects Dorothy strides along the yellow brick road. She'd been walking for at least an hour and still hears the odd tortured screams, followed by the cackle of crows in the distance. Her eyes follow them into the dull blue sky but they always land in different places, swarming around fields of dead crops.

She hadn't met anyone since she started her trek and part of her felt relieved, even though she was bored and alone. Occasionally she would sing to herself, or talk aloud to Toto, but this would often be followed by the odd rustling of bushes, and she didn't want to continue.

Dorothy feels as if she'd been watched since she stepped onto the road, though dare not bring attention to it; instead she walks calmly, listening for the slightest sound. In her stride she touches at the long grey grass, taking blades between her fingers and feeling their oily skin before they pull away. Walking past the sparse dilapidated buildings she notices some resemble those in the city, though others are terrifically different, almost archaic and she stands amazed, wondering if the munchkins used to live in them.

Dorothy takes a deep breath and huffs; she had been walking long enough to regain her appetite and hungers for fruit, though the trees are barren. She can't help but pity the land, and walking calmly she feels hidden eyes leering at her again. Standing still, suddenly feeling the presence of a body behind her she clenches a fist. Slowly turning she expected to see someone but lets out a squeal as she stares at a figure, close enough to feel the chill from its body. Wrapped in a large brown cloak he towers six feet, but Dorothy stands still, wondering how he could get so close without making a sound. Glaring at the figure, with its face hidden and limbs tucked away he stands silently as Dorothy waits, unsure what to say and needing to show her assertiveness. *'What do you want?'* she shouts, but receives no reply. Tightening her fist and trying to peer through the darkness under his hood to see a face Dorothy asks again, *'What is it you want?'* answered with a long croaked breath before he slithers the words:

'White, a witch I see, new are you? And blue...You must be for the munchkin's entertainment. They'll never find you I promise, how much sorceress?'

Genuinely confused Dorothy brushes, *'I'm sorry?'* inquisitively, as the stranger coils his words, *'For you, how much?'* and she snaps back *'I...I'm not for sale!'* She can imagine a smile creeping over his face as he continues, *'A powerful sorceress maybe, but everything is for sale,'* before pulling a scaled green hand from beneath his cloak, offering it as leeches suck at the wrist. *'Walk with me,'* he says, and Dorothy distances herself from him, turning her back to hear a leer, *'You will soon, the carnival's in town.'* About to walk further away she grits her teeth and spins her body, ready to shout vigorously but he's already gone. A cold sweat creeps along her skin, and she starts to walk quickly along the road, wondering if the creature's still watching her.

After walking for several more hours Dorothy feels her legs weaken and sits at the side of the road. With her weight pressing on the wood of a broken blue fence, she pulls a canteen of water from the wicker basket and drinks thirstily. Staring out to the vast colourless countryside she notices the murky blue skies start to darken and wonders where to sleep. Looking at the odd abandoned buildings, thinking them the best place for refuge she spies a hut, its window lit by a candle as she slowly stands. Looking harder Dorothy can see the warm face of a munchkin, one untainted by Avatonika, and she packs away her canteen. With what she knows of their kind, the young girl thinks there's no better option than to ask for help as nightfall approaches.

Walking toward the hut and crushing down the tall grey grass with her boots Dorothy can't hear their screams, and instead her attention fixes on the munchkin, who spots her and hides nervously. With a gentle knock on the door there's no answer from inside and Dorothy taps again, still without response. Unsure of how to get the munchkins attention she speaks gently, announcing, *'Hello, my name's Dorothy and I need your help.'* Not a sound comes from the house and she tries again, gently tapping the door with the words, *'Please, I'm cold and tired, a friend of Bopeia's.'*

Again there is silence, and just as Dorothy's about to turn her back, she watches the door open slowly as a munchkin woman stands scared. *'What, what is it you...'* then looking at the white and blue in her dress, and the soft blue glimmer of the girl's eyes the munchkin opens the door wider. *'Are you a great sorceress?'* she asks, and before Dorothy can reply the lady chimes, *'Only good wear white don't they, evil wears black, that's what they tell me, and the blue, so kind of you, though I have been fooled before. What do you want?'* Dorothy speaks softly as she cowers, *'Just... just somewhere to spend the night. I don't want to sleep on the grass.'* Listening to the girl's request, though her attention quickly snatched away by the shine of the silver boots the munchkin lady sparks, *'The boots, they belong to the witch,'* ready to close the door. Dorothy nervously admits, *'She's dead...I killed her,'* and with the door still open the munchkin lady replies, *'No, no you couldn't have!'* The young girl remorsefully mouths, *'It's true...please help me!'* and the munchkin lady looks at her wearily with, *'I've been tricked before,'* then points to another small weathered hut not far away, *'If you need rest sleep there, no-one will find you.'* Dorothy nods her head slowly, hoping for a comforting word though settling for shelter as she whimpers, *'Th...thank you. Could you tell me how long it is to Emerald city? I need to see the wizard.'* The munchkin looks out to the girl's lost expression, like that of a broken doll as she answers with a sigh:

'It is far and will take you many days, and be careful; you will pass through dangerous places to get there. Be warned of the wizard, he is a tall slug of a man and you best keep away unless you have business with him.'

With this Dorothy suddenly feels worried, and takes no comfort in the munchkin's, *'Take care,'* as the door closes.

Lying awake on the floor of a dishevelled hut Dorothy tries to sleep as the anomalous howls and creeping sounds of the night keep her awake. She holds a small sharp stone to her side and listens to the creaking of the floorboards, the whipping of breeze through grey grass as she peers out to the lurking night sky. Scared, she grips Toto in her arm tightly for comfort, so lost in the strange land as she whispers to him, *'Not long boy, be home in a while, see aunt Em.'* Soon she sobs herself to sleep, her reoccurring nightmare meshed with worry of what tomorrow will bring.

Sleeping better than she expected Dorothy wakes to the soft fur of Toto against her cheek as she gently places him in his bag and pulls some breakfast from the wicker basket. After eating in the beaten up hut she stands on the porch, looking out at the countryside. Determined not to feel sorry for herself today, not let anything scare her she takes a deep breath, knowing she has to push through if she ever wants to get back home. It's that simple, and as she feels the warming rays of white light on her face, she doesn't even question why she's in this land, because knowing the answer's not as important as getting home.

Walking through the grass and making her way back onto the road of yellow bricks Dorothy feels stronger this morning, prepared and determined. Even smiling a little at first, she sees the murder of crows again and watches as they land in a crop field not too far from her. They give a dreadful caw, followed by the screams of a man as Dorothy decides to follow, running along the yellow bricks toward the agonising cries.

Her heart beats vigorously, even feeling adventurous as the adrenaline courses through her veins. She speeds past a slew of dead trees, curiously staring out at an eton blue cornfield. The crows scream viciously, and now closer Dorothy can make out their features, though they may seem like crows from her own world these are very different indeed. Scared at first she's cautious, looking out to the mass of them as they gather, ignoring the dead corn but pecking at a scarecrow crucified among the crops. Dressed in a torn blue suit, tattered and well worn Dorothy looks at its face, amazed as it screams in agony and begs, *'Help, please, please!'*

Snared by the deep cutting shrill of the scarecrow she looks out at the crows as they tear at his skin, cutting at it with their beaks as they pull straw and gnaw at bare bones. Moving quickly Dorothy grabs at a stone on the floor and throws it at the birds. A slew of them pull away quickly in shock but others linger, picking at the skin as one clasps its beak around one of the scarecrows black button eyes, trying to pull it out. Dorothy throws another stone and the remainder of the crows caw at her, flying away quickly from the scarecrow as they head toward Dorothy and she crouches speedily to avoid their talons. With her basket on the floor and her arms wrapped around her head she looks up slowly to watch them all flying in the distance and rises to her feet.

Staring up at the scarecrow she hears him call, *'Please,'* and approaches slowly as her eyes scan the long thick pole he's nailed to, looking at his attire; grubby black shoes, shabby smart blue trousers resting on a skinny waist, and his jacket torn open as Dorothy gasps. His skin tight like leather holds in bundles of straw, with odd patches sewn shut by metal wire as a gaping wound exposes his insides. She looks at his skeletal frame, bones prominent through thin skin, jagged ribs protruding and straw pouring from the hole in his chest. He says something but Dorothy ignores it as she walks closer, her eyes gazing over his barely covered skeleton hands, the skin leathered and burnt by the white sun. She looks at his neck, sewn with a thick line of barbed wire, holding the burlap sack that is his head to the body of a man. It's dark brown, a different colour to his skin and misshapen, packed with straw as two black button eyes stare at her, and a small slit for a mouth, sewn almost shut repeats, *'Please help me down, they've kept me here for days!'*

Moving to the large pole Dorothy forgets her better judgement and takes no caution as she grabs at the scarecrows leg, ready to free him as if in a trance. Amazed by the suffering, sympathetic towards the pathetic thing she feels at the bony leg, puffed out with straw as she grabs at the large thick nail lodged between his bones. Pulling with all her strength, she feels it loosen and her body stumbles backward as the nail tears from the wood, then she does the same to the other leg. The scarecrow mumbles, *'Thank you, thank you, the crows will be back soon,'* and Dorothy starts to climb the pole, asking, *'Why are you hung here?'* as her senses start to tingle, wondering if he's crucified for a good reason, if he's dangerous. *'I'm a scarecrow, I...'* he answers smiling, stumbling in his words as his anxious expression turns sour, *'I don't know, was only made two days ago.'* Shocked though trying to suppress it, Dorothy climbs along the pole, thinking the scarecrow harmless enough as she tries to pull a large nail from between his skeleton wrist and asks, *'Who did this to you, why did they make you a scarecrow?'* He sighs quizzically, feeling no pain as the nail leaves his bone, answering:

'Can't remember, took my brain, no thoughts, memories, took insides too, only left with skin and bone. Woke up hanging here, been awake for days, can't sleep anymore. Like my buttons? Crows keep trying to steal them, don't want be blind.'

Wanting to offer a 'you poor thing' Dorothy thinks it too cynical a phrase and pulls the other nail from his left wrist. Dropping the heavy chunk of metal to the floor Dorothy's hands are sore and the scarecrow's limbs dangle freely as a single hook's left in his back, holding him to the pole. The girl tries to get a grip on it but her chapped hands can't hold the metal tight enough as sweat forms around her brow. *'I can't get the last one out,'* she says to the scarecrow and he smiles manically, flailing his limbs as he hangs from the pole and looks under his jacket at the metal hook through his back, wedged around his left collarbone. He grins with, *'Won't you look at that,'* and presses his hands and feet against the pole, pushing away with all his strength as the collarbone snaps and he crashes to the floor. Looking down at him as a cloud of dust and straw forms Dorothy jumps from the pole and watches the heaped scarecrow. Standing close but unsure whether to extend a hand she gazes as his head looks up at her, grinning, *'I think I broke something,'* as he shudders and stands with a ridged click of his bones. Feeling at his burlap head he insists, *'No damage,'* then looks at the shattered bone sticking out from dusty skin as his head leans to one side, *'Oh dear!'*

Still keeping a little distance Dorothy asks, *'Does that hurt?'* and half of his mouth smiles whilst the other frowns as he says, *'No mind no pain, only bone and straw, and...* ' Then swirling a bony finger around his plastic sewn on eyes he beams, *'...and buttons. I like buttons. What's your name?'* Smiling falsely with politeness the young girl answers, *'Dorothy, I'm going to the Emerald city to see the wizard.'* Curious, the scarecrow stands straight, and Dorothy doesn't realise how tall he is until he has to lean down to be face to face with her. *'Where's that?'* he asks, and the young girl looks up at him confused, answering, *'It's at the centre of Oz, didn't you know that?'* as the scarecrow squeezes his straw filled head into shape. *'Think I said know nothing, can I come? A wizard could help me,'* he requests.

Dorothy thinks for a second, believing the scarecrow to be harmless as she fancies the company and sees the benefits and security of not being alone, especially if Outika finds her. *'Yes, yes of course,'* she says, and the tall scarecrow, almost whimsical in his nature extends his arms and shuffles, his frame reminding Dorothy of thin spider's legs as he smiles then looks down at his body. With a sudden faint look of surprise he sees the hole through his chest, sticking a finger in the air and smiling, *'Great, but one minute please.'* Turning his back, he pushes his straw deeper into the hole, grabbing at handfuls from the ground and stuffing them in. Then taking a stray piece of metal wire from a broken fence he sews up his chest; piercing the dried up flaps of skin as he pulls them together and stabs the ends into the flesh. Turning back around and extending a hand to Dorothy he smiles, *'Shall we?'* Cautious at first, though determined not to be scared the young girl places her small hand in Scarecrow's long thin palm, as they step back onto the road of yellow bricks and he asks:

'Have you seen my buttons? I like my buttons, they show me such pretty things.'

7

Several hours later, the pair still walk along the road of yellow bricks, and for the second time the scarecrow asks where Dorothy is from. Reminding her of some of the children in the orphanage, the ones who needed more attention she tells him of her world again, how she woke up to the evil munchkins and how the eastern witch is dead. Amazed at first, though easily distracted by his surroundings the scarecrow makes odd sounds and points at flying insects, smiling at their unnatural thin shelled spines and webbed wings as he swings his arm with a smile. *'What are you doing?'* Dorothy asks, and Scarecrow replies, *'Playing with them,'* as he holds tightly onto Dorothy's wicker basket for her, and his skewed legs stumble along the road as it begins to turn rough.

Dorothy looks down at the yellow bricks, some damaged with only cobbled chunks left, and others removed completely to expose the black sludge underneath. Almost as if it's alive the liquid moves, trying to crawl along the bricks as Dorothy steps over it and looks out to the countryside. With the forest in front of her she tries to ignore it at first and stares out to the grey blades of grass, in the distance they almost touch the sky, and the farmhouses and odd huts stand bleak, even less inviting than the empty ones before them. With a faint putrid smell creeping through the air Dorothy's eyes catch the odd twisted trees in the distance, noticing several peculiar shapes hanging from the branches, imagining what they could be. Sinister thoughts flash through her mind but she's drawn to a building not too far away. She watches with a dry lump in her throat, looking out at the large door as it swings with the faint breeze.

Almost expecting to see someone she stands still in her tracks and looks at the slaughterhouse, wondering what animals are killed inside as the capturing stain of crimson spreads a thick line along the blue chipped path. Still waiting, watching the large door swing, as if giving her a distraction from entering the forest, she thinks she sees someone inside and the scarecrow calls, *'Dorothy what's wrong?'* She turns, facing him with a faint sigh as she walks to his side, looking back to the slaughterhouse before making her way toward the forest. The door still grinds on its hinges, ushered along by the breeze as Dorothy fades in the distance, not even noticing the odd bones scattered along the gritted path and hidden amongst the grey grass by her feet, some munchkins though mainly quadlings and humans.

Standing in front of the forest Dorothy starts to feel the fear wriggling inside her stomach again as she looks at the crooked trees, forming an archway with their festering branches. The scarecrow's unfazed by the dark woods in front of them as his head sways, taking everything he sees with a quizzical smile, fearless as he sees it all for the first time. Feeling the bright white sun fading as nightfall approaches Dorothy's skin grows colder as she stands at the entrance and scarecrow walks on ahead, not noticing she'd stopped as he walks back to the young girl. Moving toward her from the darkened forest Dorothy watches his thin skeletal frame stretching an arm, and his misshapen burlap face unnerves her. *'Come on Dorothy we're off to see the wizard,'* he comforts, and as if frozen in fear she doesn't reach out for his hand, nor even move until his bony fingers feel at hers, asking, *'What's wrong, what are you scared of?'* Forgetting the stamina she started the day off with, the young girl looks to the Scarecrow's button eyes and quietly whispers, *'The woods,'* as he holds her hand and says, *'If the road goes in it must come out. I'll make sure you're safe.'*

As he gently pulls her hand she follows him into the forest, and the cold on her skin from the fading sun suddenly feels like nothing compared to the darkness of the trees. Trying not to think of the reason why she's so frightened Dorothy holds tightly onto the scarecrow's hand, sure he'd be in pain if he could feel her grip. Looking up at his face he's still curious of it all, and Dorothy can hear the faint crawls in the distance, the odd slithers and the cracking of branches.

On edge with a clenched fist she feels the rough road under her feet and takes care where she steps as her eyes peer. Almost every tree is bare, standing dead as Dorothy hopes the lack of leaves will help her see better, but past every tree's branches is another's, as their thin arms and peculiar trunks spread through the woods. Trying to find a gap, scared of what could be waiting behind the long trees she gazes up to the sky to see noting but branches, encasing the forest as they block out most of the fading light with their stretched wooden claws.

Feeling a lump in her throat Dorothy hears the faint growl of an animal in the distance and clenches the scarecrows hand tighter as she catches odd haunting expressions on the trees faces. With carved circles for eyes and jaggedly etched mouths their thin teeth spread in the dozens, and they smile hungrily as Dorothy closes her eyes and looks again. Suddenly with the faces gone she feels sweat on her forehead, and an odd tickle at her left thigh as she looks down to swipe away a stray branch as it reseeds, coiling back to the trees as their unseen eyes leer. Watching the road in front of her bend, she cautiously continues as the scarecrow's slight humming fades into the background and she focuses on the trees. Dorothy looks ahead as they spread their arms across the road and lay still, waiting for someone to cross the path as some hang eye level and others creep along the floor.

With the scarecrow leading slightly in front the pair get closer to the stray trees and Dorothy pulls at his hand, not wanting to get too close to the branches as the scarecrow turns to her. *'Don't be scared Dorothy,'* he says, and she stutters, *'I, I'm not.'* Slightly pulling at her hand again he leads her to the branches blocking their path and ducks his head to get past them. Dorothy waits her turn and lowers her body, feeling the trees wooden fingers an inch from her face as she looks to the ones at her feet. Stepping over them quietly, the others brush through her hair like an unwanted caress and she gently stands when through, seeing the scarecrow smile, *'See, they're just trees.'*

Suddenly the branches creeping along the floor entwine around Dorothy's ankles, and the ones that stretched eye level scratch along her face. Tightening their grip instantly and pulling the girl's body backwards her hand wrenches from the Scarecrow's easily. He looks at her confused as the branches tare her body to the ground, pulling her along the rough road as she screams for help. Stretching out a hand to the scarecrow she feels wooden claws crawl along her face, her skin held firmly as she disappears into the woods, her body dragged deep inside as the trees smile crookedly.

In a dream the rain pours down through the trees, spreading past the leaves as it soaks Dorothy's body. Her blood mixed with dirt and tears, lost in the downpour she screams her lungs raw as she nurses her wounded limbs. Trying to stand she falls to her knees in pain and screams, *'Mr Clayton, Mrs Clayton!'* to hear nothing but the creeping sounds of the woods. She tried to climb out of the hole, but feels too weak to move the slightest muscle anymore.

Nine hours have passed, and as the bright yellow sky turns black, she lays in the dirt with nothing to cover her but the thin dress she's wearing. Watching the sky change she keeps screaming for help, sobbing to herself as she looks up at the hole, at least nine feet high as she tries to scram at the dirt walls. Unable to sleep, too scared to even try it's dark now and she can hear the wind lurking through the trees branches, the animals calling out hungrily, and she presses her body against a corner. Weak and unable to escape the cold rain pouring on her body, she keeps calling for help until she falls asleep, exhausted and sure she won't be saved. Shivering in the morning and almost unable to speak her stomach's empty and lips dry. Trying to drink at the rain water and call for help she feels her body get even weaker, her skin numb, cold and frail as she closes her eyes to see her parents, hoping someone will save her, praying.

She'd been down the hole for forty-two hours now with no food, no water, and she'd even lost the energy to stop the insects crawling along her face. Her throat too dry to even mutter a word, delusional she smiles at the thought of hot cocoa in uncle Henry's shed back in Kansas. Unable to even feel the cold anymore, sure only of the warm cocoa she drifts asleep again, no pain, no hunger, just black.

Shaking at her body the scarecrow listens to her mutter the names over and over, *'Mr Clayton, Mrs Clayton!'* as he looks at the vines and branches wrapped around her. Tying her to the ground the forest's strong fingers crawl along Dorothy's face, grip around her limbs and strap her firmly to a pool of murky water. Calling her name again the scarecrow tries to pull at the branches, and tares away a handful as they give an almost silent shrill and some creep away. Cutting at the vines with the jagged wire holding the seams of his hands together, he watches as they bleed a dark red substance and grins, *'How curious,'* as he manages to finally free the unconscious Dorothy from their grip. Lifting her from the murky water, he notices a large sore red patch on the side of her leg and another around her arm. He looks at the bright red skin surrounding several bloody holes as a green residue lingers, and he brushes it away, conscious of the vines that still try to grab at her. Holding Dorothy high in his arms he carries her back to the road and keeps walking along the yellow bricks as the evening turns to night.

Waking in a cold sweat Dorothy feels her back pressed against stiff floorboards and gasps for air through dry lips. Looking around at the dank room quickly she spots the scarecrow standing lifeless by the window. With his thin frame silhouetted he turns his head slowly, facing Dorothy as she reaches for the wicker basket on the floor and pulls out some water. *'W, what happened?'* she asks, but he doesn't respond, just stands still and watches her drink greedily. His shape framed by the window Dorothy offers him some water and he tilts his head, still quiet as Dorothy's about to open her mouth again. Feeling her dry tongue soften and about to repeat herself the scarecrow walks towards her in an awkward jolt, and she'd be lying if she said he didn't scare her. *'No need for water...'* he grins, *'No good for straw. Forest took you and I found you; thought you'd rather sleep in here than out there.'* Dorothy rises to her knees, finishing her canteen then asking, *'Where are we, in someone's cottage?'* and Scarecrow nods his crooked head, pressing two hands against his burlap face as he squeezes it into shape and answers, *'Maybe, next to yellow road. Didn't want to go too far in case I forgot how to get back.'*

'Thank you,' Dorothy offers earnestly, looking at the red sores on her arm and leg, the odd scabbed holes, and feeling at the scratches all over her skin. *'You saved me, didn't you?'* she asks, and he gives a creepy expression, innocently replying, *'I'm sure I did.'* Dorothy puts a hand on his and he crouches down on one knee. *'Thank you,'* she says again, this time with a stray tear and a forced smile as she continues:

'I...I'm scared of the forest. When I was thirteen, I lived with a family who had a house in the forest. They wanted to be my mom and dad, and... I wanted them too as well...' Quickly her smile quivers and the odd tears of relief turn to fear as she fails to hold them in, *'...but they had a son and, and he led me deep into the forest one day, told me he wanted to play a game. He pushed me in, into a hole and I couldn't get out and...and I stayed down there for two days. When they found me they said I was lucky to be alive, I almost died because he thought I was trying to steal his parents. That's why I'm scared.'*

Clenching onto the scarecrow's hand, expecting some sort of sympathy all he gives is another eerie smile, with a second of silence before shaking her hand, asking, *'What do you do Dorothy?'* and she wipes away her tears with a confused smile, *'What do you mean?'*

'I'm a scarecrow; it's in the name I scare crows. Everyone does something don't they? What do you do?'

'I...I learn, I have classes, I'm still just a girl. I don't do anything yet.'

'How unfortunate, when will you stop being just a girl?'

With a vacant thought, Dorothy realises what day it is, and it's already come to an end. Unsure of this world, how and if time works like back home she sighs. Back in her world, today would have been her birthday, and she forgot all about it.

'T...today, I suppose,' she quivers with a faint sigh as she lets go of the scarecrow's hand. Curling her body back to the floor, huddling herself in the foetal position she hears the scarecrow eagerly ask, *'Marvellous, what do you do?'* and she answers solemnly, *'I just want to sleep.'*

On the verge of closing her eyes, distancing herself from Oz the scarecrow tells her that he doesn't sleep, so he'll sit awake through the night, listening to the forest as Dorothy rests. Clinging onto his side and huddling her head against his straw stomach she falls asleep, as Scarecrow plays night watchman and gently places a hand atop of her brow, protecting her from the barbwire holding him together. Then slowly he pulls a small flower from his jacket pocket, a strange brightly coloured one he'd found outside the hut as he twirls it between his fingers, watching it with a smile as Dorothy dreams, hugging her new friend for comfort. That's where he sits patiently all night, awake in the darkness and thinking of nothing, stroking Dorothy's head and watching the flower peacefully.

SCARECROW

As Dorothy awakens to the white light barely breaking past the gaps in the branches, she watches through the window and pulls herself from Scarecrows side. Still sitting awake he's waited patiently for her and she thanks him as she pats at her dress and runs a hand through her hair.

'I need to find water,' Dorothy says, and standing up to stretch his arms fully Dorothy notices that the scarecrow can almost touch the walls either side of the room as he asks, *'What for?'*

'To drink, and to wash the dirt from my dress and blood from my skin,'

'How inconvenient to be made of nothing but flesh, needing to wash and drink, you're not very well made are you, but at least you have a brain. That's what I need.'

Back on the yellow road Dorothy takes a deep breath as she looks out to the forest, and feels comfort as she holds onto the scarecrow's hand. They walk for a little while, Dorothy on edge as her eyes scan along the trees, and her companion oblivious to the crooked road stumbles, his jagged frame jolting with shock as he asks:

'What does pain feel like?'

'It...It's something that hurts your body and your brain reacts to it, I suppose,' Dorothy answers, the best she can muster in such a short time as the scarecrow seems disappointed:

'Oh! I expected more,'

'Well don't you feel any pain at all?' The young girl asks,

'Nope!' Scarecrow says, bending his wrist back and forth as if it's already broken.

'But when I found you, you were screaming because of the crows attacking you!'

'I was, imagine that,' he smiles curiously,

'Yes, you were scared of them taking your eyes,' Dorothy recalls, trying to see if he remembers,

'Oh well that's different!' Scarecrow proclaims as he pokes at his burlap head,

'What do you mean?

'Well I can't feel pain, but I like my buttons...' he glows, tapping at one gently, continuing:

'I need my buttons to see, and I don't think well because I have no brain. So without my eyes I wouldn't have anything to see with, and I'd be terribly bored. I like seeing things.'

'I see,' Dorothy says looking up to her tall friend with an understanding glare, and the scarecrow smiles manically, pointing at his buttons with, *'Me too!'*

After walking for at least an hour Dorothy feels her stomach grumble and her parched throat ache, but to her amazement she spots a small spring through the dead trees. Pointing to it and swaying the scarecrows attention she feels relieved, but it seems too easy. From the yellow road the water looks crisp and clear, and it almost seems out of place. Glancing up at her silent friend he smiles at the light reflecting off the water as she wonders what could go wrong; she knows she can't walk much further without something to soothe her throat. Looking down at the cracked yellow bricks she tells herself that the spring isn't too far from the road, only a few steps, and she leads the scarecrow off track as they step over the tree's dead branches and avoid the swiping vines.

Finding a small dry patch of dirt next to the spring Dorothy sits cautiously, looking deep into the grass an arm's length away as the scarecrow walks around the edge of the water. Taking a breath and looking down into the spring before scooping her hands in, she sees the reflection looking back at her and mumbles under her breath, *'Goddamn eighteen!'* Then with a sigh, cupping a handful of water she lets it drip through the cracks in her hands, checking it's safe to drink as she tastes several single drops. Satisfied, and checking the spring itself she notices it's too deep to see the bottom and dips her hands back in. Lifting the cupped palms to her mouth she feels the soothing release on her lips then lets it drip down her throat before taking another, then another. With her mouth moist and her thirst quenched she pulls some bread from the wicker basket, offering the scarecrow some, though sure he'll say no. As he does to her relief, she tears away a lump of the bread and keeps the rest for later, sure it probably won't last her till supper as she wonders what to do for food. Making sure she keeps a keen eye out for fruit she's not confident she'll find any, but tries to enjoy her breakfast anyway. Eating quickly though trying to make it last she finishes the food to feel no satisfaction. Still hungry, she's positive she's eaten enough to keep her energy up and drinks more water to fill her stomach.

Wanting to bathe she looks across the spring at the scarecrow first, as he balances on one leg peculiarly with a queer glare, looking into the water as Dorothy calls to him, *'Scarecrow, Would you like to see something?'* Quickly standing on both legs and nodding his head he walks toward Dorothy with a smile. *'I like to see things,'* He says, as she feels at the small bag around her shoulder and unzips it to stroke at Toto's fur. Pulling him from the bag she smiles as she looks into the fake plastic eyes and kisses him on the nose, bringing him closer to her face as she presses him against her cheek to hear the scarecrow ask inquisitively, *'What is it?'* With a smile she holds him to her chest and looks at the scarecrow, *'It's Toto'* she smiles, and he tilts his head pondering, *'What's a Toto?'* Dorothy smirks, feeling the soft animal against her skin as she replies, *'He's my dog.'* With his hands poised in the air, curious though unsure of the small thing the scarecrow asks, *'Does he bite?'* and Dorothy feels a slight giggle under her breath. *'No, he's not real,'* she tells the scarecrow as he huffs, *'Too bad,'* in disappointment, poking at Toto's stomach with his curious expression turning to a full smile, *'He's stuffed like me.'* Excited he strokes at the animal to feel nothing against his bony skin, but watches as the fur flickers between his fingers. Looking into Toto's small brown eyes the scarecrow smiles ecstatically with, *'I like him,'* and Dorothy debates her words at first, but after some thought smiles back at him with, *'You can look after him while I bathe if you like?'* Scarecrow's buttons look up to Dorothy as he bursts, *'Yes, yes please,'* and gently, with caution she hands him to the scarecrow, letting him know how important Toto is to her, *'But be gentle, don't hurt him he's very fragile.'* He replies, *'Like my buttons,'* as he takes the small stuffed dog in his hands and looks at it, stroking the fur and making sure not to scuff the material with the wire keeping his hands together. With a faint smile, Dorothy watches the scarecrow with Toto and unlaces her silver boots, placing them together on the bank as she unrolls her socks and takes the bobbles out of her hair. Standing up and ready to unbutton her dress she looks to the scarecrow and his straw filled anatomy as he innocently strokes Toto. She'd always felt old fashioned, even with boys in the orphanage and calls to him, *'Scarecrow, could you turn around, I have to get undressed.'* With his hands holding Toto he gives her his quizzical expression, responding with, *'But why, I like to see new things?'* Dorothy always thought of herself as sensible, mature, but as the words leave her mouth she can't help but feel as though she sounds like one of the old ladies at the orphanage, not a teenage girl:

'It's rude to look at someone when they're undressed, um...unless they want you too. It's not gentlemanly!'

'But I'm not a gentleman, I'm a scarecrow' he argues curiously,

'But you're a male scarecrow aren't you?'

'I...Well I suppose I am.'

'Then you should act like a gentleman. You wouldn't like people seeing you without your jacket or...or without your buttons would you?'

'No I suppose not. Very well I'll turn around,' Scarecrow submits, with a tap on his mouth and a quick swivel as he faces the yellow road. Dorothy gives a, *'Thank you'* and gently unbuttons her dress, letting it fall past her feet as she looks around cautiously and continues to slide off her underwear. She doesn't want to get naked, feels vulnerable but doesn't want to get any of her clothes wet in-case they don't dry before nightfall. Looking into the crystal clear water she can't see anything but the bottomless hole as she places a foot in with caution. Her heart starts to beat harder and she steps in further, feeling the cold water at her knees, and then her waist as her body deepens and she tries not to lose her nerve. She hates not knowing what's at the bottom of the spring but needs to wash away the dry blood, the crust around her wounds. Fully emerged she hears the scarecrow talk to Toto and feels at the small black key, checking it's tight around her neck. She rubs a hand at the dry blood first, then touches the branded cross Avatonika scarred on her inner thigh. Telling herself that she's eighteen now she knows she's expected to be out following rock bands and getting drunk, or at least going out with boys, but the last few

months she's been too distracted. She didn't want to get into trouble incase it meant she couldn't get back to Kansas. She'd heard the stories of the orphan girls who caused trouble, ones who weren't mature enough and had their decisions made for them by the councillors, even when they were eighteen. Dorothy didn't want to be under control anymore, trapped in the system, and she knew she had to treat it like a prison sentence. Good behaviour gets you out and bad behaviour gets you nowhere, she knew that and thanked bad television for engraving it in her head. She'd heard it all before, the 'To hell with the system', and the 'You can't make me do what you want', but she knew they could, and didn't want to risk losing her chance to live in Kansas to something frivolous.

Deep in thought Dorothy floats in the water, not thinking of the things that could be hidden under the ripples anymore. She ignores the odd creeping sounds, the sliding of water in the distance and tries to break the thought, focus on Oz before worrying about her own world. Brushing water over her face she snaps out of her daze, looking at the scarecrow's back, unaware of the odd rippling waves of water and scaled skin close by. She hears the scarecrow mumble, *'I'm glad I found you Dorothy, like the company, Toto too...'* and she smiles, dunking her head into the water and feeling the coolness on her bare skin as she drowns out scarecrows voice for a second. Submerged for long enough and scuffling hands through her wet hair she quickly lifts her head back to the surface to hear, *'Can you tell me when I can look again, I like looking at the water, and the small things at the sides.'* Dorothy's eyes widen, her skin shivers and she shouts, *'What things?'* as the scarecrow replies, *'The shiny little things.'*
Dorothy looks underwater quickly to see what she first thought were small rocks, swimming underwater with solid skin and several eyes. She gasps, swims quickly for the small dirt bank and catches the shimmer of snakes slithering into the water from a small crack in one of the rocks. Panicking she moves faster, pushing her arms against the spring fiercely as she dares not look back, and climbs up the dirt bank without hesitation. Grabbing for her dress she places it against her bare breasts and looks down into the water, watching the camouflaged creatures swim quietly, only noticing them in the odd glimmer of light as several snakes swim peacefully in the water as others join them. Still scared, in shock she turns her head to the scarecrow, walking towards him in a huff, grabbing at his left arm as she spins him around and shouts:

'What were you thinking? You knew there were things in there and you didn't tell me. I could have been bitten, you, you need to think!'

Dorothy finds herself shouting at the innocent scarecrow as he pets Toto gently, softly answering, *'I, I have no brain,'* sadly as she looks at his buttons, condemning the man who saved her last night and protected her while she slept. Calming down quickly, ashamed of herself she loosens her grip, apologizing with, *'I, I'm sorry. It's not your fault, can you forgive me? I was just scared,'* as she softly strokes his arm. His sad expression soon changes, twisting to the frightening crooked smile she's used to, and he offers, *'It's okay, I understand,'* as he strokes Toto again, watching Dorothy hold tightly to the gingham dress covering her.

Quickly drying herself with a small towel she'd placed in the wicker basket, Dorothy stands by the spring and dresses in the same clothes, noticing they're starting to get awfully scragged. Buttoning up her dress she puts her socks back on and steps into the silver boots, lacing them tightly as she looks to the spring. Seeming tranquil on the surface, though possibly deadly in the water Dorothy watches the snakes glide along impressively. Without a care they wriggle and tap at the surface with their tales to make the spring ripple, as the odd shiny creatures glimmer along the stones.

Admiring the road from where she stands Dorothy looks to the scarecrow, in the distance with his back to the spring as she goes to stand by his side, her attempt interrupted by a deep grumble. Though the sound is quiet its tone is alluring enough to obtain Dorothy's attention, and she looks back to the spring, staring at the tip of a dark green head sticking out of the water. Taking a step toward it as the odd grumbling continues she looks at the bulbous brow, its skull a peculiar shape. Its head sticks out of the spring enough for Dorothy to see large yellow eyes as the creature groans, croaking through water as it speaks, *'Pale skin, have you anything to trade?'* Fearing that the creature will leap to the surface Dorothy keeps her distance, wondering if it was in the water with her as she replies sternly, *'No, I have nothing for you,'* about to turn her back.

Still underwater, though stretching a peculiar limb it grabs at the muddy bank, groaning calmly, *'Do you know how fast I can catch you?'* and Dorothy stands in fear, keeping her body still as she thinks of shouting to Scarecrow, but the option's cut away. *'Call to your friend and I will leap from the water and eat you. Come closer to me.'* Dorothy shakes her head, sternly saying, *'No!'* and the creature pulls another limb from the water, grabbing at the dirt with wet green skin, grumbling, *'You awoke me and I'm hungry, come closer or I'll eat you.'* Dorothy hesitates, moving forward with a solid step as she reassures herself that if the creature tries to attack her she can knock it back with her heavy silver boots. Repeating itself the creature groans, *'Have you anything to trade?'* and close enough to the spring to see its body Dorothy's skin shudders as its tentacles flail wildly in the water. Nervously she answers, *'No, I have nothing to trade,'* and the creature replies, *'What about pearls, what would you trade me for pearls?'* and Dorothy answers, *'Nothing.'* Its fins feelings at the water the creature gargles:

'You must have something to trade, the carnival is coming to town you know, you have something I need.'

Although her curiosity bites Dorothy still shakes her head and the creature offers a solution, *'Very well, I will trade you whatever you want, food, jewels. All you have to do is come back into the water and I will give you anything.'*

Dorothy pauses with a lump in her throat and the creature groans, *'Come to me!'* as it whips a tentacle from the water and the young girl slowly starts to walk backwards. Stretching another limb toward her it swipes at her arm but misses as she continues to move away; further from its reach and distancing herself from the spring as she looks back to see the creature wrapping its limbs around dead trees and broken rocks. Unsure whether it can move on land Dorothy sprints to the scarecrow, grabbing at his arm as she forces him to run along the yellow road with her as he asks, *'Why so fast?'* Meanwhile the creature lingers its tentacles around loose pearls and dead trees, its efforts to tempt Dorothy useless as it sinks back into the water, wishing it woke up just minutes earlier.

10

Walking back along the road Dorothy places Toto in her bag to keep him safe, and the scarecrow watches in amazement as peculiar flying insects flutter in the air.

Swiping at them, their wings crush with his effortless attack as some die instantly and the injured fall to the road, left for dead and vulnerable as Dorothy looks with concern. *'Why do you do that?'* she asks, and he continues waving his arms, turning his head down to the girl as he ponders, *'I don't know, I dislike flying things, take my buttons.'* She mutters aloud to herself, thinking, *'Like crows,'* as the scarecrow hears her and replies, *'Don't like crows,'* as he keeps swiping his arms.

Unsure how long they've been walking Dorothy hasn't seen anything strange since the peculiar creature at the spring, and though the trees pulse their limbs along the road they're subdued, even as they smile creepily with their sharp carved teeth. She feels the air colder now, her bare legs chilled as she catches glimpses of sun peering through the forest's wooden cage, shining between the crooked branches as it lights the path just enough to see. Dorothy listens past the scarecrow's mischievous huff as he crushes insects, and she focuses on the sound of the animals crying in the distance, beyond the trees. Wondering what they could be Dorothy can't imagine them being normal, and the thought of a typical fox or cat wouldn't suffice. She expects something fascinating, even horrific as her mind trails around Oz, wondering of its possibilities.

Her wits adrift the scarecrow pulls Dorothy from deep thought as he sounds, *'That's new,'* showing her a small tin insect struggling in his hand, half crushed with its stinger imbedded into the skin. Unable to free itself it flaps its wings relentlessly, as the sound of grating metal cuts at Dorothy's ears and she looks closer.

Glaring at the tin creature her eyes stretch along its anatomy; the small fine etched legs stick out of a complexly carved body as the folds in its rusted head spread along its main to the sharp stinger. Accurate to the smallest detail she stares at the tiniest eyes, the ridges on its wings, and the almost invisible tin hairs on its back as even two rows of thin teeth snap at her. Amazed, but unsure what to do with it Dorothy wonders how the insect works, or if it's in pain, and asks the scarecrow to drop it to the floor. Pulling the stinger out of his skin, slowly he drops it to hear tin wings scrape along the ground and Dorothy looks at the weak insect, stamping quickly to put it out of its misery. Just as she's done to all of the scarecrows victims. Pressed onto the bottom of her boot Dorothy lifts her foot to see the mangled insect, as she failed to hear the tin cry and looks at the tiniest cogs she'd ever seen, imbedded into the sole.

Walking along the road in her solid stride Dorothy tries to look through the trees again whilst the scarecrow flails his arms, wondering if he'll catch another tin creature. With her attention lost in the deep forest, she stumbles over a loose brick on the dirty yellow road, taking notice as she looks to see their path bend. With sudden amazement she stands still, looking in front of them as she pulls the scarecrow's arm, murmuring, *'Look,'* as he smiles, *'I can't believe my buttons.'*

Built atop the grey grass a house stands surrounded by dead trees, their branches spread along the structure and its exterior covered entirely in metal. Glimmers of white light shine on the clean patches of metal, though the majority rests coated in rust, dilapidated as a vicious corroded fence surrounds the house. With sharp rusted blades spread across the barrier waiting to cut intruders, barbed wire rests eager to infect, and beams of thick jagged metal stand tall. Dorothy looks at what she can only call a junkyard as the fascinated Scarecrow grabs her hand, leading her closer to the house. She follows without hesitation, finding a small gap in the deadly fence as the scarecrow chimes happily. Ducking under the sharp wire and trying to avoid the fine blades Scarecrow makes his way through eagerly, slicing a hole at the skin on his shoulder without noticing as straw pours out. Now slightly hesitant, though not enough to turn back Dorothy slides her body through the fence with concentration as she breathes in and holds her stomach tightly, so scared of getting cut as she falls to the ground in relief. Taking a deep breath and turning her head she looks inches from her face to notice a bear trap on the floor, open with its teeth hungry as she jumps to her feet and latches onto the scarecrow's arm.

Murmuring the words, *'What are we doing?'* Dorothy proceeds to walk around the yard with Scarecrow as he smiles at the new sights. Interested in the sharp pieces of metal scattered along the side of the house he feels at them to see straw pour from his fingers, looking curiously whilst Dorothy places a hand on the cold lonely building. Rubbing a palm along a small amount of metal she feels at the rust, scratching vigorously to see wood underneath. Turning to look back at her intrigued friend a mechanical roar spreads from the back of the house as Dorothy jumps and they stand together, the scarecrow asking, *'Can we go look? I want to see.'* The young girl shakes her head, quietly mouthing, *'No, we should leave,'* as she jumps backwards. Pointing with no words she looks out of the corner of her eye at a dead munchkin, and the scarecrow walks closer. Barely visible behind a large sheet of metal its body's upright as it leans against a rusty meshed wire fence. Almost intact, every inch of its visible flesh is covered in deep thin slits, spanning from the back of his legs to his stubby hands. The scars even spread along his face, encrusting an eye with thick cuts and dry blood. Scarecrow looks at the decaying munchkin's clothing, covered in thin slits with a large gorge in its chest as he curiously runs a finger along its face, one eye torn out completely as he feels at the chasm and turns to Dorothy, muttering, 'B...birds!' Reaching for his hand her panic swells as she hears the oxidized groan again, and shouts, 'We have to go!' Quickly she glances at the covered sky as a swarm of rusted tin insects hover above them, gleaming in the odd rays of light. Screaming, 'Run!' she acts on instinct as the creatures descend, positive that tin's a thin weak metal but unsure of the damage it can cause at such a speed. Heading for the house's front door the scarecrow hears a familiar sound in the distance and glares behind him as he spots a tin bird and panics.

With the grating flutter of the insect's wings in Dorothy's ears, she jumps to the porch and pulls at the door handle to feel it locked. Without thought the scarecrow runs at the door, smashing his fists into the metal encased wood as his skin bursts at the seams and straw pours from his hands. Staring back at the winged insects, followed by several birds he watches in fear as they swarm, swiftly shocked by the sound of shattered glass. With a rusted metal chair in her hands Dorothy throws it to the floor, looking at the broken window with thin layers of tin peeled away. She shouts, 'In now!' jumping inside the house first, ignoring the glass cutting at her legs as Scarecrow follows.

Inside she runs through the house quickly, pulling a large wooden mirror from the wall as the scarecrow stands idly. Wedging it into the shattered window frame she's positive the wood's thick enough and screams at the scarecrow, 'Get here now!' as they both push their weight into the mirror. With their backs along the glass they can feel the force of the tin insects shattering against the wood, but hold it strongly as the beating continues, taking the impact of what the scarecrow believes to be a bird or two as he smiles. With her eyes closed Dorothy feels strong, holding them off as she grips onto the wood, only un-tensing her muscles as the beating against her back stops. With a curious, 'Do you think they're gone?' Dorothy replies, 'I think so,' as the scarecrow shakes his head, murmuring, 'Don't like birds, scare me, scare me as much as...' He pauses and Dorothy looks at the worry on his face, 'As much as what?' she asks and he looks at her with his curious expression nowhere in sight as he timidly mouths, 'Fire.' A short silence falls between them, Dorothy unsure of what to say at first as she carefully lets go of the mirror and places a hand on his shoulder. She looks down at his skeleton hands, the skin peeled back to his wrists as she assures, *'Come on, we'll fix you.'*

Making sure the mirror's securely wedged in place they walk through the house and Dorothy's eyes scan, almost disappointed that the walls are stone, and the floorboards and the furniture's made of wood.

The mechanical roar screeches again, scraping through Dorothy's ears as the scarecrow stands with a foot on the staircase, looking to the top curiously as she calls to him. *'Don't go upstairs, it may not be safe,'* the young girl says, as he recedes and she smiles to herself, not having the heart to tell him she thinks he's as curious as a magpie. Scared of the odd mechanical groans Dorothy slowly makes her way to the back of the house, eager to leave as she walks into the kitchen. Looking at the bowls of rotten fruit, and smelling spoilt meat she puts a hand over her mouth and looks to the back garden to find bushels of straw in a small hut. Calling to the scarecrow, he stands beside her as they slowly open the backdoor, looking into the sky to make sure the tin creatures are gone as the pair step outside cautiously. With his eyes focused on the straw scarecrow opens his mouth in anticipation and extends his two bony hands as Dorothy follows behind.

Walking in the open ground she feels uneasy and looks to the small hut, her eyes drifting past the scattered pieces of junk metal as she spies the tall vicious fence and turns. Looking in the sky for tin insects she walks around the yard cautiously, passing odd pieces of junk, walking between fences and scrap metal as she suddenly stumbles to the ground screaming. Scared, she tries to shuffle backward, looking up at a tin monster as he stands fearsomely. His tortured eyes stare at Dorothy, with his mouth as jagged and hungry as a bear-trap, groaning an agonised threat as he clenches a rusted axe in his hands.

11

Dorothy grabs at a handful of dried dirt, throwing it at the tin-man's face in hope of blinding him as she stumbles to her feet, reaching at an old pitchfork as Scarecrow runs to her side. Looking at the monstrosity and waiting for it to attack, her eyes scan along its silver tin exterior, patches worn and rusty as braces and thick bolts hold him together, the joints caked in blood. Ready for the axe to swing Dorothy eyes the tin-man's hands, moulded like thick spiked gauntlets as she stares at its face; his whole head laced with metal as the jagged guard covering his mouth groans, and bloodshot eyes stare in agony.

Dorothy shouts, *'Come on!'* steadily holding the pitchfork, gritting her teeth as she looks to the tin-man, standing still as she notices the thick cross on his chest, its east point tipped with an arrow, Avatonika's mark. Carved deep into the metal Dorothy can see raw skin underneath his armour and slowly lowers her weapon, asking, *'What are you?'* as his voice chisels, *'Tin...'* then after a painful glitch, *'...man.'* Confident that he can't move she looks into his eyes, intensely staring back at her as she asks, *'What's wrong with you?'* Giving the sound of snapped brittle metal he curdles, *'Need oil...'* groaning again as blood trickles from the mouth guard as he continues, *'Small hut.'* As if exhausted his voice still groans lightly and Dorothy holds the pitchfork in hand asking, *'If we help you, will you harm us?'* to which the tin-man's throat scrapes, *'No, have...my word,'* as the blood still dribbles. Dorothy points, *'Go, go get it,'* to the scarecrow as he moves to the small hut to fetch the oil, while she stands holding the pitchfork. Quietly groaning in pain the tin-man watches the scarecrow come back, holding the can of oil in his skeletal hands as he pours it over the blood stained joints. The tin-man's neck loosens at first, then his legs, feet and arms as he drops the axe to the floor, thudding solidly whilst the scarecrow pours the remainder of the can over the metal monster. Groaning in relief, spitting out a mouthful of blood he falls to the floor happily, crouching as he feels the oil seep through the metal and over his skin. The tin-man's eyes dripping a crimson black he says, *'Thank you so much,'* as Dorothy stands, still with the pitchfork in hand as she asks, *'What happened to you?'*

Looking up at the young girl's face, the tin-man's bloody metal exterior, jagged spikes and sharp chiselled teeth seem almost less horrific as he tells his tale:

'I'm a woodsman, just as my father was...not long ago he died, and shortly after so did my mother. I still worked the yard alone, but knew I couldn't bear it much longer. Soon I found a girl, a beautiful girl who said she'd marry me if I could build us a better house, one sturdier than wood alone. So I started work on the house, and when my love told the old woman she lived with the news, she was scorned. For the old woman treated her as a slave, and could not survive without someone to torture. Then one day my love came to me with her skin roar, her eyes blackened and her wrist broken, as although the old woman was frail she had enough strength to abuse a young girl.

Filled with anger I grabbed at my axe ready to confront the old tyrant, but sadly Avatonika took a liking to the old one, even though she lived in the Quadling country...and she helped her stop our chance of marriage. Her evil munchkins took my love away from me, and the wicked witch held me prisoner, scolding my skin every day with fiery water until she was ready to begin her torture. I screamed, begged for her to tell me where my love was but she wouldn't answer me. All she said was that I was too good, in my skin and my heart, then she used my own axe to deform me; firstly cutting off my left leg, then the right, before leaving me for days. I was sure I would die but she kept me alive with her magic, so I could suffer.

Days later she summoned me again, this time cutting away the flesh and bone of my right arm, and then the left. I begged her to let me die, pleaded I'd do anything if she left my love alone...and she agreed. The witch promised me my love's safety, and then used my axe to open my chest and remove my heart. She was happy at my misery but not enough, she didn't want me to die, she preferred I suffer. That's when they replaced my heart with a machine; letting it pump blood through my body, keep me alive as she proceeded to destroy my good skin. I was fully awake when she soldered my limbs back into place, bolting them at the joints and pouring liquid metal over them, letting it set as I suffered. Then placing a metal skeleton over my body she wanted to keep the skin on my chest fleshy, so I could see the scars. After that she continued to design me in this horrific way, making me wear horrific hands and teeth of steel, though replacing most of my skin with weak tin so I could still bleed easily. Now my good features are that of a monster, and my heart stolen. I have no heart to give to my love.'

Dorothy stands with the pitchfork loose in her hand as, *'I'm so sorry,'* comes through sympathetic lips, watching the tin-man rise from the floor. Holding at the armour on his chest with a solid gauntlet he points to a circular mechanism, groaning, *'Inside's the machine that keeps me alive,'* as the young girl looks at his body; the metal a part of him as she eyes the bare pieces of flesh, his skin burnt and stitched up like a cadaver. Watching the tin-man and cooing, *'That's most strange'* the scarecrow abruptly waves his bony hands, tapping at his burlap head and offers:

'Come with us, we're off to Emerald city to see the wizard. I need his help for a brain, he may be able to help you too.'

Dorothy stays silent as Scarecrow invites the tin-man to join them, sceptical of the added company at first, though sure he'll be strong enough to help if Outika finds her. She knows she needs strength on her side, and although she feels sly she can't afford to tell the tin-man that Outika may come, so she simply agrees, *'Yes, please join us.'*

Sure that with a heart he'd be able to find his love again, and hearing through the land how powerful the wizard is, the tin-man accepts. So preparing to leave he takes a fresh can of oil from the small hut, and Dorothy offers to keep it in her wicker basket for him. The scarecrow pads his hands with straw, sewing the flesh back together as the tin-man sharpens his axe, handing the newly fixed Scarecrow a pitchfork. *'Here you may need this,'* he indicates, and the scarecrow takes it in his hand, waving it as he watches the thin spikes cut through the air, cheering, *'This looks fun, but why do I need it?'* The tin-man looks at him confused, taking a firm grip on his axe as he groans, *'The forest can be deadly, and the carnival's in town don't you know?'* to which the scarecrow smiles, *'I don't know much, I have no brain.'*

Walking through the thick woods, again Dorothy nurses Toto's bag, feeling him inside as she holds the wicker basket with the other hand. The scarecrow clenches his pitchfork proudly, swinging it in the air as he walks in front of the others, unaware of their conversation as Dorothy tells the tin-man of Avatonika's death. He seems unfazed at first, only giving the word, *'Good,'* with no happiness, not even as he notices the silver boots on Dorothy's feet as he comments, *'She was proud of them.'* Suddenly realising the pieces don't fit, her head so wrapped up in the tin-man's story the young girl asks, *'How were you rusted outside?'* as an image of the dead munchkin flashes to her, and the tin-man groans:

'One day in the heavy rain I went outside to chop wood, and as they always do the witch's munchkins crept into my yard. They would steal my

wood, hide bear traps in the grass and taunt me, though last time they attacked me and I couldn't fend them off quick enough. One munchkin stole a can of oil I had nearby and they fought me as my joints started to rust in the strong downpour. I was lucky that my pets attacked them, scared them away.'

'We saw a munchkin in your yard, dead,' Dorothy struggles to say as the tin-man groans, almost with a painful smile as chars, 'At least not all of them got way, must be why they never came back.'

Turning around the scarecrow interrupts, 'You made those flying things?' as the tin-man answers, sure he should feel sadness:

'With no heart I didn't have the strength to continue building my love's house anymore, and alone I needed company so I made tin birds, then insects, small creatures that Avatonika wouldn't find.'

Impressed at the tin-man's talent Dorothy looks amazed, though scarecrow points at him with one hand saying, 'Shouldn't make things with wings,' before walking in front again, trying to swipe at flying insects with his pitchfork. The tin-man watches him curiously and thinks of the insects he crushes, wondering for a second if he should be killing the small innocent creatures. Dorothy smiles at the scarecrow then looks back at the tin-man as he effortlessly carries his heavy axe, telling him of her journey so far, and her hopes to get back to Kansas. As she tries to trigger some sympathy from him the only thing she receives is a processed, 'As you have helped me I shall make sure you get to the wizard safely.' Smiling slightly Dorothy finds comfort in her new friends, though feels scared at the thought of what they're both capable of; one a heartless metal monster, and the other found peculiarly crucified, his insides removed. Still she wants to trust them, feels she offers at least the scarecrow that after what he had done for her so far. Sighing with guilt she hates not telling them both that Outika may come for them, though she can't risk frightening them away, not if it means she may never get back home.

Walking along the yellow road their stride is strong as Dorothy drifts deep into thought, and scarecrow dances peculiarly whilst the tin-man asks, 'Do you feel lonely if you don't have a brain?' to which he replies 'I'm not sure, maybe.' Their attention not on the road they fail to hear the large black wheels turning behind them as a wagon charges forward. Drawn by a dirty grey buffalo the wagon's large main's a deep red, and frame a rough black as speeding toward the three it goes un-noticed at first. With the sound closer, no more than several feet away the wheels grind along the yellow bricks as the tin-man turns, grabbing at Dorothy as they dive into the grass, calling to scarecrow. Turning, his eyes widen and he moves his gangly body quickly, as tall as the wagon as he steps onto the verge to wave as it passes by. Thinking it must have been so silent in its approach Dorothy looks up to the wagon, its shape baroque as she looks into the back window to see several peculiar creatures laughing. Angry and shocked she asks, *'What was that?'* as the tin-man stands, shifting his large body as he looks with a stern glare, *'The carnival, it must be tonight. It's the only reason creatures like that come to these parts.'* Dorothy looks at him concerned, thinking of the cloaked man she met when first on the yellow road, and the creature in the spring as she asks worriedly, *'What happens at the carnival?'*

'It travels through Oz with the gypsies. On the surface it's harmless, but underneath it's... you'll see,' the tin-man alludes, as Dorothy shudders, *'I don't understand.'* Lifting his axe the metal monster rests it sturdily on a shoulder, looking down at the young girl as he groans, *'Just be careful, the yellow road will pass through it.'*

TIN-MAN

12

Walking along the road again, the tin-man chops at the tree branches in their path to hear them shrill then recede. At first there were thick chunks of wood; fallen trees in their way as the tin-man took an effortless swing to split them open, throwing them back into the woods. Though now with no obstacles he still swings his axe occasionally, tearing away the flesh of the branches, cutting them to the ground as their sap drips over the bricks. Watching him chop away, almost as if he enjoys it Dorothy asks, *'Why are you still cutting at the branches?'* to which he cuts at another to watch it wriggle on the floor. *'I'm a woodsman,'* he says, and the girl continues, *'What do you know about the trees? They attacked me.'* Staring straight ahead at the forest in front of him he answers without looking her in the eye, *'They're carnivores; they bleed their prey to nourish their roots. Anything warm blooded.'* Swallowing back mild panic, thinking what could have happened to her if the scarecrow didn't come to her rescue sooner Dorothy stutters, *'Wh… why haven't they attacked me again?'*

'Like any species some are more intelligent than others. The stronger predators will wait until nightfall, feed on the weak, the wounded unexpectedly in darkness. That's why they try to block out the light of the sky. Others will try to tempt you to them or hang their braches on common paths, hoping for an effortless meal.'

With a stressed sigh Dorothy looks out to the trees, crooked and twisted, now realizing their intention as something comes to her. The tin-man's is no regular woodsman like in her own world, he doesn't simply chop down trees, he hacks away at their living timber, killing them and peeling away the meat like a butcher would. Watching the scarecrow still swiping at insects, crushing their wings as they fall to the ground Dorothy realises that she's stopped standing on them, putting them out of their misery hours ago. With nightfall soon approaching she looks through the small cracks in the trees to see the fading sun, ready to hide as she thinks of the darkness and the hungry wood. Turning her attention to the road for a second Dorothy looks to the yellow bricks as thin black ooze trails along the cracks, the same substance she found on the road when she first started her journey, but now it grows thicker.

Turning a corner the three follow the road as it bends, curving as they look ahead of them to see an obstacle blocking their path. The scarecrow walks ahead curiously, squinting his worn button eyes as he looks down to the ditch, it's neither large nor deep but the tin-man warns the scarecrow not to get too close.

Moving toward it with a slow curious step Dorothy looks down to see the trees roots, slithering and overlapping like a casket of snakes as they stretch as high as they can. Wriggling with long thin teeth stretched across their tips Dorothy pulls back and the scarecrow looks to the side of the road. Pointing at a path almost hidden amongst the tightly pressed trees he sees the wagons tracks. *'We can go that way!'* he voices, but Dorothy quickly corrects, *'No, we have to stay on the path,'* as the tin-man looks to the pit, groaning, *'Very well, but we have to be careful.'*

Scratching his head with a pointed finger the scarecrow asks, *'Hooowww?'* with his mouth stretched as the tin-man looks to a dead tree, thinking that he could make a bridge. Unsure if it will give the roots more chance of getting their prey he hears Dorothy ask, *'Can't we just jump?'* as she looks to the pit. Asking her, *'Do you think you can?'* she nods at the tin-man, remembering her P.E classes as she watches the scarecrow bob like a broken doll with, *'I think I can I think I can,'* as the tin-man asks him the same question. Preparing themselves the tin-man tells Dorothy to jump first as the roots won't have time to react, and she quietly mouths, *'Okay,'* with a deep breath. Looking to the pit, remembering what the trees did to her last time she's sure that even with her friends helping her, they won't be able to save her if she falls in.

Trying not to think she runs, not giving herself a chance to change her mind as her boots clunk at the ground and she jumps in the air. Gritting her teeth and clenching every muscle in her body she crashes to the other side, her body sliding along the yellow bricks as she gasps for air, winding herself. Next, the scarecrow runs without thought, his light bony body pushing through the air as he looks down at the pit, watching the roots as he lands on the other side and helps Dorothy from the ground.

Looking at the two of them, safely at the other side the tin-man grabs tightly to his axe and throws it across, shattering yellow bricks as it lands, and he looks to see the roots calmly rising. Running to the pit he leaps at the last minute to feel the weight of his heavy body fasten as he looks under his feet to see the roots, trying to reach for him as they stretch and flail their teeth. Ready to feel the impact of the ground he lands on his feet, barely making it across as his left leg stands on the edge of the pit, and cracked stone falls to the vines. Trying to pull his body forward he quickly feels the pressure of a root at his tin back, as two more spring like tentacles and wrap around his left arm. With her eyes keen Dorothy quickly snatches the pitchfork out of the scarecrows hands, knowing she wouldn't be able to lift the tin-man's axe as she stabs at the roots. Piercing their skin with metal spikes they shrill quietly and tense their grip, causing the tin-man to pull away harder as he feels the warm blood pouring from his joints and roars a howling scream. Forcing himself away from the pit his heavy body stretches the roots as their flesh starts to tear. One lets go quickly, shrivelling back as the tin-man rips the others from the ground, watching them wriggle on the floor as he hears a tree groan behind him. Falling to one knee the tin-man looks at his arm, moving it easily and ignoring the blood as he hears Dorothy ask, *'Are you okay?'* but he listens past her voice to hear a curdling war cry. They've awakened a Kalidah.

Shouting, *'Move now, run!'* the tin-man grabs at his axe and jolts quickly as the others follow with speed, hearing the beast. The young girl shouts, *'What's wrong?'* and he cries, *'Kalidahs! No time, we need to run, find shelter!'* Hearing only its roar Dorothy looks behind them to see nothing at first, only the woods and the yellow road as suddenly bursting through the dead trees a colossal beast stands.
Even taller than the scarecrow it roars, its thick body skinned of flesh, shaped like a bear with the head of a tiger as its long forked tongue slashes. Turning her head Dorothy runs as fast as she can, screaming obscenities to herself as the scarecrow looks back, staring at its large yellow eyes, and claws a foot long as he smiles, *'How strange!'* Shouting to make him move faster the tin-man watches as he picks up speed, his long legs quickening as he runs alongside Dorothy.
With no shelter to be seen ahead the three still run for their lives, though the tin-man soon falls behind, his weight heavy to carry and too slow to out run the Kalidah as he turns his head briefly, watching the creature jump over the pit as the roots whip around its leg. Screaming and tearing away their limbs like worms from soil it doesn't stop, its hungry teeth glare and the eyes of a hunter lock on fiercely.
Knowing he won't be able to run much further without the creature catching him, the tin-man slows his legs as the metal grates along yellow stone, and he stands still. Ahead of him Dorothy still runs, her heart racing as she turns to see the tin-man, shouting, *'What are you doing?'* as her body slows and he cries, *'Stay back!'*.
Watching the creature charge, its claws scramming along the bricks the tin-man stands still. Holding his axe in front of him he waits, his eyes fixed, the creature coming closer at tremendous speed, too fast to stop, a chance for attack. Its roar piercing, the Kalidah lifts a claw in motion, ready to swipe and only feet from the tin-man as it strikes.

The thick bone claws come down and the tin-man feels the breeze, pushing his body into the beast's as the fatal strike misses, and the woodsman's axe slices through the monsters belly. Its agonizing cry's unbearable and the tin-man dives to the trees as the Kalidah's speed continues, smashing to the ground as its blood smears over the tin-man's metal. Scraping along the ground the beast's body soon stops dead as the chasm in its chest stretches several feet, and the smell's almost unbearable.

With darkness merely an hour away, Dorothy feels the chill up her back as they trek through the forest again. They've been walking non-stop for several hours and her legs are weakening, her stomach empty as she wonders where they'll rest and eat. Then unexpectedly she hears music in the distance. Pausing in her tracks the scarecrow stands by her side, looking through small gaps in the trees branches as he sees lights, a fantastic bright neon glow as he smiles widely, giving a, *'Oooh!'* Walking behind them the stained tin-man booms, *'The carnival's here,'* as Dorothy asks, *'Will they have shelter for the night?'* The tin-man nods his head concerned, answering, *'Yes they will,'* and she looks at him to feel the scarecrow tapping her shoulder, smiling wildly as his head shakes and he asks, *'Are we going in? It will be fun.'* Dorothy looks back to the troubled tin-man, knowing that this could be the only place with shelter for the night, despite how little she knows of it. Then she places a hand on his, as well as the scarecrow's, as she feels something wicked in the air, hastily assuring, *'Yes, but we have to stay together.'*

13

Walking to the entrance Dorothy feels the grass under her feet, shorter than before as she looks out to a large clearing; every inch covered with bodies, stalls, stages and machines as the carnival's circled by carnivorous trees. They stand tall, silent though leering out at the neon lights, the swarm of bodies fumbling about each other as some slither on the ground and others walk with legs spanning from one to eight. Cautious at first, holding the scarecrow's hand tighter Dorothy looks out to the crowds, some with faces like insects, bodies like animals, and others none at all. A number of them look human, just taller, shorter and oddly shaped, though others hold their brains in jars, some have no arms, and the odd few have skin etched like pieces of a puzzle. Even those that Dorothy thinks as mortal humans are strange to her, and in amazement she stares, her streak of tiredness subdued as she looks to the scarecrow. Shaking his burlap head and fidgeting, his buttons stare as anxious and excited as a child. Turning to Dorothy he asks, *'Can we go in now?'* as the tin-man looks down to the girl and nods his head cautiously. *'I...I suppose so,'* she replies, and before she can say another word the scarecrow runs ahead, pulling her along as the tin-man follows behind and they stand at the entrance.

Dorothy looks at the odd creature at the gate, his skin covered in green blotches as he nods his head with the words, *'Come on in, enjoy!'* to the couple in front of them, but stares tiredly at the tin-man. *'No weapons inside sorry,'* he says with a sigh, and the tin-man replies, *'Do you have rooms for the night?'* Looking at him with worn eyes the gateman enforces, *'We do but you can't take in the weapons,'* as the tin-man answers, *'That will be fine, we'll leave the weapons in the room.'*
'Perhaps you didn't hear me I...' the gateman pushes angrily, and the tin-man moves in closer as his jaw grits and his hands clench on the axe, *'No, you didn't hear me.'* Placing his arms in the air the man steps backwards, easing, *'Fine, okay, okay, but put them away quickly,'* as the trio walk inside to join the crowd.

With his eyes open wide the scarecrow spots the bright colours of the stalls, the toys, peculiar games and he wrenches at Dorothy's arm, pulling her in one direction then another until she holds herself sternly. Her weight grounded she can feel the scarecrow trying to pull her, and as he turns his head she yanks him backwards. *'We find a room first,'* she states, and like a sad pet he looks back to the stalls then follows Dorothy.

The rooms are no more than small single bedded cabins, the sheets stained and the floor grubby, but with a lock on the door Dorothy feels comforted. Standing inside with the owner, a sleazy gnome he snorts, *'Well would you like the room?'* and Dorothy replies kindly as he continues, *'Good. Well what do you have to trade?'* Confused at first, though sure she should have known there'd be a price the young girl asks cautiously, *'What would you like?'* The small man puts a finger to his chin, looking up to the ceiling as he requests, *'Something, unusual.'*

As if for support Dorothy looks to the scarecrow for a second, unsure what to offer as the tin-man steps forward, storming fiercely, *'Have you not seen her boots little man, the white on her dress. Did you not know the eastern witch is dead? This is the new witch.'* Stumbling about himself the gnome mumbles at first, tapping his fingers together as he cheekily gulps, *'A good witch would pay a hard working gnome who...'* Standing next to the Gnome, the large tin-man stares down with hungry eyes, fuming, *'You greedy little man, I tell you that one of the four has chosen one of your cabins for the night, and you still wish to charge?'* Wiping sweat from his brow the gnome's flustered, unsure of what to say as Dorothy thinks quickly and approaches the owner, speaking calm and clearly as he listens without hesitation, *'If we choose not to pay you will receive nothing, though if I am satisfied with the bed and the nights rest you will be rewarded in the morning.'* Placing his hands together then giving a curtsy the owner wipes at his brow again, quickly cowering, *'Yes yes, so kind. Thank, thank you. I'll make sure no-one goes near your room, rest well,'* as he leaves the cabin and closes the door.

Smiling to herself Dorothy looks to the confused scarecrow and the emotionless tin-man as she rambles, *'I know that was wrong but...'*, *'You did well girl,'* the tin-man interrupts, placing his axe to the side of the bed as Dorothy sits on the mattress to hear a creek beneath her. For a second she thinks with an innocent smile, a room for the night with two men, that wouldn't have gone down well at the orphanage. Scarecrow looks empty and Dorothy watches him, thoughtless until he gazes through the small window, jumping, *'Carnival, can we go?'* to which the young girl smiles, her curiosity and fear meshed as they outweigh her tiredness.

In the midst of the crowds Scarecrow pulls at Dorothy's arm, darting from stall to stall and touching at the trinkets, letting the odd lights dazzle his buttons as he bounces gleefully and Dorothy smiles. Walking behind them the tin-man watches, pushing his way through the crowd as he feels their bodies glide along his metal skin. Ignoring them he keeps a keen eye on the odd faces, the ones with a gleam of hope in their eyes as they show interest in his friends. He knows there's something unusual about Dorothy, and without her he fears he may not be granted a meeting with the wizard.

The scarecrow pulls Dorothy from one stall to the next, happily pointing out the fine sights and oddities as they gleam. She laughs aloud to hear him wonder, *'What's this, what's this, ooohh I like that!'* as he places peculiar pieces of jewellery against her skin, and for the first time since she's been in Oz, she enjoys herself. *'So pretty, so pretty,'* he glows dangling golden hooked pieces of amethyst by her face, then holding an emerald chain to her neck, *'So pretty, so pretty,'* as he reaches for an amber pendant and his buttons widen. *'Ooohhh!'* he coos, holding the piece to her neck as he smiles at the dead flies and moths trapped inside. *'So beautiful,'* he raves with a malicious smile, pulling Dorothy to another stall before she notices, smiling along the way. This one beams a light red to its audience as small white horses project in the air and Scarecrow tries to swipe at them before noticing the small playing cards, over fifty of them taped to the back wall.

Pointing at the small distant pictures of kings, queens, hearts and spades he hollers, *'What are those?'* to the owner, as he places a dart in the scarecrows hand, replying, *'They're playing cards, hit the King and win a prize. First dart's free, hit the King.'* Waving the spiked tip in his hand the scarecrow's amazed by the flow of it then throws vigorously, cutting right through the chest of a queen as he turns, distracted by another stall as Dorothy stays for a moment. Sure she heard a cry, a faint whisper of agony she looks to the cards, her eyes focusing, waiting for the slightest movement as the owner offers her a free dart and she kindly refuses. The seconds linger, no movement, not a sound from the cards and Dorothy thinks herself crazy, turning around to follow the scarecrow as the Queen whispers her last words.

Dorothy looks behind her at the tin-man and smiles, following Scarecrow to the centre of the carnival as they join the crowds, gathering around an empty podium. Curious, the young girl feels comfort to have straw and dried skin pressed against one hand, as quickly cold metal embraces the other. Smiling happily she almost forgets the tin-man's warning of the carnival, though as worry creeps in her concentration's shattered by snaring drums. They pulse against the canvas quickly as a trumpet joins the rhythm, and Dorothy looks up to the empty stage to see a purple cannon fire smoke at the audience. Breathing in a quick gasp it catches her throat and she hears the crowds roar in worship, looking past the fogged stage to see a pale ivory man dressed in a tuxedo. His skin bleached, cheeks pitted with birthmarks and lips painted a bright red he smiles. The yellow teeth give no welcome, nor his green eyes surrounded by the deep red of burst blood vessels, though he scuffles his greasy short grey hair confidently. Swinging his cane in circles he looks out to the masses, rubbing his hand along the bald ivory baby head at the tip as he begins:

'Welcome one and all, I am Mr Jack and this is my carnival. Are you ready for a good night?'

The audience cheer in response, some louder than others and the ringleader snaps back to entertain, goading, *'I can't hear you!'* to follow with another roar as he smiles wildly, dancing around the stage ecstatically like a mime. Laughing a loud piercing screech he places a gloved finger to his eye, pulling away the skin beneath as he groans exhaustedly:

'As you can see I've been having too much fun recently, but that won't stop me tonight, because this is our last stop in Munchkin country.'

The crowd sigh, a mass sorrow as Mr Jack sobs falsely, rubbing at his eye and smattering his lips:

'Sad I know, but for all you stalkers the Emerald city will be our next stop. And I promise you I will be personally seeing that you all have a better night than the folk down at Quadling country did. I mean they where fun but a little, dead on their feet when I finished with em', but some people just can't handle their antifreeze can they. They're just a bit too much of a goody two-shoes place for me.'

The crowds cheer and Dorothy watches as some seem excited, clapping vigorously as others stand miserable, smiling as if they're forced to. Her eyes focus on them, their tortured expressions through stretched lips as their eyes water, screaming for help silently. Slowly a small child turns her head from the stage, facing Dorothy with a haunting smile, the skin around her lips scarred as she waves. Looking back at her, about to pull at the tin-man's arm Dorothy feels warm neon along her face and looks up to the stage as reams of distort lights flash behind Mr Jack while he continues:

'That's better. Well I'll keep this short and sweet, like a munchkin dipped in honey...though I must say, what will the bees do to him, Ha! So

enjoy the food, flesh, fun, merriment and remember...We're here to entertain you. So I shall leave you with this; the man who invented it doesn't want it. The man who bought it doesn't need it, and the man who needs it doesn't know it. What is it? Ooh, tonight I feel so...naughty.'

Hypnotised Dorothy watches Mr Jack spread his arms and laugh, surrounded by a sudden burst of smoke as he disappears and she turns back to the crowd. Her eyes scanning the bodies she looks for the child, the tortured smiles and finds nothing but genuine adoration, blaming what she thinks she saw on tiredness, her mind playing tricks on her. As bodies push against Dorothy, moving away from the podium she feels their different skins press tightly; some with brittle hair, scales like a reptile, soft and warm limbs, and even the odd cold touch. She stands still, holding her friends hands as it plays on her mind, Mr Jack's riddle as she ponders, *'I'm sure I know the answer, it's on the tip of my tongue.'* The scarecrow places two hands together, lowering his head to Dorothy's as he distracts, *'Don't think about it, lights were pretty weren't they. Let's go see more things!'*

Quickly Scarecrow pulls her arm and the tin-man loosens his grip, letting her go with the scarecrow as he follows behind cautiously. Her head still a blur and thinking of the riddle, scarecrow leads her to a small stall as she watches fairies no bigger than her little finger fly from a jar. Quickly she forgets and watches bright yellow, green and blue fairies fly from the container, fluttering around the stall before they burst into a rainbow of dust. Shocked, wondering if it's magic she feels scarecrow pulling at her again, taking in the sights of a stall as she peers through the masses. Odd insects float through the air, the hum of electricity drones in her ear and the neon constricts her pupils as she looks out to the different species; playing games and browsing through stalls just like people back home.

For a second she wonders if there's much of a difference between the worlds, watching a baby seferine bounce a ball happily. Dorothy's smile widens, watching the families wander as she catches something at the corner of her eye. Standing still, unmoved by the buzz of the crowd a figure waits, looking at her through the cover of a hood as she recognises the brown cloak and the green-scaled hands, the creature from the yellow road. Pulling at the scarecrow she points out to the crowds shouting, *'Did you see that?'* and he looks quizzically, asking, *'See what?'* Her voice drifts as she looks again, the cloaked figure gone as she runs a hand over her face, murmuring, *'He was there, I know he was.'* Feeling the scarecrow pull at her she hears his voice cheer, *'Don't worry, no need to think, let's see more,'* as her eyes latch onto the tin-man in the distance and she stretches out an arm. Keeping his space at first he moves quicker as he notices her hand reaching and presses a metal palm against her skin. Asking, *'Did you see the figure, in the cloak?'* the tin-man grumbles, *'No,'* as the scarecrow stands in front, looking to a house of mirrors as he turns quickly, encouraging, *'Can we go inside, it's free, think what we can see.'* A little shaken at first Dorothy doesn't answer, but as the faint, *'I suppose...'* leaves her lips the scarecrow's already inside as she stands at the door with the tin-man. Feeling a little vulnerable she takes a breath, telling herself she's just on edge because she's tired and hasn't eaten yet. Even if the cloaked figure is here Dorothy knows she's safe with her friends, and as she tells the tin-man, *'We should go in,'* she hears the scarecrow's voice echo, *'How fascinating,'* as she smiles and steps inside.

Dorothy gives a faint giggle straight away, looking to the gangly scarecrow as his reflection portrays him short and fat. Staring in one mirror at himself he declares, *'How peculiar,'* then moves to another which shows him even taller, thinner than usual as he scratches his head with, *'Extraordinary!'* Dorothy follows him, looking at her reflection with a smile though more interested in Scarecrow's as the tin-man trails behind, ignoring the mirrors. Looking at a peculiar child standing by a mirror the scarecrow pokes at his stretched out and chubby reflection as he smiles, *'You look so odd, such a round head.'* He taps a hand on the little one's brow and Dorothy laughs as she runs to his side. Holding his waist and keeping him in one position she stands behind him, stretching her arms to her sides as Scarecrow looks at his reflection, distort and unusual as he notices the extra pair of arms extending from his torso. Flapping his limbs he smiles broadly as his thin jagged mouth widens. *'Well, I look very peculiar, though not as much as her,'* he says, pointing to a troll woman before taking Dorothy's hand and whisking her to the next room. Looking at Dorothy's face as she laughs the scarecrow touches her lips with his worn skin, giving an enthusiastic, *'So pretty when you smile,'* before running away as his buttons adapt to the new room.

Still smiling, looking at the scarecrow to feel happy she watches him run along a wall lined up with a dozen mirrors, all showing a true reflection as he amazes himself. Quickly turning back to check the tin-man's behind her Dorothy follows the scarecrow through the maze of mirrors as the heartless metal man looks at his reflection, sure he should feel sad at what stares back at him. Pressing a cold hand against the glass he thinks of what's been taken from him, the witch who changed him already dead as he follows Dorothy's laughter, trying to ignore the face staring back at him. Her belly tightening with laughter she chases after the scarecrow as he moves quickly in front of her, touching at the glass and shouting with delight. Watching him push further into the maze, she still smiles at his reaction, turning a corner to see him moving further away as she tries to keep up. Calling, *'Scarecrow, wait,'* she watches him turn another corner, his reflection disappearing as she runs toward him, stretching out a hand and gliding her fingers along the glass.

Reaching the corner, she looks to see nothing but her own reflection, feeling a gap along the glass panels as she steps into another layer of the maze then back again. Calling out, *'Scarecrow, tin-man!'* she feels her muscles tighten, nerves peak as she looks around to see nothing besides herself, sure she couldn't lose them so easily. Running along her original path she wonders if Scarecrow disappeared through the gap and debates going back to the beginning in hope of finding the tin-man.

Distort, lost in the maze she calls out their names again, presses a hand against the glass and moves quickly, feeling at one, two, three gaps as the maze curves and she spins in a circle. Her heart beating faster and her patience brittle she runs through the maze, moving into a gap in the glass to run through another layer, then another as she starts to feel dizzy and leans against her reflection. Calling out their names again she looks ahead of her to a corridor full of mirrors, as her body slides down the glass and her head spins. Taking short breaths, trying to keep calm she notices a flicker in the mirrors and her eyes widen, waiting to see the scarecrow as the flicker of a body comes again. Catching a glimpse of thick brown cloth, a grimy cloak she panics, and before she can stand the light quickly disappears, leaving her in darkness.

14

In the darkness Dorothy clenches a fist, keeping her body pressed against the glass and stands slowly. The seconds feel too long, as a faint sound of breathing comes closer and suddenly the lights beam again. Feeling the need to scream but repressing it the young girl looks in front of her to see a cloaked figure as she readies herself to attack, sure of who it is until she see hears the feeble voice. *'Are you okay dear?'* the old lady asks, and Dorothy looks under the hood to see a wrinkled woman looking back at her worried. Her throat dry she feels relieved, and the old lady smiles, *'It's okay, let's get you out of here shall we?'* Slowly nodding back, Dorothy follows her, asking, *'Have you seen anyone else in here, a scarecrow and a man made of metal?'* The old lady shakes her head, frowning, *'Sorry dear, you're the first person I've found,'* continuing, *'you're a smart girl though, I'm sure you'll find them.'*

Slowly finding their way out of the maze Dorothy thanks the old lady, and in return she clasps her hands as they stand outside the house of mirrors. *'The honour's mine, here take this,'* says the elderly woman, handing her a small pouch, *'I'm sure you'll need it.'* Dorothy smiles thankfully though trying to pull away as the woman's grip tightens, '*Please take it, a sign of my appreciation to the new witch of the east.'* Smiling at first Dorothy utters, *'I...'* but the enthusiastic old lady presses, *'You seem kind, you'll do Oz well, please take it.'* Forcing it into her hands with a gleam in her eye the old lady walks away and Dorothy holds the pouch, shouting, *'Thank you,'* as she opens it up to see a mound of silver coins. Feeling comforted by the kind act she doesn't feel so scared without her friends and walks to the front of the house of mirrors, finding the owner who's a scraggedy man holding his brain in a jar. Dorothy asks him if he's seen her friends and he points her to the left of the carnival, telling her they came out a few minutes ago. Wanting to believe him she still waits outside the house of mirrors for a minute longer, and then makes her way through the carnival.

Watching different species play odd games she catches the odd bursts of fairy dust and smiles, looking over to a stall where a creature with the body of a child stands tall, with its legs and arms like thin spiders legs. Looking at the game he tries to play Dorothy laughs as he holds a ball between his legs, stretching them out and touching the ring as the owner taps him on the shoulder yelling, *'C'mon kid, the object's to throw the ball.'* Covering her mouth with a hand, not wanting to seem rude she looks to a stall and the glimmer of an orange stone catches her eye as she spots it amongst a handful of necklaces. Touching at it with her fingers, she holds the flat circular piece as it gleams against the light, spiralling different shapes as she holds the leather strap in her hand. Gently gasping, *'It's beautiful,'* she asks the stall owner how much and he smiles through webbed lips, *'For you my dear just one silver, that's real tangine stone y'know.'* Pulling a coin from her pouch she nods, *'I'll take it,'* as she watches the peculiar shapes move within the stone and quickly places it in her bag with Toto. Stroking her small companion she says, *'Oz isn't so bad Toto, not so bad at all,'* thinking she'd like to take him out and hold him in her arms, though doesn't want to risk losing him.

Feeling her stomach grumble she moves along again, ducking under a small rainbow as two children throw a circle back and forth, each time spiralling new colours. Smiling at her one of the children laughs, *'Sorry miss,'* and she smiles back, *'No worries,'* as she looks into the distance hoping to see her friends. Walking past a food-stall Dorothy looks at the foreign items, some insects, sweets and others things she can't describe except their unusual colours and shapes. Then she sees something that makes her curiosity quiver; two taps in front of long black curtains, as a weird shaped woman pours a glass of thick red juice and serves it to a customer.

Staring at the tough fabric, the tap moving slightly as the curtain shimmers her imagination runs wild, curious what's hidden behind it as a strong hand grabs at her wrist. At first shocked, though with a sudden relief she's sure it's one of her friends and turns around to see the cloaked figure next to her, leering a thick, *'How much?'* Pulling her arm away Dorothy looks to the figure, its scaled hand riddled with leeches as darkness hides its face. Moving quickly she turns from the stranger and walks, her legs tensed like pistons as she distances herself and looks to see the figure stand still at first, but then he follows.

Looking in the distance, hoping to find a familiar face Dorothy thinks quickly and turns a corner, running through the carnival as she dips behind stalls. Looking to see the figure in the distance, surrounded by the crowd and unsure where she is Dorothy squeezes between two tents, moving to the outskirts of the carnival. Passing a few carriages then hiding behind a small hut, she keeps in the darkness, away from the bright light of the attractions in hope the figure won't find her. Feeling the beat of her heart pound relentlessly in the cold quiet she looks again to see no one, and waits behind the hut for a moment longer. Taking a deep breath she watches the trees, closer than she'd like them to be as she remembers what the tin-man said, how they prey on the weak in darkness.

With her body pressed against the hut she realises how stupid she was coming out this far and creeps around the side. Distancing herself, scared to get any closer she looks out to the carnival to see the cloaked figure standing in her way, waiting. Without gasping she stands still, tells herself she'd be lying if she didn't expect this, but that doesn't mean she's not scared. Her lips open with no words at first, just a warm breath as she musters, *'What do you want?'* Silent, watching her fear grow the figure walks closer, and Dorothy moves backward begrudgingly, aware of the trees.

With every step the stranger takes she does the same, pulling away with, *'What do you want?'* as she watches the small hut grow distant and feels moistness under her feet, looking down to murky water slithering with vines and roots. This time screaming, *'What do you want?'* Dorothy stands still, grounding herself as she refuses to step back any further.

Silent at first the stranger keeps walking, feeling the girl's fear as she stretches out an arm, warning, *'Stay back!'* as he steps even closer, forcing her to pull back her limb in dread of touching him. Standing strong, knowing she shouldn't move back she watches the figure, closer than arms length as it groans a tainted, *'Want to trade?'*

Her lips dry and fists clenched she grits her teeth, venomously biting, *'For what?'* as the stranger lifts his scaled hands to pull back his hood, revealing his face. Looking at him Dorothy can't help but panic, muttering under her breath, *'God that's ugly!'* as she looks at its green scaled face. His mouth stretches from the tip of his chin to the side of his cheek with thick red lips, as wide yellow eyes stare with oval pupils and the main of his face flakes as if burnt by the sun. Flicking a thick red tongue he pleads, *'A kiss from a witch,'* as Dorothy thinks of trying to talk her way out of it, telling him she's not a witch, but she knows he won't listen.

Silent she wonders, daring not to run in case he's too strong, pins her to the ground as he groans again, *'I'll take what I want whether you like it or not. I need it!'* Dorothy sweats, feeling she could cry, remembering the drunken fake fathers as suddenly she realises she's not just a girl anymore, she doesn't have to be on best behaviour because of the orphanage, take the abuse without making a sound. This is Oz, and there's no strings attached, she's in control and no-one who can stop her going home.

Almost smiling in bemusement she stares at the stranger, dazed as he pushes, *'Well...'* and Dorothy smirks, uncomfortably trying to flirt, placing a finger on her lip as she asks, *'What will you me trade for a kiss?'* He slithers, *'Anything, I need this,'* and Dorothy's skin trembles, her body awkward as she takes a step closer and places a hand on his shoulder. She'd seen women do this in movies, heard stories in the orphanage of girls trying to get what they want from men, but not from creatures like this. Trying not to shake, show a single expression of disgust she feels clunky in her movements, forcing her head closer to the stranger as he opens his wide mouth and Dorothy cringes. She knows what she has to do to get home, no-matter how much she may hate it, and as the figure closes his large yellow eyes she whispers, *'Just be gentle.'*

Opening her mouth, lingering it over the creature's thick red lips she clenches her eyes shut to feel his hand along her bare leg. With his breath spreading along her face she's scared and keeps a clenched fist, feeling his scaled palm on her thigh as she quickly bites into his lip to hear an agonising shriek. Forcing her mouth shut she cuts through the flesh, pulling her head away, tearing at a chunk of meat as his blood pours and she quickly punches him in the temple.

Stumbling away from him as he falls to the floor in agony Dorothy spits out a piece of his lip and wipes blood from her chin, stepping away from the trees and watching the hungry vines suddenly latch to the fresh prey. With the thick wooden shards cutting into his skin the stranger struggles, tries to pull away as he looks to Dorothy, his deep yellow eyes begging for help as she quickly runs away. Looking back she can hear him beg, *'Help me,'* as he stretches out an arm and Dorothy shouts, *'Aunt Em' wouldn't have approved of you, no manners,'* before blowing a kiss and smiling, *'Have a nice night!'* Walking backward and watching him struggle against the branches Dorothy hears his screams fade as the wooden hands clasp at his face, dragging him into the forest as she almost feels proud, relieved that her plan worked.

Feeling safer with the lights of the carnival on her Dorothy moves back into the crowds and tries not to think too much about what she's just done. Her eyelids flutter as she sees a fairy just above her nose, its tiny face panicked as it flies into the distance, bursting into dust. Thinking of how odd it seems she turns around to watch several children playing with a stuffed toy, pulling it in different directions as the fabric tares and the fluff pours out. Walking toward them she notices the forced smiles on their faces, scarred into their skin as they run away and Dorothy's left looking down at the stuffed toy. Unsure what she expects to see she smiles, tells herself she's just tired as she lets the odd thoughts fade.

Raising her head she looks around the carnival, still amazed by the different species, the odd games as she starts to walk ahead and feels a hand on her arm, hearing the words, *'How good to see you,'* as she turns around with a smile. Wrapping her arms around the scarecrow, excited she reaches for her bag, teasing, *'I've got something for you,'* as she pulls out the tangine necklace with a smile. Holding it to the light she watches the shapes float in the stone as she gazes at Scarecrow, his buttons wide as he grins, *'How beautiful,'* touching at it with his fingers. Holding at the necklace she stands on the tips of her toes and ties it around the scarecrows neck, watching him fidget with the stone as he smiles, *'Thank you,'* and she replies, *'You're welcome, I thought you'd like to look at it through the nights when I'm asleep, so you don't get bored.'* Holding the stone between his long bony fingers he chimes, *'I will,'* as Dorothy queries, *'Where's the tin-man?'* to which the scarecrow looks at the girls face, putting a finger to his head as he struggles to think, *'He, he, um....I forgot. I'm sorry.'* Optimistic she rubs his arm then holds his hand, comforting, *'That's fine, we'll find him.'*

As they walk through the carnival, Scarecrow's spoilt for choice as his eyes drift between the new sights and the stone around his neck. Guiding him through the masses they walk past a large tent and Dorothy hears the sick cackle of Mr Jack as she peers through a hole in the fabric to look inside. Her vision's blurred as she catches the glimmer of metal hooks, making the hole bigger with a thumb as her eyes widen; looking at tortured bodies hanging from the hooks as they groan pathetically.

With a shiver along her spine Dorothy stares at them, almost naked and wrapped in tight red plastic, lamenting with their faces covered with twisted masks as they hang constricted. Unsure what she's witnessing Dorothy watches the dark Mr Jack point to two of them, deciding, *'I'll have that one and that one,'* before turning his head, giggling, *'I spy with my little eye.'* Moving quickly Dorothy pulls the scarecrow's hand, and the ringleader bursts from the tent with arms spread wide. *'You want an autograph, blood, DNA, I'm full of them,'* he greets, and Dorothy eyes him up and down, pulling a face as she pipes, *'Good for you, what are you doing in there?'*

Pointing a finger to her face Mr Jack smiles, stretching his thin lips as his yellow teeth shine with slickness, smarting, *'Ya know what they say about curiosity?'* Without changing her expression, refusing to be impressed or intimidated she boasts, *'It solved the riddle,'* and Mr Jack turns his back, muttering, *'Everyone's a comedian,'* as he flings the entrance open. Looking into the deep dark tent Dorothy watches the metal rack, hooks supporting the confined bodies as the ringleader raves, *'It's all part of the show, wanna be in it?'* Sternly replying *'No,'* as the scarecrow stares obliviously into his stone necklace Dorothy asks, *'What show?'* and Mr Jack runs a hand through his greasy hair, slithering, *'The fu...reak, shooow! Best in Oz. Sure you don't want in?'* Then his eyes scan Dorothy's body, skimming down the dress, her bare knees then her silver boots. *'Ohh, I could give you a really big part. I've never had a witch before,'* Mr Jack smiles. *'And you're not going to!'* She bites, as he groans confidently, *'Listen, why don't you come inside, I'll show you around. Backstage access!'*

'What about my friend?' Dorothy asks curiously, and Mr Jack dryly sneers, *'Lean him against a post or something.'* Looking at Dorothy's dress as he flicks at the frills, about to touch her as she grabs at his finger, bending it backwards, *'Listen, whatever you touch me with I will break off, understand Jack!'* Sulking, he pulls back his finger in a huff like a spoilt child before laughing, *'My your feisty, I hate that in a girl. Prefer them stiff as a board if you know what I mean,'*

'Real charmer aren't you?' Dorothy says sarcastically, hearing his, *'Well I do my best to please,'* as she snares, *'It would please me if I stapled your mouth shut.'* She smiles before walking away as Mr Jack shouts in one last attempt to get her attention, intriguing, *'At least come to the show. You've never seen anything like it.'* Dorothy hesitates, curiously answering, *'Maybe, b*ut *if you try anything funny remember what I can do,'* as she points to her boots and smiles. Watching them walk away Mr Jack mumbles with his efforts crushed as he lashes out at the scarecrow, bullying him with, *'Hey Scarecrow, your um, your heads misshapen,'* to which he replies innocently, *'I know, you're quite ugly too,'* as he plays with his necklace.

Walking through the carnival with a joyful stride Dorothy makes her way to the freak-show, guiding the distracted scarecrow through the crowds as he takes in the sights, pointing with a curious innocence: *'Oooh, look at that, and that, what's that one? I never saw one of those before.'* Dorothy watches children playing colourful games, and carnival entertainers dazzle their customers, as the scarecrow makes sure she doesn't miss a thing. Moving along without a care, hoping to find the tin-man, little do they know that he's lingering behind them, following in the distance. Keeping a watch over them he observes as they walk to the freak-show and decides to make himself known. *'Dorothy!'* He calls walking toward them, seeing her turn around with a smile as she takes his hand. *'We're going to the Freak-show, you coming?'* she asks, and he looks down at her, replying dubiously with, *'I better had,'* walking to the entrance as he continues, *'We'll have to be careful though the ringleader collects oddities like us.'*

15

With their bodies shuffling along the freak-show's dark corridor Dorothy holds the scarecrow's hand as the tin-man walks besides them, keeping on guard. Joined by several other visitors they walk through the attraction, just part of an audience preparing to be entertained as they hear peculiar noises coming from the floor. With the light dim enough so they can barely see their way Dorothy feels something at her legs, a small hand groping her as others feel the same and give sounds of worry mixed with mild laughter. Feeling it again, the odd pressure against her skin she looks down to see nothing and the tin-man walks calmly in his stride, fearless as he assures, *'Don't be scared, they're just gnomes, made invisible by one of Outika's spells.'*

With the odd touch of skin against her Dorothy swipes it away to hear the rest of the audience laugh in amusement as she asks, *'Are they always invisible?'* The tin-man answers, *'Yes, a punishment I've heard the witch finds amusing,'* and the thought scares Dorothy, to never be seen by anyone, not even herself. As they walk forward the tin-man feels a touch along his legs and swipes his spiked gauntlet downward without thought. A small scream echoes through the hall and the audience talk amongst themselves in jest, unsure what's happening as an invisible gnome lies on the floor, struggling to breathe.

At the end of the corridor, they walk into a small dark room, still barely dim enough to see in front of them as they sit along the two rows of chairs and look out to the stage. Covered in a thick red curtain the audience watch the platform, waiting for the show to begin as Mr Jack's voice staggers through the darkness:

'Welcome one and all, prepare yourselves because I have all the wonders of Oz to show you!'

Suddenly the dim light disappears, and left in darkness the audience flutter as Dorothy holds Scarecrow's hand tighter, preparing herself as the crowd's voices flicker in the dark. Waiting in the cold tense seconds without warning a bright spotlight shines onto the thick red curtains before they open, and what can only resemble a kalidah roars at them. Chained to the ground it swipes a claw several feet from their faces and they grab tighter at their chairs, pushing their hands against the cold metal as the creature watches them hungrily. Looking closely at the beast Scarecrow's fascinated as he looks to what seems like a tiger, though with its body skinned of flesh and the head of a bear as it lashes a forked tongue. Mouthing *'How weird,'* the scarecrow pats his chin and Mr Jack walks onto the stage, this time dressed in a red suit as he twirls his cane and smiles fiendishly:

'This my friends is a kalidah believe it or not. Though quite deformed, he still has the killer instincts of his pureblooded brothers, yet is the only one of his kind. He is a rare breed and quite a sight wouldn't you say. Now which of you is brave enough to give him a hug?'

The crowd sit obediently, some laughing mildly and others groaning in shock as Mr Jack hears a voice above the others, a heckling jeer, *'That's not real, it's just a tiger in a mask!'* To which the ringleader licks at his lips, pointing his cane to the man, *'I assure you a skinned tiger doesn't look like this, though if you don't believe me you're welcome to try and pull its head off....'*

With his cane still pointed at the audience Mr Jack waits for another response, a sarcastic reply but hears nothing as he quickly clicks his fingers. Abruptly two masked men come into spotlight and grab at the creature's chains, leading it off stage with force as a small cage rolls on in its place, wrapped in a silk sheet. Walking alongside it the ringleader glides a gloved hand along the material as he continues: *'Now this little thing is, well I suppose unique is the right word to use but I'd say he looks rather...two faced.'*

Tearing away the silk sheet, one of Avatonika's munchkins stands in the cage, screaming out to the crowd as it squeezes his hands through the bars trying to grab at Mr Jack. With a unified sound of awe, the audience mutter amongst themselves as they watch the munchkin savagely attacking its prison, focusing on the creature's two heads as one screams and the other slumps lifelessly. Pointing a finger to the munchkin Mr Jack smiles, teasing it before he looks out to the crowd cheerfully:

'You see, this rarity is one of Avatonika's rejects. As when she tried to make what we all know now as munchkins, there were of course certain, deformities, and this one was born with two heads, although one is rather lifeless, and I'll tell you why. You see, this little creature is a savage bundle of flesh, and used to have two fully working screaming, seeing and

hearing heads. Although one day it decided to attack itself and beat one of its own faces to death. It's odd I know and how could it still live? Why has the other head simply not rotted? Well my friends these are types of oddities my show brings.'

Again, by simply clicking his fingers two masked men roll the cell backstage and Dorothy watches curiously, no longer holding the scarecrows hand as they both stare with amazement. Unsure whether she should be worried or not she knows that the tin-man was right, all three of them are the kind of oddities that Mr Jack would like to twist into a unique show, but she's not scared. Intensely she watches the stage as the ringleader confidently boasts, bringing on a hammerhead with no arms or legs, then conjoint goonlens, followed by the bound humans on hooks, and finally a snake woman. Begging for help she stretches her arms out to the audience, pleading for her suffering to stop as the top half of her body's scaled flesh, whilst her lower torso is nothing more than a thick snake's tail. Mr Jack walks around the caged woman, tapping his cane along the bars as he looks down to her twisted spine then back to the audience.

'This young woman was a gift from Outika, the western witch. Apparently, she was a normal human slave girl, who found herself a victim to the queen because she simply refused to eat meat. The witch was shocked, appalled at such insolence and turned her into this thing you see, and I assure you she suffers greatly. Even more so that now, changed into this...thing, the poor creature craves only meat, and of course prefers her prey alive.'

Dorothy's curiosity turns cold, the amazement at such sights soured as she realises the suffering these creatures must feel. With a sickness in her stomach she knows she can't leave, doesn't want to make a spectacle and draw attention to herself in a place like this. Instead she sits silently, prepared for what's to come as Mr Jack prances around the stage, smiling, *'I promised you unusual sights didn't I!'* Then sitting on the edge of the stage he's in the centre of the spotlight as the curtain closes behind him. Laughing manically at first, smiling to the audience like they're children his jagged voice creeks:

'Would you like to hear a story...of course you would. Once upon a time, there was a family who were stricken with poverty, so much so that the hut they lived in had holes in the roof, and their beds were sold long ago to buy food.

The father had lost his job because he cut his own fingers off when chopping wood, what a silly man, and the poor mother was so sick she could barely walk. Though the worst was that in sickness and with no money they had to raise two ten year old boys. So for months the family sold their possessions for food, but made sure that they kept their warmest set of clothes. First the tables, chairs and beds went, and the poor sick mother had to rest on the floor. With no furniture they had enough food for a month, and that month was good, until there was nothing left to eat.

Then the Father tried to pick fruit from barren trees and hunt for fare, only to be attacked by a lion and lose one of his eyes. Quickly he sold his tools to feed the family, and didn't even think of paying to see a doctor. Content on rationing their food they ate for another month, though the mother's sickness was getting worse with so little to eat, and the father ate less to give her more.

Then the next month the father sold everything but the blankets they had to sleep on, and the clothes on their backs. The children's toys went too, how sad they were that day. Then that month the father ate even less and gave more to the mother, as did one of the boys. His father was so proud of him, though understood why his other son would not share, as they were all so hungry.

Soon they had run out of food again, though this time had nothing to sell, and the father's blindness quickly spread to the other eye.

With the parents too sick to leave the hut they sent their two young boys to try and find food or money. That day the father told them to be careful, and understood why they may not want to come back to such a poor miserable home, but he begged them to be kind and bring back food for their sick mother, as he had suffered so much to feed them all and loved her so.

Now alone in the wide world the brothers set out, one who tried his hardest to find food and money, and the other who simply didn't care. At first the good son sat at the side of the yellow road begging for money day and night whilst his brother played games and slept contently. Waking in the night the bad son would creep into the forest and eat bread that he'd been stuffing into his pockets for days, not wanting to share.

Soon without food, and having made no money at all the good son decided he had to try to hunt, even though he hated the thought of it. Unsuccessful at first he persisted all day and night even though he was tired and weak, starving whilst the bad son trailed behind eating pieces of bread and crushing insects happily. That night the good son struggled through the dark forest, trying to keep awake as he hopelessly hunted for food, and by chance he stumbled into a lion cub. Scared at first and his hunger ravenous he didn't know what to do, but when the cub told him that his family was killed by a pack of kalidahs and he was lost in the forest, the good son couldn't bear to harm him. Though the bad son eagerly grabbed at a shard of wood when he saw how weak the cub was, wanting to kill it even though his stomach was full of bread. The good son protected the animal, and that night they slept together in the forest as the bad son crept away to eat his supper.

Over the next few days, the good son and the lion survived on leaves and grass alone, begging for money at the side of the yellow road as they played games and kept each other warm through the nights. Then one day the bad son realised that he had run out of bread, and as he watched his brother and the cub begging he didn't know what to do. Their begging had gotten them no money and later that day as they walked along the road, the bad son noticed that a small deformed munchkin was imploring passers-by for loose change. He watched as they looked down at the cripple's broken legs and misshapen features, either laughing as they passed or sighing out of pity, throwing money in the small creatures can.

Later that night having eaten leaves from a dying tree the good son was ill, and the cub laid next to him, keeping him warm as the bad son watched, feeling a rumble in his stomach. He was not starving yet, but he was hungry, and because of that he waited until his brother and the cub slept, and then found the heaviest stone he could lay his hands on.
Deforming his good brother beyond belief he knew the cub would protect his friend, and tore out chunks of his hair, threatening, 'If you harm me lion I will kill my brother.' Scared that his only friend may die the cub was obedient and protected his friend, begging that he not be hurt anymore.

The following morning the bad son made the cub carry his deformed brother, and they waited by the side of the road for passers-by. As they came, the bad son exhibited his brother, showing him off to the crowds as he begged for help, pleading through a shattered jaw and nursing mangled bones. That day the bad son earned enough money to feed himself, and within a week he earned enough to buy a small cart: which he sat in, and made the lion pull as well as carry the good son on his back.

Now as the months passed, the bad son had become very successful in exhibiting his brother, and made so much silver and gold that he couldn't count it all. In fact he earned so much money he could feed himself, his brother and the lion, but more importantly he made sure that the lion was tamed, and he paid men to make his good brother look even more horrid than ever before.

Then one day he bought a carriage to travel in, and he continued to travel around Oz, scorning the lion for silver as the crowds watched in amazement, and presenting his brother for gold. After some time the bad son, now eleven years old, decided he should go to his parent's dreary little hut. So after days of travelling he finally arrived, and as he stepped inside the home he grew up in, he saw his parents dead on the floor and simply turned his back.

Now children, with that in mind I have some very bad news, and that is that one of our special guests died yesterday...'

The crowd groan sadly, almost humouring the ringleader as he pulls a mock frown: *'But don't be sad. As it has taken years to perfect this special exhibit, and he is a true rarity, I didn't want you to miss out. So although he's a little cold I present for his last public appearance, the good son, and the lion.'*

Dramatically the curtain opens, the folds quickly pulled aside as Mr Jack moves with them, not wanting to obscure the spotlight on the shows stars. Dorothy looks out to the stage as she covers her mouth, astonished and sickened by the sight as Scarecrow stares, tilting his head confused, *'Don't think I like looking at this.'* Propped up in a chair the good brother sits lifelessly, and the lion crouches on all fours with a broad metal collar around his neck, chaining him to the floor. With his thick brown coat dirty and his mane dishevelled, broad scars spread along his muscular body and patches of his skin stand out a dark pink where he's be sheered brutally. Roaring to the audience his thick white teeth gleam and he stares fearsomely with a single yellow eye as a scar stretches through the other; leaving it a dead crystal white as the wound spans from the tip of his forehead down to the left side of his snout. Moving his feet along the stage his thick black claws cut at the wood effortlessly, and suddenly he stands on his two back legs, stretching to seven feet before hunching its back like a human. With the veins bulging through its strong body the creature stands tall again, its tail lingering above the floor as the fierce beast lifts one of its front legs to wave at the audience like it's been taught, snarling occasionally with a sad glare. The crowds watch in awe at the lion, as Mr Jack clicks his fingers and animal roars a fierce battle cry. Dorothy stares, amazed at the size of the creature, as its head alone is half the size of her. She'd never seen a lion before, not even been to a zoo as she watches a gnome walk onto the stage. Mr Jack proudly smiles to the audience, twirling his cane again as he allures:

'Now my dear audience, this looks like a fierce lion does it not?'

The crowd groans in compliance, smiling with their comments as the ringleader stretches a hand out to them and places it against his ear, taunting, *'I can't hear you!'* as they groan again, this time louder as some cheer and Mr Jack responds:

'Well I beg to differ...As you have seen he can stand like a human and he's been taught to wave, but I'm going to demonstrate to you, how I Mr Jack have tamed the king of the beasts.'

With a click of the ringleader's fingers, the lion folds his body down to the floor and stands on all flours again, looking with a hungry glare at the audience as its fearsome jaws slowly open. Dorothy watches the beast, its sad yellow eye watering as Mr Jack shouts out to the audience:

'Are any of you brave enough to put your head in this lion's mouth?'

Suddenly the odd mutters, the groans of entertainment fall silent and the audience looks to the smiling host. Lingering on their lack of response he laughs to himself, pointing his cane first to an elderly hammerhead, then at Dorothy as she looks back at him with contempt. Retracting his stick he places it on his shoulder adding, *'Tough crowd!'* as the gnome steps from beside him and approaches the lion. Watching him with disgust the animal thinks of sinking his teeth into the flesh of the gnome this time, but as the ringleader plays to the crowd he feels the small hands against his lips and waits obediently.

'Well lucky for us we have s a small friend that's braver than you!' Mr Jack goads as the gnome places his head into the lion's mouth, feeling the saliva along his brow as he smiles to the audience, accepting their cheers. Dorothy watches unmoved, refusing to take entertainment in the creature's

misery as he stands solemnly, waiting for it all to end. Then as the gnome removes his head, the lion closes his mouth, unable to get rid of the sour taste as Mr Jack clicks his fingers:

'Now I know that looked fun, but I'm sure you know that the best way to prove you've tamed an animal, is to do your worst to it.'

With a carved smile stretching along his pale skin he runs next to the lion, screaming in his ear, *'Your mother's a squirrel!'* as the audience laugh and the beast stands still, preparing himself as a hooded man hands the ringleader a cat o' nine tails. Throwing his cane to the assistant Mr Jack holds the whip tightly, standing next to the lion as it tenses his muscles, waiting for the pain as the ringleader stresses:

'Ladies and gentlemen I give you, the cowardly lion.'

Then the whip comes down, again, and again as the creature feels himself weaken, letting the pain and blood spread over his body as Dorothy closes her eyes, unable to watch as she whispers, *'Poor thing'*, to hear the whip crack its skin open. Thinking she should do something, make it stop she knows she can't, not if it means risking her chance to get home, and her own selfishness tears her insides apart.

Soon the lion lies bleeding on the floor and Mr Jack drops the whip with a smile. The show's over, and as the tortured beast is dragged offstage the blood smears under him as the ringleader boasts:

'Well I hope you enjoyed the show, it is my pride and joy. And remember kids, if you know anyone unusual, I want them. Goodnight!'

Abruptly the curtains close, the spotlight disappears and the dim light re-emerges as Dorothy finally opens her tearful eyes. Looking at her the scarecrow sulks, *'Wasn't good to watch was it?'* and she wipes away the tears, shaking her head as she grits her teeth. Without another word she stands from her seat and walks back into the dim corridor, letting her friends follow behind her as she feels the invisible gnomes groping at her legs again to give a solid kick, and then another as its yelp echoes and she leaves quickly.

Outside she catches her breath, running a cold hand along her face as she clears away the moistness from her eyes and watches Scarecrow and the tin-man coming closer. Tilting his head the scarecrow gently places a hand against Dorothy's shoulder, looking at the bitter expression as his thin mouth opens. *'What's wrong?'* he asks, and the girl tries to hold in her temper as she looks at him fiercely, *'You don't understand do you?'* Shaking his head slightly, confused he slowly replies, *'No,'* as Dorothy continues, pointing to the tin-man, *'He was right, this place...we...'* Then at the corner of her eye the girl watches the twisted ringleader approach suavely, stretching his long thin red lips and asking confidently, *'Enjoy the show?'* Dorothy doesn't say anything at first, just looks at him in disgust, wanting to tell him how she feels as she holds her tongue, knowing it won't help. As the silence grows Mr Jack groans, and a thought sticks into Dorothy's mind, imbeds itself firmly as she smirks:

'I know the answer to your riddle; the man who invented it doesn't want it. The man who bought it doesn't need it, and the man who needs it doesn't know it,'

'Please do tell,' the intrigued ringleader smiles, to which Dorothy confidently answers, *'It's a coffin, and I hope you're in one soon,'* as she turns her back on Mr Jack, walking away with tin-man and the scarecrow. Watching her leave a sick smile cuts along his face as he looks at the glimmer of her silver shoes, and scratches an un-gloved hand against his cheek. The jagged nails cut at the skin and he chatters, *'Hate the game not the player sweetie, you may be part of it soon.'*

Walking through the carnival in silence Dorothy ignores the sights, doesn't care about the games or the bright colours. Instead she thinks, plans as the scarecrow asks, *'It's very dark, are you tired Dorothy?'* and she answers with fury in her eyes, *'Yes, but we can't sleep here tonight.'*

THE COWARDLY LION

16

In the small hut they intended to spend the night Dorothy waits, looking out of the window as the carnival's crowds slowly die down and she struggles to stay awake. She'd been keeping watch for an hour now, maybe longer as she'd seen the masses leave whilst the stall owners packed away their things. Now the carnival seems empty, and confident there's not a body in sight the girl moves from the window, looking at her friends as she tells them again:

'Tin-man, when we find where the cages are kept I need you to keep watch. Scarecrow you come with me, and when we're finished we leave quickly and get as far away as we can before stopping. Agreed?'

The tin-man nods his head with a metal creek and the scarecrow looks confused, scratching his burlap sack as he nods, *'Sure thing Dorothy, whatever you say.'* Still with the thin bag wrapped around her body Dorothy feels at Toto and grabs the wicker basket, as the tin-man clutches at his axe and the scarecrow picks up the pitchfork with a smile.

Leaving the small hut Dorothy closes the door quietly, watching the scarecrow look around, amazed at the quiet stalls, the neon lights now dim as he's about to speak. Quickly Dorothy places a finger to her lips, shaking her head as the scarecrow mimics then smiles, trying his hardest to understand. Creeping through the barren carnival Dorothy feels the dirty ground under her feet, listens for the slightest sound and looks up at the trees surrounding them, fully aware of their capability. Quietly she takes a deep breath as they make their way back to the freak show, sneaking along the stalls and behind small tents as they find themselves at the entrance. Listening carefully Dorothy hears voices in the distance and orders the tin-man to keep watch as she creeps toward them. With the scarecrow beside her she makes him crouch down as his thin body scurries along the floor and she moves in front, creeping along the back of the freak show as she looks to a large tent. With voices coming from inside she's curious and points to the scarecrow, whispering, *'Stay there!'* as she gets closer, checking there's no-one on guard as she moves, pressing her body against the thick plastic sheets to hear Mr Jack's voice. He croaks a wriggled, *'Well do any of you sadists want to take this one home, she was a gift from Outika y'know,'* and Dorothy looks at the thick plastic sheet, finding a small hole as she moves to it and looks inside.

She watches Mr Jack standing in front of a row of caged creatures, tapping his fingers along the snake woman's cell as he barters with a masked man in rags. Selling her he smiles with, *'Now she's yours,'* as a feeble couple approach the ringleader, pushing a pram in front of them as Mr Jack pulls away a blanket and looks inside. Stretching his arms the crooked keeper's ecstatic as he screams, *'What a horrid little child, I'll take her. Do you have anymore?'* Looking in shock, her throat dry and limbs tensed Dorothy pulls away from the tent and looks in the distance to see a row of cages as she creeps towards them and the scarecrow follows. Her eyes looking to the dozen cells she dashes past them quietly; the first one empty, the second, the third, and then she stands in front of a beast's cage, watching as the cowardly lion looks out at her.

Grabbing at the thick metal deadbolt across the cell Dorothy pulls with all her strength, swinging the door open as she stretches a hand inside. Cowered in a corner the lion presses its body against the bars and the girl climbs in, calling, *'Come with me, it's okay,'* as the animal raises a claw in the air and growls. Snaring its teeth at Dorothy and ready to swipe its strong paw the girl slaps the lion's scarred face as hard as she can, sternly pressing, *'Don't you dare, we're here to help you. Come with us!'* Lowering its claw the savage looking beast withdraws its teeth and timidly growls, *'I can't, he, he killed my only friend.'* Quickly snapping Dorothy bites, *'That's why you have to come with us, or you'll be next.'* The lion feels tears drip through its fur, whimpering a deep, *'I don't care, can't leave, he'll find me...have no courage.'* With a quick thought, one of scarecrows few he offers, *'We're going to see the wizard, maybe he can...'* but Dorothy snarls at him, *'Not Now!'* Turning to the beast, baring her teeth the girl's voice stresses, *'We've risked a lot coming back for you, and look at yourself. You have nothing left to lose, he's taken everything. You're coming with us now!'*

Grabbing at the lion's mane, she pulls firmly and he follows her out of the cage. Jumping to the floor Dorothy guides him out as his solid weight lands on the ground and the cage gives a thud of relief. Looking down at him as he stands on all fours Dorothy lets go of his mane with a firm, *'I need you to be quiet and stay close to us,'* as he stares at her with a gruff, *'I'm scared.'* Feeling her eyes begin to water Dorothy crouches down, placing a gentle hand against his face as she looks at his scarred white eye. She strokes at his soft snout, feeling the warmth of his breath against her hand as he leans into her, feeling a comfort he'd long forgotten. *'You don't need to be scared,'* she says softly, *'but we have to leave!'*

Creeping back through the carnival the three of them find the tin-man, standing strong in his monstrous frame as the lion arches his back, giving a growl as Dorothy comforts the animal with, *'He's our friend.'* Quickly they all make their way to the carnival entrance, as quiet as possible as they walk toward the gates, so sure they hadn't been spotted. However, as they're about to leave the scarecrow sees a man, his body shaking and his eyes nervous as he screams at the top of his voice, *'LION!'* Without hesitation the tin-man strikes, knocking the man to the floor as Dorothy looks back to the carnival as swiftly she hears faint voices and watches scattered lights turning on in the distance.

Screaming, *'Run!'* Dorothy and the others move as fast as they can along the yellow road. The lion's quicker than the rest, with his legs of solid muscle as he runs ahead, leaving the others in the distance as he looks back to the girl. So scared of being caught he thinks of running further, leaving them behind at first but waits, looking back as Dorothy and the scarecrow get closer. Thinking quickly he runs past them, toward the carnival as he approaches the tin-man. Knowing he's too slow to outrun the horde the lion growls, *'Get on!'* carrying the tin-man's heavy weight as he feels his wounds re-open, the sharp metal cutting into him. Enduring it, running back to Dorothy and further ahead, so scared of being caught the lion roars, *'Faster!'* Quickly, watching the lion speed in the distance Dorothy shouts, *'Carry me!'* to the scarecrow and he drops his pitchfork, taking her in his arms as his tall legs jolt along the path.

A while later, having travelled far along the yellow road and sure they've distanced themselves enough from the carnival they stop to rest on a small patch of grass. The lion's body's sore and he licks at his wounds as Dorothy feels her stomach ache for food. The scarecrow's content, looking around the dark forest aimlessly, and the tin-man stands watching them all with little desire to do anything. Still, Dorothy holds the lion tightly for warmth as they rest on the grass, thinking that they need to build a fire, but sure it would attract unwanted attention. Opening her wicker basket Dorothy offers some bread to the lion even though there's barely enough for herself. Refusing kindly he tells her he'll find his own food later, and along with the scarecrow she tells the animal of their journey to the Emerald city. Feeling the comfort of the girl against his fur, the lion thinks of a friend he lost long ago and asks:

'Do you think the Wizard will be able to fix me? Give me back my pride, stop me being a coward? Give me e...enough courage to go back to the carnival one day?'

Dorothy strokes his head, caressing his scars as she asks, *'He may, but why would you go back there?'* and the poor beast replies, *'To find Mr Jack,'* with a snarl. Kissing his snout Dorothy throws her arms around him, imagining how much he's suffered. She holds him tightly, kisses him again as he sobs, *'I miss my friend, so much,'* and she tries not to cry, hoping the wizard can help him and praying he's not as heartless as some rumours say.

After eating her bread Dorothy and the others walk along the yellow road again, even though the young girl's exhausted. Too anxious to leave the forest and not wanting to sleep on the ground at night she doesn't want to stop moving, so the scarecrow insists on carrying her. Taking his hand she says, *'Thank you,'* as he picks her up, holding her securely in his arms as the lion feels his stomach rumble. With hunger setting in he asks, *'Could you please wait here a second? I need to find food.'* The tired girl yawns, *'Of course,'* and he replies, *'Are you still hungry? I could kill something for you?'* Dorothy shakes her head, disgusted by the thought as she nods, *'No thank you,'* and the scarecrow queries, *'If you can kill an animal that means you're not a coward?'* To which the lion stares grimly before hunting for meat, *'No, it means I know how to survive.'*

17

With the sun creeping along her face Dorothy slowly wakes, even though she's only been asleep an hour. Feeling warmth blanket over her as she lies cradled in the scarecrow's arms the young girl slowly opens her eyes to look up at his nightmarish face, feeling content as he smiles, *'Good morning sleepy head!'*

Gazing in front of her Dorothy stares out to the distance, thinking she's still dreaming at first as she looks at the beautiful crisp green grass and the soft blue sky. With the dark woods behind them they walk along the glowing yellow road, pathed with pristine bricks and surrounded by beautiful trees, plentiful with fresh fruit as Scarecrow lowers her to the ground. Smiling at the scarred lion he greets, *'Good morning,'* and Dorothy strokes his head, looking to the heartless tin-man as he solemnly strides, and she offers, *'Good morning.'* Replying in his cold mechanical tone Dorothy hears him and turns around, looking at the twisted forest behind her as she stares at the tall brooding trees, so relieved to be out.

Moving to the nearest tree she pulls away some fruit, biting into it hungrily as the juice pours down her hand and the scarecrow points, *'How odd, what's that?'* Lapping at the liquid she walks toward him, telling him it's an apple as the sun glistens against its insides. Smiling she looks at the path ahead again, its yellow bricks leading to the edge of a cliff as she runs in front of the others.

Standing close to the peak of the road she feels stone crumble below her feet and looks to the other side, the sights picturesque as her eyes slowly drift beyond the yellow path. Turning to her right she looks to see the forest she'd passed through, miles long as the deflowered Munchkin country lies beyond it; its once green fields surrounding a small city as the dilapidated skyscrapers leer entwined with vines.

She even tries to look beyond them but can only make out a dull shade of yellow surrounding Oz, the deadly sands. Then she turns to her left, looking down along the river as her eyes follow through miles of marshland and hills, then above the tall trees to see small villages and forests further away. To the south, the land is scattered with red mountains, deep forests, and as she squints she can see a porcelain white terrain.

Then Dorothy looks to the land at the centre of Oz, as past the river, above the hills, and beyond a vast terrain stands the Emerald city. Blinking her eyes at the sight, a great wall with bright green bricks spans for miles, surrounding the large metropolis and containing the buildings as their rustic roofs peer over the wall, a deep green glowing in the sky above them. Still, she finds none as impressive as the wizard's castle. Within the city, it rests on a tall hill as the bottom of the castle aligns with the tips of the tallest buildings, and the thick mound beneath it stands three hundred feet. Its winding path treks through weathered grounds that appear to be nothing more than a vast graveyard and Dorothy can't believe her eyes. She looks at the tall trees aside the gothic castle, as it gleams an emerald green and its ominous spires stab crookedly into the sky.

Her eyes railing away she follows the distant yellow road, leading from the great wall as it passes along a hill, through tranquil fields, curving through a distant village and miles of poppies, almost forming a single shape in the distance. Reseeding further, the road bends through another field and behind a hill as it twists to the cliff in front of her, where her eyes focus on the fallen bridge. Underneath its weak bricks, along the jagged rocks and down the tall cliff she stares to the river as if it's a distant death. Hypnotised by how far down it is she watches the waters current crash fiercely against the rocks, peeling away layers of stone like acid and tearing away limbs from hanging trees.

Turning around Dorothy stares at her friends as they look down the face of the cliff, and her smile slowly fades as the lion hesitates, *'We'll...we'll have to climb down.'* Looking at him she asks, *'And then what?'* as the tin-man interrupts, staring at the riverbank, *'I can see trees down there, we'll have to make a raft to get to the other side.'*

Ready to descend Dorothy feels her stomach pressed tightly against the crumbling peak as her hands grip at loose bricks and her legs dangle over the edge. Struggling to find secure stones at first her boots press against the structure as she lowers her body and looks down to her friends. Scarecrow was the first to climb down knowing that the others would need a secure path to follow, and that if he fell to the bottom he wouldn't be able to feel it anyway. Behind him the cowardly lion follows even though he doesn't want to, as despite being his idea Dorothy still had to persuade him that if they didn't move quickly Mr Jack would surely find them. Hesitant with every move the lion's heavy body causes loose stones to crumble between his paws as Dorothy starts to descend.

Climbing down the face of the cliff she concentrates, feels her muscles taut as she watches the lion and calculates her next step with the shuffle of her body. Struggling at first, scared to lift a hand from one stone to another she soon becomes more confident, terrified of falling but left with no other choice than to follow the yellow road. Quickly glancing up she watches the tin-man climb down the rocks as she feels gravel fall to her face and holds her breath. Glad that she asked the tin-man to climb last she watches the stones crush in his palms, even the solid ones, as she's sure if he descended first he'd have left them with no safe rocks to cling to.

Trying not to focus on it and sure she needs all her concentration to climb safely Dorothy can't help but think of the wizard of Oz, as his macabre castle dominates the land. Uncertain whether she can trust him, the young girl's confident she has no other choice, no one else who can send her back home. She's heard of his power, whispers through the carnival of his wonders, and warnings of how brutal a ruler he is as she wonders if they're just rumours. She hopes he'll be kind like Bopeia, and suddenly the rocks beneath her feet perish.
Dangling from a single stone her nerves burn like seared meat, unsure what to do as she feels her hand slick with sweat and looks down to the savage river. Her strength weakening, fingers' slipping from the rock one by one she flails her legs in panic, trying to find a secure ledge as a solid grip crushes her wrist. She looks up to the tin-man scared, his strength cutting off the circulation to her hand as she stares into his tortured eyes, trusting him. Swinging her legs she rests on a ledge, pressing her body against the surface as she feels the tin-man's grip release. Whimpering, *'Th...thank you,'* she massages her aching wrist and rests frozen against the wall.

After climbing down the cliffs deadly face Dorothy falls to her knees, taking handfuls of dirt in her palms and smiling with a slight wince. Looking to the lion she can see him trembling and watches the scarecrow wander without thought, picking up odd stones and scratching his head as the tin-man reaches the bottom and looks to the brutal river. Without the need to stop he finds some nearby trees and starts to chop at the trunks as Scarecrow pulls pieces of fruit from their branches, placing peaches and plums in Dorothy's basket.

As they slowly build their raft Dorothy and the lion find thick vines to bind the wood, scouring along the dirty bank of the river as they grow tired. Watching the two try to secure the odd pieces of wood already chopped the tin-man kindly says, *'Rest, it will take time to make the raft,'* though his generosity comes from a heartless chest as his mechanical tone cuts bluntly. Soon the lion and Dorothy rest on the bank as she huddles against his chest and thinks about Outika, wondering if she's scouring the land for her. She'd heard of the witch's horrors, her dark domain, people whispering her name in fear, and Dorothy closes her eyes, drifting asleep as she hopes Outika never finds her.

Awaking refreshed Dorothy looks to the river in surprise as a wooden raft waits at the edge of the water and she wonders how long she'd been asleep for. Thanking the tin-man and quickly waking the lion, she eats a peach the scarecrow hands her and smiles at him before sitting in the raft. Clenching tightly to the thin bag around her shoulders she feels Toto inside as the cowardly lion clambers beside her, pressing his body against hers as his weight causes the raft to tip and he grumbles, *'Don't like water.'* Next the scarecrow steps onto the raft, so light he almost falls in the water as the vessel rocks. Pushing the raft away from the bank the tin-man quickly steps onboard in fear of getting his joints wet, as he hands the others long poles to guide them across the river.

Despite the strong current they do well at first, their poles pushing at the rocks and mud beneath the water as they make their way to the middle of the river. Feeling the raft shake, water splashes onboard as they make their way to the other side, but without warning the current gets stronger, starting to pull them downstream as the cowardly lion stutters, *'C, can't go that way, not west.'* Dorothy panics at the thought of what Bopeia said; to avoid the west as Outika shall surely make her a slave. Thrusting the long pole along the bottom of the river with all her strength she looks downstream in fear, as she screams at her friends and they try to push against the current. Fighting the waves and trying to resist their pull the tin-man forces his pole through the water, rowing fiercely as the wood in his hands lodges between the rocks, snapping as Dorothy weakens and the lion trembles, dropping his pole in the water.

Dragged downstream the raft sways, crashing into a set of jagged stones as they tear the vessel apart. Falling with the crash Scarecrow's frail body's impaled on the sharp rocks, breaking several of his bones as he looks to others in the raft, forced downstream as the harsh waves pull them away. Looking down at his chest he sees the skin torn open, two of his ribs snapped and the jagged stone holding him in place, muttering, *'Oh Dear!'* as he watches the raft get smaller and waves goodbye.

Looking downstream the lion remembers everything he'd heard of the western witch, the stories Mr Jack would tell to give him nightmares, and his back arches in fear. Baring his teeth to the water the coward acts on instinct, scared of what the witch will do to him as he roars to Dorothy, *'Grab my tail!'* Doing so quickly she watches the lion's face cringe, leaping into the water as he almost drags her with him, but the strong tin-man acts quickly, clenching the girl's hand as he holds onto the raft.

Panicking in the water the lion's swept back with the current at first. His mouth filled with water, fear crystallised in his eyes he pulls with all his strength, struggling upstream against the tide as he eventually heaves the raft ashore. With his claws dug deep into the dirty ground he feels an aching pain in his poor tail, and Dorothy and the tin-man jump ashore before the raft is swept away. Crawling along the ground the lion slumps to his side, panting as the sun dries his fur and Dorothy watches the abandoned scarecrow. With his poor burlap face frowning he looks at Dorothy and she stares at his sad button eyes as he waves.

Whispering to herself, *'I can't leave him,'* she looks uphill to the yellow road, this one not as steep at the other side's as she turns back to Scarecrow, *'I'll find help, don't move okay!'* Nodding his head the poor man says, *'I'll try to remember,'* as the sparkle of his tangine necklace caches his eye and he smiles. Moving to the lion Dorothy stokes his head, *'I know you're hurting, and you've been very brave, but we have to get Scarecrow help.'* His legs sore he struggles to get up but extends his body as he stands on all fours, wanting to rest the limbs he'd used so vigorously to push against the current. He looks up at Dorothy, breathing deeply with, *'No, I'll stay here, make sure he stays on the rocks,'* and the girl smiles at him. Asking, *'Can you save him if he falls in the water?'* the lion hesitates, offering, *'I'm, I'm too scared...but I'll try,'* as the young girl strokes him, looking out to the scarecrow one last time before running up the muddy bank.

With the tin-man behind her she moves quickly, looking up to the grass mound as she claws at the mud and pulls her weight up the hill. Feeling the soft blades along her skin, she knows she should be happy to see the beautiful greenery but ignores it, forcing herself up the mound. Reaching the top Dorothy doesn't struggle, and instead runs to the yellow road as the tin-man soon joins her side. They move quickly along the path, looking in the distance to a poppy field as Dorothy starts to pant, feels herself tire. With her mouth dry and her legs sore she wants to stop but continues along the road, screaming loudly as she sees a bird fly above her head, *'You, come here! I have silver.'* The winged creature turns its head, looking down to the girl as it gets closer, wheezing, *'Silver?'*

Unsure what the animal is Dorothy presumes it's a stork, taking no notice of its irregular shape or cobwebbed wings as she grabs at her small pouch of money and pulls out a handful of silver. The creature's orange eyes glow and it asks, *'What do you want?'* as Dorothy tells it of the stranded scarecrow. Clicking its neck and eerily grinning, *'Give me the silver and I shall carry your friend to safety,'* Dorothy smirks at the crafty bird, telling her that she can the silver when her friend's safe. Squawking at her with its sharp beak the creature flies away quickly, down to the river as Dorothy watches it disappear. Thinking of running back, unable to see the scarecrow from where she is the tin-man places a hand on her shoulder, clenching her tightly, tempting, *'Rest, you'll need your energy, no need to run back.'* Looking at him and nodding her head hesitantly she knows he's right, but worries about her friend.

Down at the river Scarecrow suffers as the waves crash into his body, pressing him into the jagged rocks as his bones scrape against the stone. Straw pours from under his skin and worriedly he looks ashore to the lion, hearing his voice but too terrified to reply as he watches a winged creature descending towards him. The scarecrow screams, so scared the bird will try to take his eyes that he pulls his body furiously, chipping his bones against the rocks and tearing open his skin. Flailing his arms at the bird, swiping at its body Scarecrow fights and the stork-like creature moves quickly, squawking, *'Keep still, you're worth money to me.'* Grabbing at the scarecrow's frail neck with her beak the bird pulls him from the jagged rocks, barely hearing his bones snap as his terrified shriek stabs at her ears.

Deciding to sit on the floor Dorothy looks at the yellow bricks to notice how clean they are, without a single crack, and not a trace of black ooze crawling between the stones. Resting she keeps a watch at the top of the bank in the distance, waiting to see Scarecrow and the lion. Unable to hear a sound from the river at first Dorothy quickly stands, incapable of keeping still as abruptly the lion bounds from the distance. Smiling at him she looks to the sky, watching the stork-like creature carry Scarecrow as he screams, *'Not my eyes! Not my eyes!'*

Flying through the air and hovering in the sky above Dorothy the creature holds the scarecrow as he struggles, flailing his limbs as his saviour wheezes, *'Throw my silver to the ground or I will drop him,'* through the side of her mouth. Throwing the money to the yellow road the pieces roll along the floor and the winged creature swoops in, dropping Scarecrow as he lands on his feet and she aims for the silver. Peking at the pieces and collecting them in her mouth she greedily glares at the girl. Running to the scarecrow Dorothy wraps her arms around him, asking, *'Are you okay?'* as he pats his worried burlap sack into shape, *'Was so scared the bird would take my buttons!'* She watches him touch at his chest, trying to push the broken ribs back into place and hold in the straw as he mumbles to himself, *'Bird, so scared, my eyes, so scared.'* He tries to stretch the dry skin over his wound but Dorothy knows it won't reach, it's torn too badly torn and instead she buttons up his jacket. Quickly looking at his back to see the hole she sighs, unsure of how to cover it as she tries to comfort the traumatised scarecrow by pointing out to the crisp green grass, the blossoms and scarlet poppies in the distance. Looking out at them Scarecrow mumbles incoherently, but as his buttons fill with the bright colours of the land his voice slowly fades and a fragile, *'How...how pretty!'* eases his trauma. Dorothy watches the scarecrow run ahead of them; sure that whatever mind he has is trying to avoid thinking of the stork as he speeds to the field.

Standing tall amongst the big yellow blossoms he spots blue, white and even purple ones besides great clusters of poppies. With the deep scarlet catching his eye he coos, *'Oh my, how beautiful,'* plucking one and skipping back to Dorothy as he hands it to her. She glistens with, *'Thank you,'* as she looks into his eyes, care free and child-like again as if he's already forgotten about being stranded on the river. Then she looks at the amazing colour of the poppy, sniffing at its spicy scent as she feels herself light headed and stumbles to the floor.

Reaching for her with concern the scarecrow asks, *'Are you alright?'* and she nods her head, still lightly struck by the scent as she smiles at his obscure face, stroking at the burlap sack as she sways, *'Fine, just fine.'* Picking the young girl up the tin-man takes the flower from her hands and throws it away as scarecrow looks sad, confused as the tin-man warns, *'You must be careful with the poppies...'* Even though the lion hears the metal monster's voice he doesn't listen, and instead looks out to the amazing colours and the thick carpet of grass. Unable to contain himself he bounds out to the field ecstatically as the tin-man continues, unaware of the lion's absence:

'...They are not normal flowers, they're deadly, their scent can put you in a coma if you smell them for long enough.'

Far in the distance the lion runs through the poppy fields, smiling at the bright colours as soon he notices how few blossoms there are the deeper he runs. Still he swipes at the heads of poppies without a care as he feels the soft grass beneath his paws and dances in the field. The creature's been caged for so long, deprived of such sights he never thought he'd see again, and he runs with no fear as suddenly his friends see him in the distance. Calling out to him, their voices are unheard and he breathes in the poppies scent, feeling happy, euphoric until he notices something in the grass.

Standing still his body starts to weaken and he looks to see bodies, not a few but dozens, all dead in the field of poppies.

Suddenly with a burst of energy he runs back, desperate to get to the yellow road as he feels his body grow heavier, his limbs harder to move. Still he pushes through, rushes past the poppies and crushes them under his paws as he looks to Dorothy, getting closer and closer until he can't fight the poppies affect any longer. With his legs buckling and eyelids heavy he falls to the ground, crashing with a thud as he churns up the grass and lays unconscious.

Not too far from the yellow road Dorothy screams to him, ready to run into the field but scarecrow stops her and the tin-man looks down, unsure why she's so upset. Still, he throws his axe to the ground and walks steadily into the field of poppies, approaching the lion and grabbing his tail, dragging him back to the yellow road and dropping him to the floor. Sure that this is what a man with a heart would do he watches Dorothy dive to her knees as she strokes the lion's mane with horror in her eyes, whispering, *'Wake up, wake up.'*

Feeling warm breath push through his mouth and placing a hand against his chest as he breathes heavily, the young girl screams, *'What do we do?'* and the tin-man bluntly answers *'Nothing.'* With his playful expression fading the scarecrow gently holds his hands in front of him, looking concerned at the lion as he wonders, *'He looks peaceful, but that's not good is it?'* Looking to the two of them worrying over the lion, the young girl's eyes start to glace and the tin-man says bluntly, *'He wasn't in the field long enough to suffer the full affect, he'll wake soon.'*

Looking at the lion in deep sleep Dorothy runs a hand along his snout gently then pats his face, looking up at the tin-man as she stumbles in her words, *'What...what if you're wrong, what if he doesn't wake up?'* and the tin-man replies with no sympathy, *'Then he'll die in his sleep.'*

18

Soon they walk along the yellow road again, and the tin-man carries the sleeping lion because Dorothy asked. After a while his arms slowly weaken, and they find a small spring and rest as the lion sleeps unaware. Stroking him again and whispering in his ear so he'll wake up Dorothy rests with the lion for an hour before sitting next to the spring.

Swilling her face and cleaning pieces of gravel and dead insects from her hair she tries to scrape the mud from under her nails but finds it too much effort. Her dress is stained and tatty, skin almost tanned with dirt and her teeth feel uncomfortably slick. First she eats a juicy peach, resting by the small spring with the others as she cautiously sits next to the water, fully aware of what could be lying deep inside. Then pulling at a leaf she wipes it along her teeth and swills her face once again, refreshing her eyes as she looks to the hefty lion as he starts to move.

Rushing to his side she rubs a gentle hand along his snout and the scarecrow watches, smiling as the sleepy lion raises his head and yawns. Rubbing a paw along his face he stretches, *'I should have been afraid of the poppies shouldn't I?'* but Dorothy doesn't answer him. Standing on all fours, then up on his hind legs the lion stretches with a huff and brushes his body against Dorothy as she smiles, looking at his eyes in relief as within no time they all walk along the road of yellow bricks again.

The insects are fewer here, the air fresher as scarecrow searches for small flying things, ready to crush their wings as he looks out to the beautiful carpet of green with a smile. The deadly poppies still lurk amongst the grass, clusters of them besides odd fruit trees and a few hidden alongside the road, ready to catch unexpected travellers as Scarecrow forgets how dangerous they are and tries to pick one up. Dorothy stops the silly scarecrow and points to the beautiful crimson carpets that spread along the lush fields, telling him it's better to watch them than to touch, and his buttons widen. Following the road as it bends they look out at the path ahead in surprise, feeling they've finally found civilization after trekking the dark forest for so long. A village waits ahead of them, and both Dorothy and the scarecrow's eyes widen having never seen a sight like this before. Beautiful green grass carpets the land, painted green fences guide the way, and small homes, huts and farmhouses are all covered in the same emerald tone, glistening in the sun.

Passing through the village with buildings surrounding the yellow road, the gentle calm that Dorothy started to feel from assuming she'd found civilization soon fades. The path is empty, houses locked and curtains closed as not a single sound travels through the air. Soon they find themselves deep in the village and Dorothy notices there's not even a breeze, nothing but empty houses as the lion stays close to her side, whimpering, *'I'm scared.'*

Walking behind the girl Scarecrow looks around the village with a curious glare, admiring the green houses as he spots a window, the curtain inside shaking as a pair of eyes peer from behind them. He smiles unthreatened, and as they continue he looks at the concentrating Dorothy and spots another window, but this one's without a curtain as he makes out a shadowed figure deep inside. Without a worry, and admiring the glistening green he starts to sing to himself, skipping with his jagged body as Dorothy holds his wrist, whispering, *'Shhh!'* Nodding his head and tilting it to the side, confused he keeps quiet.

Moving next to the tin-man the young girl asks, *'What do you know about this village?'* and his mechanical voice groans, this time quieter than before answers, *'Only that it's close to Emerald city.'* Then she asks the lion the same question, watching him shake his head, quivering, *'Nothing,'* as they walk through the village.

Soon the sun starts to fade and Dorothy feels nervous, wondering where they'll rest for the night. They walk as the dusk creeps in front of their eyes, and a sudden shrill comes from behind the emerald houses. Turning in panic Dorothy looks out to the buildings, wanting something to catch her eye as the cowardly lion whines.

With their eyes glaring through the evening sky the sly shrill comes again, playful and menacing as the scarecrow looks to the girl, asking *'What's wrong Dorothy?'* She doesn't look at him, just answers, *'That noise,'* as she stares beyond the yellow road to hear the scarecrow giggle, *'It's just the people Dorothy!'* With a lump in her throat she looks at his face, almost dumbfounded as she asks, *'What people?'* to which the scarecrow smiles, *'The hidden people.'* Grabbing at his wrist as the strange noise creeps along the air again she sternly orders, *'We have to move, Now!'* as darkness spreads over the sky and their bodies shuffle quicker.

Suddenly the strange shrill stretches from one side of the road to another, lurking behind each house, first beside, then in front of the travellers. Dorothy looks up to an empty house in her stride, barely making out a body and a horrid face in the window. Panicking she moves even quicker, feeling the smooth yellow path under her feet as she stares into the distance, amongst the cold stark houses to see one with a light. Getting closer she's unsure what to do, whether to run past or beg for shelter. Confused she can't decide, and as they get closer she can hear the lion mumble in fear and peers beyond the lit house, seeing nothing but darkness. Making up her mind she points, ordering, *'Quick, to the farmhouse!'* as the light suddenly extends from a single room to the whole house, and the front door opens.

With the creeping shrill surrounding them Dorothy feels a cold breeze down her spine, and reaching the house they rush to the front door, standing on the lit porch as they look out to the dark empty village. With the strange sound still ringing in Dorothy's ears she looks inside the house with a knock on the open door, noticing its no different from the farmhouses in Kansas.

Moving smoothly through the kitchen an elderly woman greets Dorothy, wearing a thick black fabric that covers everything but her old pale eyes. Almost out of breath but trying not to pant as she speaks Dorothy asks, *'Can we please come inside?'* and the woman looks at the girl's company, asking *'Is the lion tame?'* as she replies, *'Oh yes, very tame!'* Nodding her head slowly the old woman's throat creaks, *'Of course, you are welcome to shelter and food,'* as she walks back into the kitchen.

Nervously stepping inside, Dorothy doesn't trust the house, but would rather be indoors than out as she hears a voice call to her from another room. *'Guests? Come in here,'* echoes through the house, and Dorothy turns to check her friends are still behind her as she makes her way into to another room, whilst the tin-man closes the front door, looking through the glass out at the darkness.

Walking into the living room Dorothy looks to an elderly man as he sits on a small sofa, wearing the same black garment, leaving only his eyes visible. His voice crackles like burnt plastic, *'My what strange company!'* as the lion huddles next to Dorothy and the scarecrow looks to the old man with a smile, *'How odd you look?'* Quickly stopping the scarecrow from saying anymore at the risk of offending their peculiar hosts Dorothy apologises, *'I'm sorry for my friend, he has no brain,'* to which the man sits silently at first then says, *'Sit!'* As they all crowd into the room and take seats the old-man looks unthreatened by such guests, and simply asks, *'Where are you going?'* to which Dorothy replies, *'Emerald city, to see the wizard.'* The man's laughter pulls like a choking animal and the girl looks at him blankly, noticing an odd liquid drip from the bottom of his black cloth as he creeks:

'The city is full off...amazing sights, though I doubt the wizard will see you. Word has it, he lets no one in his presence, not even his servants. He simply stays in his castle, though if you did see him you may not even know it!'

Confused, wanting to ask about the village she walked through Dorothy finds herself intrigued by talk of the wizard, asking, 'What do you mean?' as the man's sick laughter starts again, and he continues with a peculiar gasp:

'The great wizard can change his appearance. To some he may be beautiful, and others ugly, man, animal or beast. He will only show you what pleases him and nothing else. No-one has ever seen the true face of Oz!'

Dorothy feels her skin crawl, a deep fear that the wizard may be as the rumours described him, and instead of being a great ruler, he may be a tyrant or something worse. Her thoughts drift, crossing paths she'd hoped not to see and faces she'd never dreamt to encounter as the man asks, 'What do you want from the wizard?' Her mind still on a strange plane the girl doesn't say a word, but the scarecrow smiles, 'I want a...um...' The tin-man interrupts as his deep mechanical groan grates, 'He wants a brain, the lion courage, and I need a heart. Do you know if he'll be able to help me?' The old man rests in his corner, wheezing through the black fabric as Dorothy suddenly comes too, hearing, 'The wizard has a throne of hearts, brains in jars and courage he feeds the dead. He can give you what you want, if he chooses to help you.'
On edge Dorothy assumes the elderly man will ask her what she wants, so she asks a question quickly before one comes her way, 'What's happened outside, in this village?' She pushes, and silent for a second the man wheezes hesitantly, 'It's the poppies child,' as unexpectedly the elderly woman slams a palm against the wall, silencing her husband as she obtains her guests attention. 'Food is ready!' she calls as the tin-man stands and Dorothy asks the elderly man, 'What were you going to say?' as he cackles, 'I cannot child,' and his wife strictly presses, 'Food will go cold.' Leaving the room Dorothy looks at the old man, the grey liquid dripping from beneath his cloth as she asks if he'll be joining them for food, and he replies, 'No, I'll eat much later.'

Walking into the kitchen and very weary of the house Dorothy looks at the table to see it spread with fresh meats, plates of bread and vegetables, and bowls of fruits and porridge. Hesitant the girl sits, asking the elderly woman, *'Are you going to join us?'* but she sneers with, *'Guests eat first, we eat later,'* as she takes a seat and watches her company for the night. Without hesitation the lion smells the meat, fresh from the bone and takes plenty in his paws before chewing ferociously. The tin-man and Scarecrow eat nothing, and as the woman's eyes fix on Dorothy she simply takes a look at the porridge, lumpy and grey as she settles for a piece of fruit, hungry but cautious as she smiles falsely, *'I'm not that hungry.'*

After sitting at the table for a while and trying to avoid watching the hungry lion feast Dorothy stands and her friends follow, she thanks the elderly woman for her kindness then makes her way to the door, not wanting to go outside but worried about staying in the house. Watching her slowly move closer to the exit the elderly woman stares with her beady eyes, standing in-front of the door as she gasps, *'You should not be out at night!'* Unsure of the old woman and trusting nothing about her Dorothy asks, *'Why's that?'* and the elderly woman hesitates at first, though quickly replies, *'In-case you lose your way and stray into the poppy field dear. We have rooms ready for guests, come with me!'* Moving past Dorothy she walks upstairs, looking down to the young girl as she follows wearily, sure that the dark village's outdoors would be a worse place to sleep than a cold room with a closed door. Following her host Dorothy walks into a rickety guest room to see a readymade bed as she jumps slightly at the sound of the woman's voice. Looking at the scarecrow's back as straw pours from a large hole the old host taps, *'Come with me, we'll fix you up,'* and the scarecrow smiles, *'What needs to be fixed?'* Turning to Dorothy and the others the woman ignores him, advising, *'Sleep now, I'll bring your friend up when he's finished...,'* and only now noticing the young girl's silver boots the host stands still then leaves in a hurry. Scarecrow follows the old woman out of the room curiously, and before Dorothy can say a word the door slams shut and the three friends stand in the cold bedroom.

After some time Dorothy lies on the bed, waiting for the scarecrow to come back as the lion sleeps by the door to keep guard, and the tin-man stands in the corner of the dark room without hesitation. Wondering if she should go downstairs, check Scarecrow's all right Dorothy slowly drifts asleep even though she tries to fight it. Forcing her eyes open, looking across the black room to a small broken porcelain doll on the floor she feels her eyelids grow heavier. Despite her struggle she soon falls asleep, waking sometimes to the sound of tapping glass and having nightmares of the distant shrill through the village.

19

In the morning Dorothy wakes, springing from the bed and making her way through the house as she calls, *'Hello, Scarecrow!'*
With no answer, not even from her hosts she goes downstairs and her friends slowly follow behind, moving into the kitchen, then the living room. Again she calls, *'Scarecrow!'* to hear nothing, and without a sign of the elderly couple. Then she looks to the small couch the elderly man sat on last night, curious where he is. Moving toward it she looks at a small doll on the seat, its white porcelain face cracked and scarred with black stains as it reminds her of the one in the guest room. With her eyes still focused she hears a, *'Hello!'* from outside and moves quickly to the kitchen, opening the front door to see a small green shed beside the house.

Without hesitation she runs to it, recognising the voice as she swings the door open to see Scarecrow smiling back at her. With his thin mouth open wide he bursts, *'They fixed me last night but left me in the shed, it was good I had this,'* fidgeting with his necklace as Dorothy takes his hand. Assertively she voices, *'We're leaving!'* walking past the house to see a thick black cross painted on the door, unaware of it last night as she quickly turns around, facing the village behind them. Looking out to the green buildings they seem less threatening in the sunlight, though the macabre black cross is painted on most of the doors, and few are bare. Curious, but not enough to stay Dorothy moves quickly and her friends follow, passing through the village in hope of not seeing a single person.

Soon, with the village far behind them the group look out at the vast Emerald city as it glistens in the sun, and their eyes follow the road of yellow bricks, ending at a vast jade wall. They walk along the road as the sweet scent of fresh grass environs them and Dorothy notices a gate in the great wall surrounding the city. Covered in green diamonds Scarecrow coos at their amazing glare, though the sceptical girl looks above the wall, even higher than the green thatched roofs. She stares at the wizard's horrific castle, standing on a thick graveyard hill as she sees the tombs and resting places clearly from outside the wall.

Walking to the large emerald gate, almost unable to believe that the yellow road has come to an end Dorothy turns around and looks behind her with mild relief. She smiles awkwardly, telling herself she's closer to home, and amazed she's made it this far thinks of all she's had to pass through. Then looking to the gate its diamond studded locks unbolt as if by magic and it swings open without a sound. Smiling at such a sight the scarecrow says, *'How pretty, I want one'*, as even the cowardly lion almost smiles, his fear entwined with excitement whilst the tin-man stands without care, waiting for a heart. Taking a deep breath Dorothy walks through the gate first and the others follow, finding themselves in a box room gleaming with emeralds as a man no taller than a munchkin stands in front of them. Amused by the green clothing he's wearing, even the light green tint to his skin Dorothy tries not to laugh at the thought of him reminding her of a child in a cheap Martians costume. Yet despite how amusing he may appear to the young girl, the man raises a hand to the group, asking very sternly, *'Business or pleasure?'* Unsure what to say Dorothy gently mouths, *'Excuse me?'* as the guard mutters under his breath, *'Damn tourists,'* before loudly inquiring, *'What do you want in the Emerald city?'*

'To see the great wizard,' Dorothy replies meekly as the guard squints, pushing effortlessly:

'No-one has asked to see the wizard in years and I doubt you will be allowed in the castle...'
Determined to get inside the girl bluntly presses, *'Please, it's urgent!'* as the guard nods his head:

'Very well, but I am ordered to warn you; if you are to waste the wizard's time you will be punished by methods he deems fit, and suffer the likelihood that after your admittance you may not be allowed to leave the city. These are the rules for those seeking an audience with the wizard, do you accept?'

Dorothy looks to her friends for guidance, finding herself in control of their fate as they stare blankly and she faces the guardsman, confirming, *'Yes, we accept.'* She follows with a shy, *'Is he a good man?'* as her imagination turns grim at the thought of a wizard who would trap people within his city. *'He is, and a wise ruler,'* the Guardsman continues, *'though to those who are not honest, and disobey his will he is cruel and...I should not say.'* The girls curiosity aches, pleading, *'Please, say!'* but the guard feels nervous, rubbing a cloth over his sweating brow as he leads the guests to a large machine:

'P, please, this way. This is a phoropter; you must place your head on the rest and look into the lenses. The brightness of the city will blind you if

you do not have your eyes scanned, but after you have you'll see that everything inside is a magnificent green.'

Dorothy looks at the machine, its teal metal structure reminding her of something she'd often seen when having her eyes tested back home. Going first she places her head against the rest, looking into the lenses as the guardsman presses a button at the back of the machine. Quickly a bright light temporarily blinds her and she feels something press against her eyes before moving away, squinting and rubbing at them furiously. Next the tin-man places his head against the machine, followed by the scared lion as Dorothy holds his paw to comfort him. Finally Scarecrow approaches the phoropter, asking, *'I have buttons, it won't hurt my buttons will it?'* The guardsman shakes his head, and as Scarecrow places himself into the machine he fiddles with odd dials, poking at cogs as he queries, *'What's this? What's this?'* Quickly pressing the button the guardsman hears the scarecrow glisten, *'Oh my!'* as he moves from the phoropter to feel his sight slowly coming back into focus.

As they all stand ready to enter the city the guardsman takes a gold key, chained to his armour as he places it into a green gate. Opening one lock, then another Dorothy watches him, feeling at the small black key around her neck as she wonders how it will help her get back home. Opening the fifth and final lock the guardsman swings the gate open, and the Emerald city of Oz waits before them.

The scarecrow taps his buttons with amazement and Dorothy looks out to the emerald streets, blinking energetically, wondering what the flash of light could have possibly done to her eyes. Still she looks out at the cobbled streets, houses built with green marble and their roofs either thatched or laid with cracked slate. At first Dorothy imagined the city to be beautiful, but now inside it seems old, dirty and poor, despite the sparkling green emeralds. The guardsman directs, *'Walk straight to the graveyard hill, you'll be expected,'* and as the visitors step onto a crooked street the large gate closes, locking them inside.

Walking slowly along the streets Dorothy looks up to the sky, tinted an odd green as suddenly she watches the residents of the city. Not at all like she expected they're dressed in green, their skin tanned with it and they bustle along the streets; some pushing others out of the way, and stealing things from their pockets as Dorothy clenches tightly to Toto, feeling him in the small bag. Watching the peculiar people the girl's eyes widen as she looks amongst the crowd, noticing that some of the men, woman, and even children wear wooden masks. Most of them walk around normally, with eye holes cut into the wood, though some stumble along the pavement, sit on the floor begging for money as the mask covers their eyes. Approaching one of the men Dorothy asks, *'Excuse me, why are people wearing masks?'* and he snaps vigorously, shaking a metal can at her, *'How would I know I'm blind, refused to have my eyes fixed, now look at me. Any change?'* Quickly ushering her away from the man, Scarecrow points to shop windows showing Dorothy green lemonade and candy as he smiles, but she's not interested.

As they continue to walk through the city, the cowardly lion treads carefully as the people point at him, some hiding away as he approaches them, whilst others watch with threatening glares. He moves close Dorothy as the tin-man walks behind them all, and scarecrow holds the girl's hand, looking out at the new odd sights with a grin. Though Dorothy doesn't smile, she thinks of the city; the old houses and dark emerald alleyways, the crowds like animals and the dank smell. It reminds her of history class, the plague of London and she watches as people move away from them, the masses parting as she wonders if it's because of the lion.

With her curiosity building, the reason for the masks still a mystery Dorothy approaches a woman, asking, *'Excuse me, why do you wear a mask?'* The lady's voice shuffles fraily, *'Because I disobeyed the wizard, though he only scarred my face, how kind he is.'* Pointing out to the crowds, dozens of them wearing thick wooden masks the young girl enquires, *'All of these have been punished by the wizard?'* and the woman replies, *'Yes, and he has used his magic to weld masks to our face's so no-one can see our scars.'* Dorothy's horror cuts deep and she asks, *'What did you do to deserve this?'* and the woman shakes, *'I crept into his throne-room and saw his face.'*

Moving in closer the young girl pushes, *'What did you see?'* to hear her whisper, *'A head the size of a house, no body. How wonderful the wizard is.'* Dorothy snaps, bitterly roaring, *'Wonderful! He sounds like a di...'* though the woman grabs her dress with a strong hand, pulling her in closer as she whispers with fear, *'Careful, he can see everything.'* With her eyes looking up to a building the woman pushes Dorothy away, warning, *'You'll get me into trouble,'* before walking away.

Stepping back, moving from the curb the young girl looks up at the building, her eyes focusing along the green bricks as she notices a discreet emerald box, occasionally flashing a small jade light.

Walking through the cobbled streets, the group reach the bottom of the graveyard hill, standing at its gate as a sharp thick metal fence circles the mound. Scared, the lion holds onto Dorothy's dress, cowering, *'I don't want to go up there, I don't need courage,'* whilst tin-man's unfazed, and the scarecrow smiles. His eyes peer over the small tombs, up the dirty track of fresh graves and along the green marble crucifixes and sarcophaguses as the oddities amuse him.

Standing at the bottom of the grim graveyard Dorothy looks up the hill at the wizard's castle. Her eyes look past the gravestones, creeping over the exposed skeletons and crawling along the dead ground. She's terrified, the path ahead reminding her of a nightmare as she thinks of the only person who can send her home, a monster. Though having gone through so much already, and with nowhere else to go she's ready to put her life in the hands of a dark stranger, as she stands shaking in the cold breeze of death, just a young girl in witch's boots.

20

After persuading the cowardly lion to join them the travellers ascend the graveyard hill, and although it's not too steep their journey is long. The tin-man pays no attention to the dead and ignores their resting places as he walks over the graves, his weight crushing odd bones as he treads over newly buried bodies.

Dorothy treads behind him carefully, trying not to think of the bodies underneath her as skeletal arms stick out of the soil and she looks straight ahead to the castle. Meanwhile the lion walks very hesitantly, watching the ground ahead of him as he takes each step, trying to ignore the rotting dead and their horrific smell. Though the scarecrow treks with glee, his gangly legs taking him all over the graveyard as he points to one skeleton with, *'That's what I look like underneath,'* admiring the glisten of emerald statues and running a finger along the thin peculiar fences.

Reaching the top, they look up to the castle as Dorothy feels a lump in her throat and hears scarecrow coo behind her as the lion whimpers. Standing beside a row of dead trees Dorothy pushes through them, feeling their twigs cut at old wounds as a cold chill comes from the castle. She stares up at the gothic architecture, the solid green bricks, and twisted spires before looking to the huge doors in front of her. Walking to the entrance the group look at the two guards either side, both in emerald armour and holding spears as one informs, *'You're here to see the wizard, I'll tell him you're here!'*

Watching him open the large doors Dorothy tries to peer inside, seeing nothing but darkness as it closes and her heart races, finally here as she notices the other guard. His gaze lingers on her, sliding up and down her body as she barks, *'Hey, keep looking at me like that and I'll send you down the hill.'* Quickly he turns his head, looking out to the city below as Dorothy smirks.

After waiting a little while the large doors open, creaking horridly as the guard rushes out of the castle, flustered and trying to catch his breath:

'The...the wonderful wizard will grant you an audience, though he will only admit one of you into his castle each day. There are rooms set for you so you may rest, and you will be summoned when the wizard is ready for you.'

Dorothy wants to argue the suggestion but knows no good will come of it. She follows the guard's orders as he commands, trying to assert himself after showing how scared he is of the wizard: *'You are to leave the castle now, and servants will be waiting for you at the bottom of the hill.'*

Reaching the bottom of the hill after trudging along the graveyard again Dorothy watches two men drop a body into an open grave as they look at her expressionless, their faces hidden behind thick wooden masks. Waiting for Dorothy, a woman dressed in green bows, her face pretty and unmasked as she greets, *'If you'll follow me ma'am, I'll show you to your room.'* Ready to lead the young girl away from her friends the green woman continues: *'You'll each have to sleep in separate quarters, that is the wizard's orders and you must not disobey them.'* Reluctantly Dorothy trails behind her guide, not wanting to tempt the wizard's wrath as the tin-man groans, *'I'll find you!'* and she watches her friends get smaller in the distance.

Following her guide through the cobbled streets, and walking for at least ten minutes Dorothy stands in front of a house. It's less decrepit than the others; with no cracks in the structure, broken windows or stones missing, even though it stands right beside the rest. Opening the entrance the guide walks into the house and Dorothy follows, closing the door behind her to breathe in perfumed air opposed to the stench of the streets. Showing her upstairs the guide walks quickly ahead and Dorothy follows her into a beautiful green bedroom, as flowers rest on the windowsill and a beautiful silk green bed awaits her. Glancing at it with no care at all she asks, *'Where are my friends?'* to which the woman smiles, *'You'll see them later, rest now,'* as she leaves a front door key and exits the room quickly. Giving a huff Dorothy looks to the beautifully carved green desk, a grand bookshelf and opens a cupboard to find it full of silk dresses, all an emerald green and the perfect size for Dorothy. Picking one up but dropping it to the floor with ease she realises how little she cares about the room and leaves abruptly, grabbing the key her guide left behind. Closing the door to the room and then locking the house, the young girl wonders why she's been separated from her friends, and roams the city in search of them.

As time goes by the green sky soon darkens and Dorothy doesn't feel safe in the streets. Hopelessly she'd wandered down a cobbled path in the chance of finding her friends, then another, and another as she rests besides a building to catch her breath, looking into green windows to see families fighting over food. With an odd smell in the air, one even stronger than the stench of the streets she follows it, reminding her of the poppy fields as she comes to a small house. Looking through the window she can't see anyone inside, but notices a small door around the corner. She walks toward it, pushing it open slightly as the smell gets stronger.

Hearing scattered laughter, peculiar noises she slowly takes a step down into the basement, then other as the voices get clearer, and even clearer again as she gets closer. At the bottom of the stairs she can hear their unusual groans, peculiar sounds as she pokes her head around the corner to see a cold damp basement, with dozens of bodies laying still on the ground. With some holding long green pipes in their hands, Dorothy looks to a wall to see 'Kill the memories' carved into the green stone. As the bodies murmur amongst themselves, fidget in their sleep Dorothy makes her way back upstairs quietly, uncertain of what she's found but sure that she may not want to find out.

At the top, still curious of what she's seen Dorothy closes the door to walk along the cobbled pavement once more, feeling it's time to go home even though she hadn't found her friends.

Memorising the now dark streets the young girl walks back to her house, afraid to go deeper into the city in case she gets lost. Making her way along an avenue, then turning another she hears distant sounds, muffled voices and cries coming from a dark emerald alleyway. Curious she walks toward it at first, though denies her inquisitiveness as she continues along her street, spotting a woman on the corner who shouts, *'Bit young aren't you?'* Ignoring the woman Dorothy approaches her temporary home and opens the door, sure she's being watched as she locks it quickly, running upstairs to bolt the bedroom door behind her too. Moving the bed and wedging it against the door she's unable to sleep at first, though pulls Toto from his bag and holds him tightly as she slowly drifts off, wondering if she'll have nightmares.

Scared of what lurks in the streets at night Dorothy wakes occasionally, as her friends sleep in pleasant rooms scattered through the city. The tin man stands looking out of his window all night, thinking of what he'll do when he has a heart, and the scarecrow looks into his tangine necklace, laying awake as the lion sits behind a bolted door, scared of being alone.

As morning comes, Dorothy hears a knock on the front door and makes her way downstairs, opening it to see the woman who guided her through the city. Looking at her she quickly asks, *'Where are my friends?'* and the servant replies, *'You'll see them soon, but first the wizard wants to see you.'* With a sigh, unsure if she's happy or nervous Dorothy nods her head and the woman informs, *'You are to wear one of the green dresses in your wardrobe, the wizard would like it.'* The young girl quickly snaps, *'No,'* and the servant looks amazed, *'But you must, the wizard wants you to.'* Dorothy shakes her head with, *'Not happening,'* as she shuffles her silver boots, *'Is that a problem?'* The woman's stunned, unsure of what to say so she simply finishes, *'Very well, as you wish...come with me.'*

Following the woman to the bottom of the graveyard hill Dorothy feels her stomach in knots, terrified of what will happen in the castle, so she insists, *'My friends, make sure they're here when I come out,'* hoping they will help her if she's in danger. The guide nods her head, quietly replying, *'If you come out they will be waiting for you ma'am,'* before leaving as Dorothy mumbles, *'That's encouraging,'* before she treks up the hill again. In her stride she ignores the skeletons this time, has no thought of the dead beneath her as she stamps on the soil, her mind drifting to what the guard said when she entered the city. When asking him if the wizard's a good man he simply replied, *'He is...though to those who are not honest...he is cruel...'* Dorothy feels her skin splinter with cold, the thought of what the wizard will do to her if he knows she's lied to her friends. She didn't tell them of the dangers she carries, that she'd been marked by the wicked western witch since she killed Avatonika. Feeling the guilt burn in her stomach Dorothy reaches the castle, the large doors open as if by magic, and she ignores the guards, stepping inside and hoping the wizard will send her home, praying he'll overlook her lie and not hurt her friends.

Standing in the castle's emerald darkness Dorothy feels the large doors close behind her, as the cold silence pricks at her skin. Stepping forward into nothingness she expects a voice, something to guide her, but all she hears are faint echoes through the grim castle. Following the distant sounds, clenching a fist she walks through the dark corridor, sure it's grand and amazing though unable to tell. Turning a corner, she stretches out a hand to feel a carved marble pillar and looks in the distance to see a lit room. Walking toward it, fearing there could be something in the darkness behind her she moves quickly.

Running through the empty castle she reaches the lit room, stepping into the light without hesitation as her mind plays tricks on her. Standing in the courtroom her eyes amaze at its grand architecture and she looks to the walls, both left and right as she stares at a dozen ladies and gentlemen. All dressed in fine outfits they remain seated, with their hands folded and eyes flickering as Dorothy approaches the strange company. Cautious if this could be one of the wizard's tricks she looks at their skin, textured like wood as long thin pieces of wire stretch from their limbs and disappear into holes in the ceiling. Unsure if they're real people or an elaborate puppet show Dorothy looks past them to a small door and slowly makes her way toward it.

With company either side of her she looks to them as she passes, watching their flickering eyes, like that of dolls as she hears one voice, *'Are you sure you want to see the face of Oz the impaler?'* Looking at his synthetic expression Dorothy says, *'Yes, if he will see me,'* and another voice answers, *'If he knows of your silver boots he'll see you,'* whilst a third groans, *'He knows everything.'* Turning around swiftly, looking at all of the seated members she tries to see whose speaking and asks, *'Who are you?'* One voice answers, *'We are the ones who refused to leave!'* then another speaks, *'We are the ones who wish to see the wizard!'* as a final voice utters, *'We are the ones who wasted the wizards time!'*

Spinning in a circle, unable to tell which one's talking a dozen separate voices continue, *'Now shall never leave!', 'Can never leave!', 'Now shall never leave!', 'Can never leave!', 'Now shall never leave!', 'Can never leave!'* Breaking their madness a deep husk roars, *'ENTER!'* and Dorothy looks to the small door as it opens. Running to it, and having to crouch to get under the frame she looks into the wizard's throne room. Amazed at how a doorway so small could lead to a room so grand Dorothy stares in awe; looking at the machinery spread along the thick room, arched ceilings and an elaborate emerald glow as she walks deeper. Staring to a throne at the tip of the room, hidden behind a dull panel she looks around again to see chunks of wood, metal skeletons, workbenches and tools, though not a single window. Looking back to the empty throne, approaching it slowly a deep dark voice licks at Dorothy's skin, booming through the room as she feels her eyes water. A voice so terrifying it's how the young girl imagined the devil would sound:

'I am Oz, the great and wonderful, the reaper and the terrible. I have many names and faces, what do you want from me?'

Looking around the room at first, hopelessly trying to find a figure to put with the voice Dorothy gazes back at the throne, though this time it's not empty, and she stares at the shadow of a horned man. Fear flows through her veins like never before and she whimpers:

'I...I am Dorothy, j...just flesh and bone, and I need your help.'

Looking at the horned wizard's silhouette, sitting in his throne in front of her eyes she hears a voice behind her, as it touches at her shoulder and leeches into her ears, *'Why should I help you?'* Trembling, so scared to move, feeling him behind her she begs, *'Please, I just want to go home,'* and his voice smashes against her skin like thunder as she falls to her knees, *'Where did you get those silver boots?'* Trying to answer, her body frozen she mutters, *'I...I got them from the eastern witch....I killed her.'* The wizard's voice touches against Dorothy's skin, slithering up her body as he asks, *'And the key?'* She whimpers, *'Bopeia,'* closing her eyes and clenching her teeth as the ruler's voice stretches along her neck, slithering, *'And what do you want from me?'* With her eyes clenched tightly, feeling scales and blood touch at her face she softly moths, *'Kansas, I just want to go home to my family, my...my aunt and uncle.'*

Silence falls, the voice leaves Dorothy's skin and creeps through the grand room, *'I will help you, but you must do something for me in return!'* With her eyes still closed, a lump in her throat she asks, *'What?'* only imagining the horror ahead of her as the wizard's voice penetrates into Dorothy's skin. Biting like a hundred snakes he hisses, *'Kill the witch of the west!'* Dorothy cries, *'I cannot!'* as her cheeks glisten with tears and she slams a fist to the ground. Whimpering again, she feels all hope is gone, her task impossible as she sobs, *'I can't go through Oz anymore.'* Crashing against her skin like a brutal wave the wizard commands, *'You will!'* as she opens her eyes to see him standing in front of her.
Crawling backwards, too scared to even scream she pulls her weight along the marble floor and stares at the terrible wizard; Standing seven feet tall he towers over the girl, his skinned muscular body made of nothing but raw dripping flesh, held together with an armour of bones. Reaching for her face with a large taloned hand she feels his long cloak against her bare legs and looks up at his face, almost like a bleeding humans, though thick bones spread from his temples. He screams, *' I can do with you as I wish!'* as Dorothy looks at is mouth to see no teeth, just two thick fangs like a spider as she stares at his eyes, almost human as thick mounds of meat surround them. Then the God walks away, his blood dripping along the floor as his voice slices at Dorothy's ears:

'You will kill the witch or never leave Oz. I'll make sure of that.'

Leaving the castle Dorothy sees her friends at the bottom of the hill, running to them as she wraps her arms around scarecrow, crying, *'There's no hope.'* His face frowning quizzically he holds her tightly, caressing her head with a gentle hand as he asks, *'What's wrong Dorothy?'* She sobs, pushing her face into Scarecrow's burlap head for comfort, *'He'll only send me home if I kill the western witch.'* Looking up to Dorothy, horrified for her the lion stands on his hind legs as he wraps his front two around the girl and scarecrow, cushioning her head with his mane as he squeezes them both gently. Pressed against the two of them Dorothy sobs, *'I'll never get home'* as the heartless tin-man places a hand on her shoulder, looking into her crystal blue eyes as he groans, *'I am so sorry.'*

Soon she goes to her room, laying in bed as she cries, thinking that she'll never see aunt Em and uncle Henry again. She'd been so good back in her own world, followed all the rules, and suffered the fake families, all for nothing. She cries, holding Scarecrow's hand as tightly as she can, laying next to him on the bed with the lion on her other side. Sleeping heavily, like a lazy cat she feels his heart beating against her back as she rests on her side, letting his deep breaths tickle her ears, and his paws hold her closely.

Sandwiched between the lion and Scarecrow on such a small bed Dorothy looks into the straw man's buttons as he frowns. Feeling nostalgic, she tells him stories of when she was younger, about the farm on Kansas as she remembers how aunt Em would sit on the porch drinking lemonade, teaching her how to knit as uncle Henry would reap the crops. She tells him more as the hours pass, looking over his shoulder occasionally at the tin-man as he watches them, unsure how to interact. Remembering everything she had when she was a young girl Dorothy smiles every now and again, though the tears don't stop and Scarecrow asks, *'Is that what it's like having a heart?'*
She nods, whimpering, *'It hurts,'* with a sad smile as Scarecrow shakes his head, *'I'm glad I don't want one,'* but Dorothy looks at his curious burlap face. Feeling the lazy lion holding her, Toto squeezed between them and the tin-man watching, she touches Scarecrow's round plastic buttons, smiling as she thinks of her family in Kansas and her friends in Oz as she says, *'No, it's worth it.'*

THE WIZARD OF OZ

21

The next morning Scarecrow's summoned by the wizard, and leaves his friends at the bottom of the hill as he treks through the graveyard without worry. As he walks through the castle a faint stab of fear cuts into his empty head, though not of the wizard, only the dark corridors, thinking his buttons are broken until he sees a light in the distance.

Moving into the courtroom he smiles wildly at its grand architecture, boasting, *'Oh boy, oh boy!'* as he looks to the seated ladies and gentlemen. Touching at their fine outfits and tapping at their wooden skin Scarecrow pokes, *'How odd you are,'* as he looks at their long thin pieces of wire, stretching up to the ceiling. Tapping each of them on the head he says, *'Hello?'* expecting a response, but they sit silently as the small door ahead of them opens. Struggling to get through such a small door Scarecrow feels his twisted limbs buckle, but soon forgets when he's inside. Looking at the machines spread along the vast throne-room, the odd pieces of wood, metal and tools he runs to them, touching everything he possibly can as his voice echoes, *'Oooh shiny!...peculiar!...what's this...and this...oooh!'* Then abruptly the curious scarecrow turns quickly as he hears a soft voice, looking to see a beautiful woman draped in fine green silk. With crystals in her hair and emeralds sparkling along her gown Scarecrow stretches out a long crooked hand as he utters, *'You're beautiful!'* Walking toward the woman he hears her soft gentle voice whisper through the air, touching at his strands of straw:

'I am Oz, the great and wonderful, the beautiful and the kind. I have many names and faces, what do you want from me?'

The scarecrow scratches his head as small pieces of straw fall from his burlap sack, trying to think, sure that he wanted something, and then it comes to him as a smile spreads along his eerie face:

'I want a....a....a brain! Can you help me?'

The beautiful woman does not move, and her lips barely open as her voice drifts through Scarecrows strands of straw, stroking at his bare bones:

'I will, but you will do something for me in return. You must kill the western witch!'

The scarecrow nods frantically, happy at first that she can help him, but then the tiniest of thoughts comes to him, so he asks, *'Didn't you ask Dorothy to kill the witch?'* The woman's voice turns colder, as brittle as ice as it freezes along the scarecrows burlap sack:

'Yes. The witch is to die! I don't care who kills her, but until she is dead you will never have your brains. I shall not make you a wise man!'

Leaving the castle without a worry Scarecrow skips down the graveyard hill, happy to spend more time with Dorothy as he reaches the bottom and tells his friends that the wizard is a beautiful woman. Asking Dorothy what she saw the young girl tells them of the horned man and the lion shakes in fear.

Soon they walk through the cobbled streets, arriving at Dorothy's house as masked servants wait for them at the door. Expecting a punishment for letting her friends sleep in her room last night Dorothy's hesitant at first, but the servants come baring gifts. Bringing fresh meat for the lion, bundles of fresh straw for Scarecrow, oil for the tin-man and food and drink for Dorothy. After they have eaten, the servants tell stories to entertain the guests and Dorothy sits silently, sceptical of the generosity. Finally as nightfall creeps over the Emerald city the servants leave, telling Dorothy that her and her friends can all sleep under the same roof tonight, though they must not leave the house until morning.

Watching the servants leave Dorothy waits at the window, looking out at the dark streets as she spots discrete boxes, one on each building as they flash a tiny jade light. Abruptly she closes the curtains, running from each room to the next, doing the same, making sure the windows are closed and checking that no one can get inside the house. After some time she lies in bed happily with the lion and Scarecrow, falling asleep as she thinks of the western witch, wondering how she can kill her.

As the morning sun spreads over Emerald city there's a knock on the front door and a soldier waits, ready to escort the tin-man to the graveyard hill. Without a second thought he walks through the cobbled streets, following the soldier as he stands at the bottom of the graveyard mound. Trekking up it with no fear, only the desire to obtain a heart, he crushes bones beneath his feet and stands in front of the castle. As the large doors open he journeys through the dark corridors to stand in the lit courtroom, feeling no amazement by the grand room, or even curiosity of the twelve seated puppets. Looking to the small door ahead of him one of the costumed crowd asks, *'You dare see the wizard?'* as another follows, *'You dare see the wizard?'* to which the tin-man approaches the seated bodies. Putting his hand against one's face, he crushes it in his palm with a look of disappointment as the small door opens, and he struggles to fit through such a small frame.

Walking into the throne-room his eyes do not drift, and he looks up to the wizard without the slightest threat. Towering over the tin-man the wizard is no longer a beautiful woman, and is instead a vile creature whose head touches the ceiling. With five eyes spread along its bulbous face the monstrous wizard sits with its spindly legs perched, as five tentacles and arms point to the tin-man. Looking up at the monster the tin-man's patience wears thin, he has no time for games and wonders if slaying this beast will show him the true face of the wizard. *'Is this supposed to frighten me!'* the heartless juggernaut roars through bear trap teeth, and the beast does not move. Its mouth rests shut, though a scaled voice crawls along the floor, touching at the tin-man's weak metal, burning through the sheets like acid:

'I am Oz, the great and wonderful, the monstrous and greedy. I have many names and faces, what do you want from me?'

The tin-man stands strong, untouchable as his voice booms through the throne-room, as loud as the wizard's as he says, *'I need a heart great wizard, will you help me?'*

The wizard's anger flares like a burst sun, yet his voice does not echo through the vast room, or smash into the tin-man's thin sheets. Instead it creeps softly, piercing the metal and leeching into his brain as the words stab and linger like the teeth of a parasite:

'You should fear me tin-man, for what is metal I can melt, and what is flesh I can consume. I will give you a heart, though you must join the girl and kill the witch of the west first.'

The tin-man looks at him without expression, nodding his head as the thick metal around his chin grates at his chest, *'I will kill the witch for a heart, but I do not fear you great wizard, nor will I pretend to.'*

Soon enough the tin-man leaves the castle and meets his friends as he tells them what he must do. The scarecrow smiles at the thought and Dorothy tries to contain herself, feeling much more hopeful of getting home with the tin-man helping her kill the witch. Yet the lion cowers, feeling his dead eye weep as he whimpers, *'If I could I'd roar my loudest and scare the wizard so he'd give me courage, but I know what he'll want from me in return.'* Nodding her head slightly Dorothy's sure that the lion's right and crouches down as she strokes his snout. *'Don't be scared,'* she tries to comfort, *'If he wants you to kill the witch at least you'll be safe with us.'* He looks up at her with a sad eye, rubbing a paw against his face as he huffs and nods his head, licking Dorothy's hand with, *'You're right, but I'm still scared.'*

After walking around the busy streets for an hour Dorothy and the others go back to her house, and soon after they arrive the masked servants bring them gifts again; meat for the lion, oil for tin-man, straw for Scarecrow and food for Dorothy. They eat and rest for a while as the servants entertain them with more stories, and as they're about to leave a masked girl says:

'Again you can all sleep under the same roof, and feel free to wander around the city tonight. Though be careful.'

Closing the door on them Dorothy moves into the kitchen where she picks up her pouch of silver and places it in Toto's bag. Then they walk through the streets as the green night sky spreads over them, unleashing the oddities of the city life. Walking next to the tin-man Dorothy looks at his grim body, monstrous despite his tortured human eyes as she asks, *'What will you do when you have a heart?'* The cold mechanism replies swiftly without thought, *'I will try to find my love. I've been cold for too long.'* Behind them the scarecrow looks at the lion's rugged fur, his dishevelled mane and scarred flesh as he points, *'You don't look happy, are you in pain?'* The lion huffs, *'Constantly, my scars are deep. And even though I look fierce I'm scared inside, it's torture.'* Nodding, the scarecrow's head falls to its side, curiously asking, *'Are people afraid of you?'* as the strong animal replies, *'Yes, haven't you seen the crowds run away from us?', 'I have,'* says the scarecrow, *'Though I thought it was because of tin-man, he's a little shiny but unpleasant to look at.'* The lion laughs, but the tin-man remains silent as Scarecrow grins, *'I like to look at nice things, my buttons are my best quality.'* With a wide smile along his scarred face the lion asks, *'How about me, am I unpleasant to look at?'* and the scarecrow shakes his head, *'Because of your eye and your scars you look sad. But I think you look fluffy, like Toto?'*, *'What's Toto?'* the lion asks curiously and Scarecrow stretches his stitched mouth, *'It's Dorothy's dog.'* Turning around to the lion the young girl smiles, *'Yes, I'll show you later,'* as she realises neither tin-man nor the lion have seen her little black dog, still it's good to keep him hidden in his bag, he's safer that way.

As they walk through the dark streets Scarecrow spots a woman in the distance, as she waits on a corner and the street light shines brightly on her. His buttons widen, expressing glee as he walks ahead of his friends and looks at the woman's jewels, glistening slightly. Stretching out a hand to him, unsure of what to say Dorothy keeps quiet and smiles discretely as the tall creepy scarecrow bows to the woman. *'How are you?'* he asks, *'You look very shiny,'* and she stumbles for the right words, announcing, *'Sorry, don't do scarecrows,'* as the tall man of hay tilts his head, *'What an odd thing to say.'* Walking toward him Dorothy takes his hand and leads him away, smiling to herself as the scarecrow looks up to a streetlight, watching the flies swarm around it.

Looking through a green window at what seems to be a tavern Dorothy's intrigued, and her curiosity grows as she leads her friends inside. She'd never been in one before and watches the men and women sitting at their tables, interrupting their drunken rants as they look to the strange guests.

Some spill their drinks and others groan at the sight of the company, expecting them in the streets but not in one of their taverns. Ignoring their fuss the tin-man walks past them, whilst the scarecrow waves his hand saying, *'Hello,'* to all the gasping faces. Yet the lion, sure the people are afraid of him isn't so scared here, and instead walks proudly, strutting his solid figure as he looks to a man's plate to see a hefty steak.

Staring at the meat he approaches the man, stretching so he stands on his hind legs and asks, *'Are you going to eat that?'* Looking at the lion's head, the scars spread along his face and the dead eye staring back at him the man mumbles at first and hides under the table. Smiling at the backside of the man the lion eyes his food, lifting a paw to reach for the steak as Dorothy slaps his furry leg. Retracting it and cowering the lion rests back on all fours, stepping away from the young girl as he mutters, *'I...well I suppose it was overcooked for me anyway.'* Then looking to the burrowed man's bottom the lion coyly says, *'Sorry.'*

Walking to a table the tin-man looks down to a man sitting alone and the metal monster sits next to him, his heavy weight almost breaking the seat as the small man drunk in his swagger smiles at first. Then looking at the tin-man beside him, and to the lion approaching he begs, 'P...please don't eat me,' and the lion sniffs at the air with a faint smirk, 'I wouldn't dream of it, you smell gone off.' Hiccupping, the intoxicated green man says, 'I think I've drunk enough,' as he stands and looks at the tall grim scarecrow staring down with a smile, 'Hello!' Waving a hand back at the scarecrow the man moves along, looking at Dorothy to hear her offer, 'please don't leave because of us.' He sways slightly with, 'It's quite fine you're....' and then looking down at her boots he gazes back up at her sweet face to say, 'Your majesty, um...your highness, no...your witch, oh bugger I'd better go.'

Watching him swagger away Dorothy smiles as they all sit, and a young woman comes to their table. 'What can I get for you?' she asks, and the lion licks his lips, 'I'd like a deer please,' as she replies, 'How do you want it cooked?' Looking at her he grins, 'I don't, and can I have a whole one?' to which she curiously asks, 'You want a whole deer, to eat here?' Nodding his head he says shyly, 'Well I am a lion,' and she replies, 'I can see that,' as Dorothy interrupts with, 'He'll have whatever you can fit on a plate, but raw please.'

A little while later the lion sits with a full stomach, rubbing his belly as he smiles at the three empty plates in front of him. Still looking at the lion licking his lips the scarecrow gasps, 'That was fascinating,' as the lion says, 'Dorothy are you sure you're not hungry?' to which she wheezes slightly, 'I've lost my appetite.' After resting for a while longer, and letting the lion's stomach settle Dorothy looks at the people in the tavern, all keeping their distance and most ignoring the strange guests, though some watch with a greedy glare in their eyes.

With the strong lion giving a fierce yawn Dorothy starts to feel tired too, and even though Scarecrow and the tin-man don't sleep, they all make their way out of the tavern.

Walking through the shady cobbled streets as thin lights shine on scattered lengths of their path, Dorothy notices a small crowd of men following them. Ignoring it at first she keeps quiet, though concentrates as she occasionally glares over her shoulder at them, assuming they're just drunk.

Turning a corner, walking for a while then taking another the young girl notices they're still being followed, and brings it to her friends attention in a whisper as the tin-man sternly replies, *'I know!'*

They keep walking as the lion shakes, terribly worried whilst Dorothy looks over her shoulder to see the three men smiling, waving at her. The tin-man still walks calmly, waiting for an attack as the scarecrow whistles without a worry. Still, they walk home, turning another corner and walking along a dimly lit street as without warning three men appear out of an alleyway ahead of them.

Looking to gang, then turning quickly Dorothy can see they're surrounded with three strangers either side as they walk closer. Shouting, *'What do you want?'* Dorothy bares her teeth in anger as one of them smiles, his sleazy voice echoing through the streets, *'You'll see pretty!'* Giving a fierce roar to scare them away the lion stands in fear and they laugh, one of them shouting, *'He's timid as a cat!'* as the tin-man regrets the mistake of leaving his axe in Dorothy's room.

The men walk closer, surrounding the strange crowd as they stand still, unsure of what to do until they hear a man scream, *'Now!'* Suddenly the men charge as one of them attacks Scarecrow, throwing him to the ground as two men grab at Dorothy, their strong hands squeezing against her skin as she struggles to fight them. The scared lion roars as a man comes at him, punching at the beast with a spiked glove. Despite being cowardly his instinct flares as he claws at the man, mauling him ferociously as another attacks, stabbing at the lion as the blade cuts into his skin and he runs away scared, leaving his friends.

With scarecrow struggling to stand the two men grab at Dorothy, trying to hold her arms still as she struggles, breaking a hand free. Scramming at one of them, her nails dig deeply into his face and she tears away a chunk of flesh as the other man punches her in the face and she falls to the floor. Moving quickly, his frail jagged body twisted from the fall the scarecrow swipes a hand at Dorothy's attacker, cutting him to the bone as the rusted barbwire holding the scarecrow's hands together blinds the man.

Looking to the tin-man Dorothy watches three men attack him as the one she wounded joins them. Running to his side she watches his thick spiked gauntlets tare a man in two, then break both of another man's arms as a sly man holds a knife steadily, thrusting it deeply into the thin layers of metal around the tin-man's chest. He falls to his knees in pain. Dorothy runs to the attacker as he stabs her friend again, only to be thrown to the floor as the other man starts to cut at the tin man, piercing the thin metal as blood pours from the wounds and the tin-man roars. Despite the pain he struggles to his feet, flailing a forceful hand as he snaps one man's neck and reaches for the other.

Grabbing tightly at his attacker's throat the wounded tin-man falls back to his knees, keeping the grip firm as he looks down at the man, as suffering human eyes lay imbedded in an iron-monster's head. *'What do you want?'* he roars, and the attacker chokes, spits out blood as the tin-man's vice-like grip tightens and he stares at his victim almost with a smile.

Helping Dorothy from the floor the scarecrow watches the tin-man, looks at his deep wounds as he holds the man, his cackling voice uttering, *'You don't know how much your metal's worth!'* Without hesitation the tin-man roars, grabbing at the man's head with his other hand as he twists the skull from its neck, tearing his head from his shoulder like it's nothing more than flicking the head from a flower. The blood pours through the street and the tin-man groans, stretching a hand out to his friends, chiselling, *'Help!'* as the wounded lion lies bleeding in an alleyway.

Soon the wizard's servants come to the aid of the strange friends; stitching the lion's deep wound, fixing the scarecrow and trying to stop the swelling on Dorothy's face. Though none are in more pain than the tin-man, as the servants have to solder his wounds; melting at his thin metal and flesh, fusing them to seal the tin.

They all lay awake for many hours, and when their wounds have been treated they join the tin-man in the cold damp workshop. The cowardly lion cries, *'I'm sorry, so sorry I'm a coward,'* and Dorothy simply strokes him, wrapping him in a thick blanket as she looks at the new scar stretching along his side. Soon he falls asleep on the floor, and Dorothy lays on the cold metal workbench beside the tin-man, gently with her arms around him as trickles of blood drip from his eyes as the young girl asks, *'Does it still hurt?'* His grim mouth moans, *'It's agony,'* as she wipes the blood from his cheeks and falls asleep holding his cold metal. Lying awake, with nothing to do but suffer through the night the tin-man rests with his eyes open, feeling Dorothy beside him as the scarecrow stands, looking to the tortured tin-man as his burlap sack frowns, *'This isn't good to see.'*

22

Morning had passed and the strange friends still rest in the windowless workshop, as cold and dark as it had been all night.

Dorothy's skin feels chilled, even her eyelids icy, almost too heavy to open. She looks to the tin-man as he breathes heavily, his tortured eyes staring at the ceiling, caked with blood at the rims. Yawning slightly Dorothy can feel the bruise along her face stretch, as she imagines the burst vessels tanned a deep red. She touches it lightly with a cringe and opens her mouth widely to feel a severe crack in her jaw.

Looking at the scarecrow, she watches his sad smile peer back through the darkness, effortlessly waving at her as she slides her body off the workbench. Stepping over the lion gently Dorothy watches his tired heavy breath and moves to the door, opening it a crack as the light beams a faint line on her face, warming the cold skin.

Within the hour a masked servant comes to the workshop, ready to escort the lion to the wizard's castle. After a long stretch and a hungry yawn the lion walks through the cobbled city begrudgingly, nervous of the passers-by, even children, as he walks past the street where he was attacked last night. His back arches and he bares his thick white teeth, watching people as they wash away the blood spread along the cobbled bricks.

At the bottom of the hill, the cowardly lion's still struck with fear, worried that the wizard will know he killed a man last night, and even worse, he'll want him to kill the witch. As his paws press into the soil of the graveyard hill he re-enacts his attack, though not the one inflicted upon him, he had suffered far worse at the hands of Mr Jack. Instead he thinks of how he mauled the man last night, his claws tearing away chunks of flesh like it were another animal in the forest. Although he doesn't have the courage to admit it the lion smiles inside, proud of himself for fighting back, though so ashamed of leaving his friends behind that he tries not to think of it anymore. With a snarl he whimpers, *'C...coward!'* to himself as he walks up the hill and notices a cart of bodies to his right, the servants throwing them in a single grave one by one, the attackers from last night.

At the top of the hill the cowardly lion cautiously walks between the guards, his sharp teeth on show to make them think he's strong. Yet his body shakes as he walks through the large doors, stepping into the darkness as he takes a few paces and snivels, *'Don't need courage, don't need courage.'* Turning his back, ready to leave the dark castle the lion winces as the large doors close behind him, and he claws at the wood unable to open it. Reluctantly moving through the darkness he finally finds himself in the grand courtroom, but the beautiful emerald marble doesn't catch his eye, instead he keeps his distance from the disturbing puppets, watching their carved bodies keenly. Even though they're silent he's still cautious, unsure if they're alive or not as he looks past them at the small door. Sure that's where he must go he waits, and his eyes flicker from left to right as he watches the seated company, whose expressions change with the blink of an eye to taunt the animal. His body tenses, the thick legs ready to run as the silence lingers, and his eyes widen as the small door opens quietly. Bounding on all fours, he dashes past the seated folk as fast as he can, running into the wizards throne room without thinking as he struggles to stop. Sliding along the emerald marble at first he digs his claws into the ground to slow himself, standing on all fours and looking out to an empty throne.

With no sign of the wizard, the lion quickly begins to walk backwards, heading toward the door, as rapidly a circle of flames bursts through the floor. Trapping the cowardly lion in the centre he cowers, trembling as he looks up to the circle wall, at least eight foot high as he feels the heat against his skin. Whimpering, the lion closes his eyes, burying his head between his paws as a scolding voice spreads along the fire:

'I am Oz, the great and wonderful, the beginning and the end. I have many names and faces, what do you want from me?'

The lion doesn't answer, petrified he simply keeps his head cowered, shaking as the flames burst with strength, and the wizard's voice commands:

'Answer me beast! What do you want?'

Feeling a lump in his throat and the muscles tense in his neck, his dead eye weeps as he looks to the flames, reminding him of the burns he'd suffered at the hands of Mr Jack. His deep voice breaks the lion, and the animal begs, *'Courage, so I can be strong, like...like a lion should.'*

The wizard's voice stings in response, his wall of fire unfurling beautiful deadly flames as they taunt the lion:

'I will grant you courage, but you must do something for me in return. You must join the others and kill Outika, the witch of the west. She must die and you will bring me her heart, or you will forever be a coward, and my flames will be your prison. Do you understand?''

The lion cowers again, his eyes tightly shut as he whines, *'Y...yes!'* Trapped within the fire he feels the heat press against him, and as quickly as the air burst into flames the wall holding him disperses, vanishing as he opens his eyes and runs away. Charging though the castle, clawing at the large doors, they open and he sprints down the hill with tremendous speed. Making his way to the workshop, he runs past the servant who was supposed to guide him, refusing to stop until he finds his friends. Bursting into the small shed he startles Dorothy and hides in a corner, licking at odd patches of fur where the fire had burnt him. Mumbling to himself at first he groans, *'He...he wants the witch's heart as proof,'* trembling on the floor in fear.

Still recovering, laying still on the metal bench the tin-man's voice scrapes, *'We must go west, toward the land of the winkies,'* as Dorothy remembers what Bopeia told her of the winkies. She had been warned that they're an evil race of clones made by Outika, their teeth and fingers razor sharp and eyes sewn shut. The good witch told her not to go near one, not even to go near their land in the west, but the young girl knows that she must. She has to go west and kill the wicked witch for the wizard, otherwise she'll never get home, and she will have to suffer his wrath.

Throughout the remainder of the day Dorothy and Scarecrow prepare for the journey ahead of them as the lion and tin-man rest their wounds. Knowing they'll set off early in the morning Dorothy sneaks into a tavern, finding herself in the kitchen as she searches for food.
She knows that if she had asked the wizard he may have let her take as much as she wants, but the young girl didn't want to disturb him for something so small. So she fills her basket with fruit and cooked meat, finding a butcher's knife as she holds it in her hand, feeling the cold steel before placing it in the wicker basket. Then she joins scarecrow, sharpening the tin-man's axe on a myrtle grindstone whilst he fills a can with oil. Finally they stuff the scarecrow with hay, finding a pitchfork as he holds it in his hand, forgetting he'd held one before as he admires the thin harlequin green spikes and smiles, *'How shiny!'*

Again sleeping in the workshop at night Dorothy rests on the workbench next to tin-man, as the lion sleeps on the floor and Scarecrow stands next to the young girl. Holding her hand he looks down at her face, worried as she struggles to close her eyes.

'What's wrong?' Scarecrow asks, and she looks up to his twisted face in the darkness with a lump in her throat, whispering, *'I'm scared.'* Holding her hand tightly his thin mouth smiles, stretching creepily along his face as his wide buttons stare, *'Don't be scared, we'll look after you, Toto too.'* Smiling up at him Dorothy soon falls asleep, again comforted by her friends as the tin-man still stares at the ceiling, his wounds almost healed as he thinks of his love, wondering where she is now.

As morning comes, even before the sun rises the group set out on their journey as several servants guide them through the city to the west exit. The tin-man's joints ache from lying still for so long, and although his wounds are healed, they're still sore. Clenching his axe tightly he feels comfort with it in his hand and watches the others in front of him. With a slight whimper the lion walks next to Dorothy, his new scar camouflaged with the rest as he fears the trek ahead. With a large gate at the front of the castle opening they look in the distance to see a wagon rolling onto the cobbled streets, as Mr Jack sits upfront with a sinister smile. The lion quivers, *'The...the carnival,'* and they move quickly as Dorothy shouts to the servants, *'We have to hurry!'*

As fast as they can, they make their way to the edge of the great wall, far away from the large door that brought them into the city as the servants tap at the bricks. Watching the wall with amazement Dorothy sees three of the large stones dislodge themselves and swing open like a gate as the scarecrow gleams, *'What an oddity!'* Whilst the other servants wait by the wall one walks inside, leading the strange friends as they enter another small room without hesitation. Looking at the dull green viridian walls the group walk inside and the tin-man's the last in as he watches the stones close behind him, feeling the room slightly shake. The masked servant walks to another jade phoropter, touching at the machine as he timidly asks, *'Please look into the device, if you do not scan your eyes you will not be able to see properly outside of the city.'* As they each take their turn Dorothy realises the room isn't as green as before, neither is Scarecrows pitchfork and she squints for a while. Still, she watches the servant as he pulls aside his gown to unveil a thick metal strap, grabbing at a thick key chained to it. The strange company watch him undo all five locks of a gate covered with stone as he struggles to push it outward.

With the glare of white light outside, Dorothy smells the fresh air and turns to the servant, asking, *'What road do we follow to head west?'* Shaking his head at first and pulling a small compass from his pocket, he hands it to Dorothy, answering nervously, *'No road will take you there, you must head west where the sun sets.'* With a rickety breath the girl nods her head, asking, *'Have you ever been west?'* and the masked man trembles, *'Never, never left city, it's forbidden.'* Surprised, Dorothy gasps, *'What?'* but the man pushes them out of the room quickly, repeating, *'Please, please you'll get me into trouble!'* scared to step outside himself, as he pulls the exit shut behind them.

Forced outside and standing by the wall Dorothy still tries to shout at the small masked man, but she watches the door close, shutting to look like just another set of green bricks in the great wall. Taking a deep breath the lion's relieved to be outside of the city, so scared that Mr Jack may find him. Staring with amazement the scarecrow touches at the wall, tapping the stone with, *'Very impressive,'* unsure of what happened to the door as the others walk away from the Emerald city.

Looking out in the distance, they stare to the west and Dorothy drops the compass to the floor as a look of defeat scars along her face. Miles of carpeted green fields spread in front of them, dotted with buttercups, daisies and several small huts, though beyond that is nothing but shades of yellow spanning as far as they can see. A barren icterine land of perishing stone and sand's scattered with skeletons, as amber hills and cliffs form behind them, and jagged golden mountains shaped like arms tower the land. With no sign of the witch's domain, nor civilization or shelter Dorothy crumbles inside, this is what she'd imagined the land to be like, and now she has to endure it.

Trying not to shake, her throat already dry at the thought of hiking across the terrain Dorothy knows she has to push through, she's undergone too much to give up now. So with a quick breathe, trying to focus on the journey ahead she opens the compass to see a small piece of paper inside. Unfolding it curiously she reads, 'Please help us!' as the dark chill of the wizard's voice pricks at her skin, and she thinks of his cruelty and the people trapped inside his city. Hideous thoughts of his domain run through her head, the masked servants, the silent, the blind, and the scarred children. Wondering the depths of his cruelty she feels sick, thinking of the tortures he's capable of as the task over her head seems far more dangerous than ever before. What will the wizard do to Dorothy if she fails him?

23

Walking along the deep green fields the strange friends ignore the fresh grass and blooming flowers, focusing on the yellow valley ahead as Scarecrow's buttons stretch widely with intrigue.

Soon they find themselves at the border of the west, as the icterine yellow country lays a step ahead and they move forward into the dead land. With miles of sand and crumbled rocks surrounding them they walk through the barren terrain, pathed with skeletons as the sun gleams against their crisp white bones. Scattered like breadcrumbs for birds the bones are of various species, some of small creatures and others bigger than elephants, all impeccable. Without a single broken piece, or the slightest of marks to the skeletons frames they spread through the west, and Dorothy looks at the husks of amazing animals and the bones of dainty creatures, wondering how they all died.

After marching for hours, the group soon loses count of the dead, and even the cowardly lion grows used to such sights, yet Scarecrow's amazed with every new species he finds. Some of the bones are from humans, others of animals, large insects, and as Scarecrow sees winged skeletons he crushes them with his pitchfork, mumbling, *'No wings, no wings.'*

Dorothy and the lion soon find themselves tired, they'd been walking all morning; treading carefully and avoiding the deep cracks in the ground, and now the chrome yellow sun reaches its peak. The bright light burns at them as Dorothy feels it stinging her neck, and even the tin-man's thin metal chest heats vigorously. With her mouth dry and her limbs aching the young girl struggles on for another mile, knowing that they need to get to the witch, and as far from Mr Jack as possible. After a while she gives in to herself, panting, *'I need to stop,'* as they find the skeleton of a large elephant and rest. Looking up at the burning sun the tin-man walks to the dead animal's skull, hacking away its head from the spine and snapping several of its ribs as the scarecrow helps him build a small shelter.

Shaded under the clear white bones Dorothy gulps at a canteen of water, and then the lion gently laps some from her cupped hands. Knowing how timid he is Dorothy underestimates his strength, ignorantly letting him lick at her palms without thinking that his tongue is so strong it can scrape meat from bones. Still he laps at the water as gently as he can, panting as the heavy weight of his body is almost hypnotizing. Waiting a little while for the sun to die down Dorothy opens the small bag around her shoulder and pulls out the little black dog as Scarecrow gleams, *'Toto!'* and the lion eyes up the small creature. Sniffing at it at first he huffs, blowing the fur along the little dog's back as the scarecrow gently rubs at its head. Turning to the lion Scarecrow asks, *'Do you like it?'* and the lion tilts his head unsure, squinting his good eye as the straw man scuffles the lion's mane, smiling, *'You should, you're both fluffy.'* Dorothy giggles at the two of them and the lion groans, *'Don't you think I look fierce?'* to which the scarecrow says, *'Yes,'* so the lion starts to feel proud, raising his head smugly before the straw man continues, *'As fierce as Toto!'* The lion huffs again, *'I'm a lion I'm supposed to be fierce,'* and the scarecrow nods repeatedly, *'I know, and I'm a scarecrow....but I don't scare crows. It's a mad world.'*

After resting for a little while the group walk through the land, trekking for hours as the scarecrow dances along the way, admiring how his tangine necklace shines in the light as Dorothy tries to think where all the skeletons came from. They're whole, undamaged but not a single one has an ounce of flesh left, perhaps the chrome yellow sun burns so brightly sometimes it can melt flesh from bones. Either that or they died a long time ago, and no one dares cross the land anymore. Dorothy ponders then turns to the tin-man, gallant in his stride as she asks, *'Do you know anything of this land?'* to which his warm metal jaw crunches open, *'Only one thing, but you'll have to see it yourself.'* Curious, the young girl can only imagine what waits ahead, and soon they stand at the bottom of the amber hills.

Looking to obstacle in front of them Scarecrow's the first to attempt climbing it, though Dorothy quickly pulls him back, kicking at a stone to watch it quickly sink into a pool of sand. Telling him, *'Do what I do!'* she takes a few steps back and runs, jumping onto the rocks as she digs her boots into the mound, trying not to drop her wicker basket as she starts to climb the steep hill. With no trouble the others join her, and finally reaching the top of the first hill they look back at the Emerald city.

Amazed at how far they have travelled in such little time Dorothy looks out to the miles of dead land and the Emerald city behind it, still so grand on the outside. She can see the dull Munchkin country and the dark forest in the background, turning her head to stare across the yellow land, seeing shades of red to the south and deep purples to the north. Smiling in amazement at the countries, taking in how beautiful it all is her thoughts are disturbed as a voice echoes, *'Eat please!'* The group look into the rock formations in front of them, the tin-man waiting to see a figure as he tightly grips his axe, and the lion cowering backwards.

Staring at the thick jagged walls of stone Dorothy watches a man peer from a small cave; his pale grey complexion standing out amongst the amber as he limps toward them. With his festered skin covered in small rotten mushrooms, the scarecrow scratches his head at such a sight, as the fungus spreads over every inch of the man's body and he pulls one from his skin. Watching the stem break, he holds a mushroom in his hands, another growing instantly in its place as he stretches his arm out to Dorothy. *'Please eat, you must be hungry,'* he says as the girl looks at his tongue, layered with fungus as his pitiful eyes stare. Shaking her head she orders, *'Get back into your cave,'* as she slowly reaches into her wicker basket for the butcher's knife. *'P...please just eat one,'* he begs, *'I am cursed, and if a passer-by eats just one of my mushrooms I will be free.'* Clenching at the knife in the basket Dorothy is ready to attack but the tin-man charges in front of her, wielding his thick axe as he approaches the grey man. *'You're wasting our time, move or I will hack you in two,'* he shouts as the man cowers backwards, begging:

'Please don't, I cannot die, I'll only suffer more. The, the witch cursed me, making me forever this way. Can you help me? Just eat one, please?'

A dirty liquid drips from his eyes and he trembles by the tin-man's blade, staring at Dorothy. Feeling heartless she orders, *'Get in your cave!'* and the man crouches to his knees, crawling backwards as he sits in the small hole. Still holding the axe to him the tin-man watches his friends pass, then pulls away the weapon away, roaring, *'Follow us and you will suffer.'* Moving along the hill Dorothy climbs another mound of rocks, unaware that the poor grey man was once a human, and the mushrooms he offered would have caused her no harm despite how vile they looked. This is his curse.

Atop the next hill Dorothy and her friends rest for a minute, then climb another, this one even steeper, and they finally reach the top exhausted. Out of breath, Dorothy stands at the edge looking out to the vast Oz, and then down to see how far they had climbed. Feeling dizzy she quickly pulls away, hugging a large stone wall. Looking deep into the rock formations Dorothy stares up at the mountains above them, amazed that they stand almost as tall as the Emerald castle. Looking like stone arms atop of the cliff, she feels at the warm yellow rock and looks to a gap between the mountains. Moving carefully along a precarious ledge they make their way to a rough path through the mountain, as Scarecrow coos, *'What a sight!'* Looking behind them at the landscape of Oz he walks toward the ledge, smiling widely at the approaching night as the tin-man places a strong metal hand on his chest with a stern, *'Wrong way!'* Nodding his head the scarecrow turns around and joins the others as they walk between two golden mountains, seeming like ants in such a vast amount of rocks. The path is long and dark as the mountains block out the chrome yellow sun, and Dorothy feels a sudden chill against her skin as a slight breeze drifts through the passageway.

Walking through the damp opening until they can see the other side of the land only metres away Dorothy squints out to the darkening sky. Trying to decipher what's ahead of them she can hear faint cries in the distance, deep peculiar sounds as the tin-man's mechanical voice crunches, *'We should stay here for the night!'*
Dorothy looks back to him, challenging, *'We can still cover more ground,'* but he drops his axe to the floor, refusing to move as his curious words echo through the passageway, *'You will not want to rest down there in the day or night, not until we're past the river.'* Walking toward him she presses, *'River, what river? This land is pretty much a dessert, what's out there?'* The enigmatic tin-man refuses to answer, not offering a single relief to her curiosity, instead he groans, *'You don't want to know before you sleep.'*

After a while, Dorothy sleeps on the ground as a draft whips between the mountains, and she lays with her head pressed against the lion's chest as he drapes his paws over her. Feeling the warmth of his breath against her face and his thick coat against her skin she still shivers in her sleep. With nothing to do but watch them both Scarecrow and the tin-man stand idly by, as scratching his burlap head the scarecrow whispers, *'If I had a brain do you think I'd feel sleepy?'* The tin-man looks at him with a blank glare, quietly moaning, *'Maybe,'* as his jaw creaks open and Scarecrow frowns, *'Too bad, it looks boring...'* Then bursting, *'I like shiny things,'* he startles himself, amazed his screech didn't wake Dorothy as he looks down at her with a thin finger against his mouth, whilst the tin-man replies solidly, *'I know you do.'*
Listening to the western night the tin-man can hear faint cries still echo through the valley, but nothing nearby, not even a single groan or whimper from the smallest of creatures. Reaching for his axe the tin-man says, *'Stay with them,'* to the scarecrow, as he watches him nod his head and walks out of the passageway, standing alone on new ground.
Looking out he can see the agonies of what morning will bring and patrols the mountain, walking further from his friends as he struggles to

hear a single sound except the faint breeze. Little does he know that in this country, despite how loud the cries of agony may be, one of its predators is always silent, the deadly wolves. At first only a few wait in the shadows, watching the tin-man as he walks along the rough ground. Yet as he moves, his jagged metal sends vibrations through the rocks, and suddenly over two dozen yellow eyes of the night stare at him. The wolves are miserable creatures, with their fur naturally tarred a thick black, and faces like dead dogs as their spiny teeth drip with saliva. On the prowl, their soulless eyes hunt hungrily, scouring the night for meat and ready to tear it from living flesh for the enjoyment. They all watch the tin-man with their presence unknown, and they can tell the meat will be sparse, but that won't stop them attacking.

They linger patiently as the tin-man rests his axe on a shoulder, waiting for the slightest sound, but with the silence in his ears he slowly walks back, lowering his weapon to the floor. Now the wolves are ready to strike.

Attacking in pairs, though with dozens leaping from the darkness the tin-man hears their hungry growls, looking to see one in mid-air, ready to feast. Acting on reflex he swings his axe upward, decapitating the creature and quickly forcing his weapon back down, aiming for a sly wolf on the ground as he cuts it in half.

As the next wave attacks, then another, he cuts at their bodies with the axe, feeling one on his back as he throws it from the mountain and kicks the next one, shattering its skull. The blood sprays against his tin body and a wolf gets close enough to bite at his hand, howling in agony as the metal spikes pierce its jaw and the tin-man throws it aside, breaking another's legs. Swinging his axe in a fluid motion to cut two bellies open at once the attack seems endless but he fights them like a gladiator, tearing their bodies apart without stopping.

Watching his kin get slaughtered by the tin-man, at least two dozen dead the leader of the pack waits, watching his allies get thrown from the mountain, their bodies torn open as only a few still breath.

The remaining wolves attack, and the tin-man kills them easily as the leader arches his back, leaping through the air with his fierce mouth ready to bite. Moving with great speed its body's close enough to attack, the tin-man quickly drops his axe, grabbing at the wolf's throat with a single spiked gauntlet. Growling at first, snapping its teeth the tin-man watches him and walks to the edge of the mountain. Tightening his metal grip the wolf soon whimpers, his eyes filled with hatred as the tin-man dangles it in the air.

Looking at the creature, with no hesitation of what to do the tin-man opens his bear-trap jaws and bites into the wolf's side. The animal howls in agony and the metal gladiator throws it back onto the ground as blood drips from his jagged teeth. Whimpering, the wounded wolf looks at him, baring his teeth as the tin-man groans, *'Follow us again and I will kill more of your kind!'* Bleeding severely but still wanting to attack the wolf whimpers in agony, begrudgingly turning its back and limping into the night.

The tin-man waits for another attack, standing on the mountain as his metal body drips with blood. He lets an hour pass then grabs at several dead wolves, ones still intact as he pulls the tarred fur from their skin and scrapes away the gore as best he can.

24

In the morning Dorothy wakes, her skin as warm as can be as she opens her eyes to see the black fur draped over both her and the lion. Trembling at the sight of the blood stained sheet she looks up at the tin-man, bewildered as he grumbles, *'You were cold, needed warmth.'* Unsure of what to say she pulls the blanket of fur from her body and hesitantly thanks the tin-man, trying to ignore the smell of dead meat and the fresh blood staining her dress.

After Dorothy eats some fruit, and the lion some meat the group are ready to explore the new land as they look out of the passageway at the bright terrain ahead. Walking from between the mountains Dorothy looks to her left to see a countless number of dead wolves, their blood and insides spread along rocks as she turns away quickly.

Feeling the sun on her face, already hotter than she expected the tin-man holds out a wolf fur, sewn delicately together and ready for her to wear. She looks confused at first and the tin-man groans, *'I used some of Scarecrow's wire. It will stop the sun burning your skin.'* Seeing sense in his words, though still begrudging her actions she takes the fur from his hand and pulls it over her body, feeling the blood press against her as she wonders if she'll get used to the smell.

Looking out to the journey ahead Dorothy walks to the edge of the mountain to see the others already staring, their eyes leering at the horror of the west. The yellow land is no longer barren, and instead the amber mountains ahead are more of a prison than a landscape. At first Dorothy refuses to admit such a place exists, but hell stands before her and thousands of living bodies mesh into the amber stone. Screaming their throats raw the suffering souls are part of the land, and spread through the vast mountains as they all beg to die.

Looking out at them, some with limbs flailing from the ground, and others nothing but half a face with stone between their teeth Dorothy feels her stomach turn. Past the mountains of bodies she looks to a cliff, its wall a large agonised face as the tin-man points to the cave that's inside its mouth, *'That's where we have to go.'*

Walking across the rough mountains the scarecrow looks at the bodies imbedded into the land and sees a face staring at him. Sticking from the rocks with its mouth sealed shut the head moves its eyes vigorously and

Scarecrow touches the stone skin curiously. Stepping over the grasping hands and keeping away from the walls the group make their way across the mountain silently as Dorothy looks over the edge, now with no sand below, only jagged rocks past a thin layer of mist.

Walking for a mile or so the land's screams stab at Dorothy's ears and she tries to ignore them, shuffle past the desperate hands and the begging mouths as suddenly the group of strange friends come to a sharp edge of the mountain. Watching the pieces of rock disintegrate in front of them, Dorothy's eyes follow as it crumbles and takes an imbedded screaming body, plunging to the mist. Looking to the wall beside them the tin-man notices carved ridges in the stone, leading to the next mountain as he calls to the others. Looking at the distance they have to climb across, the scarecrow goes first and they watch him move along the wall as he smiles, *'My, ever never seen one of those before, how odd.'*
As he reaches the other side Dorothy throws across his pitchfork, then the wicker basket, along with tin-man's axe. Next in line the young girl holds on to the rocks, shuffling along as she suddenly notices bodies trapped between the ridges. Yet unlike those imbedded in the stone these are trapped inside transparent amber, unable to move as they look at Dorothy pathetically, their eyes barely able to blink. Looking at them with pity she turns her head from the wall, unable to watch the tortured faces anymore. Reaching the other side she looks to the large face carved into the mountain ahead of them, waiting for her friends to cross the gap before they walk through the blistering chrome yellow sun again.

They trek a mile along the suffering mountains, then another as Dorothy feels hot and flustered, so warm with the fur around her but sure she would have been burnt now without it. She can smell the wolf skin heating in the sun but pays no attention as finally they stand before the vast stone face. The friends stare up at the hideous head and Dorothy half expects it to move; sure that what lies ahead will be worse than what they've already seen.

Walking toward the face they enter through its mouth, feeling at the yellow stoned lips as darkness creeps over them and they feel relieved to be out of the sun. Looking through the dark claustrophobic tunnel Dorothy stares into the distance, past tarred bodies spread along the walls to the other side of the mountain. Seeing nothing outside the tunnel but a clear white mist, it entwines with vapour, spiralling through the air as it blankets everything beyond it.

Walking through the passageway Scarecrow looks at the black walls to see odd lumps, touching at one of them to watch the skin on his finger melt away. Then suddenly the walls scream and the dormant bodies open their eyes as hot tar pours from inside the tunnel, dripping over their raw bodies. Stretching out their arms and trying to grab at the strange company, Scarecrow feels a hand clench his coat as the material melts. The lion watches, as a hot tarred hand reaches at his fur, and he screams, *'Run!'*

The souls' agony echoes off the walls, the tar coating their suffering flesh as they scream for help. Quickly Dorothy and her friends charge through the tunnel, as tortured burnt hands grope from the darkness and they finally stand at the other side of the mountain, seeing nothing but a bone white mist. Feeling at the edges of the passageway behind them Dorothy looks back through the dark tunnel to see bright yellow in the distance, but looks at the path ahead to see nothing.

Almost unable to see her stretched out hand she looks down to the boots on her feet as she realises they're standing on a crumbling ledge, and beyond it lies a river of mist, pure emptiness. Watching as the yellow mountain glimmers faintly past the white in front of his eyes, the tin-man knows the thin ledge won't be able to support all of their weight much longer. He looks out to the thick curtain of mist in hope of finding a way up the mountain, but the keen eyed scarecrow points a hand to the river, seeing a faint shape in the distance as it floats towards them.

Whinging, *'Wh...what's that?'* the lion's body trembles as he struggles not to move, pressing himself against a wall. Watching the shape gets closer the tin-man says, *'It's our way across,'* as a small boat drifts gently towards them. Curiously voicing, *'That's very odd!'* Scarecrow looks closer at the peculiarly vessel to see it's made of nothing but limbs, hundreds of pale arms holding tightly at each other as they overlap and entwine.

Drifting next to them the boat knocks against the crumbling ledge as the lion uses all of his strength not to cower into the tunnel, and Dorothy looks in amazement. Grabbing at a fleshy grey arm the tin-man holds the boat steady, squeezing it tightly to test if they would let go of each other if forced. Bruising the limb and lightly cutting its flesh he watches it drip a black substance, but still holds tightly to the other arm.

Shouting, *'Get in!'* the tin-man knows the ledge they're on won't hold much longer, and Scarecrow shuffles his body into the boat without worry, touching at the limbs with a curious grin. Next Dorothy clambers into the vessel, feeling the cold flesh against her as she looks to the steering wheel;

nothing more than a limbless chest, and the handles are small spines thrust through the main. With some persuasion the cowardly lion hesitantly gets onboard and the tin-man follows behind him as he moves Scarecrow away from the wheel, pointing into the mist with, *'Look over there!'*

Taking the spines in his hands tin-man looks to Dorothy with, *'He'd kill us, steer us into a pretty rock,'* as the distracted Scarecrow looks into the emptiness. Smiling, Dorothy looks to the tin-man's stern monstrous face, then to Scarecrow as he watches the mist glide gently, and the lion as he sits nervously in the middle of the boat.

Pulling a large skeletal lever next to him and turning the steering wheel, tin-man guides them away from the mountain as they drift into oblivion, whilst Dorothy looks to see nothing but white, not even a sign of the mountains or the sky.

25

Floating through the void Dorothy guides the tin-man, holding out the compass as they head west. With the lion still sitting in the centre of the boat he shakes, *'Don't want to drown! Don't want to drown!'* whilst Scarecrow pulls himself from the edge of the boat, tapping at the animal's head as he gleams, *'Don't be afraid, I'm sure we can't drown. I think we'll just fall, there's no water!'* The lion huffs, *'That's not comforting... well what, what's underneath us?'* rubbing a paw at his weeping eye as the scarecrow taps his burlap head, *'That's a very good question!'* Walking to the edge of the boat he sticks his hand into the mist underneath them at first to feel nothing, then as his inquisitive smile widens he holds onto the edge and leans his head overboard. Watching the scarecrow's skinny legs lift into the air the lion pounces at him, latching a claw into his skin and throwing him back into the boat. The lion roars, *'What were you doing?'* and the scarecrow innocently lifts his arms in the air, shaking his head as he grins, *'I wanted to see what was underneath us!'*

With a subtle growl the lion holds his body strongly, walking atop the severed arms as he asks, *'Well...did you see anything?'* The scarecrow shakes his head, sitting on the base of the boat as he looks to the pale limbs and waves, *'Oh, nothing!'* The lion feels relieved and lets his tense muscles relax as he looks to Dorothy and the tin-man as they guide the boat. Then the scarecrow pokes at his burlap head again, his mouth open wide as he says, *'Well nothing pretty anyway!'*

Looking back at him the lion feels a slight panic whip along his face as he asks, *'What, what do you mean nothing pretty?'* and the scarecrow replies shaking his head, *'They look miserable, boring. Take a peek!'* As a mild curiosity slides under his skin the lion walks to the edge of the boat, slowly looking overboard to see nothing but pale ivory sheets of mist. Turning his head to the scarecrow he says, *'There's nothing there,'* hearing him reply, *'Look harder, use your buttons.'*

Carefully he leans back over the edge, his cowardly eye peering beneath the white vapour carpet as he watches bodies reaching up from the nothingness; some animals and others people as their voices go unheard, the surface of the mist out of their reach. Turning his head to Dorothy the lion yelps, *'There...there are bodies under us!'* but the young girl crushes his worry, shouting, *'That's the least of our problems!'* as the boat starts to rock.

Staring in front of them Dorothy watches an elephant's head surface from the mist, its dead skin grey and eyes white as its body stretches into the sky, standing to unveil long thick spider legs spreading from the head. Treading through the thick white, it wails at the top of its voice as another surfaces from the river of mist, walking in front of the boat as the vessel shakes. Shouting back to lion and the scarecrow Dorothy screams, *'Hold on!'* as they grab at the grey arms and watch the tall creatures walk past them. Keeping the boat steady the tin-man lets it hover, not wanting to drift away as suddenly one of the animal's bends its long spider legs.

Leaning as far down as it can the elephant's head rests just in front of the boat as Dorothy stares into its white eyes to feel the tusks touching the vessel. As its cold breath pushes against the group, the cowardly lion closes his eyes and the scarecrow smiles intrigued. Looking at its dead skin Dorothy's terrified, close enough to touch its trunk as it waves above their heads. Too scared to move, even to breath she feels cold sweat dripping down her face and hears the other call in the distance, its cry echoing through the void. Quickly it rises, pulling away its head as the spider legs straighten, standing tall as the elephant's head becomes invisible in the mist. Walking away they trudge through the river, stretching their legs with speed as the tin-man starts to steer the boat once more.

Wiping a palm full of sweat from her head Dorothy looks back to the others with relief, shouting, *'It's okay, they're gone!'* to the lion as she stares back out into the mist, amazed at what she'd just seen.

Hours pass and they still head west, surrounded by nothing but layers of haze as they drift along the hopeless river. The lion sleeps heavily, stretching his paws and clawing in his sleep as the scarecrow watches him and tickles his whiskers to watch the animal rub at its face. Still up front, the tin-man steers as Dorothy holds out the compass, yawning as she covers her mouth, rubbing at her eyes to keep them from closing. Catching her in the corner of his eye the tin-man offers, *'Rest, I can hold the compass,'* as she hands it to him and rubs his metal arm, *'Thank you.'*

As the boat drifts calmly without the slightest disturbance Dorothy rests against the lion, still wearing the wolf fur to keep her warm as she holds Scarecrow's hand and he flicks at the coarse hairs. Before falling asleep she pulls Toto from her bag and hands him to the scarecrow, watching a happy smile creep along his eerie face. *'Toto!'* he says enthusiastically, and Dorothy whispers, *'take care of him,'* as she falls asleep comfortably between Scarecrow and the lion.

Thoughts drift through the young girl's mind, dreams of Kansas, how aunt Em would tell her stories by the fireplace, and how Uncle Henry would let her sleep in their bed when she had a nightmare. She smiles, dreaming that she wakes up in a lush green field, running through the farm as she sees her mom and dad on the porch. They look so happy, smiling as they hold hands, daddy shouting, *'C'mon kiddo, food will go cold.'*

She looks at him with glee in her beautiful blue eyes, younger now, ten years old as she raises her arms and pretends she's an aeroplane. Zooming along the farm she runs to the porch, smiling just like she remembers, jumping over the puddles and charging toward her parents as her arms wrap around them. Dad winces like always, holding her close as he says, *'We got a little titan here, c'mon kiddo lets have food, then we gotta go home.'*

Dorothy holds them tighter, clenching her teeth as she begs, *'Don't want to go home, not in the car,'* and hears her mother's voice, feeling the touch of her hand against a cheek as she says, *'Oh sweetie, don't be scared, we'll be home in no time.'* The little girl closes her eyes and feels a tear drip down her cheek as she squeezes her daddy tighter, opening them to look up to a strange face as her world changes.

Through the darkness a red light flashes, sirens echo in the distance and she sobs to the stranger, her body bruised as she whimpers, *'Where's daddy, m...mommy?'* He looks down at her, his grim face dripping with rain as a cold voice matures the little girl, *'I'm sorry kid, they're...'*

Forcing herself from the dream Dorothy gasps for air, sobbing as tears stain her pink cheeks and Scarecrow asks, *'Are you alright?'* She shakes her head, trying to stop the pain, sobbing, *'No...bad dream,'* as she wraps her arms around him and Toto. Thankful for the comfort she's glad she's not in her bed at the orphanage anymore, or the fake parents', that's where the dream always hurt more, almost every night.

Soon Dorothy stands up front with the tin-man again, watching as the white mist starts to darken. They drift for a while longer, the lion still sleeping and Scarecrow looking down at the tortured souls overboard as Dorothy stares in the distance, waiting anxiously until they finally see land. Smiling she shouts, *'Look!'* as the tin-man groans, *'I know,'* and Scarecrow claps his hands, *'More sights.'* Getting closer they look to the shore, seeing the aureolin yellow landscape shimmer, glow in the darkness as the tin-man looks to the black mist in-front and roars, *'Hold on!'* Dorothy asks, *'What is it?'* and Scarecrow wakes the lion quickly. Looking to the dead river the tin-man points to several white lumps floating just ahead of them, unable to see what the shapes are until they get close enough. Squinting her eyes Dorothy looks at the heads of what seem like crocodiles, mouthing, *'Oh God,'* as they get closer, several of them circling the boat. The lion quickly grabs at the curious scarecrow, keeping him in the centre of the vessel as they watch the scaled white heads float atop the mist, their tentacles reaching into the air. Staring at the creatures Dorothy cringes, *'That's not good!'* as without warning their limbs grab at the boat and the young girl screams to the lion, *'Roar!'*

He looks back at her confused, too scared to move, and she knows he won't scare them away. Quickly Dorothy grabs at Scarecrow's pitchfork, jabbing the lion in his side as he lets off a tremendous sound and the creatures quickly move from the boat, their tentacles reseeding rapidly. Watching the three of them float away Dorothy drops the pitchfork and touches the lion, looking at the small wounds as little drips of blood pour from his side.

Placing her hands on his snout she feels herself on the verge of tears, rubbing at his soft fur as she begs, *'Please forgive me, I'm so sorry, I didn't know what else to do.'* Pulling his head away from her hands he nurses his wounds, licking at the small cuts as he moans, *'I understand why you did it!'* giving her a cold shoulder and refusing to forgive the attack.

As the boat finally reaches shore Scarecrow jumps to the yellow stones first, looking at them as he points a finger in the air, *'Different shades, how elaborate!'* Next Dorothy steps onto the land, watching the lion leave the boat with a huff as he sees her smiling but turns his head away. Jumping down to yellow stones the tin-man looks back at the dark mist, and the group watch the boat pull itself back out to the dead river, drifting into the distance. Walking along the yellow shore Dorothy glances at the sad lion and looks out to the dim path ahead of them, trying to make out the hills in the distance as they stand upon barren land once more.

They trek for a mile or so and Dorothy starts to feel her limbs tire, struggling to see the compass, and barely able to make out what's in front of her. Getting closer to mountains and odd rock formations the tin-man walks ahead, searching for shelter as he finds a small cave and groans:

'Rest there tonight, it's too dangerous to go any further in the dark, we're getting too close to the winkies territory. The worst is yet to come.'

Finally settling into the cave Dorothy feels a chill up her body, despite the fur keeping her torso warm. Laying on his side the lion watches her shiver, huddling closer as his mane tickles her face and she looks at him sorrowfully. *'I'm sorry,'* she whispers, and as a faint silence lingers he huffs, *'I know, they used to do that to me in the carnival.'* She looks into his eyes, sadly as she mouths, *'I'll never do it again,'* and the lion lifts his limbs over her, pulling her close to him as he smiles with a sigh. Holding Dorothy he thinks of his old friend, remembers how they used to lay together like this through cold nights at the carnival. Sad that he's gone the lion feels tears drip through his fur, knowing he'll only ever see him again in his dreams as he sobs himself to sleep, so happy to have Dorothy beside him.

As Dorothy and the lion sleep, Scarecrow and the tin-man find themselves watching the same scene as they have for days. Playing with his tangine necklace at first Scarecrow looks to the solid tin-man, querying, *'Do you ever feel like you're just standing around?'* The tin-man turns his head, looking to the scarecrow as he answers, *'I don't feel much,'* and the silly straw man looks at him in surprise, tapping him on the shoulder with, *'I forgot that.'* Then smiling he glows, *'I'm going outside, look for pretty things,'* as he leaves the cave.

With a big stretch he feels his bones click and notices chunks of hay sticking out from his skin as he moans, *'Oh dear, that's not good.'* Poking them back inside he walks along the barren land, whistling to himself as he swings his pitchfork. *'Where are you?'* he frowns, *'No pretty things, nothing shiny. I don't think I like the west,'* he huffs, as he stands atop a small mound of rocks.

Looking into the distance, he watches tiny lemon yellow eyes in the sky, dozens of them as he smiles at first, asking, *'What are you little things?'* Waving a hand to them his expression soon changes as he hears their flutter, watching dark wings flap in the sky as the crows squawk. Terrified he screams, *'Not my buttons!'* as they swoop down at him, pulling at his straw and pecking at his skin. With his shrill echoing through the night he swings his arms at the birds, cutting at them with his barbwire stitching. With a look of fear sewn along his burlap face he stabs at the crows with his pitchfork, killing them as they squawk in agony, and he screams, *'Not my buttons, can't have them, mine, Mine!'*

Waking to the scarecrow's voice Dorothy looks up at the tin-man, standing at the opening of the cave as she asks, *'Can you hear that?'* He nods, ready to investigate as the young girl walks towards him, insisting,

'Stay here, I'll shout if I need you.' Leaving the cave she walks quickly through the barren land, following the scarecrow's voice, but it soon stops. Hearing nothing but the breeze, no squawking and no screams she edges her way through the darkness, calling out, 'Scarecrow!' She clenches a fist; walking further from the cave with a lump in her throat, as she calls again to hear a giggle in the distance. Silently she follows the eerie sound and her eyes open wider, her heart pounding as she looks to see Scarecrow cowering on the floor. Walking toward him, his evil giggle echoing through the dark she places a hand on his shoulder, looking at the dead crows spread along the floor as he turns to face her. With a fearing look in her eyes his curious smile stares back at Dorothy, watching her walk backwards as he crouches on the floor. Leaning over several dead birds he pulls his fingers from ones stomach, leaving the others open wide as their insides lay on the ground. Looking as the young girl backs away he stands, holding his pitchfork as he walks towards her saying:

'What's wrong Dorothy? They tried to take my buttons, pull me apart. I just wanted to see what their insides looked like!'

Cautious, holding her breath at first she grabs at his arm and leads him back to the cave as he pleads, 'I don't understand, what's wrong?' Thoughts buzz around Dorothy's head, unsure how to act as she hesitantly mutters, 'Nothing, nothing's wrong!'

When they reach the cave Dorothy whispers to the tin-man, 'Keep an eye on him, don't let him wander off,' as she distances herself from the scarecrow. Resting next to the lion and still cautious of the straw man she lays awake, looking at him as he sits quietly, glaring into the tangine necklace happily, as she eventually falls asleep.

As morning creeps along the sky Dorothy feels a hand stroke her head, slowly she opens her eyes to see the scarecrow smiling, holding fruit in his palms as he greets, 'You look pretty this morning, want some food?' Taking the apples she smiles back at him, confused as he says, 'You should come outside, it's nice and bright, so much to see.' Dorothy watches him run out of the cave as she rubs her eyes, holding the fruit in her hands and wondering if what happened last night was a dream.

Journeying through the barren land once more Dorothy feels the chrome yellow sun warming her hair, and the lion walks slowly, panting as the hours pass. They'd stopped for lunch briefly, resting a short time before they continued their journey, not wanting to be this deep in winkie territory when night comes. With nothing but odd rocks and occasional mountains, the young girl feels relieved not to see bodies imbedded into the landscape, but as they reach the edge of a hill a peculiar sound comes from the distance.

Slowly walking toward it Dorothy presses a finger to her lip and shows the scarecrow, whispering, 'Shhh!' as the young girl reminds him again what it means. Getting closer to a mound of rocks the group hide behind them, hearing a grim hiss through the land ahead as they look down the hill to see a number of winkies scouring the area. Watching the creatures turn over rocks and creep through the dunes they listen for the slightest of sounds as Dorothy stares at their decaying bodies; with rotten thin teeth and cracked white skin. They walk with their eyes sewn shut, rifling long gruesome hands through the rocks as their sharp bone fingernails cut into the stone.

Suddenly they all stand still. With small holes where their ears and nose should be, Dorothy wonders if they can smell her and her friends, or hear them breathing. Silently they watch, listen to the winkies communicate as without warning one dives into a cave, pulling out a lone wolf. Stabbing sharp thin nails into its side the animal howls, thrown to the ground as it looks at the winkies.

Surrounded by them the wolf bares its teeth as a warning, but several of the winkies leap for the creature, not even giving it a chance to run as they pull it open with their nails and teeth. Turning her head Dorothy hears the animal cry, unable to watch as the tin-man taps at her shoulder.

'We have to get past them don't we?' he asks, and Dorothy looks at the compass, nodding her head with, 'How?' as he points down the hill to a cave. Looking closely at the small opening, Dorothy spots a beehive and the tin-man pulls a piece of fruit from her basket. Grating at their ears as quietly as he can the tin-man says, 'We have to move when they're distracted,' and Dorothy and Scarecrow nod their heads as the lion looks at him worriedly.

Moving as quietly as he can the tin-man watches the winkies devour the wolf, raising his metal arm and looking down at the cave as he throws the fruit at the beehive, cracking a hole in their lair. Standing from their meal the deadly winkies listen to the sound of the broken beehive, hearing the bees come toward them as blood drips from their teeth. Quickly the swarm attack and the winkies slash at the tiny bees, trying to crush their bodies as tin-man leads the group down the hill. Moving slowly, cautious of the winkies strong hearing they climb carefully, reaching the bottom with the deadly creatures no more than a metre away. As the bees sting at the hunters skin Dorothy and her friends move carefully, trying not to make a sound and stand on the loose debris, but unexpectedly the lion roars in pain. Looking at the cowardly animal the young girl sees a horde of bees surrounding him, getting the winkies attention as the tin-man shouts, *'Run!'* Turning their heads to a different prey, smelling the new flesh and hearing their steps, the winkies let the bees' sting, ignoring the pain as they charge at the fresh meat.

Running up the other side of the hill the tin-man knows he's too slow, and watches scarecrow run in front of him as they reach the top. Looking back at the deadly creatures the lion speeds, as his legs pound at the ground and he runs ahead of his friends to see a chasm in front of them.
Running too fast to slow down, unable to stop he leaps in the air as he jumps over the gap, several feet long as he looks down to see the white mist miles below them. Landing at the other side his body crashes to the ground and he bares his teeth, watching his friends run toward him as the tin-man straggles at the back.
Readying his sharp claws the lion hesitates but runs back, jumping over the chasm as he barely makes the gap. His body lands on the edge and he claws at the stone, pulling his heavy weight up as he runs past Dorothy and the scarecrow. Charging back at the tin-man he roars, *'Grab on!'* as he feels a winkie's nail cut at his fur, centimetres from the flesh as he runs forward again. Looking behind him as the creatures get closer, Scarecrow doesn't say a word, and instead he turns to see the chasm and jumps as high as he can, dropping his pitchfork into the void. Clearing the gap he looks back to Dorothy, the horror on her face as she runs close to the edge and the lion speeds past her, unable to stop as he carries the tin-man through the air. Landing at the other side the animal smashes at a pile of rocks, cutting his skin on impact as the tin-man dents his frame.

Dorothy looks to her friends, throwing her wicker basket to the other side then turning her head quickly to see the hideous winkies getting closer. Gnarling their teeth the young girl holds her breath, pressing her boots against the edge of the ground and she jumps in the air. Flailing her limbs, looking at Scarecrow on the other side her eyes suddenly widen as she feels a thick cut along her back. Her body jolting at the pain she reaches out a hand to the scarecrow and he tries to reach for it, unable to catch her in time as Dorothy's body falls, missing the ledge as she descends to nothingness.

26

Looking down into the deep white mist Scarecrow shouts, *'Dorothy?'* wondering where she's gone as the tin-man pulls him from the ledge, swinging his axe at the winkies who try to jump the chasm.
'She's gone!' he growls, cutting a winkie in half to see more of them scurrying through the air. The metal giant tries his best to kill the creatures, slicing at odd limbs but they're too quick, reaching the other side and dodging the tin-man's blade. Turning his back ready to run he knows he can't fight them, feeling one jump on top of him and another latch on quickly as the lion looks back with a roar. Trying to throw them to the ground tin-man feels their sharp nails cut deeply into his side, piercing the metal as they scrape against his ribs. Weakening quickly, in one last effort of defence he grabs at one of the winkies, clenching onto its neck as he throws it into the chasm, but the other won't let go.

Thrusting its thin nails into the tin-man, the winkie squeezes at his insides whilst Scarecrow stands watching, confused at what to do as the cowardly lion runs to his aid hesitantly. Leaping at the winkie the lion sinks his claws into its chest, pulling the creature to the floor as he pins it down. Lashing his nails in the air the monster tries to cut at the lion's skin, not giving him a chance to attack, as suddenly its head rolls to the floor and the thick sound of metal smashes into the ground. Looking at the axe imbedded into the stone, the lion's eyes pan along the handle. Watching the tin-man crouch on the floor, blood seeps through his metal armour, with his visible pieces of flesh torn apart.

Spitting out chunks of blood and oil the tin-man collapses to the floor as Scarecrow runs to his side, scratching at his burlap head as he says, *'Didn't know what to do,'* but the tin-man doesn't hear him. At first the only thing pulsing through his head is the turning of cogs and the clicking of pins as his fake heart releases blood.
Leaning over the wounded tin-man the lion looks at the holes in his sides, shivering, *'You really have bad luck don't you?'* as he grabs at Dorothy's wicker basket and pulls out a towel. Trying to put pressure on the wounds he hears Scarecrow walking to the edge of the chasm, muttering, *'Dorothy!'* Looking down at the nothingness below he waves a solemn hand, moving to the others as he frantically shouts, *'Dorothy, we have to save Dorothy!'* Barely conscious and biting back at him blood pours from

the tin-man's body as he groans in agony, *'Gone, she's gone, if you want to find her jump down yourself.'*

Nodding his head the sad scarecrow walks to the chasm, looking down again as he lifts a foot in the air to feel his weight falling forward. Unexpectedly the lion grabs at his body, throwing him back to the tin-man's side as he growls with his skin still trembling from the attack, *'What are you doing? We...we can't go down there.'* Then the tin-man's voice grates at them, his sharp teeth slick with blood as he slowly tries to stand, feeling his metal legs give way:

'The best we can do is find the witch; she may be able to bring Dorothy back.'

Confused, the scarecrow scratches his head, asking, *'But aren't we supposed to kill the witch?'* and the tin-man leans against his axe, *'We will, once she does what we want!'* Trying to stand, the tin-man supports himself with his weapon, hobbling ahead of the others as blood squeezes from his body with every step. Joining him the scarecrow's thin legs move quickly as he watches the feeble tin-man, remarking, *'Good thing you're sturdy,'* as the lion follows, groaning to the metal gladiator, *'Get on, you're not walking!'*

Then the three of them start on their journey again, as the lion carries the tin-man on his back, and Scarecrow holds the young girl's wicker basket, walking behind them as he keeps repeating, *'Can't forget Dorothy, think, can't forget Dorothy!'*

Deep inside the mist Dorothy falls, unable to see above or below her as she screams. Flailing her arms, trying to grab onto something she feels the pain of descent, gravity pushing against her body as her shoulders arch to feel the deep wound spread along her back. Sure she'll die and just waiting for the inevitable she closes her eyes, thinking of home as she feels a sudden pinch at her skin.

With a faint whimper her stomach turns and her body jolts, no longer descending as she opens her eyes to see a winged monkey carrying her. Confused, wondering if she had died she looks to its pristine black fur and thick bat wings as a strong face stares down, holding her with his feet as he comforts, *'Don't worry girl, you're safe.'*

Lifting her in the air, pushing through the thick mist the monkey soars into the sky, above the chasm and high above land as Dorothy looks down to see her friends. Trying to call to them her voice's muted and her breath thin as she gets higher in the sky, closer to the sun as the monkey hovers in the air.

Feeling the heat beat onto her skin she looks out at the west, unable to blink as the monkey glides through the barren land. Dorothy watches the miles of yellow beneath her as she spots dozens and dozens of winkies below, hungrily patrolling.

They fly for only minutes, but at such speed, they cover more land than the young girl believes possible. Then suddenly, amidst the barren yellow land is the largest canyon she'd ever seen, and inside a beautiful golden palace. Watching in awe, they descend towards it, Dorothy closing her eyes in fear as she gets closer, feeling her stomach turn, as quickly the monkey uses all of his strength to slow his speed. Opening her eyes, no longer feeling her body push through the air she looks down at a grand balcony just below her feet, as the monkey lets her go. Landing with a thud she looks up to the winged creature, watching him fly away into the sun as he waves briefly.

Suddenly Dorothy feels a chill along her skin, the dripping gorge in her back the least of her worries as her scared mind numbs the pain. She'd spent so long trekking through the horrors of the west that she didn't want to think of the witch that would be at the end of the journey. Now Dorothy stands in her palace, the one responsible for the millions of tortured souls spread along west, and she has to cut out her heart. With no other choice she thinks of the evil witch, and what the wizard will do if he doesn't have Outika's heart. There's no other way for Dorothy to get home and she's scared, wondering how an ordinary young girl can kill a witch so powerful.

With a lump in her throat she walks toward the open door, stepping inside the grand room as lavish yellow spreads along the walls; a crystal chandelier hangs from the ceiling, and the soft sound of a violin echoes through the palace. Dorothy's come this far and she knows she can't turn back, there's nothing but miles of hell behind her, and an evil wizard who wants the witch dead.

Taking a deep breath she walks through the room, listening to the beautiful music as she spots a desk and runs toward it, ignoring the crisp letters and other oddities as she reaches for a paper knife. Quickly clenching it in her hand she walks slowly through the palace, leaving the room as she looks out to a beautiful landing. Sulphur crystals imbed themselves in the walls and she stares up to see a glass dome in the centre of the ceiling. Following the soft music Dorothy slides her body along the walls, listening for footsteps as she edges her way into an open room. Carefully treading along the floor she silently peeks around the corner, looking into the grand amber yellow ballroom to see a woman sitting alone in the distance. With her back to the young girl she plays softly with a sorrowful glare in her eyes, letting the notes dance around the room like ghosts, tenderly caressing each other with the softest of touches as her gentle voice pirouettes to the young girl's ears. *'Please, come in,'* she says, and Dorothy feels her hairs stand on end, her clumsy grip on the sharp letter opener tighten as she steps into the room. *'Such a beautiful young girl,'* the witch says lightly, continuing, *'Please, come in,'* with her back facing Dorothy as she plays a long lost ballad.

Feeling the music touch at her skin the young girl moves closer, walking through the large ballroom as she ignores the pristine paintings on the wall and the deep set yellow stones as she looks to the witch.
Almost close enough to touch her Dorothy tightens her grip on the weapon in her hand, shaking as she tries to lift her arm, though stopped as the witch's calm voice whispers, *'Please don't.'*
Then lifting the bow from her violin the witch places them on the floor, standing as Dorothy drops the letter opener, but refuses to step back. She thinks of reaching for the blade, thrusting it into the witch's heart, stabbing her before she turns, but Outika moves quickly, though as gentle as a butterfly as she faces Dorothy.

Almost shocked, expecting her to look as gruesome as the other witch the young girl stares at her soft face, looking no more than thirty years old as long black hair flows down her body, and she gleams sincerely with Aureolin eyes and ruby red lips.
Walking toward her Dorothy looks at the black satin corset studded with yellow sapphires, as layers upon layers of thick taffeta flow from under it, laced with yellow diamonds as the skirt spreads to the floor and trails behind her. Stretching out an arm, black satin gloves stretch from the tips of her fingers up to her forearms as she tries to shake the young girl's hand. Reluctantly Dorothy decides to step back, ignoring the glare from citrines around the witch's neck, clenching her teeth with, *'You're the western witch aren't you?'* She looks at the young girl with sadness in her eyes, a faint sigh as she nods her head, *'Yes, but call me Outika, oh I almost forgot.'*
Then she clicks her fingers as Dorothy feels a sharp pain in her back, touching at the gorge to feel it healing, even the mild swelling on her face gone. Shocked the young girl mumbles, *'That, that's impossible...'* and Outika smiles, *'After all you've seen you still think things are impossible.'*
Gliding gently through the ballroom the witch holds out a hand as the young girl takes it, wondering what would happen if she refused.

Escorting Dorothy through the palace, the witch looks around and smiles, almost reluctantly remarking, *'Beautiful isn't it?'* as her eyes trail away in thought. The young girl nods her head, wondering if the witch will change into a serpent, or if she's leading her to a dungeon. Her heart races, the possibilities of torture are endless and she stays hand in hand with the witch, knowing she has to bide her time, catch her unexpectedly.

Despite her scepticism Dorothy follows Outika, as she leads her to a beautiful balcony much like the one she entered, then simply flicking her wrist to pull a golden chair from under the table. Smiling gently, the witch undoes the wolf fur around Dorothy's neck with a slight gesture of her hand as she politely asks, *'If you don't mind?'* The young girl is silent, almost grateful to have the warm fur removed, watching as it lifts itself from her body and drifts to the floor.

As they both sit down Dorothy watches the witch, leaning an elbow against the railing as she stares out into the chrome yellow sun. *'I know why you're here,'* she says, and the young girl panics, clenching a fist as she replies, *'You do?'* Sighing, Outika's eyes still focus on the bright sun as she asks, *'What did the wizard ask of you?'* Dorothy hesitates; unsure if she should say, but assumes if the witch really wanted to know she'd pry her lips open. So she returns, *'To kill you,'* and Outika smiles, asking, *'Why do you think he sent you to kill me?'* Dorothy feels the pressure rising, mouthing, *'I don't know,'* threatened by the calm witch. Slowly looking away from the sun Outika's faint smile fades, and a grim cloud casts over Dorothy's illusion of Oz as her words creep along the air:

'Because he knew you would die trying! And if Bopeia wanted to help you she would have taken you to the wizard herself, not guided you through the deadly woods.'

Dorothy opens her mouth, trying to speak but nothing comes out, so the witch asks, *'What have you heard about me?'* Bewildered, the young girl looks blankly at Outika, feeling lost in the strange world. *'You're wicked,'* she insists, and the calm witch looks the scared young girl in the eyes, placing a gloved hand on her cheek as she softly mourns:

'I am not wicked child...It was because of me you had a boat to cross my land, I was protecting you in the mist and Adam saved you from your fall. I've done nothing to harm you, and I don't intend to. The wizard thought you would die in the west, assumed you'd never even reach me, but he was wrong, you're safe now.'

Dorothy grits her teeth, still strong and ready to fight the witch's words as she exclaims, *'But the things you've done!'* Leaning toward her, removing the gloved hand from her cheek Outika asks, *'What have I done? Tell me,'* and the young girl bites, *'The people...the dead ones in the west.'*

Leaning back, looking to the chrome sun again the witch presumes, *'You have much to learn about Oz. I suppose you even think I'm evil because I wear black?'* Young Dorothy mutters, *'I was told that white means good, I...'* and as the words leave her mouth she realises how gullible she may have been, so terrified in the strange world that she believed every kind voice and superstitious prattle she heard. Outika moves from the table, standing in clear sight as she lifts her arms, motioning:

'So you think black simply means evil, and good is white? What colour is Toto young child?'

Dorothy grabs at the thin bag around her shoulder, feeling the little dog inside, thinking Outika must be a powerful witch to know the things she does. Then with a simple smile the witch's black clothing changes to a bright white, as pure diamonds gleam in the sun and she looks at the young girl:

'I think I need to tell you more about this strange world.'

OUTIKA

27

Looking out at the yellow canyon and the chrome sun blistering in the sky Dorothy watches winged monkeys soar through the air as she wipes sweat from her brow. Landing on the balcony's railing they clench at it tightly with their feet, bringing bowls of fruit and plates of cake as they place them on the table. The young girl smiles politely without a word as one brings a pot of tea, and another gently pours her a cup. Listening to their odd chatter, even seeing a slight smile on their faces the young girl says, *'Thank you!'* as they bow their heads and one delicately places a napkin on her lap. The witch smiles at them and they jump to the railings, flying away as Dorothy watches, wondering how her friends are.

Still looking out to the canyon the young girl hears her gracious host voice, *'Please, you must be hungry,'* and Dorothy turns to look to the food with a smile. Still with her friends in mind, worried that they may be hunted by the winkies she's cautious of her words, requesting, *'Please...if you are not evil...can you bring my friends to the palace?'* Outika smiles lightly, offering, *'Of course, that is where my monkeys have gone,'* as the young girl feels an uneasy reassurance, her curiosity on edge.

'Thank you but...but how do you know everything you do?' she asks, and the witch smirks, almost forgetting how curious guests can be, *'I can see almost everything in Oz, I even saw you arrive in the Munchkin country.'*

'You, you saw me kill Avatonika?' Dorothy asks curiously, almost with guilt. *'No, though I wish I had,'* Outika replies, following:

'I am powerful enough to see the whole of Oz, but cannot see inside the other witches' dwellings, and I dare not try to attempt the wizard's.'

Dorothy feels a lump in her throat and reaches for the tea, sipping at it to feel the warm liquid comfort her, prepare her as she asks, *'You said I needed to know more about Oz, what did you mean?'* With a cold remembrance creeping through her bones, a deep wound reopening, the witch tastes lament and her sad eyes look at the curious girl:

'Very well, though you may not believe what you hear...I've seen almost everything you've gone through in this world and you are indeed brave, though you've been misled. The cunning Bopeia's true form is only

visible to those who know her sins, and despite what Oz portrays me to be I am the only good witch left.

Long ago, even before creatures walked this earth, it was declared that the witches of the four corners were to protect Oz. We were to rule the land and bring peace, but the north and south had black in their hearts despite their pale white cloth. They waited patiently for many years, let our civilisations grow, then they created war, the first our world had ever known. The people of my land and the country of the munchkins were not prepared, we didn't know what war was, but like a plague the people of the north and the quadlings of the south spread, slaughtering many.

It was during this war that a wretch now known as Avatonika raped the land of the munchkins and...and killed my sister, claiming herself to be my new kin. Little did I know that Bopeia and Notou had planned this all along; to bring in new blood to overthrow my sister, and soon enough the three brought their armies to the west. Still, the witches' pact with the east was never known to their people. They forced them into war and watched the ones they were supposed to protect slaughter each other, along with my people. That's when I cursed the eastern witch's skin, scarring every inch of her body for what she had done to my sister, though I was not strong enough to fight the three, and it didn't take long for them to destroy my kingdom. They erased the beauty the west once had and killed my people, they slaughtered the winkies and...and I let them. I was a coward then, and could not bear make more of their race in order to save them. I knew that anything I created would suffer at the hands of the three corners.

The witches left me with a barren land, the queen of a dead country and cast a spell on me. One that lets me leave the palace only three times each millennium, and if I leave a fourth, then my home will smoulder to ash and all of my creations will die. Though this wasn't enough for them, and they used all of their strength to bring every soul that died in the west back from the netherworld. They created a purgatory of my land, leaving me the ruler of a million tortured dead.

Then the wizard came, taking a small piece of each of the corners as he claimed the centre of Oz as his own. From then on, I knew the witches would not harm me, despite how they'd defile my land with their dead, and kill anything I created outside the palace. They feared him so much that they left me in peace, though made sure that my name was tainted, frightening the land of Oz into conforming to their order. The stories grew and soon I became the monster, my good nature was the irregular in an evil world and I took the mantle of the wretched, unable to convince Oz otherwise. So the witches kept their pact hidden; spreading word of Avatonika's wretched rule, which she accepted happily, making hers a country almost as feared as the west, whilst Bopeia and Notou persuaded Oz that they were the only good witches left.

After many years in solitude, Queen of a dead land I grew lonely and created new life, Argus who you'll see shortly, and a dozen or so more. They lived in the palace with me, like friends not servants, though one day they left, merely for a walk through my cursed land. I warned them not to leave but couldn't force them to stay, Argus never left my side but the others did and the witches knew, so Avatonika showed no mercy. She had finally twisted the munchkins in her own image and they slaughtered my few, ate them in front of my own palace and hung their skin clearly for me to see. So...I created no more.

However, as time passed I watched Oz change, and I knew I couldn't stay dormant any longer. I made the winkies, the evil ones that scour my land, as I feared making an innocent breed, couldn't bear to see them die. The winkies are not for comfort and show no love, though they are loyal to me, and most of all, they are killers, made only to protect the west from the other corners. They've existed for a long time now, and when I saw what they would do to trespassers I felt confident to bring new life to the west again. That's when I made the monkeys, Adam and the others, giving them wings so they could fly away from danger. I understand how sceptical you must be, but I have no need to lie to you.'

Dorothy looks at the witch, pulling a hand from her strained eyes as she stares out to the chrome sun again. The young girl's speechless at first, lost in all the lies she's been told and unsure if she can trust the accused wicked witch, asking, *'You said when the wizard came the witches left you in peace, why?'* Turning to Dorothy Outika smirks in distain:

'The three needed me to fill the circle, and couldn't risk having me dead. It is said that the four corners could rule the whole land of Oz together, with the infinite power to create and destroy. They thought that to defeat Oz the terrible the four must join, so they couldn't risk a dead witch...but you've taken that hope from them, and they were wrong.'

'What do you mean?' Dorothy asks as she feels the chance of going home slipping farther away.

'The wizard is a demon, but one that can be killed, just like a witch, and by the hands of any man or creature. '

'You can't kill him! I need him to send me home...' Dorothy bursts, slamming her hands on the table as she stands, finding herself shouting at the witch, *'...You said they lied, Bopeia...the wizard, can he send me home?'*

'You must understand...' Outika says sitting calmly,

'Can he send me home?' Dorothy persists, clenching a fist against the table with a scream.

Outika looks up at the girl, strong yet weakened with desperation as she lets the silence rest in the air, hoping it will calm her as she gently utters, *'He has the power to, but I doubt that he will. '*

Standing with a grim expression smothering her face Dorothy suddenly sits again, reverting to child-like tactics as she begs the witch, *'You! You're powerful! Can you send me back home?'*

'I'm sorry,' Outika replies pressing a gloved hand against the girl's, *'Only the wizard is powerful enough to send you back, but I will help you.'* Dorothy feels a pressure lift from her chest, though entwined with uncertainty as she wonders if the key around her neck has a purpose, and hesitates trusting the witch as she falsely utters, *'Thank you, thank you!'* Smiling kindly at the young girl Outika looks at the food on the table, and the tea now cold as she touches the cup lightly to make it steam once again. Extending a hand she says, *'Please indulge, then I'll show you around the palace whilst we wait for your friends,'* and Dorothy looks at the witch, waiting for a reason not to trust her.

As the witch leads Dorothy through the palace, the young girl's amazed by such elegant sites. Looking up to the sky from the fine library window, she stares through the isabelline glass to see the yellow sun start to fade with the night. Meanwhile her friends still trek through the barren land, with no compass to guide their way as they walk a straight line through the west. Still repeating the words, *'Can't forget Dorothy, think, can't forget Dorothy!'* the scarecrow ignores everything else and follows the lion, who carries an injured tin-man on his back. His wounds haven't stopped bleeding, but he assures the lion that by morning he'll be able to walk on his own again. With night creeping over them the lion starts to struggle, his energy fading with each step as the tin-man's jagged metal digs into his skin.

Walking for another mile the lion's ready to collapse, and he feels relieved as the tin-man points to a small cave, grunting, *'We'll wait in there until morning,'* but Scarecrow argues, *'Can't stop, What about Dorothy? I can't forget!'* Reassuring him the tin-man replies, *'I'll make sure you won't forget,'* and they make their way into the cave as the lion's relieved of the tin-man, and collapses to the floor. Having walked for so long in the sun and exerting all of his energy he falls asleep quickly, whilst tin-man keeps guard and the scarecrow sits patiently for morning, murmuring, *'Dorothy, can't forget,'* as he rubs at his tangine necklace.

In Outika's palace, a curious Dorothy feels the cold night seeping through the corridors with a breeze, wondering how long it will be until her friends are brought from the dead lands. Asking the witch again she's comforted with a delicate hand placed on her shoulder as Outika says: *'They will all be back soon I hope, though my monkeys cannot see too well in the dark. Still, I assure you they'll be with us by morning.'*
Leading her through a thin corridor the yellow walls seem darker, even though lit with a candle as Dorothy stands in front of a room, whilst the witch opens it gently. The heavy wood creeks open, swinging backward as the young girl looks to her host, receiving a slight nod of the head. *'Please, you will need somewhere to rest until morning,'* Outika says, and Dorothy looks around the room, dazzled by the golden four-poster bed shimmering in the candle light. She eyes the wardrobes, the yellow marble dressing table and the grand window, smiling slightly as she turns to the witch.

Jumping back at first Dorothy looks at Outika, still standing in the shadowed corridor as a man waits beside her. Dressed in black and gold to match the witch, Dorothy looks at his face, nothing but a plain round piece of clay, unmarked and featureless as Outika smiles, *'Please don't be frightened, this is Argus, my treasured proteus creation.'* Cautiously looking at the lump of clay atop his human shoulders Dorothy utters, *'His face,'* and the witch presses a hand over the matter, closing her eyes as hair sprouts from its head and definition forms around its face. Watching curiously the young girl's amazed as a pair of bright lime coloured eyes, slim lips and other features form, carving themselves from the clay. As Outika removes her hand Argus smiles, and the witch looks to Dorothy, *'I must rest now, but please, if there's anything you need Argus will tend to you. Goodnight.'* Watching her turn her back and ready to walk away, the young girl quickly shouts, *'Wait...You said you would help send me home, how?'* Looking back to her Outika gently smiles, with a gleam of hope as she replies, *'I'll explain in the morning, when your friends are with us, now rest.'*

Disappearing through the corridor Dorothy watches the witch's dress trail behind, then looks to the clay man as his grey face smiles. Leering at her he opens his mouth, asking *'Is there anything I can do for you?'* as he reminds her too much of the fake fathers, the ones who'd drink too much. Shaking her head Dorothy places a hand on the heavy door as she pushes, *'Goodnight,'* closing it on Argus as she quickly draws the bolt.

Stepping away Dorothy hears his feminine voice scratch at the door, lingering, *'Goodnight Dorothy,'* as she moves around the room, feeling at the walls and looking behind the furniture. Tapping at the thick stones with her knuckles she feels for loose edges, looks for hidden doors, a passageway, but nothing.

There's no way in or out of the room besides the heavy door and she stares, watches a small gap between the wood and the floor as she sees Argus' shadow, standing still. Telling herself he's there to guard her she slowly blows out the candles in the room, making her way into bed as she leaves the one beside her lit. With her eyes lingering on the shadow she lifts the bed sheets and crawls inside, not removing a single item of clothing as her head touches the pillow.

With her eyes still open she watches the door, yawning as she refuses to sleep, but feeling herself slowly drifting. Thinking of Outika Dorothy knows she can't kill such a powerful being, and finds herself torn between who to trust; a pale witch who sent her through a deadly land, or the one known through Oz as evil. The decision riddles through her mind, and she knows right now there's no choice but to trust Outika. Despite which witch is evil the wizard is the only one in Oz who can send her home, and only the western witch can help her, either dead or alive.

Eventually falling asleep Dorothy feels a cold draft along her face as the bed sheets around her body lift from her skin. Murmuring in her slumber she dreams of the wizard, locking her in his dark castle as she sits huddled in the corner of a cell. Looking out of her prison she see his horned form walk toward her, the bloody flesh dripping from his body as a voice crawls through her skin like a burrowed insect, *'You'll never leave me.'* His thin fangs glisten with saliva as he watches her hungrily, scraping his talons along her metal cell as she fights her way from the nightmare, screaming with relief as she lays still in Outika's golden bed. With her eyes open she looks to the door, seeing nothing through the darkness as a cold sweat breaks along her skin and she closes her eyes.

Drifting again, though this time somewhere else the fields are green, and water pours from her hands as she looks out to the farmhouse, smiling to a woman in the window. Swilling the water over her face, deep inside another world Dorothy can't feel the two bare hands creep through the bed. Touching at the silver boots a clay face turns sour, and nails scratch the leather as his hands feel at her bare legs. Caressing her milky skin they slither up her body as the grey face smiles, its body arching as teeth chatter through the palace's dark corridors.

Dorothy's body jolts and she kicks her legs in panic, looking up to the open door to see Argus standing silently. Clenching her teeth and staring at the clay-man with anger she snarls, *'How did you get in here?'* and the gentle man looks at her blankly, touching the door with a finger as he says, *'The door I, I didn't mean to scare you. I heard you scream.'*
Staring at him, ready to gouge his eyes out if she has to Dorothy screams, *'I locked the door,'* and confused he softly replies, *'If you locked it then I wouldn't have been able to get in, but here I stand.'*
Leaping from the bed Dorothy forces Argus out of the room, slamming the door behind him as she draws the bolt. Grabbing at a blanket from the bed she quickly wraps it around her body and pulls Toto from his bag, leaning against the wooden door as she waits; either until morning or until someone appears in her room.

28

As the morning sun glows through isabelline glass, Dorothy feels the heat against her skin and wakes to look around the room in shock, expecting another nightmare, or worse. Pulling herself from the floor she throws the blanket back to the bed and unbolts the door, wondering if she dreamt that Argus was in her room. Taking a breath and holding it she swings the door open expecting the clay-man to be waiting for her, but looks down the empty hallway. With the curtains still drawn she walks through the dark corridor, pulling them open to light the way as she stops, unable to hear a single sound.

Making her way through the palace there's no sign of life, not even the distant chatter of monkeys, or music as she walks down a flight of stairs. Unsure where she is Dorothy thought she knew her way back to the main hall at first, but as she proceeds along another corridor, nothing looks familiar. She thinks of calling for help but changes her mind at the possibility that Argus will find her alone. Whether what happened last night was a dream or not she doesn't trust him, and oddly enough fears him more than the witch.

Walking down another narrow corridor Dorothy opens more curtains along the way, letting light fill the palace as she turns a corner. Moving, her legs feel stronger, her body healing from being crouched by the door all night, and she starts to walk quicker, turning another bend to realise she's truly lost. Looking down the corridor, she stares at a dead-end with nothing ahead of her but a small door, so she walks toward it. Stretching out a hand, she presses it against the door, pushing lightly to hear the wood faintly crack as it opens. Looking to a small spiral stairwell Dorothy places a hand against the cold wet wall to guide herself, making her way down the stairs as she reaches the bottom to hear a lingering moan. Standing still and listening to the muffled sounds, she waits at the bottom of the stairs, wondering if the witch's words were lies as a man jumps at her.

Ready to slam a fist into the figure she looks up to its face in shock, as the scarecrow wraps his arms around her and she looks over his shoulder to see lion and the tin-man. *'We found you, we found you!'* the gangly straw man repeats, and Dorothy smiles as she feels his skewed bones press against her. Looking at Scarecrows button eyes she feels comforted, then noticing the tin-man's wounds she runs to his side, worriedly screeching, *'What happened to you?'* as he grunts *'The winkies!'* With a pained face she places a hand to her mouth, gasping as he groans, *'I'm healing, just a little weak.'* Running a soft hand along his cold metal face she hears the lion grumble, *'The monkeys brought us here, one said he knew where you were.'* Walking to her side and nuzzling his head against her stomach he groans in contentment, sighing in relief, *'Glad we're all back together,'* then looking up to her with his one good eye as he whimpers, *'Don't like flying though.'* Hugging his neck she kisses at his snout, smiling at how attention seeking he is as the tin-man says, *'Took a lot of them to bring us here,'* and the lion interrupts, *'They almost dropped Scarecrow, he wouldn't stop screaming.'* Turning her head to him she looks at the smiling scarecrow as he waves, and she reaches for him, holding his hand and pulling him into the group as she asks, *'Are you okay?'* He nods his head lightly, poking himself in the chest as he mumbles, *'Don't like wings.'* Thinking how traumatic it must have been for him Dorothy hopes he forgets soon, looking at his innocent face as the tin-man roars, *'Where's the witch?'* trying to stand tall even though he's still wounded.

After telling her friends the same story that the imprisoned witch bared to her, the lion looks to Dorothy as he asks, *'Who are we supposed to believe?'* and she shakes her head with no definite answer: *'I don't know, but Outika said she'll help me get home, and I'm sure she can help you too.'*

Holding his axe firmly the tin-man ignores the open wounds, tightening his grip as he roars; *'No, the wizard's powerful enough to help us. We have to kill the witch!'*

Dorothy rebukes, subconsciously taking the witch's side as she battles:

'What if he chooses not to? You saw what his city was like, and his people nearly killed you. If he were a good wizard he wouldn't let his city become the way it has. And he wouldn't scar children, have slaves or frighten us into killing for him. We can't trust him!'

As a silence drifts through the air the lion says, *'But we can't trust the witch either,'* and Dorothy sighs, *'I know...'* her energy in defending Outika depleted, unsure of who to trust. Wiping a hand along her face, feeling this decision could tear the group apart she hears the tin-man's metal voice and stares at his fierce mouth, chiselling, *'We can't afford to make the wrong choice, but whatever you decide, I'll follow you.'* With a faint sense of hope Dorothy smiles at him then looks to the scarecrow, who bursts, *'Me too, I'll stay with you,'* even though he doesn't fully understand what's happening. With a huff the lion looks up at Dorothy, listening to her as she asks, *'Who do you think we should trust?'* Hesitating, shuffling his paws on the ground he points his nose at her with, *'You?'* as the possibilities run through her head. Looking at him, the fear pooling on his face she says, *'I...'* then closing her eyes tightly, decides, *'Outika, I...I trust her.'* With a lump in his throat the lion's too afraid to make a choice of his own, unsure what the consequences could be as he sighs, *'Okay, the witch it is.'* Trying to give a relieved smile Dorothy can't help but feel responsible for whatever comes next, already blaming herself for not telling Scarecrow and tin-man she only wanted their company because she thought the witch would attack her. Now things have changed, and it's her decision that binds them to the Outika.

Suddenly a winged monkey flies to an open window, perching on the frame as Scarecrow looks to him and hides behind Dorothy, ducking down as he repeats, *'Wings, monkey, don't like em', don't like em.'* Folding the wings behind his back the monkey places his hands together graciously, bowing his head as he greets:

'Dorothy and the scarecrow, the Queen requests your company, if you would kindly follow me. As for the lion and the tin-man, she knows of your wounds and asks that you stay here. Someone will be sent to tend to you as soon as possible.'

Looking to the tin-man first, almost as if for approval Dorothy watches him nod his head and then answers the monkey, *'Of course.'* Politely smiling at them like a gentleman would, his face wrinkles and he stretches his hand to the door, clearly asking, *'If you please?'* Dorothy looks at him and crouches down to the lion, stroking at his mane and whispering in his ear, *'Don't be scared, I'll be back I promise,'* as she kisses his cheek and stands. Taking scarecrow's hand she leads him to the door as he walks behind her, keeping his distance from the monkey as Dorothy looks to the tin-man with a solid nod, and notices the lion's worried frown.

Following the monkey through Outika's palace Dorothy pays little attention to its yellow beauty as she hears Scarecrow coo, *'That's pretty, what's that? Ooh shiny, I like those.'* Pointing at the diamonds and touching the beautiful tapestries he simply smiles and doesn't even notice the worry on Dorothy's face. Scared of what she'll have to do to get home the young girl watches the monkey swing a large door open as she feels fear pouring from her skin, hoping she doesn't lead her friends down a hopeless path. Escorting them into a large seating room they follow patiently and scarecrow smiles wildly at the glisten of a yellow diamond chandelier, and twitches his fingers at the sight of golden seats. Gesturing to them the monkey offers, *'Please sit, can I get you anything?'* as Dorothy smiles, *'No thank you,'* and the scarecrow simply shakes his head, saying, *'No monkey.'* Watching him leave the room Dorothy quickly asks, *'Where's Argus?'* still curious about last night as the winged animal replies, *'He's resting; he stayed awake outside your room for most of the night in case you needed anything.'*

As he exits Dorothy takes a seat and looks to the scarecrow, who stands, watching in awe as the sun shines through a window, dancing along a mural of crystals as every shade of yellow dazzles his buttons. Letting them sparkle in his eyes Dorothy hears footsteps and watches the beautiful Outika walk into the room, as Scarecrow turns his head, exclaiming, *'Oh my!'* Walking toward her guests she smiles at Dorothy and extends an arm to Scarecrow as he holds out his hands, looking at the witch's face as he gleams, *'Never seen a witch before, so pretty.'* Politely smiling at him she says, *'It's good to see you in person, so nice to have guests,'* and he nods his head, *'Nice to see you too, so nice.'* Admiring her corset studded with yellow sapphires, and her skirt laced with yellow diamonds his eyes drift to the citrines around her neck and she looks to Dorothy as they both smile at the scarecrow's curiosity.

Gently pulling her arm back the witch takes a seat across from Dorothy as the scarecrow lingers above her, standing beside her golden chair as he admires her beauty and the glow of her jewellery. Looking at Dorothy the concerned witch comforts, *'I know you're scared, but you don't need to be.'* Curious, the relief meshed with worry she frowns, *'Really?'* as Outika smiles slightly, pressing a gloved hand against the young girl's skin as she gently replies, *'I promise.'* Her throat dry Dorothy asks, *'what...'* then she gazes at the curious scarecrow watching over Outika, *'What do we have to do?'* Looking into her beautiful blue eyes and holding her hand tightly the witch smiles at the young girl's supple life, mouthing, *'That's easy, you just have to convince the wizard I'm dead.'* With her eyes almost chrysalised, seeming more naive than ever Dorothy asks, *'How? He said he wants you're heart as proof,'* and smirking at her Outika replies:

'My dear I can create life, and can make a heart that will convince the wizard it has been pulled from my own chest. I could even give your friends all the hearts, the courage and brains they need, but that would only arouse the wizard's suspicions, and he may not send you home.'

'*But...but what if he refuses to help us?*' Dorothy asks, and the witch softly answers, '*I have planted many seeds deep in this land, if he refuses you then I shall use all of my power to persuade him.*'

'*But how?*' the young girl pleads curiously, determined for answers as the witch feels a lump in her throat. Her eyes dry she tastes the hatred welling inside of her, the suffering brought to her country:

'*Do you know what makes a queen out of a prisoner? Freedom, as despite the life I can create, all the power in Oz is nothing if you are a prisoner. I have been in solitude for so long, and finally, seeing you has made me realise that I can't stay trapped in this palace any longer. I can't let the wizard and the witches destroy this land...and as soon as you're sent home safe I shall restore peace to Oz.*'

The witch feels her blood warm, the strength she once had surface again as she looks to Scarecrow, placing a hand upon his as she stares at Dorothy, her face as solid as stone, '*And I will make sure that your friends are safe when you're gone, I promise.*' Smiling sincerely, happy at the kindness she's found Dorothy whispers, '*Thank you,*' as she feels herself closer to the end, almost home.

After feeding both the lion and Dorothy, mending the tin-man's wounds and letting the scarecrow wander through her beautiful palace Outika readies her flying monkeys to take them back to the Emerald city. Standing in the Grand main hall Dorothy holds the scarecrow's hand as she looks to the monkeys, chattering amongst themselves as she notices that none of them speak. Curiously she asks the troop, '*Excuse me, can you talk?*', and one in particular steps forward, the monkey who'd saved her from the mist and led them through the palace. Standing straight and smiling at Dorothy, she looks at his strong face and pristine fur to hear him answer, '*Only me I'm afraid, I'm the leader.*' The young girl says, '*What a shame, well I...I just wanted to thank you, for everything you've done.*' Bowing to her Adam replies, '*My pleasure,*' with a slight smile as the scarecrow looks at him sceptically, whispering to himself, '*Don't like wings, don't like em.*' Standing ready the tin-man looks to the large door in front of them, and then through the palace, groaning, '*Where's the lion?*' as Dorothy says, '*I don't know,*' wondering if the poor animal is lost in the palace. Looking up at the tin-man she pushes, '*We'd better go and find him,*' as Outika appears at the top of the stairs. Staring up at the witch Dorothy asks, '*Have you seen the lion?*' and she steps aside to unveil the cowardly beast behind her, answering, *'He was lost,'* as they walk down the stairs. Touching at the lion's fur Outika smiles, and the animal whimpers, pulling back with fear in his eye as Dorothy asks, *'What's wrong?'* Silent he moves quickly down the stairs, toward the young girl as he shudders, *'D...don't, I... Don't want to fly, don't want to go to Emerald city, carnival might still be there!'*

Crouching down to him the young girl opens her arms as the beast nuzzles his head against her, his sad face brushing against the key around her neck as his scarred eye weeps. He trembles in her arms, *'I'm scared'*, feeling her warmth comfort him as she strokes his head, repeating, *'It's okay, it's okay.'* Calming the lion as much as she can Dorothy watches the monkeys open the large front door as Outika smiles at the light spreading over her body. The tin-man looks at the witch silently, staring at her face before leaving the palace, still wondering if killing her is an option. Walking outside the scarecrow follows him, ushering the lion along as he repeats, *'I don't like flying either, don't like the wings, but we have to, otherwise I won't get a brain and you won't get....um.'*

Watching her friends walk with the chrome sun upon their bodies Dorothy stands in the doorway of the palace, looking at Outika as she says, *'I can't thank you enough.'* Smiling at her the beautiful witch replies, *'You don't need to, just take my hand,'* as she offers a gloved arm, and Dorothy feels the satin against her skin, their fingers entwining as the witch asks, *'Please, escort me outside.'* The young girl panics, *'What if......'*, but Outika insists, *'Please,'* as sorrow bleeds in her eyes and her ruby lips quiver:

'It's going to be a beautiful day, I don't want to spend it as a prisoner.'

Holding her tightly Dorothy smiles at Outika, moving toward the chrome yellow sun's fresh rays as she walks her out of the palace and a beautiful smile of happiness spreads along her face. Lifting her empty hand the witch looks into the young girl's eyes, as suddenly a leather pouch appears in her palm and she hands it to Dorothy with the words, *'Give this to the wizard, it's my heart.'* Taking it from her Dorothy says, *'Thank you, if this works I can go home. I'm free,'* and Outika smiles happily. Leaning toward the young girl she sees how simple her soul is and kisses her gently on the lips, whispering, *'You have freed me too Dorothy,'* as the winged monkeys lift her from the ground and she journeys to the Emerald city.

29

Flying through the air Dorothy clenches tightly to the leather pouch with one hand, and holds Toto's bag with the other. Looking down to the Emerald city she feels relieved as the monkeys slow themselves, descending to the ground as she hears Scarecrow struggle. Close enough to the floor she feels the tight grip on her shoulders loosen as she lands gently and watches the lion's body shudder as he hits the ground. Standing on all fours, relieved to be out of the sky he groans lightly and watches the others land as Scarecrow runs to Dorothy's side, as grateful to be out of the sky as the lion. Looking up at the monkeys Dorothy shouts, *'Thank you,'* and the leader nods his head as he watches them enter the city.

Walking through the first gate they find themselves in the small room again, scanning their eyes in the phoropter as Dorothy tells the guard she has cut out the western witch's heart. Surprised at such news he fumbles for his keys in excitement, unlatching all of the locks as the strange friends walk onto the city's green cobbled streets. Looking around the sights as if he'd never been here before the scarecrow smiles, *'How odd they're wearing masks,'* as he points a finger, and Dorothy takes his hand. Refusing to spend any more time in the wretched city she forces her way through the centre, remembering her way to the graveyard hill as her friends march beside her. Cautiously lingering by the tin-man's side for protection, the lion looks at the people and the dingy streets, worried that he'll be attacked again. Feeling his fur on end he keeps quiet, glancing at the tin-man's expressionless face occasionally, comforted by the metal monster's strength as he wonders if the carnival's left the city.

Soon they find themselves at the bottom of the graveyard hill, climbing their way to the top as Dorothy feels her hope swell, determined to get back home. They trek the mound and the lion tries to be confident, thinking that he'll have his courage soon and be a king of the beasts, but the thought of what will come still sends shivers up his back.

Standing in front of the large castle Dorothy lifts her arm in the air, shouting to the guards, *'I have the witch's heart, let me see the wizard!'* as they push the doors open and stand aside, one voicing, *'He's expecting you!'* Suddenly the young girl feels fear crawl under her skin again, wondering how the Wizard could expect them. Still, she walks through the dark castle strong; almost convincing herself the witch is dead as she clenches the leather pouch in her hand.

Eventually finding themselves at the courtroom leading to the wizard's quarters Dorothy and the tin-man ignore the finely dressed puppets, though the lion's scared and the scarecrow points with a smile, forgetting he'd been here before. Looking to the small door in front of them Dorothy stops, her adrenaline burning as she suddenly wonders what form the wizard will take. She'd tried not to think about his voice biting at her like snakes, his dripping flesh, and what he could do to them if he finds out their lying. The thoughts burn, her fingers twitch and she storms towards the door before she loses her nerve, trying not to think of how much the wizard scared her before.

As they get closer the entrance opens for them, though no macabre voice greets as they make their way through the small door. Instead there's silence as they walk into the grand room, and they look beyond the machinery and pieces of wood, staring at a horned figure who sits in his throne, hidden behind a thin dull panel.

Standing in front of her friends Dorothy can only imagine what horrors such an evil man could bring, and she lifts her arm in the air, trying not to tremble as she holds out the leather pouch. Suddenly a voice creeps around the group, tasting like brimstone in their mouths as it strikes upon their bodies like acid:

'I am Oz, the great and wonderful, the deceiver and the damned. I have many names and faces, what do you want from me?'

Almost proud, believing her own lie again Dorothy screams, *'The witch is dead!'* as her voice echoes through the room, but the wizard doesn't answer. Instead a thick wheeze comes from behind the panel, and the strong horned shadow moves in his throne, letting his voice dissect their skin as he calmly scorns, *'I know...now leave me!'*

Even though she'd expected such a response Dorothy's aware of how small she is in the large room, just a young girl at the foot of a powerful wizard, whimpering, *'But...'* Feeling the boom of his voice cut away pounds of her flesh she stands still, trembling as the monster's roar drowns the room:

'Leave me or I will strip your bodies and make you my slaves, burn out your eyes and cut out your tongues!'

Petrified, feeling her friends behind her but too scared to move Dorothy could cry, crawl along broken glass to get home, but instead clenches her teeth, neither screaming nor cowering as she forces the single word out of her lips, *'No!'*

The wizard's voice grinds through her insides, squeezing tightly and pulling them apart as he returns:

'You dare challenge me! I will deny your requests and will torture your soft lives. Leave!'

Again the determined girl forces a strong, *'No!'* from her lips, refusing to be denied as the tin-man moves from behind her, clenching his rusted axe as he throws it through the air, shattering the dull panel hiding the wizard. Looking to the throne, the group stare at the ruler, his skinned body dripping with raw flesh, protected by an armour of small bones as his bloody face stares back at them. Marching to the wizard with speed the tin-man roars:

'I will strip the flesh from your bones wizard, and feed them to the lion if you refuse our requests.'

The great wizard of Oz doesn't move, instead his taloned hands dangle from the throne and he sits almost lifelessly. The horned monster watches the group approach him, the thick mounds of meat covering his face shaking as he shouts, *'No closer!'*

Walking toward him, Dorothy, the tin-man and Scarecrow stand in front of the wizard whilst the cowardly lion watches from the distance. Rapidly picking his axe up from the ground the tin-man presses it against the wizard's throat, roaring, *'You will not deny us!'* as Dorothy looks at his eyes, pressed deep within the devilish body. Stretching out her hands to touch the wizard's dripping flesh she feels his face, sure that if he were powerful enough he could have destroyed them all by now. Yet as Dorothy takes a handful of gory flesh all the great Oz does is give a weak shrill, begging, *'Please, no!'* as she rips away layers of dead meat, furious to see the face of a weak man beneath it all. Pulling the fangs from his mouth and grabbing at the horns upon his head she throws them to the floor, digging her nails deep into his cheeks as she accuses, *'You are not a great wizard are you?'* Feeling the girls thick nails cut into him the blood drips down his face, and the tin-man pulls the axe away from his throat, letting him beg, *'Please no, don't hurt me I...I'm just a man.'* Tearing her nails through the wrinkled skin Dorothy feels his blood on her fingers and screams, *'You never intended to send me home did you?'*

The frail man looks to the young girl, his eyes like a dead animal's as his head shakes slightly, *'I am sorry.'* Filled with rage Dorothy leaps at him, sending the throne crashing to the ground as she scrams at his face, punching at the old man to feel his teeth shatter against her knuckles. Screaming at him, giving him no chance to defend himself she spits in his face, digging her nails into his skin and tearing through the flesh as she punches until her hands are soaked in blood, roaring:

'I've suffered Oz for nothing...because of you. I...have killed, and...and I have survived, I....'

Her anger stalled, the hatred turned to fear she slams a fist into the wizards face and beats at his chest, brought to tears as the scarecrow lifts her from the man's weak body.

Taking her in his arms she cries, holding onto Scarecrow tightly as she feels his jagged bones stick into her body. Pressing her face against him she sobs, and the lion looks at Dorothy, then to the bloody mess of a man on the floor as he steps backwards, cowering with a shameful look in his eye as he silently leaves the throne room.

Touching at the side of the weak man's face with his axe, the cold steel presses against bloody flesh as the tin-man groans, *'Why shouldn't I kill you?'* Spitting out blood the fake wizard's hands tremble, raising to the tin-man as he wheezes, *'I can still help you.'* Wiping the tears from her eyes Dorothy looks at the concerned scarecrow and rubs a hand along his burlap sack, nodding gently to him as he lowers her to the ground. Shouting to the tin-man she orders, *'Lift him up,'* and the metal monster clenches a gauntlet around the throne, pulling it back to its legs as the feeble man sits inside. Watching him spit shattered teeth to the floor Dorothy asks, *'How, how can you help us?'* walking toward him as he covers his face in fear, mumbling fraily:

'I'm not, not a great wizard but I am a great man. I can give you hearts, c...courage, brains. I just need time.'

Pointing a finger at him, clenching her teeth and ready to attack she asks, *'Can you send me home?'* He trembles, wondering what the strange friends could do to him as he scrambles for the right words, muttering:

'I...I have a balloon, can, can get back home in that but I need it, from...I'm from Omaha and only, only one person can fit inside.'

'I'm taking the damn balloon, you can rot here! Do you understand?' Dorothy forces as she points to the weak man, watching him shiver in fright as she continues, *'You have three days to prepare everything, and that's it. I don't care if you're in pain, I don't care if you're too weak. You'll give us what we requested, and you won't stop until you're done. Work as if your life depends on it.'*

Turning her back on the old man Dorothy starts to walk out of the throne room as the tin-man and Scarecrow follow. Leaving the defeated wizard to work, the young girl hears him call, *'Wait!'* falling from his throne and crawling along the floor. On his hands and knees, the young girl watches him beg, his feeble face broken and pleading, his body encased in a wizard's suit of flesh as he trembles:

'P...please don't tell anyone I'm human, not a great wizard. No one else knows and...and they'll burn me. The witches, my people will torture me please...please.'

Dorothy looks at the pathetic man with disgust, grovelling at her feet as she condemns him:

'Just in case you decide to cheat us and try to leave the city, you should know that Outika isn't dead, and you will suffer unless we get what we want! I'll make sure of that.'

Turning her back on the fraud Dorothy exits and her friends follow, leaving the stain of a man crying on the floor as she hears his sobs echo through the halls. The dark castle seems pathetic now, without power or threat she walks through the shadows, feeling stronger than ever before. With her face still like stone, her temper waiting to boil again she looks to the heartless tin-man, asking sternly, *'Did I do well?'* and he nods his head, groaning, *'If it's in his power he won't dare try to cheat us now.'* Tapping his fingers together the scarecrow sprites, *'Lion's gone!'* and Dorothy nods her head, concerned about the animal as she says, *'I noticed, he must be hiding somewhere!'*

As they reach the large castle doors the tin-man pushes them open and the three friends stand atop the graveyard hill, watching over the city as Scarecrow looks to a guard. Putting a hand on his face and swiping it up and down the burlap sack he voices, *'It was so weird, his face was...'* Quickly pulling him by his arm Dorothy puts a finger to her lips and shakes her head, whispering, *'Nope, can't tell anyone!'* as she fears that if the city finds out they'll storm the castle, ruining her chance of getting home. She knows she has to expose the wizard for the sake of the city's people, but not yet, not while still there's so much to lose.

Calling at one of the guards Dorothy asks, *'Did you see the lion come past here?'* and he answers promptly, *'Yes, he ran straight down.'* Nodding her head at him the young girl continues to make her way to the bottom of the hill, as her friends follow and Scarecrow sings. Skipping over the graves he screams, *'I'm going to have a brain!'* and Dorothy asks the tin-man, *'Are you excited that you'll have a heart?'*
With his tortured eyes fixated on her the metal monster grates, *'Not yet, I don't trust the wizard.'* She smirks with distain, remembering how she feared the wizard, and thinking of how frail he actually is as she utters, *'Neither do I.'* Despite how weak he may seem Dorothy still doesn't trust him, he may just be a man but he was cunning enough to convince a world he was a wizard. She wonders how he did it; looking out at the masked faces and the green glow of the city, deciding to ignore his lies for now, there's too many to decipher.

Reaching the bottom of the hill Dorothy looks back up at it, her eyes creeping over the gravestones and staring at a castle fit for a king. Taking a breath she sighs, *'Almost home,'* and thinks how best to expose the wretch, whether to let his people tare him apart, or give him to Outika so she can punish him fairly. Dorothy ponders on the thought, finding a masked servant girl and asking, *'Have you seen the lion?'* as she answers with panic in her voice, whispering, *'Yes, yes he ran to the west gate.'* Nodding then walking away the young girl hears the servant mutter, *'Terrifying creature,'* under her breath, and Dorothy smiles, thinking of how fierce the lion may seem. Remembering him being too cowardly to leave the carnival, or how he'd cower in fear of the smallest things Dorothy worries, wondering where the poor animal's hiding.

Time passes and the three friends walk along the cobbled streets, keeping out of the way of the people they watch them at a distance, some fighting over food and others begging for coins as they bustle in the streets. Their voices mesh into one; a unified cry of poverty as they barter over rotten fruit and the drunken ones cry profanities. Walking to the west gate the tin-man remembers the way and leads the scarecrow and Dorothy, as they trudge through the city. The young girl calls out, *'Lion! Lion!'* to hear no answer, and they walk for ten minutes, getting closer to the gate as the young girl looks to two the children playing games on the floor. She smiles at them but a crowd catches her eye, screaming at the top of their voices as they run through the streets. Curious, Dorothy reaches for the tin-man's arm, holding it as he turns to see the screaming civilians, grapping at each other, begging *'Help me!'*

Unable to see past the crowds at first Dorothy and her friends look out to watch a thick black liquid oozing along the cobbles, reminding the young girl of what she saw on the road of yellow bricks, but stronger. It spreads across the ground quickly and the people flee, leaving several struggle as the liquid reaches from the stones. Leeching at the civilians and trickling up their bodies, it smothers their skin and clothes, carpeting them as one man screams, *'Please!'*

Reaching out to the group, the black substance lashes from his legs like a lizard's tongue, whipping at his arm as he tries to pull it away, tearing at layers of his skin. In shock Dorothy stands still, watching the thick black spread along his body and ooze toward his face as it drips into his mouth. Grabbing the young girl firmly the tin-man roars, *'We have to go!'* pulling her through the streets as she watches the hordes of people, trying to run as the black expands under their feet. Like a shadow it consumes the emerald ground, surging along the stones and reducing the bodies to nothing as it flows over them like lava. Whimpering, *'Li...lion, we have to find him,'* Dorothy tries to struggle against the tin-man, pull away from him but the scarecrow ushers her along, shouting, *'Can't go through the city.'*

The screams of agony are deafening, the streets covered with bodies as they try to escape, finding themselves victim to the carnivorous black, leeching at their flesh and devouring them. Moving quickly the tin-man pushes through the crowds, leading the way for Dorothy and the scarecrow, as they look to the west wall to find it smothered with bodies. Civilians scram at the concrete, trying to find the secret door as they trample one another, standing on the bodies of their friends as they scream. Looking behind him the tin-man watches the streets, its ground slick with black as smothered bodies lay heaped in the ooze. Turning to Dorothy he grates, *'It's getting too close!'* as it flows towards them, drowning hundreds of people like a tsunami. Watching the lives simply disappear in the liquid, the young girl feels hopeless against it, hearing a sudden chatter as the witch's winged monkeys descend to the city. Grabbing at Dorothy and her friends they don't struggle, not even the scarecrow as he covers his eyes, mumbling, *'I'm not flying, don't see wings, no wings.'* Lifted from the ground Dorothy looks down to the people, trying to find the west gate hidden behind the wall as the liquid surges towards them. They scream, reach their arms up to the sky and Dorothy can't turn away, she watches the black consume them, leech at their skin and crawl down their throats. Yet the further away Dorothy gets the more she sees; a whole city overwhelmed as the ooze carpets the streets, and hundreds, if not thousands scream, suffering and begging for their Wizard to help them as they drown.

The young girl's eyes drip with tears, watching them fall through the sky she thinks of the lion, closing her eyes tightly as the image of him being consumed in the city stabs at her mind. She screams to the monkeys, *'The lion, have you seen him?'* watching the one who can speak carry the tin-man, ignoring her voice as they fly to the west.

30

Dorothy sobs as they fly over the dead-lands, letting the monkey carry her weight as she tries to wipe away tears from her eyes.

Even though she's thankful Outika's creatures saved them she still can't stop thinking about the lion, hoping he left the city. She can't help but think of his soft mane, the heat of his breath against her face as her eyes close, but suddenly her concentration shatters. Looking down to the barren yellow land Dorothy ignores the burn of the chrome sun behind her and stares deep into a canyon, looking at Outika's palace, no longer golden as it drips with thick black liquid.

Screaming, *'What's going on?'* to the talking monkey he ignores the young girl, and quickly they descend. Dorothy feels her stomach turn and Scarecrow keeps his eyes closed, mumbling to himself as the monkey's fly lower and hover above a balcony. Dropping Dorothy further from the ground than before, she crashes to her knees and cuts her leg. Gritting her teeth she watches the scarecrow land beside her, his thin body hitting the floor with a snap as he pokes at one of his ribs to feel it shattered. Looking back up at the monkeys Dorothy shouts to them and they drop the tin-man, though he lands on his feet as the weight of his body sends a crack along the floor.

Hearing the same solemn tune echo through the palace as before, Dorothy listens to the gentle music and looks inside the room. Followed by her friends they enter cautiously, looking at the fine shades of yellow and making their way to the landing, amazed that the black ooze hasn't found its way inside. Following the music Dorothy calls, *'Outika!'* walking to the grand amber ballroom as she looks inside. Again, the witch sits at the far end of the room with her back to Dorothy as she caresses the violin softly. The young girl looks to the witch curiously, and her eyes widen as she sees the lion beside her, relieved as he roars, *'Dorothy!'*

Looking at the happiness on her face and her arms stretched open the lion stands, ready to bound into her comforting embrace as he struggles to move. Looking at the thick collar around his neck, and a chain leading to Outika's wrist Dorothy notices his blood on the floor and utters, *'I don't understand!'* Delicately the music fades and the witch removes her bow from the violin, standing elegantly as she turns to face her guests. Smiling beautifully Outika walks toward then, leading the wounded lion beside her as he looks out to them with a sad glare. With the distance between them still vast the witch's delicate voice glides through the air softly, gently touching Dorothy's ears as the betrayal comes from tender red lips, *'I used you child!'* Dorothy shakes her head, looking into the witch's deep eyes as she moans, *'No...no, I trusted you,'* but a sinister smile spreads along Outika's face, one the young girl had never expected to see as the words cut her to the bone:

'You were a lot stronger before you met me young Dorothy, what weakened your judgment dear, my sad story, my sorrow?'

Feeling rage build inside of her, a defeat so simple the young girl holds back whatever tears she wants to shed and spits her words with venom, screaming, *'You lying whore!'* The witch simply laughs, walking gently towards her guests as she smiles, pulling at the lion's chain with an air of satisfaction:

'Don't bother fighting, you're mine now, and this pitiful creature helped me. My little informer came straight to my side when you unmasked the wizard, and without his help I wouldn't have dared look inside Emerald city, let alone flood the streets with death, but I did. Though I suppose you're to blame too Dorothy. Still, if your cowardly lion hadn't betrayed you you'd have all gotten what you wanted from the lying wizard, and I'd have been none the wiser. He may have even sent you back to Kansas, but instead you're here with me.'

Cowering his head the lion looks at Dorothy, sadly quivering his lips as he stutters, *'S...so sorry Dorothy, she, she said she'd send me back to Mr, Mr Jack. I was so...so scared'.*

Almost as if he'd broken her heart Dorothy looks at him emptily and suddenly the tin-man roars, the witch close enough to attack as he swings his axe in the air and runs at her. His tortured eyes filled with rage he's ready to cut the witch in two, but as his blade descends Outika simply smirks and he's defeated. Without warning his hands force open, each finger snapping backwards before his wrists shatter and his elbows collapse into themselves. His agony roars through the palace and he crashes to the floor as oil and blood pool around his body. Breathing heavily with a mechanical grunt he tries to stand but the witch forces him down, confining him to the ground as she smiles:

'Don't worry, flesh or metal I'll fix you, then break you all over again.'

Crippling the metal monster without moving a limb the witch watches Dorothy and the scarecrow run to his side, quickly controlling their bodies with her magic. Holding Scarecrow to the ground she makes Dorothy walk backwards, and then holds her still. As she stands straight, Outika walks toward the frozen girl and leads the timid lion, pressing a gloved hand against her face. Dorothy's attempt to move is useless, and Outika leans toward her, pressing her ruby red lips against the young girl's ear. She gently whispers, *'You have something I want,'* with satisfaction, then simply smiles to make her lose consciousness.

As time passes Outika leads the lion out of the palace into a rotten courtyard. The greenery's dead and nothing grows, but still she chains him to the ground and points her hand to scattered pools of water. Smiling at him the beautiful witch shows her blackheart, caressing his forehead as she rewards, *'You're a good traitor, for that I won't send you to Mr Jack...'*
The lion looks up at her with a sudden hope, almost feeling relief in his stomach, but she cuts it away instantly: *'Well not for a few days. You can stay here until then, but you'll have to share with my pets.'* The fear bites at him as he looks at her face, begging, *'P...please no,'* watching her leave. Scared, he looks around, watching the pools of water as a nest of snakes slither from the depths, hissing at him as he cries pitifully.

Meanwhile, in a dungeon below the palace Dorothy wakes to the smell of burning coals as she opens her eyes to see nothing but darkness. Struggling to move, she's hung from the ceiling with chains, her confined hands hold the weight of her body and she feels them wrench, ache with pain. Trying to move her legs, pulling them she feels restraints around her ankles, shackling her to the floor and she refuses to scream. She hangs in the dark dungeon for an hour, awake with her eyes blindfolded; unsure of the time, or even where she is, as from nowhere Outika's gentle voice unexpectedly lingers in her ear. *'Do you know the population of Emerald city?'* the witch asks, and Dorothy refuses to speak, clenching her teeth tightly together as the witch continues:

'Thousands...thousands of men, women and children, and you're responsible. The lion may have helped me but I gave him no other choice, unlike you. I couldn't have done it without you Dorothy; I wouldn't have been freed from my prison. I owe you something for that, because there was a reason why Bopeia warned you not to come to the west. I'm a trickster and she knew you were naive enough to believe me...how does it feel to be responsible for the death of thousands?'

Dorothy breaks, her silence shattered as she shouts incoherently, condemning the witch as she simply smiles in response, letting the young girl's throat wear itself out before she clicks a finger to silence her screams, whispering in the young girl's ear again:

'They didn't die quickly either. The black is a parasite, and although its touch is like acid it likes a warm place to nest, guess where? Then it takes the prey several agonising hours to be digested from inside out, and it leaves nothing but bones. But let's talk about you, are you at all curious how little sweet Dorothy saved the evil witch? It's because of your good little soul, and all you had to do was walk me out of this prison. You see the witches' knew I could never create a good soul, find one in my land, nor could I force one to free me, but you Dorothy, you did it of your own free will. So for that I'll give you a choice. I want those boots on your perfect feet, and if you give them to me I'll send you home...but if you don't, then I'll torture you until you do...What will it be?'

Clicking her fingers the witch lets Dorothy talk and waits for a response, but the young girl doesn't say a word. Instead she takes deep breaths, wondering why the witch wants the boots, why she can't simply tare them from her feet. She wonders if they're powerful in a witch's hand, and the young girl knows she can't let her have them, not at the thought of what she may do to Oz. Outika's grim smile quickly fades and she threatens calmly, *'Answer me or I will burn you!'* touching the young girl's face delicately. Dorothy's thoughts flood, everything she's suffered, all she's been put through. Perhaps she's not meant to go home she wonders, maybe she's never supposed to leave Oz.

Dorothy smiles mournfully, letting the tears run down her face, kissing her chance of going home on the lips and letting it go as the hope of seeing Kansas, uncle Henry and aunt Em slips away. Despite how selfish she could be Dorothy knows what she has to do, and as the tears stain her face she smiles, lets it stretch across her face as she groans, *'Go to hell.'* Outika stares scornfully, smiling at the pain to come as she replies, *'I'm sorry sweetie but this is hell, and you're here with me.'*

Suddenly Dorothy screams, her agony sirens through the palace as the wretched witch thrusts a searing hot spike into her thigh, whispering delicately in her ear:

'My land's filled with tortured souls, welcome to the fold Dorothy!'

31

The next day Dorothy hangs restrained in her cell, but the witch doesn't even enter the dungeon, instead she wanders through the palace, occasionally torturing the tin-man as she lets the girl starve, and her body dehydrate.

A day after Dorothy wakes to the smell of blood as she stretches her dangling body to feel the muscles sting. With her eyes still blindfolded, she can't tell if it's day or night, and hungry and thirsty she licks at her lips as a voice sends shivers down her spine. *'Awake are we,'* the witch says, running a finger along Dorothy's body as her gentle voice presses through the air, whispering, *'Shall I tell you what I've done to your friends?'* Dorothy tries to move, pulls at her chains in fear, her face cringing at the thought as the witch watches her struggle. *'Well...'* Outika says calmly, her voice as soft as velvet though her words like nails as she scrapes:

'The tin-man is confined to a table, and yesterday I went to him and healed his wounds...then I slit his throat and burnt the thin metal from his skin. After letting him suffer through the night, I'll heal him today, and then I'll start again. But I can make it stop, if you give me the boots!'

Dorothy bares her teeth, grinding away at the enamel as she bites, *'No,'* thinking of the poor tin-man, wondering if he could ever forgive her. Outika smiles, *'Very well,'* and the young girl waits in the silence, feeling her dress open at the back as the zip unfastens and the witch's voice lurks:

'Do you like leeches, being scolded, whipped? You know, I could plant an insect in your stomach and let it burrow its way out...but let's start gently first shall we.'

With her fingers pressed to the zip on Dorothy's dress Outika spreads the fabric, unveiling the young girl's bare back as she runs a finger along the soft skin, mouthing the word, *'Fresh!'* Dorothy shivers, she doesn't want to give in to the witch but she knows she'll suffer for it, and so will her friends. Yet the thought of what Outika could do with Avatonika's boots scares her, if she can slaughter a city without lifting a finger, how powerful would she become with something of another witch's', and what would she do to Oz.

So Dorothy waits in the darkness, hearing nothing but footsteps and the twist of leather, feeling only cold air along her skin as she screams to the witch, *'C'mon!'* Outika watches the young girl patiently, lets the anxiety build in her mind at the thought of what will come next. The witch makes her wait and hears her scream again, demanding Outika punish her to get it over with, but the cruel torturess watches her patiently. Expecting an attack at any moment, readying herself for it Dorothy taunts:

'Lost your guts witch? ...I've suffered my world I can suffers yours... What are you waiting for? ...What are you waiting for?'

Yet the witch lets an hour pass, walking around the room so Dorothy knows she's not alone, lets her scream, beg for the pain. Then finally, when the young girl's energy's gone and her throat's raw the witch strikes, whipping Dorothy's back with a cat o' nine tails as her flesh tares open and she screams. Fingering at the knots on the tip of the whip Outika feels the metal wire she'd wound around each strand, admiring her work as she walks to the front of her prisoner. Dorothy shivers, her moaning lips open as she tries not to cry. Thrusting a small piece of wood into her mouth the witch gently offers:

'I'll be generous, bite on this and tell me when you're ready to give in.'

Feeling the piece between her teeth Dorothy spits it out, cursing, *'You're wicked!'* but the witch smiles, pressing her ruby lips close to Dorothy's ear as she whispers, *'No darling, not wicked, evil.'*

Then she lashes at young Dorothy thirty times, looking to the bloody skin, eventually bored at the girl's determination as she hears her scream, still refusing to give in. Having punished her enough for now the witch speaks, leaving the room and gently letting her words murk in the dungeon as she suggests:

'Give me the boots and there will be no-more pain...I'm going to visit your friends now, and I'll be back with salt for your wounds.'

Leaving the girl, hearing her sobs echo in the distance Outika walks through the palace, smiling at how she almost feared Dorothy before, a simple child who killed the eastern witch and stole her boots. Now she's a prisoner and all the witch has to do is make her take off the silver boots, then her power's limitless and she'll mould Dorothy into whatever she wants. The evil one smiles, proud of herself and free from the good witches' curse. She's already taken Emerald city, and the black she'd planted through the land now wakes, devouring earth and life. Her happiness gleams at the agony and she opens the courtyard's gate, seeing the lion resting on his side. Cursing, *'What have you done?'* the witch watches him stand, cowering backward as she looks at the dead snakes spread along the ground. The lion had been bitten many times, but despite the blood he lost and the attacks he suffered, when the beast eventually caught the snakes he tore them to pieces.

Outika clenches her fist, gazing into the lion's dead eye as she opens it to hear a grumble from within the small pools. Looking at them hesitantly, scared of what will come next the lion whines and the witch smiles, cutting with, *'If you manage to kill these, you'll see Mr Jack much sooner,'* before leaving him alone with the unknown creatures.

Soon nightfall creeps over the palace, and after healing the tin-man's wounds just to torture him again Outika returns to Dorothy. Entering the dungeon she can hear the young girl singing:

'When I walked all alone I felt so scared, wanted to go home, When I walked all alone...'

Curiously asking, *'What's that?'* the witch locks the door behind her, looking to the confined girl as Dorothy hisses, *'A lullaby, did your mother ever sing to you, or were you just hatched?'* Smiling at her the Witch returns, *'Feisty, I like that,'* as she reaches for her violin, tapping at Dorothy's cheeks with the bow as she says, *'You're not sleeping tonight girl, I'll make sure of that.'* Taking a seat the witch plays her violin, softly at first, gently enough to send Dorothy asleep as she suddenly scratches the strings, making the highest pitch possible as it screeches through the young girl's ears. Shaking her head she begs, *'Stop!'* feeling the deafening pitch stab at her skull, pulsing through her veins as she screams.

Despite the pain, the torture of starvation and the piercing sound, Dorothy doesn't give in, not even as the witch scars her skin when she drifts asleep, depriving her of unconsciousness.

32

With the morning sun shining onto the Palace Outika's aware of it and looks to Dorothy, shaking as she mutters to herself.

The young girl hasn't eaten or drunk a drop of water for days and the dehydration sets in as she twitches her chapped lips, murmuring to a hallucination as the witch opens a window in the dungeon. She tears away Dorothy's blindfold and the young girl screams, taking the light into her eyes after days of darkness as she focuses on the beautiful witch. Smiling at the weakened girl, Outika whispers, *'Shall I show you what I've done to scarecrow?'* as she points outside. Unable to focus at first, wondering if it's all just a hallucination Dorothy squints her eyes, looking out to the yellow canyon as she screams to see the scarecrow, nailed to a cross as crows swarm around him. The young girl struggles, tries to free herself as she watches her friend, begging for the witch to stop, but Outika gently whispers, *'Only you can stop it.'*

Scarecrow screams, *'Please stop, please stop!'* as the winged creatures hack at his insides with their beaks, pulling away straw from his body as Dorothy closes her eyes. The young girl cries, moistening her dry skin as Outika places a hand on her face, *'If you close your eyes I will cut them out next, understand?'* Dorothy's lip quivers and the witch simply clicks a finger to force Dorothy's eyes open, making her watch her friend's suffering. The scarecrow can see her through the window and calls, *'Dorothy, Dorothy!'* as the crows pull away his skin, gnawing at his bones and eventually trying to peck away his eyes. The young girl sobs as she watches scarecrow suffer, hearing him scream as they gnaw at his buttons, pulling one loose and unravelling the stitching throughout his body. The witch whispers, *'You can stop his torment, just give me the boots,'* and the torn Dorothy screeches, *'I'll rot first!'* as Outika smiles, *'Then so will the poor scarecrow!'*

Trying to close her eyes Dorothy's forced to watch Scarecrow suffer, and as the crows pick at his body, disembowelling the tortured soul they peck away at both of his eyes, tearing away the string so his buttons fall to the floor. Blind, the scarecrow screams, *'My buttons. No, no not my buttons. Dorothy... Dorothy!'* as he begs for help, unable to save himself. The cruel witch looks at the crows, making them fly away with a simple suggestion as she whispers, *'We'll have to save some for tomorrow won't we!'* Looking out at her tragic friend the young girl stares at his open body, the straw blowing away with the slight breeze as he calls out curiously, *'Dorothy I can't see...I can't see Dorothy.'* Feeling the tears stain her face she screams, suffering the witch's evil wrath as Outika laughs, gently placing a hand on the young girl's eyes as she makes her fall asleep.

Waking to the sounds of agony Dorothy opens her worn eyes, feeling them almost glued with dry tears as she feels her body pressed against a cold stone floor. Struggling to swallow she feels her dry face ache and looks to the tin-man to see blood and oil spread along his body. His legs are broken, the metal's been pulled from his skin and his thick bear-trap jaw's torn completely from his face. Struggling to move her body the weak Dorothy looks to the scars cut into her wrists from the shackles, and her legs shake as she stands, frailly leaning against a wall as she walks to the tin-man.

She wipes a shaking hand across her face as she tenses her limbs, trying to get the feeling back in them as she staggers to the metal table. With her sight fading and her mind adrift she touches at her friends face, looking down at his mangled body as tortured eyes stare back at her. She's barely able to utter, *'What has she done to you?'* as the tin-man roars in agony. His wounds abruptly heal, snapping back into place and cutting deeper into his defeated skin as Dorothy turns to see the witch. Gazing into the young girl's eyes Outika looks at her weakened body, making the tin-man scream with her magic as she softly thrashes:

'How long has it been Dorothy, without water, food, two days...well I assure you you will die of it soon enough, but I won't let you. I'll feed you to make you stronger then starve you again, torturing you and your friends until I get what I want, but for now I'll just kill the tin-man.'

As the witch stretches her arms the young girl looks around, the room filled with jars of thick black liquid, resting on shelves and waiting to consume. She trembles slightly, looking at the contained carnivores as they wriggle within the glass, whipping their bodies like tentacles as the witch leers:

'I will feed your metal friend to my beloved creations, and they will burn through his metal and suck at his flesh, killing him very slowly. Then I'll do the same to your other friends. Do you want that to happen?'

Dorothy struggles to clench a fist, her weak body still standing as she pushes, *'No,'* from between her dry lips, too feeble to fight as the witch allures, *'Good, because if I don't have those boots I won't stop with your friends either. I will slaughter thousands until you remove them, do you want that on your head after everything you've already done?'*

Dorothy mutters, *'No,'* turning to the tin-man as he lays healed, waiting to be tortured as he suffers because of the young girl, because of the choices she'd made. Then she finally breaks, falling to her knees as she whimpers, *'You...you win...'* She sobs with her hands trembling, her eyes glazed as she mourns, *'You...you are strong and I am weak, y...you are a god and...'* Then she feels it, the courage she had now eaten from her soul, and her strength crushed like fruit, *'...and I'm just a little girl.'* Her fingers tremble as she undoes the laces, unthreading one as she looks at the key dangling from her neck, thinking of everything she's gone through just to go home. Slowly sliding the boot from her foot she clenches it in a weak hand, shaking with hopelessness. Feeling a lump in her throat and watching the look on the witch's face, the anticipation and pleasure, Dorothy screams violently, launching the boot across the room. Smashing at a glass jar the witch looks in fear, unable to move or even use her powers quick enough as the black takes her.

Leaping to her skin it drips along her chest, stretching itself across her body as she screams in agony, trying to tear it off as her flesh peels away. Moving quickly Dorothy reaches for the tin-man, undoing his chains and freeing him as she watches the witch fall to her knees, too overwhelmed to use her powers as the tar consumes her. She screams, crawling along the floor to Dorothy as the ooze drips over her body, burning through her beautiful skin while the agony bleeds in her begging eyes.

Moving to the door Dorothy feels the witch's hand along her dress, trying to pull her to the floor as she grabs handfuls of fabric. Looking down at Outika, suffering as she's devoured, the black leeches at her face, creeping into her mouth as she tries to pull it away. Feeling chunks of skin drip to the ground, the substance stripping her to the bone she screams her last venomous words, *'Not a little girl, you're the devil in witches boots.'*

Grabbing at Dorothy the tin-man opens the heavy door, pulling her out of the cellar as she stares at the witch's body, watching the ooze spread along the floor and consume the silver boot. Now nothing but a mound of black the young girl smiles at the witch, whispering, *'Not so wicked now,'* as she locks the room, letting the black digest her slowly, eating her from inside out.

33

Threading barbwire through thin skin and burlap Dorothy's weak hands are numb, pricked with holes and covered in blood. She'd stuffed Scarecrow with hay and sewn his skin back together, removing the broken jagged bones and fixing him the best she could. Still exhausted and thirsty her dazed eyes look down at the scarecrow, laying in the main hall as she lastly stitches his buttons back, not wanting him to see what the crows had done. With one eye already sewn on he looks up at Dorothy, touching at her face gently with a bony finger as he says:

'It's good to see again, but you don't look well, I like to see things but don't like birds, look, look, they didn't take my necklace!'

Fingering the tangine stone around his neck he smiles, so grateful to be in one piece again as Dorothy threads wire through the other plastic button and attaches it to his face. Almost falling asleep, her skin slices under the wire as she tightens a knot and listens to Scarecrow gleam, *'Oh boy! I've got two just like before!'* Smiling at him, too weak to say anything Dorothy feels herself drifting away and the scarecrow stands, taking her limp body in his arms as he looks to the poor girl; her skin dry and eyes sunken with blood caked around her wrists, her body bruised and her dress stained with red. With her eyes barely open she lifts a weak hand to the scarecrow's burlap face, touching at the fabric as her chapped lips quiver, *'Help tin-man f...find...the lion.'* Watching her pass-out with exhaustion the scarecrow nods his head and carries her to an empty room, laying her on the bed and wrapping her in a blanket as he turns to see the tin-man enter behind him. Jumping in shock the scarecrow pops, *'Didn't expect to see you there,'* then leaning in closer with a smile he taps his plastic buttons, *'I've got my eyes now.'*

The tin-man looks at him blankly and grunts, *'Lion's not on this floor,'* turning to see Dorothy unconscious on the bed. Looking at her worn face, he's sure she should eat something and orders the scarecrow, *'Follow me,'* as they search the palace for a kitchen. Eventually finding one they take water and bread to the young girl, watching her eat and drink a little as she mutters, *'Lion,'* again, and her friends let her rest as they search for him.

Together Scarecrow and the tin-man traipse the palace, walking through the bright yellow corridors, elegant rooms decorated with yellow crystals, and the dungeons carpeted with bones. Despite the tin-man's torture he walks steadily through the palace as Scarecrow bangs at his metal chest, prancing, *'What's this?'* and, *'Oh that's odd.'* Acting without fear, almost forgetting his savage attack he runs from room to room, shouting, *'I want to live here, so pretty!'* and the tin-man moves along quietly, as a sudden roar echoes through the halls. Screeching, *'That sounds familiar!'* the scarecrow runs through the palace, toward the noise as the tin-man's heavy body follows behind.

Bounding to the courtyard Scarecrow opens the gate, running inside without hesitation as he suddenly stands still, looking out to dead greenery and the peculiar animal carcases piled on the floor. Unsure what the large beasts are his eyes look past the bodies and he tilts his head quizzically with, *'Most peculiar,'* as he spots the lion. Staring back at Scarecrow the lion lays on his side, groaning with blood around his mouth as the curious straw man asks. *'I remember you, fluffy. What's wrong?'* Burping, the lion feels wounds spread over his body and struggles to stand, moaning, *'I ate too much,'* as the tin-man enters the courtyard. Looking down at the animal the metal monster watches him stand, blood still dripping from his body as he lowers his head in guilt, gently offering, *'I'm sorry,'* as Scarecrow stands oblivious and the tin-man groans, *'Did she feed you for your good behaviour?'* Defending himself the lion grumbles, *'Her creatures almost killed me, I ate them to stay alive,'* but walking toward him tin-man grunts, *'I don't care, but the girl may, she almost died.'* Ignoring the dead bodies he grabs at the lion's chain and the animal cowers, stepping away from the metal giant in fear. Looking at the dread in the animal's eyes the tin-man pulls the chain apart, leaving the collar around the lion's neck as he roars at the beast:

'I understand why you betrayed us, you're a coward, and even if you didn't the witch would have seen us as soon as we left the city, but that's not the point....We trusted you!'

Turning his back the tin-man leaves the courtyard, his voice echoing, *'Follow me lion, Dorothy may be happy to know your alive,'* as Scarecrow looks at the dead animals and shouts, *'Fluffy you ate them?'* Groaning, *'Yeah,'* under his breath the lion walks through the palace painfully, his body wounded and sore as he carries guilt on his shoulders, feeling the straw man pat his back. *'Never seen that before, they looked dangerous and you killed them, that's brave,'* he cheers, but the lion huffs, *'No, it's surviving,'* as he looks to the scarecrow's face, gently offering, *'I'm sorry for what I did.'* Smiling wildly at him Scarecrow taps his buttons happily and shouts, *'Never mind, I can't even remember. Birds took my eyes and I'm just happy to see.'* Leaving the lion with a bitter taste in his mouth he carries the guilt of how the witch tortured his friends, knowing he doesn't deserve to be forgiven, and wondering if he even deserves the wizard's help.

Watching Dorothy sleep the lion slowly walks into the room, looking at her worn face as his sore pads press against the floor, walking to her bedside. Lifting his head he places it on a pillow, letting Dorothy sleep as he stands silently, grateful for what she's done for him, and so sick that he's such a coward. Feeling the heat of his breath along her skin the young girl smiles to hear his slight huff, as she struggles to open her eyes. Looking at his dishevelled face she wants to leap out of bed and wrap her arms around him, but too weak she simply lifts a hand, feeling his cold snout as she whispers, *'So good to see you.'* The lion smiles, jumping onto the bed as he rests his head against her shoulder, brushing his mane along her face as he whimpers, *'I'm so sorry.'* Combing a hand through his fur Dorothy gently whispers, *'It's okay,'* as she forgives the creature easily, too weak to express how hard it will be to trust him again. Soon enough they rest quietly, whilst Scarecrow and tin-man walk into the room, watching as Dorothy sees them standing in the corner, patting the bed with a smile. Looking back at her Scarecrow happily jumps to her side, sandwiching the young girl she holds his hand, and the tin-man watches over them as a strange sound creeps through the palace. Unsure if it's the chatter of monkeys or something else the tin-man waits outside the closed room, keeping guard as nightfall comes, curious if the black will spread from the cellar.

With the morning sun creeping through the window and spreading along her face Dorothy doesn't move, and instead feels herself pressed between fur and straw as she closes her eyes again and waits a few more hours before waking. With the chrome sun set in the sky the young girl's eyes slowly open and she looks at the scarecrow lying next to her, who'd occupied himself through the hours by simply looking at his necklace. She smiles at him, feeling her body stronger now, her energy almost restored as she pulls herself from the bed and stretches her limbs. Still sore she feels her bones ache and touches at her back to feel blood, small wounds that opened during her rest.

After eating hungrily Dorothy bathes, feeling the layers of crusted blood peel from her body as she soaks in the water before slipping into the same dirty dress, drying her hair as she thinks about Toto, hoping the witch hadn't laid her hands on him. The young girl left tin-man and the scarecrow searching for their belongings, wandering through the palace in hope of finding Toto, her wicker basket and the tin-man's axe. The witch took their possessions when she captured them, and Dorothy sighs at the thought of not finding her little dog. Still not fully healed she feels the cuts along her wrists itch, and although the warm bath soothed her bones, the slits along her back and the scars on her thighs stung enough to bring her to tears. Putting her right foot into a random black shoe, and slipping her left into the silver boot she pulls the lace tightly and thinks of going back down to the cellar, even though she saw the black consume the other boot. At first she tries to convince herself she could sneak in, and perhaps if the boot's magic it may not have been devoured by the substance, but she knows she can't risk opening the cellar door, it's too dangerous.

Waiting outside the bathroom the cowardly lion sits cleaning himself, watching the door open as he looks up to Dorothy and smiles, hearing a scream abruptly call from the front of the palace. Running through the hall and making their way into a bedroom, blunt chattering gets louder, followed by screams as they move quickly to the balcony. About to step out of the room the lion pulls Dorothy back, shaking his head as he says, *'Black on the walls,'* and Dorothy suddenly remembers the tar she'd seen smother the palace. Leading the lion along the room the young girl presses her face to a window, looking down to the ground as she watches Argus screaming at the top of his voice. Stumbling in circles he holds several knives in his hand as the winged monkeys hover in the air, chattering as they look down to several of their dead. With their bodies impaled the clay man throws a knife into the sky, screaming, *'We must die, she's gone!'* as he aims for a flying creature and spots Dorothy in the window, turning his attention to her as his feminine voice screeches, *'You, you're the one responsible, now we have to die, everything dies when the witch is dead!'*
Confused she watches him, her body unexpectedly torn to the floor by the lion as a butchers knife smashes through the isabelline glass. Pulling her away from the window the lion looks to see the black creep along the rim of the windowsill and hears a sudden scream. With Argus distracted the winged monkeys attack, swooping from the sky and tearing away pieces of his body as he stumbles to his knees. Screaming at them the clay man pleads, *'You don't understand, Outika's...'* and Adam, the monkey leader soars toward him, tearing away the clay head from his body as he slumps to the ground dead. Chattering in celebration the monkeys circle

the palace, gliding happily through the air as Dorothy pulls herself from the floor to see Adam burst into the room. Walking toward her the thickset primate brushes dust from his arms and the lion watches him, baring his teeth with a growl. Looking to the animal the leader leaps onto a stone dressing table and addresses Dorothy politely, *'Please, I am Adam, we mean you no harm.'* Looking at him confused, wondering if his words are lies she bites curiously as she looks to his gentle face, *'What about the witch, you served her, brought us to her so she could torture us!'*

Sighing, Adam rubs a hand along his face and looks up to the young girl, holding his grief inside as he replies, *'You don't understand, we were loyal to the witch because we had to be, and bringing you to her was only out of fear of what she would do to my people if we refused. We were slaves, your friend here knows what it's like to be forced by Outika, and you yourself know what it's like to be punished by her too. She may have tortured you for several days but she created us long ago, slaughtering many in her imprisonment. Once we were hundreds and now we are dozens, what would you have done in my situation? I take no pride in how I have acted, but I do not regret a thing I've done. I would walk on glass for my people and sell anyone's soul.'*

Looking into Adam's eyes Dorothy nods her head, admiring the loyalty to his people as she mouths, *'I understand,'* and watches him stand straight, bowing his head to her as he continues: *'My people owe you our lives and we will serve you if you need us, though do not take my kindness for granted. You have no power over my kind.'* Smiling lightly at him Dorothy says, *'Thank you,'* stretching her hand out to Adam as he shakes it with his strong arm, replying *'How can we serve you?'*

With the afternoon gone Dorothy and the lion eat and drink plentifully, and they ready themselves for their journey back to Emerald city. Finding his axe the tin-man feels comforted to have it in his grip, and Scarecrow hands Toto's bag to the young girl, smiling, *'I found him!'* to feel the little dog's still hidden in his bag. Dorothy clenches it to her chest, peeking inside briefly as she thanks the scarecrow. Then soon enough the winged monkeys take a hold of the strange friends, flying them back to the Emerald city as Scarecrow tries his best not to struggle, and the lion feels his stomach turn. Silently the tin-man rests in the monkey's grip and Dorothy feels a hesitant smile stretch along her face, thinking that it's almost over, she can finally go home.

34

As the monkey's fly over Emerald city Dorothy looks down to see the streets smothered with black, the screams of when the chaos struck distant, and the civilisation dead. Descending to the Wizard's castle, they watch the ooze slithering along the graveyard hill, half way up as it leeches on the newly dead in their graves, having already depleted most of the city's population. Slowing their speed the monkeys reach the castle doors, gently lowering Dorothy and her friends to the ground. At first as they stare out at the city, the green streets black and the carnivorous liquid crawling along the buildings, searching for food as it scales the hill.

With a keen eye the tin-man notices bones floating in the thick dark water, bare of flesh as a sudden yell echoes in his ears. Looking out to the green buildings, some already covered in black and others awaiting the darkness Dorothy points to a distant house, as a man inside calls to them from the attic window. He screams, *'Please, please help us!'* begging as his arms wave in the air and he looks at the ooze spreading to the second floor of his house. With a faint glimmer of hope Dorothy shouts, *'How many survivors?'* and he yells, *'There's eight of us, please help, it's inside the house!'* Looking to the building the young girl watches the substance spread through open windows, creeping inside every crevice as she turns to Adam. *'Please,'* she begs, *'Do you know how to stop it?'* and he shakes his head, *'No I'm sorry, but we can fly the survivors out of the city.'* Grateful the young girl pleads, *'Please, yes! But...you'll come back for my friends, wont you?'* Looking at her with a stern face, like that of a soldier and not a slave he answers, *'You have my word, and I hope the wizard sends you home!'* Taking to the sky with a chatter his people follow and they separate through the city, searching for survivors. Looking out at the buildings and the man waiting in his window Dorothy nods her head, feeling sick at the thought of the witch's tyranny. Yet the wizard disturbs her more as she notices that the city's gates are still locked, containing the blackness inside the walls and giving his people no chance of survival. Gently muttering, *'My god,'* under her breath, Dorothy finally accepts that although the wizard of Oz was nothing but a fake, he has always been terrible, a man to fear.

Making their way through the dark castle the lion thinks of the city, imagines the survivors hidden in basements, locked inside their houses, waiting for the ooze to consume them. He shivers with his nerves on edge as he looks frantically into the shadows, clinging next to Dorothy as he expects the darkness to spread towards them. Excited, the scarecrow dances through the halls, shouting, *'I'll be able to think things,'* as Dorothy doubts the wizard's abilities, sure that they can't trust such a wicked man.

Walking into the wizard's throne room the strange travellers watch him hunched over a table, this time dressed in beautiful green robes as he wears his true face, that of a feeble old vulture. Startled by them his beaten face looks at Dorothy with surprise as she smiles at the damage she'd done to him. *'I...I am ready, you are lucky that you left the city when you did. The witch's evil's spread,'* he grumbles, turning to two servants as he shoos them along with his hands, commanding, *'Go, go prepare!'*

Watching them leave the fake wizard asks, *'Have you killed the wicked witch?'* as Scarecrow beams, *'Yup, brain please,'* to see him smile sinisterly. Ending the old man's curiosity the tin-man groans, *'Do your people know you're a liar?'* as he grins with satisfaction, *'To them this is just another of the wizard's faces.'* Staring at him with disgust Dorothy thinks of condemning the man, have the lion tare him to shreds for what he's done to the city, but biting her lip she knows she should wait until he fulfils their requests.

Looking to his guests who demand so much of him the fake wizard thinks carefully, sure that if he granted the lion courage first he may be mauled, and if he were to give the Scarecrow a brain he doesn't know what could happen. So choosing wisely he decides to help the tin-man first, hoping a heart will calm the metal monster as he points, *'You, I...I shall give you a heart. You, you must follow me.'* Walking to a curtain the feeble man pulls it open, unveiling a metal table with a clinical, *'You must lay here,'* as he opens a drawer and the tin-man follows. Shuffling through his tools the fake wizard takes out what he needs and watches as his patient lies on the bed, putting his axe to the floor, within arm's reach. The wizard straps the tin-man down, hearing him groan, *'If something goes wrong, I will kill you,'* and the old man trembles, *'I, I'm sure you will,'* as he places a velvet pouch on the table. Watching him unravel it Dorothy looks to see a fresh heart beating, and the scarecrow coos as the young girl shouts, *'Wait, that's the witch's heart isn't it?'* The elderly man shakes his head whilst the tin-man's eyes stare, ready to pull the liar apart. *'No, no, no,'* says the fake wizard, looking to the strange friends as he defends himself:

'Many a wise man has requested the presence of the great wizard, and brought amazing gifts to pay tribute and appeal to my kindness. This heart

belonged to a nobleman and was touched by the great witch Notou so that it could beat forever and save the life of a dying soul. Now please...you must be quiet whilst I work.'

Pulling the curtain around himself and his patient the wizard uses his tools to open the tin-man's chest plate, staring past the scarred flesh curiously. Tapping at the metal heart's container he uses a key to open the cover, looking inside at the tubes and mechanism keeping the tin-man alive. Staring him in the eyes the old man says, *'You will be without a heart for seconds while I fix you. Don't struggle, I cannot afford to make a mistake and if I take too long you will die. Do you understand?'* The tin-man nods his head whilst Dorothy and the others watch the shadows behind the curtain, waiting patiently as time passes.

After a while the tin-man's friends grow worried, scared to shout to the wizard in case they cause him to make a mistake, then finally the curtain opens. Looking to the tin-man Dorothy watches him sit up from the table, his heavy body clinking as he stands. Running a gauntlet along his metal chest plate he looks over to his friends, his eyes tearing as his monstrous metal face looks no different. Walking toward them gently he feels his insides warmer than before, remembering how it feels to have a heart. Smiling at him the scarecrow asks, *'Are you okay?'* and he nods his head, looking at the worried expression on Dorothy's face, and the fear in the lion's eyes as he groans, *'This is what it feels like isn't it?'*
'What?' the young girl asks, looking up at him as he stretches a hand out to her, watching his friends as kind words creep from his rusted jaw, *'To feel...happy!'*

Calling to them the fake wizard yells, *'Lion, lion come here if you want your courage,'* and the tin-man looks down to him, groaning, *'You're safe with us here,'* as the coward slowly walks away from his friends. Approaching the wizard, he watches him fumble through a cupboard and cowers backwards when he spots a needle in his hand. *'If you want my help you'll come here,'* the fake wizard proclaims, and the lion trembles, *'That...that will make me brave, give me courage?'* Nodding his head the wizard assures, *'Yes it will!'* and the lion closes his eyes, walking toward the needle as his claws cut into the green stone beneath his feet. Feeling the metal in his skin the lion groans, and injecting him quickly the wizard steps back to watch the lion stumble as he stands. *'What...what have you done to me?'* he roars, and the wizard moves further away, trying to calm the beast with, *'Once it settles in your bloodstream you will be fine, and you will have your courage.'* Pointing to Dorothy he shouts, *'You and the tin-man, look after him whilst I fix the scarecrow, come, we must hurry!'* Looking at the odd man Scarecrow smiles, squeezing Dorothy's hand before he runs to the wizard's side, whispering, *'Gonna have a brain!'*

Leading Scarecrow to the same table that he used to examine the tin-man, the fake wizard asks him to lie down and straps his body tightly. Again searching for the right tools he pulls them from a drawer and straps the scarecrow's head to the table as he mutters under his breath, *'hope this works.'* Cutting a line along the burlap cranium with a scalpel the fake wizard pulls away the top of the fabric to hear Scarecrow scream. Quickly looking down at the patient with a panicked expression the Wizard stares as the scarecrow smiles, *'Just kidding, can't feel a thing.'* Sighing the wizard feels pressure, still sure that with courage the lion would maul him if he killed the scarecrow. Working on the tin-man was easy enough for the fake wizard, as despite how odd it looked, it was just like fixing a machine, but fixing the scarecrow is different. Grabbing at the skull saw the elderly man presses against the exposed cranium, pushing into it with one hand and turning the handle with his other as the blade cuts jaggedly.

After sawing at the bone, the top of the skull is severed and the wizard looks inside to see nothing but straw. Reaching to a shelf he holds a jar steadily in his hand, looking inside at the brain as he places the container on a table and puts on a pair of thick rubber gloves. The brain was another gift from a begging stranger, giving it to the wizard in hope he was satisfied enough not to punish the minion for stealing bread. He said the brain was taken from a great tree in Oz, one that grows organs from its branches and feeds the creatures of the south. Even though the fake wizard has doubts about its origin he places it into the scarecrow's head, stapling the skull back into place as he sews the open burlap sack back together.

Looking to the scarecrow the fake wizard asks, *'Do you feel any different?'* and the straw man shakes his head, curiously mouthing, *'I don't feel...'* as he suddenly shrieks aloud, his entire body jolting. Running to his aid Dorothy tares the curtain open, looking inside to see him screaming, *'Help!'* His body taut as the old man nervously shouts, *'It's settling, just settling.'* Watching him in horror the young girl places a hand over her mouth and the lion walks toward her, observing the scarecrow with a stern face as his skeletal body suddenly turns limp. Mumbling to himself the straw man smiles, his mouth occasionally twitching and his buttons staring at the ceiling as he mutters, *'Pretty things, need pretty things to open, pull away the skin like paper see what's inside, like the crows, the crows, their insides were good.'*

Scared, Dorothy calls his name, placing a hand against his as her voice touches gently at his burlap head. Looking at her, his twitching stops and a confused expression stretches along his grim face, as he cries savagely, *'What's happening to me, I keep...keep thinking bad things.'* The young girl's worried and the wizard says, *'Lie still for a while, try not to think too much just yet,'* as the scarecrow mutters to Dorothy, *'I, I think I'm scared.'* Watching the wizard move away from her friend Dorothy looks at him as the lion threatens, *'If you don't fix him I'll rip you apart.'*

Smiling lightly the old man says, *'I'm sure you would, but then I wouldn't be able to send your other friend back home. I see you have your courage now though.'*

Growling at him the lion's proud, happy to feel strong but he doesn't say it, he knows a lion can't seem vulnerable to his prey. Meanwhile the tin-man stands quietly, looking down at the scarecrow with a sad expression as Dorothy questions the old man: *'How did you do this, how did you give the scarecrow a brain if you're just a human, how did you give any of them what they asked for?'*

Putting away his tools the old vulture leers: *'I m a great man, child. And although I am no wizard I have learnt new tricks since I have been in this land.'*

With her hand still holding the scarecrow's the curious Dorothy pushes, *'How, why did you convince Oz you were a great wizard?'* and the old man smiles, looking at the young girl confidently as he sits on a stool and distracts the strange travellers:

'You of all people should know Dorothy, you've seen how evil this world can be. Just like you, I didn't come here of my own free will, but when I landed I made the best of what I had. I was happy back in Omaha, a ventriloquist and an illusionist, but then the cyclone came and changed my life. I was flying in my balloon above the circus when the weather turned. All I could see was clouds until I awoke here, grounded as a race of freaks greeted me. But do you know what the strange thing was? They thought I was a great wizard...'

Slowly the old vulture stands, a sinister smile stretching along his face as he clenches a fist, and his eyes fill with power as he continues:

'I became a God, and I made the people build me a city. Their kind are stupid ones, and when I showed them my tricks, my illusions and my magic, they feared me. That is how I am known as the great one through this world, fear. Though underneath it all, as you know I am just a man, so when I found that real witches ruled this world I could only imagine what they would do to me, either the good or the bad.

So I covered my body in the flesh of the newly dead, convinced my people I could change form, become any creature I wanted, and fear of the great wizard spread. I made my people build my castle atop a hill and surround it with their deceased so my power could be seen all over Oz. I had to convince the world I was a monster so that the witches feared me, and they did. Still, I hid myself away in this castle for years, I was young when I came here, and now look at me. I couldn't even fly my balloon out of this world in case the witches shot me from the sky.

The truth is Dorothy I feared you at first, I thought you were a witch because you wore the boots, and that's why I sent you to the west, in hope that either Outika or you would die. But I should have known you were just a girl, you even lost one of the witch's boots. See, I may just be a man, but I fooled the entire land, even you were convinced with my illusions, my talents, that I was a fearful wizard. All of you believed I was a God, but now I'm nothing, because of you and because of Outika.'

Dorothy looks at the wizard, sickened by his feeble frame as she hisses:

'You let a city of people live in fear because you were scared, they worshipped you and you abused them and scarred their skin so word of a powerful wizard would spread?'

The fake wizard smiles jaggedly, proud of himself as he looks out to his company:

'Not quite, as despite how evil you think I am I never harmed a single one of my people. I am a very intelligent man and I didn't even need to, not to a race as stupid as these. I simply told them that magic held the masks to their skin, and if they remove them their faces would simply peel away. Everything in my city is a trick and you should know that by now, the city isn't really green and how do you think I could see everything? I am a

modern-age man in a primitive world, and I made them think I was a God! For a girl from my own world you almost remind me of one from Oz.'

Dorothy huffs, pulling her hand from the scarecrow's as tin-man stands silently, saddened as the lion stares with anger in his eye. Staring at the wizard, the young girl feels hatred burn through her chest, she'd never met a human with such a lack of humanity, and screams:

'I understand now, you let 'your' people waste their lives for you, suffer at your command because you're an egotistical coward. Do you know that the people in this city died screaming your name, calling out for to you to help them!'

The wizard smirks, standing swollen with pride as he places a finger to his wrinkled chin, proudly announcing:

'That's truly sad but I couldn't let them leave. The witches dare not look in at my city, but I know as soon as anyone is outside the walls they will know, and they would have seen my people leave. They'd have known I was weak and they would have attacked. I am feared by the good and the evil, they'd have killed me. Besides, my people died thinking I was a great wizard, and they'd have happily given their lives for my safety, as they have. I have done nothing wrong, only what a king would...'

Suddenly a servant enters the room, calling to the fake wizard as his placid voice yelps, *'Master, it's ready,'* and the wizard nods at him as he looks to Dorothy, clenching his teeth tightly as he presses, *'Wait with your friend and I'll get the balloon for you your highness, then I can be rid of you for good.'* Moving through the throne room the wizard walks quickly as Dorothy yells, *'Where are you going?',* and the scarecrow shouts:

'You can't let Dorothy leave can you? You have to leave in the balloon because you know you're ruined. Whether it's the witches or the people, someone will make you suffer for what you've done, so you have to leave, and with Outika dead you can fly away in your balloon, right?'

His pace quickening the old man yells, *'I knew I should have given you a diseased brain,'* as he runs to a wall and the lion bounds after him. Roaring fiercely the creature chases, but the frail wizard opens a secret hatch, slipping through a gap between the stones. Waiting for it to open fully the lion squeezes through and claws at the hole, as Dorothy follows behind him and tin-man frees the Scarecrow.

Running along a rooftop the wizard moves quickly around the back of the castle, looking down at the graveyard hill to see the black ooze at the top as he looks ahead to the air balloon. Waiting for him, he smiles at the hope of leaving Oz, an escape plan he'd devised years ago as the lion roars behind him. Turning his head quickly the fake wizard sees the animal and speeds to the basket below the balloon, pushing his servants out of the way as he cuts the ropes and dives inside. Running behind him Dorothy watches the balloon slowly float into the air as her hopes of Kansas slip further away, and the lion runs at the wizard without fear.

As the balloon drifts from the castle the fake wizard condemns, *'Girl, you can be the queen of my dead!'* so close to leaving Oz as the lion runs toward him, leaping fearlessly from the castle as his claws sink into the basket. Yelling at the animal the old man tries to force him off as the balloon starts to float over the city. Ready to punch at the lion's face the old man screams as a claw cuts through his arm and tares a hole in the basket. Nursing the bloody limb he watches the lion struggle to hold on, sinking his claws into the wicker and gouging holes in the vessel as he suddenly loses his grip. Falling through the air the lion's silent, crashing to the roof of a building as tiles crack underneath him, imbedding into his skin as he jumps to his feet. Roaring up at the wizard the lion watches him struggle to stay in the basket as it sways, the vessel torn apart as he holds on for his life. Looking at the balloon Dorothy stands on the rooftop, watching the wounded wizard drift away as he screams:

'Do you know what that's like Dorothy, to have ultimate power? I would have reigned their king until the day I died if I hadn't had let you into my throne room, but now you can take my place in Oz.'

Slowly smiling the young girl watches him float away into the night as she stares at the broken basket holding him, sure to fall to pieces when the wind changes. Waving her hand she feels comforted at the lion's courage, letting the great ruler of Oz drift into the clouds, knowing that he'll fall from the sky, dying just as the wicked wizard deserves.

35

Sitting alone in the throne room Scarecrow rests as his friends clamber along the rooftops. Hearing winged monkeys cry, and the sigh of young Dorothy he watches his friends walk back into the room as he sits in the wizard's throne. With an empty expression on her face Dorothy feels the tin-man's hand on her shoulder as he groans, *'We'll find another way to send you home, we have to.'*

The lion walks proudly beside them, with his head held high as he thanks Adam and the other winged monkeys that follow behind him, for if they hadn't have lifted him from the distant rooftop the black would have soon found him. Proud of what he did, it makes him confident that when Dorothy's home safely, he'll find Mr Jack. Watching the Scarecrow as she approaches him, Dorothy's eyebrows raise as she looks at his crossed legs, and a hand poised under his chin whilst a menacing expression's cuts into his face. *'What are you doing?'* she asks with the tin-man standing close by, trying to comfort her with his cold metal touch as the Scarecrow looks down at his friends:

'Just thinking, thin...king. Some thoughts that I suppose I should not say, some thoughts that are mine alone. Do you ever feel that there are so many thoughts in your head you could just burn, burn...no, no, don't like fire can't burn. I shouldn't think of that but I just can't stop thinking...thin...king, thin...king. How clever I like that, that could be me!'

Concerned, Dorothy looks to the Scarecrow as he seems more ghoulish than ever before. His eyes no longer glare innocently and his expression isn't as curious as it used to be. Instead, a thin grim smile stretches along his face, contemplating as his skinny hands twitch. *'What's wrong with you? what do you mean?'* Dorothy asks gently, and the scarecrow shrieks eerily, *'I can rebuild the city, I can be its thin...king!'*, *'But the black, it's taken over,'* The tin-man groans, *'This city is dead, its people.'*

Standing from his throne the scarecrow opens his arms, spreading them snidely as he boasts:

'You can repopulate a city, make the people better, stronger. I just need to kill the black first. Everything dies everything can be killed.'

'*You cannot kill the sky,*' The lion says, '*You can pollute it!*' Scarecrow smirks, '*You cannot kill love,*' The tin-man groans, '*You can taint it!*' The scarecrow howls, suddenly falling back into the throne, nursing his burlap head as he shakes his body. His wicked smile fades and the innocent expression creeps back, looking out to his friends as he dithers, '*No no, not at all, it's all wrong, not thinking right. We need to send Dorothy home.*', '*But how?*' the young girl asks, feeling no sadness that the wizard betrayed her, she'd expected it long ago. Instead she's persistent, even more adamant to get back to aunt Em and uncle Henry than before as everything pushes her back. Poking at his head, knowing that there's something inside the scarecrow looks out to his company and bursts, '*Monkeys! Can you fly Dorothy out of Oz, at least past the moving sands?*'

Stepping forward Adam shakes his head regrettably, his strong voice slightly echoing through the hall as he looks up at the Scarecrow, then to Dorothy: '*I'm sorry but we can't, we're creatures of Oz and were made by the western witch. As far as I know no one has ever gotten past the desert, and I cannot risk my people trying. The magic that created us confines us to this land, and it may be rejected by your world. I'm sorry.*'

'*We could make another balloon,*' the tin-man groans, but the scarecrow interrupts, standing quickly as he puts a finger to his mouth. '*The witch, the witch, the witch!*' he repeats at first, bursting, '*Dorothy can go north or south and one of the witches will help, but will they be powerful enough to send you home?*'

Adam answers again, with a strict attitude and a firm voice as he reports: '*Notou is more powerful, and even if we wanted to we couldn't fly north. When we evacuated the city we saw the purple path covered in black, we cannot risk flying over it with the night sky. We can take you to the south, but not as far as the Quadling country, despite being a good witch her land can still be dangerous, and the hammerheads would shoot us from the sky by without warning.*'

'*Then that's it,*' the lion growls, '*We'll take Dorothy in the morning,*' but the scarecrow exclaims, '*No, we have to leave now. It won't take long for the black to devour the city!*' Looking at her friends, proud of how courageous the lion is, and so happy that the tin-man and Scarecrow have what they wanted the young girl asks meekly, '*Are, are you coming with me?*' Walking toward her with a gentle smile the scarecrow brushes a hand through her hair, twitching slightly as his button eyes open wide, '*If I didn't come with you I wouldn't have much of a brain would I?'* Holding his hand she looks at him warmly, hearing the lion's strong voice echo, *'You saved me,'* as his dead eye weeps and he looks at her compassionately, *'You became my friend, and I can't let you go alone.'* Stepping toward her he rubs his head against her neck, letting his mane tickle her face as he whispers in ear, *'But I don't want you to go.'* Feeling a tear in her eye she looks at his sad beaten face, feeling his cold snout against her skin as she realises how it must feel for him, after losing the only friend he had to Mr Jack's carnival, the one who took his place is leaving him too. Wrapping her arms around the lion, tears stain her cheeks, almost wondering if she even wants to go home. She suddenly feels relieved she didn't get in the balloon, because she doesn't want to say goodbye to her friends, not just yet. Looking up past the lion's fur to the tin-man she asks, *'Will you come with me too?'* though not just for protection, but because he's become a part of her life in Oz. She thinks of the times he's saved her, how she felt when he was attacked in the streets, and how she laid by his side in the cold workshop. Seeing the hesitation in his eyes she asks, *'Please,'* and he looks down at the young girl, feeling a swelling in his chest he had almost forgotten.

'I'll come with you to the south,' the tin-man groans sympathetically, *'I want to see you home safely but I'm scared. Do you remember what I told you about my love, how she lived with an evil old woman...her house is in the south too, and I must go there, I...'* Gently moving from the lion Dorothy holds the tin-man's gauntlet, careful not to prick her skin as she looks into his eyes, *'I understand, but don't be scared, she'll be happy to see you. Come with us, we'll be beside you...don't leave me yet.'*

As quickly as they could the strange travellers were soon flying through the air, leaving the Emerald city as Scarecrow looks behind him at the morbid green castle. Now covered in back the ooze it drips along the steeples and clings to the spires, spreading along the buildings and creeping over the great wall as it whips into the sky hungrily. So concerned with the city he almost forgot how much he hated flying before, but now with a brain he smiles, sure that if anything with wings would try to harm him he'd simply be intelligent enough to catch the creature and open it up like he did the crows.

Flying over the red lands of the south Dorothy looks down at a forest of moving trees, watching their branches flail in the night as the monkeys slowly descend. Staring at a high wall made of clear white china, and a delicate village within it made of such beautiful colours Dorothy's amazed, though the scarecrow doesn't coo like he used to, and instead he looks inquisitively, thinking what kind of people live here. Gently lowering the travellers into the town the monkeys float above their heads and Adam bows to the young girl, asking, 'Is there anything else you want of us?' and she smiles up at him, 'No, your free, thank you for bringing us this far.' He looks at her with a modest smirk, announcing, 'Yes we are, and we have you to thank,' before flying higher into the sky and shouting, 'We wish you the best of luck,' as they disappear into the night.

Looking out at the dainty china village Dorothy smiles in amazement, from the sky she hadn't noticed, but its houses and barns are no higher than her waist. Staring at such a brightly coloured village she looks at the animals kept in a pen, the cows no taller than ten inches, as without warning a swarm of people crowd the streets. Watching them Dorothy and her friends step backwards, but not the lion, he lets the horde come closer and stands his ground. Their footsteps clatter at the delicate white floor, and the animal had never seen such strange people. With bodies, and even their brightly coloured clothes made of nothing but china, they stand with emeralds and jewels imbedded in their fragile skin, as the tallest is only as high as Dorothy's knees. Dressed in beautiful robes and jewels, one wears a crown and some pointed hats, as milkmaids, clowns and royalty are painted the brightest of colours. Yet they still look horrific, as all of their china heads are broken; cracks spread along all of their faces, across rosy cheeks, through painted lips and eyes, as almost a hundred surround the guests.

Staring at them worriedly, Dorothy's reminded of dreams she had as a child, one of evil dolls, the hideous broken toys hiding under the orphanage beds. Sure that he could just smash them to pieces the lion shows no fear, though to his surprise the crowned china man politely says, 'I am the king of this village, what do you want? We do not take kindly to guests at night.'

Stepping forward Dorothy looks down to the small king, pleading, 'Please Sir, we mean no harm. We're on our way to see Notou and need a place to spend the night.'

Looking up at her the king's sick painted smile catches her eye as he courteously says, 'If that is the case you are more than welcome, though you will have to sleep in our barns, as they're the only buildings we have that are big enough for giants to rest in.'

Nodding at him the young girl says, *'Thank you so much,'* as she feels herself growing tired, and suddenly realises that every single china person is smiling at her. With a pair of sick red lips spread across every broken white face she hears the king shout, *'Back to your homes, Princess, show them to the barn.'* As the horrid broken dolls walk back to their homes one small woman stands in an elegant pink dress as cracks spread along her face to the back of her blond hair. Looking up at the guests daintily she requests, *'Follow me,'* as she leads the travellers through the china village and shows them to the barn. Looking to the woman Dorothy thanks her and can't help but ask, *'What, what happened to you all, how are you all cracked?'* Without shame, the princess replies with a brittle voice:

'The reverend said the time would come, and no-one believed him at first. Then one day as the sun shone on our village brightly, a hundred birds came from the sky and tried to take us to their nests. Some were dropped from too high up and couldn't be fixed, but the rest of us were mended, and now our whole town's pretty again.'

Looking at the daintily white woman Dorothy stares at her sick smile, and watches her gently curtsey before uttering, *'Good night,'* and leaving them beside the barn. Watching her walk away, looking over the silent china village Dorothy whispers, *'Do you believe her?'* as the Scarecrow replies, *'Not at all.'* Still, after a while Dorothy and the lion crawl into the barn, knowing they dare not move too much in case they break it. So holding each other they gently fall asleep, as tin-man lies on the ground beside them closing his eyes, thinking of finding his love again and wondering if she'll remember him. While the others sleep the scarecrow crawls through the village curiously, listening to the slightest of sounds as he wonders what the people are hiding. Eventually he spots a lit church and lies in the distance, watching through a window as he spots a china girl. With her face a pristine white she smiles with pretty colours spread all over her, and wonders why her head's not broken. Lying still, with his body hidden in the darkness he watches her for an hour, wondering why she doesn't move from the chair she's sitting in. Then after some time the scarecrow witnesses a crowd of broken dolls walking into the church, as he realises the girl's tied to the chair. Curiously, he watches without thinking of saving the girl, instead he prepares himself, sure of what will happen as the king appears and holds a small hammer in his hands.

Without warning or sorrow, the ruler smashes the girl's china face to pieces, letting her white skin clatter along the floor as the Scarecrow finally understands the responsibilities of having a brain, and the power of being a ruler.

36

As morning comes, the travellers leave the china village without seeing a single person, or hearing a voice through the empty streets. The scarecrow keeps what he had witnessed last night to himself, and soon enough they reach another white china wall. Climbing over it carefully they find themselves in a red marshland; full of bogs, and covered with tall thick grass as they wade their way to the south. Still with her compass, Dorothy checks the direction occasionally, leading them into a swamp as they struggle to find solid ground.

Surrounded with murky water, small mounds of ground and tall-deformed trees, the travellers struggle to see past a thick layer of fog, as a peculiar scuttling sound echoes through the land. Feeling water at his feet the tin-man fears he may rust, but keeps focused on his surroundings as the scarecrow treads cautiously, wondering what's beneath the swamp. Smelling the fresh air the lion leaps from one dry mound to the next as he feels the moss crunch between his paws and looks eagerly into the murky distance. Smiling at Dorothy he says, *'I like this place,'* curious of what creatures live in the land as he bounds happily, thinking that the carnival would never come to this part of the country. Listening to the distant flow of ominous waters a loud howl suddenly travels through the swamp and the lion turns to his friends. *'Get back!'* he growls, smelling a new scent as several figures charge from the fog ahead.

With a fearful roar the lion marks his territory, and as the animals emerge from the thick grey he watches one stumble into the swamp as the others scream, *'It's back, it's back!'* Slowing their pace they run to the lion as he watches the different species joined in fear; antelope aside wolves, capybaras with jaguars and other strange species he'd never seen before. Looking to the animal drifting in the swamp the lion whimpers, he'd never seen a lioness until now, and he watches her dead body float with two large holes in her ribs. With his good eye weeping he growls, *'What did this?'* and one of the peculiar animals howls, *'The female, she's back, the eggs are hatching!'*, then a she-wolf steps forward, limping as she informs the lion:

'Spiders, bigger than elephants. Two came and devoured many of our family, then they spread their eggs around the swamp and left. Now the female's back. Some of the animals here aren't fighters, they'll die, Please help us.'

Shocked, the lion gently nods his head, growling, *'I will!'* as he stares at the dead lioness. The she-wolf thanks him and turns to the other animals, ordering, *'The wounded go, those still able come back with me,'* as she looks at the lion, *'Come, we're heading south.'*

Trudging through the swamp the lion and the she-wolf walk in front, as various animals walk behind, and Dorothy, Scarecrow and the tin-man trail at the end. With a keen eye the she-wolf watches the path ahead as the other animals look deep into the swamp surrounding them. Watching for spiderlings, sure their eggs will hatch soon the she-wolf leads the way, hearing the lion huff, *'Are there anymore of my kind here?'* Her keen eyes suddenly turn sympathetic as she glares at him, *'I'm sorry, there were before the spiders came, but not anymore.'* Saddened, the fierce lion asks, *'You live here in peace, all the different species?'* and she smirks ironically, *'We try to, but I don't even know how many are left anymore. I sent the weak and the ones unable to fight into hiding, but some of our strongest are dead, that's why we need your help.'*

Walking at the back Dorothy looks through the swamp, eyeing the fog and looking in front of her at the capybara as she whispers to Scarecrow, *'Is that a four foot hamster?'* Just as he's about to open his mouth the creature turns around, looking the young girl in the eyes as he shouts, *'Hey, I'm not a hamster!'* Smiling lightly with, *'Sorry,'* she looks at the capybara as the jaguar next to him licks his lips, *'Sure smells like one though.'* Then with a light attack the rodent hits the jaguar on the nose, confusing him as he shouts, *'I told you that's not funny, and at least I don't look like a rug!'* Dorothy hears the big cat murmur, *'So cruel,'* as she giggles lightly, looking to the lion ahead of them with a smile.

Swiftly with a sniff of the air the she-wolf cries, *'Spiderlings!'* as the jaguar turns his head to see them crawling along the marsh and dangling from the trees. The lion roars to threaten the arachnids but they leap in the air, ready to attack as the she-wolf howls, *'Watch out, their poisonous!'* The spiders jump from the ground and dive from trees as the fierce animals swipe at them with their paws, whilst the weaker ones try their best to attack, and Scarecrow and the tin-man protect Dorothy. Cutting the arachnids in half with his axe the tin-man swings the blade with force, as the scarecrow swipes his arms in the air, cutting away their limbs with his barbwire stitching. With each spider a foot high, spewing from the marshland quicker than they can be torn down the she-wolf howls, *'Retreat! Quick carry the slow, now!'*

Without hesitation the strong carry the weak and the lion leaps to the tin-man, sure he's the only one able to carry such a weight. Finding herself quickly thrown onto a jaguar's back Dorothy grabs tightly as they speed through the marsh, and she watches behind her to see some of the animals fall, the spiderlings eating them immediately.

They run for miles, dashing past the newly hatched spiderlings and avoiding the eggs that spread through the swamp. Smelling the scent of the large female spider and finally reaching even ground the she-wolf orders the others to stop, watching their bodies slow as she goes ahead alone, her legs in agony from running as she gently limps again. With the scent stronger she *barks, 'Hide those unable to fight, she's close,'* warning her pack as the tin-man walks toward her, ready to battle. Marching ahead the lion pushes him back, roaring, *'No! Look after Dorothy, this is my fight!'* and the tin-man nods as a peculiar red animal escorts the strange friends with the weak, hiding them in an empty cave. Walking toward the shelter Dorothy looks around the land; filled with hills, and beautiful green trees, as she spots dead animals scattered along the ground, some half eaten and others trapped in spider webs.

Following the she-wolf, the lion and a pack of other animals tread carefully as thick webs surround them, and they walk into a forest filled with oak trees. Looking in the distance, they see the spider sleeping on the ground, as fierce animals lay trapped in spider webs, and dozens of eggs surround the arachnid. Slowly approaching the monster the lion looks at its huge black body; its head striped with orange and twice the size of him. Getting closer to the sleeping spider, planning to attack while it's asleep a tiger moves in first, baring its teeth and leaping into the air as the monster opens its four purple eyes. Reaching for the animal with a long leg it pulls the creature into his mouth and devours with sharp fangs as it stands, as tall as the trees, running at the others.

Howling, *'Pull back!'* the she-wolf and her pack retreat, running through the forest as the spider chases quickly, knocking down the trees, spinning webs at the animals and crushing them under her legs. Side by side the she-wolf and the lion run, but as the arachnid hammers trees to the ground they separate and she pursues the wolf. Running with all of her strength, her injured leg in agony she knows she can't fight the spider on her own, and as she starts to tire she looks up at the beast. Staring at its evil eyes the she-wolf watches in amazement as the lion leaps from a hill, roaring as he dives at the spider, latching onto its head as he claws her eyes out and sinks his teeth into her face. The fierce animal hacks away at her head as she shrieks in pain, her legs giving way as she crashes to the ground, pulling apart the trees as the she-wolf dives out of its way.

Hearing its last cries the she-wolf turns to see the large spider, dead on the ground as the brave lion stands on its head, roaring out at the forest. Smiling at him the she-wolf walks towards the dead arachnid, looking her hero in the eyes as his scarred face stares down at her with pride. Then the she-wolf gives a strong howl, echoing through the land as animals of all species and sizes slowly come out of hiding. Looking at the lion atop the dead monster they cheer in howls, grunts, squawks and cackles, free of the spider as Dorothy and the others watch their friend, proud of him as he leaps to the floor. Running to him the young girl wraps her arms around the strong warrior, and the tin-man and Scarecrow congratulate him as the she-wolf bows her head:

'We have much to thank you for, it will still take time to be rid of the spiderlings but we couldn't have killed the mother without you. We have to rebuild our society, we are a pack, a herd...a pride, and we would be honoured to have you in it, please stay!'

Looking at her, and the land of strange creatures around him the lion feels at home, but turns his head to Dorothy, thinking of how he once betrayed her trust, and how she saved him. Then he thinks of a promise he made to avenge his lost friend, to kill the vicious Mr Jack. So with strength, a confidence he's never felt before the lion thinks of what matters most to him, and looks at the she-wolf as he answers:

'I can't, the girl needs my help, but I'll come back, I promise you.'

Gently the lion turns to Dorothy, watching her open the compass as he looks back at the she-wolf one last time, asking, *'What is your name?'* Strongly she replies, *'Ealora, yours?'* and the lion shakes his head with, *'I was never given one,'* as she she-wolf smiles, *'We'll have to change that when you come back.'*

37

Heading south, the four travellers pass through the rest of the forest safely, watching out for the spiderlings and crushing as many eggs along the way as they can. After journeying through the almost endless land they finally rest at the bottom of a very steep hill, one that Dorothy hopes will take them to the Quadling country. Looking up at the tall mound of rocks Scarecrow scratches his head as the young girl watches him ponder, wondering how his new brain will change him. He seems different to Dorothy, and as she asks, *'Are you okay?'* he mutters to himself as he walks ahead, ignoring her. Following him she calls his name, but he doesn't answer, and when she places a hand on his shoulder he turns around with an evil grin. Calling, *'Scarecrow...Scarecrow!'* she shakes him, his button eyes gazing into oblivion as he suddenly looks Dorothy in the eyes and smiles, just like he used to. *'I'm sorry,'* he says, *'I was just thinking, thinking things I can't say because...well because. Let's send you home.'* Stretching a hand out to her, the gangly scarecrow leers and she takes his bony palm begrudgingly, wondering what's wrong with her friend as he leads her up the hill. Mumbling to himself at first Dorothy wonders why he's not surprised anymore, why he wasn't interested in the pretty china village, or the strange animals. Thinking about the Emerald city scarecrow suddenly raises a hand in the air, shouting, *'The witch will help me get rid of the black won't she. Then I'll be king. I'll be like the wizard.'* Pulling her hand away from his Dorothy looks him in the eyes, worried as she shudders, *'I don't like the way your acting!'* With a quizzical expression at first the straw man taps at his head and points at the young girl:

'I know why...you preferred me when I didn't have a brain, when I couldn't think. But now I can and so much is in my head, too much. There's things I want to do but shouldn't, and things I think that I don't want to. There's too many voices to know which ones are right and they won't stop. Do you know what that feels like, feels like fire, and it hurts. I need to get back to the Emerald city, it needs, it...'

Looking at Scarecrow, unsure of how to stop his madness the young girl simply utters, *'You're scaring me,'* and his thin mouth twitches as his buttons suddenly widen. Then gently he extends his hand to her and quivers, *'So sorry, so sorry. I'm just confused, think the wizard gave me a bad brain...let's take you home.'* Still uneasy Dorothy takes her friend's hand, feeling sorry for him as she smiles sympathetically. She can't imagine how it must be for him to suddenly have more thoughts than he's used to, and holds his thin arm tightly, worried. Behind them the lion walks up the rocky hill and looks back at the forest as he smiles. *'Soon,'* he whispers under his breath and turns to the tin-man, who hadn't said a word in such a long time. Looking at his monstrous face, a pair of sad eyes hiding in between the metal, the lion asks, *'What's wrong, shouldn't you be happy?',* *'I am,'* scrapes the tin-man, *'But I'm scared too, scared that my love won't recognise me, that she'll be scared of me because I look like this.'* With a slight huff the lion steadily lifts a paw, patting the tin-man on the back. Although he doesn't know the tin-man's story he knows how he feels, being feared because of his appearance even though he's gentle inside.

Finally reaching the top of the hill Dorothy and the scarecrow look out at the land, the beautiful red country spread before them as burgundy houses rest on lavish vermilion grass. Cardinal brooks flow under stone rose bridges, chestnut trees grow along the clean carnelian path, and beyond it lays a beautiful crimson castle as the sky above it glows a bright cherry red. Smiling at such a sight Dorothy's eyes widen and even the scarecrow coos again as he turns to Dorothy and presses, *'Please, if I act odd help me, I don't mean to.'* Squeezing his hand tighter she gently offers, *'I know,'* as tin-man and the lion walk behind them.

Ready to make their way down to the Quadling country, the lion hears a rumble along the rocky hill and Dorothy turns to see a short stout man; with no arms, a heavily wrinkled neck and a large flat head, almost like a hammerhead shark. Standing atop the hill his husk voice chars, *'No way past!'* as all of a sudden a slew of them stand from the rocks. Looking at the deformed wild people Dorothy stares, she'd seen men like these at the carnival, but not dressed the same. The others wore normal clothes made of fabric, but these are clad in stone, wearing it like armour as it covers everything but their wrinkled necks. Gripping tightly at his axe the tin-man's ready to attack and the lion roars, trying to dominate the unusual men as Dorothy pushes, *'We're passing whether you like it or not!'*

Chuckling boisterously the hammerheads jeer, as the one in front of Dorothy sneers, *'Go back little girl!'* Gritting her teeth, and with no fear of what these wild men could do she ignores the landscape of scars over her body, her blood crusted to the gingham dress and screams, *'I've come too far to have you stand in my way!'* With a clenched fist she lunges for the hammerhead, punching him in the throat as he falls down the hill and his wrinkled body buckles with every rock. Hearing their friend cry at the bottom of the mound the wild people back away and Dorothy watches them, ready to send every single one down the hill if she has to. Slowly retreating, the hammerheads grunt and mesh with the rocks as the young girl and her friends make their way down to the Quadling country.

Reaching the bottom of the rocky mound the strange friends walk along the carnelian path as the scarecrow thinks it would be good to whistle, starting to feel like his old self. Watching his thin happy smile, and the way he looks out at the chestnut trees Dorothy wonders if it's being further away from the Emerald city that's made him happier. So close to the end of her journey the young girl feels Toto in the bag around her shoulder and smiles at the red country. Walking along the path, they pass a scragged wooden hut and look ahead to the beautiful houses and barns. Dorothy and the scarecrow walk in front, arm in arm towards the village as the lion roars and the young girl turns, looking back as the tin-man stands still, frozen outside the dingy hut. Walking to him quickly Dorothy asks, *'What's wrong?'* and he solemnly looks at her young face, for a second almost reminding him of his lost love as he groans, *'I have to go inside, it's where she lived, where my...'* Stopping him Dorothy whispers, *'It's okay, it's okay, go inside, be brave,'* as walks to the hut and leaves his axe outside, opening the door.

Remembering the tale the tin-man told her, how an evil old woman treated the girl he loved like a slave, and didn't want her to marry, Dorothy wonders how such an evil person could live in a good witch's land. Still she waits patiently with her friends outside the hut, looking in the distance past the red village as Notou's beautiful castle glows, hoping they'll reach it by nightfall. Then abruptly the tin-man walks out of the hut, picking up his axe along the way as Dorothy smiles, *'Is she still there, is she happy to...'* but she suddenly notices the fresh blood along his metal skin, dripping from his gauntlets as his eyes fill with tears. Looking at him concerned Dorothy asks, *'What's wrong?'* and he feels the tears in his eyes, not caring if he rusts as he mourns, *'I don't want a heart anymore,'* and walks past them. Watching the tragic tin-man move along the carnelian path alone, his friends run to his side, unsure of what happened but trying to comfort him the best they can, though now he feels more hopeless than ever before.

Walking through the beautiful village the strange travellers are welcomed by the quadlings, short round people with rosy cheeks who curiously come from their houses and greet the strangers. Bringing water and bread to them, Dorothy smiles at their hospitality and watches the tin-man's eyes glisten as one friendly old man says:

'So good to have visitors, now don't go letting that evil old woman give you a bad impression of us.'

Sceptical of their politeness Dorothy smiles the best she can, and when one family offers that they stay for the night she kindly refuses. Still, the courteous villagers offer food for their travel and give Dorothy some fruit as she slowly warms to them, unable to think how folk like these could be less than genuine. Asking them, *'How long will it take to get to the castle?'* Dorothy feels relieved as one short woman says, *'No more than two hours, just follow the path.'*

The group of friends walk for a while longer, the scarecrow smiling at the different shades of red and the lion proudly strutting his body as children run away from the beast, shouting in excitement. Still the tin-man walks emptily, sad as Dorothy tries to hold his gauntlet without cutting herself. Trying to smile at him and still unsure what happened in the hut she says, *'You'll always have us, we're like family, and when I go you'll have Scarecrow and the lion by your side.'*

The tin-man groans, his tears still glistening slightly as he utters in pain, *'No I won't, when you're gone the Scarecrow will go to the Emerald city and the lion will find the carnival or go back to the other animals. I won't have anyone, I'll be alone. I may as well just rust in the rain again.'*

Looking into his eyes Dorothy tries to comfort him with, *'That won't happen, you can help Scarecrow rebuild Emerald city, you can...'* but a sudden wail of people interrupt her as children shout, *'The carnival's back!'* and the young girl quickly turns to the lion. Dorothy continues to comfort the tin-man as she notices the animal approach a short round man, asking, *'Is it true, the carnival's here?'* and the friendly fellow smiles, not even afraid of the beast:

'Yeah they're in the forest, heard they couldn't head north so they came back through the west, mighty brave of them!'

With a sudden glint in his eye the lion turns to his friends, looking at Dorothy as he feels pride in his heart and says, *'Follow the path, I'll find you before you reach the castle, I promise.'* The young girl nods at him as he presses his fur against her skin, giving a heartfelt, *'Good luck!'* worried about what may happen to him as he bounds fearlessly into the woods.

Soon nightfall creeps over Quadling country, and the lion sits patiently in the forest. He'd waited next to Mr Jack's trailer for an hour, watching him, waiting for him to be alone as he pushes away the odd families and screeches to himself, *'Goddamn quadlings, I hate the quadlings, and now I can't go north, lost my damn star attraction, perhaps I should start digging up a new act.'*

The lion keeps a keen eye on Mr Jack, watching him walk to his trailer as the animal cracks a twig with his paw, moaning pathetically as the creepy ringleader hears the sound. Listening carefully to a faint whimper he looks into the forest and shouts, *'If you're trying to mess with me remember I own shoes made of many species and I ain't picky!'* Looking through the dark red night at the outline of the lion, Mr Jack's dry lips stretch and his dirty teeth gleam. Walking closer with a big smile the ringleader smatters, *'It can't be,'* as he slowly pulls a chaney-knife from his pocket and approaches the animal. Lying on the floor, whimpering like a cub and looking to the skinny Mr Jack with fear in his eye, the lion watches him crouch down and lets him gloat, *'I never thought I'd see you again my little coward.'* Holding the knife firmly and ready to stab, the ringleader pokes at the lion, looking at the seemingly pathetic beast as it suddenly groans, *'Do you believe in fate?'* Mr Jack smiles, *'What's that, can I smoke it?'* and the lion growls, attacking quickly. Giving a terrific scream the ringleader tries to run away as the lion bites off his hand, playing with his food as he refuses to kill the vermin, just tear off enough pieces to make him look...different.

Getting closer to the castle Dorothy and her friends walk hand in hand, as the tin-man buries his hurt for now and the scarecrow tries not to think about Dorothy leaving, spotting the lion in the distance. Running toward them with his head held high he makes a satisfied sound and leaps to the path, brushing his mane against Dorothy with a smile. As excited as she is at the thought of going to Kansas, seeing aunt Em and uncle Henry again she'd be lying if she said she wouldn't miss Oz, but the thought of being home overwhelms her. She can imagine them living at the farmhouse, her aunt and uncle probably too weak to sew the crops and milk the cows, but when she gets home she can do it for them, look after her Henry and Em like they wanted to look after her.

Dorothy smiles, so happy as they approach the castle wall, wishing Notou can send her home as she imagines no more fake-families, no more orphanage, just home, just Kansas.

With a nervous hand young Dorothy presses her palm against the stone wall, whispering, *'Please,'* as she closes her eyes tightly and knocks at the Castle gates. With her eyes still closed she hears the sound of metal screeching, letting her heart beat anxiously as the gates open and a soft voice whispers through the air, *'Come to the garden Dorothy!'*

Smiling at her friends, tin-man and the scarecrow hold the young girl's hands whilst the lion walks beside them, entering the castle grounds. Bedazzled by its beauty they walk under the vermilion archway, looking up at the castle as they wander through the domain and stare out at a lavish garden. Cardinal grass spreads through the grounds, with orange-red hedges and alizarin trees of many shapes and sizes. In the distance lies a small rosewood maze, a Persian red bridge over a still cerise pond, and in the centre of it all a large circle of ruby pebbles, as Notou sits on a throne made of red emeralds. Even though the strange travellers are far away from the witch, her gentle voice still breezes softly to their ears; calming the anxious Dorothy, the saddened tin-man, a confused scarecrow and even the joyful lion. *'Please come forward,'* she says, and the friends walk along the grass and admire the beautiful rose flower archways along the pebbled circle. Smelling their sweet scent Dorothy smiles, and the lion twitches his nose trying not to sneeze.

Gently letting go of her friend's hands the young girl walks in front, stepping into the ruby circle first as she looks at the witch. With her red hair flowing in ringlets, her face so soft and gentle she smiles delicately and asks, *'What can I do for you, my child?'*

Walking closer Dorothy kneels before the witch, feeling the pebbles press into her skin as she clenches her hands together tightly. With her dry lips trembling, her eyes glazing at the thought of finally going home she says:

'Please help me. I'm not from this land and I...I need to get home. My, my uncle and aunt need me and I miss them so much. I need to...'

'Get back to Kansas,' Notou says lightly, and the young girl gleams, *'Yes, yes!'* in excitement, looking at the witch as she leans forward.

Kissing the young girl lovingly on the cheek she smiles, her face glowing as she speaks: *'The silver boots can carry you over the dessert and take you home.'*

Just about to smile, feel a sense that home is only a breath away young Dorothy crumbles to the floor, sitting on the pebbles as she looks to the silver boot on one foot, and an odd black shoe on the other. Her lips trembling she says, *'I...I lost one of the boots, can...can I still get home?'* as the beautiful witch stands from her throne and offers the young girl her hand. Helping her up from the floor Notou smiles softly, *'Bless your dear heart,'* as she lifts her hand in the air. Then the slightest of breezes gently comes, and from nowhere the lost silver boot appears in her palm. Amazed, so happy she could cry Dorothy looks at the witch and takes the boot excitedly, asking, *'How did you do that?'* and the witch replies with a gracious, *'I'm very powerful I'll have you know.'* Throwing the black shoe to the floor Dorothy slips her foot into the silver boot and looks at the witch, whispering *'Thank you,'* as Notou says:

'The silver boots have many powers, and if you want them to take you home, simply concentrate and knock your heels together three times.'

So excited, her eyes filled with tears of happiness Dorothy looks to the witch and thanks her again, turning to her friends quickly. Running to them she wraps her arms around the lion, so hard that she almost chokes him as he huffs, *'I'll miss you,'* and she sobs *'I'll miss you too,'* kissing his big head and stroking his mane. Then she looks up to tin-man, staring into his sad eyes as he cries, mumbling, *'Having a heart hurts.'* Dorothy hugs him lovingly, not even caring about his jagged metal as she smiles, *'It's worth it, otherwise we wouldn't feel love.'* He nods his head, and the young girl sobs, *'I hope you find your place,'* to him before looking at the poor scarecrow. So sorry she's leaving him more confused than when she found him she holds his skinny body, and he wraps his arms around her as she cries. Rubbing her back he comforts, *'Don't be sad Dorothy, you're going home,'* and she whispers quietly in his ear, not to upset the others, *'And I'll miss you most of all.'* Letting him go gently, she steps backwards as he holds the tangine necklace between his fingers, smiling innocently, *'I'll never forget you Dorothy.'*

Sad at the thought of losing her friends she realises that without meaning to she found the family she always wanted, the ones who protected her, always stood by her, and made her feel loved. They had all been through so much together, with each of them forming part of a bigger picture, one she almost can't imagine living without.

With a lump in her throat and tears in her eyes Dorothy taps her heels once, then again as she cries, *'I'll miss you all so much,'* but as she goes to tap them a third time the witch stops her. Notou's gentle voice presses, *'I can't let you go just yet Dorothy,'* and as the young girl asks, *'Why?'* the beautiful red garden suddenly bursts open as thick black liquid spreads along the ground. The witch's beautiful eyes swiftly fill with darkness and her young skin shrivels to a wrinkled corpse as she falls to the floor, shattering to the ground as behind her stands a figure cloaked in black tar. From the dark robes, two monstrous hands pull back a thick hood slowly, and underneath, Outika's hideous face stares, deformed with one eye in the centre of her burnt myrtle head as she cackles:

'I am the reason you woke in this world child, I am the beginning of Oz and I am the end. Without you I wouldn't be free, but you tore the beautiful skin from my body, and for that I wanted you to see my true face. You've served your purpose child, and now I would rather see you suffer at the power of the silver boots than have it myself just yet.'

Terrified, Dorothy's unable to move, her body held still by the witch's magic as Outika gives a hellish scream and black ooze shoots into the air. Sprawling through the grounds and carpeting the once beautiful garden, the substance forces the young girl's friends closer to the witch as tarred winkies submerge from the liquid. It drips from their deadly bodies as they screech in hunger and the lion roars, running at the evil witch. Leaping into the air he opens his savage mouth, ready to attack as Outika easily casts him to the ground, and the tin-man runs at her, wielding his axe and ready to chop her in half. Watching him charge Outika simply opens her hands as the curious scarecrow bursts into flames, screaming as Dorothy cries, unable to move. Laughing, the witch looks to the young girl, clicking her fingers and controlling Dorothy's feet as her heels tap together one last time, her body lifting into the air.

Screaming, reaching out to her friends the young girl hears Outika scorn, *'Home Dorothy!'* as she tries to force her way to the ground, unable to fight the power of the silver boots as she watches the witch throw tin-man to the floor, and surround the lion with deadly winkies. With her throat raw and her limbs weak Dorothy swipes at the air, her body ascending to the red sky as Toto's bag slips from her shoulder, and she watches him fall to the ground. Quickly the carnivorous black consumes the country, spreading all the way to the dainty china village as her friends get smaller in the distance, and she cries as she watches tin-man and the lion fight for their lives.

The silver boots tare the young girl through the red sky, away from Oz, giving her the only thing she wanted since she awoke in the land. Now the last thing she sees is the poor scarecrow, and the flames devouring him as he looks up at her, waving his hand as he sadly smiles,

'Safe home Dorothy, safe home!'

Waking in shock, her body in agony Dorothy feels the soft padded cuffs around her wrists and her body tucked under warm bed sheets.

She opens her eyes in the crisp white room to feel a torture more horrific than any Oz had to offer, and looking down at her feet she sobs, they're bare with nothing to help her escape. Trembling, remembering everything that happened she feels her heart bleed, the burn of loss inside her as she prays Oz is real.

Lifting her torso she screams, her hair wet and blood still caked around the slits spread over her body, stretching like cracks in concrete up to her forearms and along her back. Raw, her throat begs to be heard, her dry eyes burning as she flails her body, trying to get free, and aching to leave as she screams:

'No! No, I don't want to be here. I don't belong here, how to I get back, how to I get back?'

Hours pass, and eventually after the questions and accusations, the curiosity why her body found in a gutter beside the highway she lays in bed mournfully, so scared of this world and truly alone. She listened to what they had to say with tears in her eyes, their apologies and condolences reminding her of the fake voices she'd hear in the orphanage. They said it was peaceful, her aunt and uncle died in their sleep but she couldn't believe it, how cruel the worlds had treated her, without even a chance to say goodbye. After everything she went through to come home, she was too late, and no-matter what she'd say no one would believe her about the scars, or where she disappeared to.

Lying awake again, she can't stop thinking of aunt Em and uncle Henry, missing them and wishing she were back with her friends in Oz. At least in that peculiar land far away there's still hope for the young girl, and she knows it.

Each night as she sleeps she prays she'll wake in Oz, lying next to the lion as Scarecrow coos at butterflies and the tin-man watches over them. Only in dreams does Dorothy find peace, but even then the witch creeps in to remind her that she left her friends for dead.

Through the days of slow torture, the medication and psychiatrists Dorothy notices that with every face, she sees there's disappointment, pity in their eyes as she hears the occasional whispers of, *'Poor kid,'* and, *'perhaps she couldn't take it.'* So slowly, the 'real' world attempts to strip her of Oz, and despite how hard she clings to it, the dreams try to fade away, but she makes herself remember. She can't afford to lose that piece of her.

After a week, her wounds healed and her mind supposedly on the mend she's finally discharged, feeling as though she'd just left Outika's dungeon, but this time there's no one waiting for her outside. Instead she's given medication, appointments with doctors as a nurse brings a plastic tray into her room. Hearing the muted, *'Here's the stuff you came in with,'* Dorothy feels defeated, looking to the gingham dress as she slowly slips it on, wondering where to go from here. Then she looks to the tray to see the small black key she was given by Bopeia, clutching it in her palm as the grim stare she'd been prescribed by the doctors slowly fades.

Sitting silently in a taxi Dorothy watches the rain pour along the streets, the drab colours with disgruntled faces, every single one looking the same. She'd thought of going to the graveyard, placing a flower on her aunt and uncle's stones but chose not to. She remembers the last time she saw them, years ago before the orphanage, and that's how she wants to remember them, before they became too sick, before they just became names in stone. She mourns as the car drives through the countryside, even the green grass and distant hills muted in colour, their warmth eaten away by her broken heart.

After an hour, the taxi finally pulls up at the old farmhouse and Dorothy steps outside, feeling the rain on her skin as she looks at a place she used to call home. The thoughts of evenings falling sleep on the porch and staring up at the stars flood back, times when uncle Henry would try to teach her how to milk a cow but she'd stroke its head for hours instead. Even that day when she had to leave her aunt and uncle comes back to her, and she walks to the porch slowly.

Her body drenched and the taxi long gone she feels the gauze sticking at her skin and thinks of the lion as she smiles. 'Before he had his courage I bet he hated the rain' she thinks to herself, and suddenly realises that if the tin-man were here he would surely rust...but he's not. So walking onto the porch she looks out at the farm, smells the damp air and watches the rain bead off the corn, wondering how her friends are now. She tries to convince herself they're fine, they beat the witch and ruled Oz together, but she doesn't believe it. Instead she watches the rain pour onto the farm and rubs her side, feeling even more alone as she thinks of poor Toto, trapped with her friends in Oz.

Then at the corner of her eye she spots a familiar face and leaps from the porch. Running into the cornfield the rain soaks her to the bone and she moves as fast as she can, screaming, *'Scarecrow, Scarecrow!'* But when she reaches him she stands in disappointment, touching at the pathetic figure as she sighs, *'Not even buttons to see,'* cursing Outika for sending her back to this cruel world.

With a whimper, the young girl's tears get lost in the rain and she thinks of her friends in Oz, so scared for them as she looks to the small black key around her neck. Clenching it in her hand she takes a deep breath and closes her eyes, gritting her teeth as she lets out a cry, all of a sudden remembering what Bopeia had told her:

'It will send you home when you need it the most,'

Then the young girl shivers as she feels a strong wind coming from the north; the crops blow with a fierce breeze as fences get pulled into the air, and the farmhouse creeks wickedly. Suddenly nothing seems strange and Dorothy softly whispers, *'I need to get home, I need to get back to Oz!'*

For more information on;

'Dorothy- The darker side of Oz'

or the author, please contact

s.stanford@darkersideofoz.com

or visit;

www.darkersideofoz.com